SEVERANCE

N. N. BRITT

Dear reader,

Thank you so much for picking up this book.
I'm grateful that you are willing to give Alan's story a chance. As an author, I try not to shy away from discussing difficult topics, and this particular subject is something I have been wanting—and needing—to write about without sugarcoating for a while now. By no means, this read is an easy one because a devastating event touched upon in this work of fiction changes the lives of survivors forever. It cripples them emotionally, it alters the way they see the world, it alters the way they react to the simplest things, it alters the way they express their feelings. It alters the way they love. I tried to be as accurate as possible with certain mental health information. Any mistakes are my own. I advise caution if you are sensitive to the themes of gun violence, PTSD, or depression.

Sincerely,

N. N. Britt

PLAYLIST

Bury Me Deep Inside Your Heart - HIM
Fascination Street - The Cure
Pretending - HIM
Black No. 1 - Type O Negative
(Don't Fear) The Reaper - HIM
This Fortress of Tears - HIM
Sweet Pandemonium - HIM
Tears On Tape - HIM
Passenger - Deftones
The Kiss of Dawn - HIM
Play Dead - HIM
Salt In Our Wounds - HIM
Love You Like I Do - HIM
Circle of Fear - HIM
Love You to Death - Type O Negative
Last Dance - The Cure
The Path - HIM
Change - Deftones
Let It Go - James Bay
Bloodflowers - The Cure

For all the lost ones...

PROLOGUE

February 16, 2019
Saturday

They say you hear a pop.

Or at least, that's what I read online once. But that's not exactly accurate, because it's extremely hard to identify a specific sound in the middle of a rock concert when seven hundred people are clapping and singing along with the band. It's too noisy to distinguish between a pop and a drummer's new trick.

A distorted guitar riff is what I hear first, and my heart leaps into my throat for all the wrong reasons. Initially, I'm under the impression Dakota messed up his guitar solo. Although the thing is, my boyfriend doesn't make mistakes like that. He's number five on Portland's Guitar Players to Watch Out For in 2019 list.

But when the song goes from a jumbled clutter of unrecognizable notes and offbeat pounding to nothing in less than a second, I realize something's wrong. Really wrong.

My pulse begins to sprint.

The stage is full of fog and there are silhouettes moving rapidly against the darkness. A wave of screams and booted footsteps roll through the club like thunder.

"Gun!" a voice shouts from the crowd.

People start running and pushing as panic and chaos spread through the room. Bodies crash into each other, sending me down. I fall forward, my palms and knees skidding against the sticky wood floor that's covered with debris. The satin skirt Jess talked me into buying last weekend rips and twists up around my waist. Only, it's not the skirt I'm worried about—or the fact that potentially dozens of people could be staring at my naked ass. I'm terrified for Dakota because when I turn my head, I don't see him anywhere. He was there a moment ago, standing next to the microphone. I see Blaze's boots— they're black with studded skulls and hard to miss—charging through the fog and past me toward the side stage exit, and I see the huge sweaty stain on the back of Luke's t-shirt moving behind the scattering bodies.

Now the gunshots that rumble through the club are loud and clear.

Bang! Bang! Bang!

My ears are ringing. My eyes are full of tears. My blurry gaze examines the stage, nervously darting from one indistinct form to another. I blink repeatedly to try to discern if the dark blobs on the floor are bodies, but there's too much fog and not enough light.

Bang! Bang! Bang!

More screams and then a sea of footfalls rush through the cluttered backstage area.

"Where's Alana?" Jess shouts from somewhere above me. "Alana?"

I try to push myself up, but I'm trembling so much that my arms and legs refuse to cooperate.

Bang! Bang! Bang!

Oh, God. Please make it stop!

"Get down!" a ragged voice hisses as a body—large, warm, and oddly familiar—collides with my back and forces me to the floor. My cheek slams against the tacky wood and I feel crushed glass stab into my skin.

"Shhh, keep quiet," he says in my ear, covering my head with his palm. This is when I realize that it's Mikah. "Stay down! Don't move." He's like a firm blanket, solid and heavy.

Squeezing my eyes shut, I draw a deep, shaky breath and bite the inside of my cheek to suppress the cry that threatens to escape. The taste of my blood on my tongue is weird. It's not really salty or sharp or metallic, far from the way I've heard it described. It's mostly just bland and a little nauseating.

"We're going to die," I whisper in panic, my eyes closed and my body shivering.

"You're not going to die, Alana," Mikah says against my cheek. Then his hands cover my ears and I don't hear or see anything that happens after that.

1. BEFORE

"How about him?" Jess giggles, nudging me on the shoulder.

Her current victim is a bulky guy in a jean jacket and a pair of leather pants that don't look quite right. He's part of the ragged or, as my father would say, "bohemian-looking" group to our right that my best friend has been checking out since we arrived at the club.

"You can have him. He's definitely your type." I shift my gaze to the empty stage. The main floor is packed, just like it should be, because the last time Black Rose played Portland was four years ago, and tonight, this is definitely the place to be in town. I begged my father to let me go back then, but he wouldn't budge since I was a minor.

Now that I'm eighteen and in college, things are different, but he still likes to set a curfew and I like to push my luck a bit and be fashionably late.

My main goal for the evening, apart from enjoying the music, is to try to not get ensnared in another male catastrophe like the type that follows Jess and me—mostly Jess—every time we go out.

"I think he'd be perfect for you." Her skinny arm wraps around my neck.

She's been on this stupid mission to find me a boyfriend ever since we became besties in elementary school. A million attempts and twelve years later, Jess Tiller, best friend extraordinaire, is still at it. At this point, I'm surprised she hasn't put up flyers.

"It's not even acceptable not to have a boyfriend at eighteen," she adds.

"In what universe?" I ask as I draw her arm away before the curls I worked on all afternoon turn into an irreparable disaster.

"Oh, come on." She tugs on the sleeve of my jacket. "Just look at him. He's tall. He's got gorgeous blond hair."

"He looks like he's on a breakfast, lunch, and dinner steroid diet," I counter.

Jess likes her guys big and buff. She says the sensation of being dominated makes her feel like a real woman. I have no idea why she'd want such a thing.

Although I might not be the best person to judge. My father has never allowed me to date, so most of what I know about guys is from books, the ones I read in secret when I was growing up. And I suppose fictional men aren't quite like real-life ones, the majority of whom, according to my father, aren't serious about relationships. He did try to pair me up with the pastor's son once. And then a boy from the church choir. Neither was very interesting, but I bet my father wasn't looking for interesting. He was looking for someone stupid enough to believe couples shouldn't have sex before marriage.

This guy is also a definite no. Besides, my father's blood pressure would jump through the roof if I were to bring someone like him home for dinner.

There's a special name for families like mine. Traditional.

If not for Jess, I'd probably still think angels brought children from heaven. Jess is the best bad influence friend there is. Besides the guy thing, she's the one who got me into rock music. My father wasn't too thrilled when I put up my first band poster on my bedroom wall at the age of thirteen. And proving that Black Rose was a band without satanic tendencies turned out to be a challenge.

"How about him?" Jess motions in the direction of two guys who've just joined the group.

"Which one?" I shift my focus back to the circle of male specimens to make my girlfriend happy.

"The short hair," Jess whispers in my ear, her auburn curls tickling my cheek. "Since you don't like the blond hunk."

I snort out a laugh, evaluating the guy with the, as my father would say, "decent" haircut. However, his dark blue hoodie, which has a very *in*decent version of the Keep Portland Weird slogan that has the F-word after the name of our beautiful green city, disqualifies him from being an acceptable dinner date with my family.

My eyes slide to his friend's back and drink in his black leather jacket. It's snug and accentuates his shape perfectly. Then the moment I catch myself staring at his ass, heat floods my cheeks. Not that it isn't a great looking ass—he knows how to wear his jeans like a pro. It's the fact that my eyes linger on his body longer than necessary, which is shameful according to my father, and Jess obviously takes notice of it.

"Ohhhh!" she hoots, almost jumping for joy. "You like 'em dark and brooding."

"Shut up." I shake my head and avert my gaze.

"He's hot."

"You determined that by looking at his back?"

"A guy with an ass like his can't be ugly." She gives me a toothy smile and twirls a lock of my blond hair around her index finger. "I think we should go say hi."

"No!" I grab her shoulder in panic.

"You're no fun at all." She pouts.

"We're not going over there, Jess," I almost squeal. When it comes to guys, I'm extremely brave in my mind, but in reality, I stammer and blush like a sixth-grader. "It's weird."

"How is it weird?"

"I'm not going." I fold my arms on my chest, trying not to look across the room. But my eyes are traitors. They're ogling Mr. Leather Jacket again within seconds. He's not as tall as the steroid guy, not as big either. His body is lithe and very *male* with broad shoulders, a narrow waist, and long legs. His hair is dark and shiny, and it cascades over the collar of his jacket in the most sensuous way a guy's hair possibly can.

He looks like he belongs on the cover of some dark fantasy book. When he turns to his friend, a teasing smile on his lips fills my stomach with a blissful flutter. However, as if on cue, my father's voice then enters my head. *Shame on you, Alana*, he says, his tone stern and authoritative.

He's obsessed with keeping the male population of the entire planet away from me as much as Jess is obsessed with finding me a nontraditional-looking boyfriend.

The question is, who will succeed first?

"Ooh!" Jess pulls me out of my thoughts. Her blue eyes widen. "He has an earring. Wonder if he's pierced anywhere else?" She waggles her brows at me.

"You're horrible." I almost cover my face with my palms to hide my flaming cheeks, but I don't want to ruin my makeup. Although what I've done with my eyes and lips can hardly be called makeup. My mother has always taught me to keep things simple and only use enough to bring out my natural beauty, but right now, I secretly wish I'd agreed to Jess's earlier offer to give me smoky eyes. Unlike me, my girlfriend was born to rock the sexy glam look. Over-the-top suits her in a way it doesn't normally suit other people. She isn't tall, but she wears short skirts and high heels like a model, even in winter. Something I tried once but failed.

"Ohmigod!" Jess says in a breathy voice, fanning herself with her hand. "He's looking at you." Her excitement is palpable.

"No, he's not," I cut in, my knees weakening. My gaze is still trained on the empty stage, specifically on the lonely microphone that's set up at the center. I remind myself that I'm here to see the band I adore, but my heart leaps into my throat at the thought of the cute guy checking me out.

Jess and her stupid boyfriend quest.

Guys don't ever have this effect on me. This is possibly the first time in my life I've felt flustered because a specimen of the male persuasion, who happens to look like a dark gothic prince with questionable intentions from a forbidden novel, may or may not be glancing in my direction.

"Yes, he is. Throw him a bone, girl." Jess murmurs and nudges my shoulder again.

"You seriously need to stop it." I rub the sore spot right above my elbow that she's been assaulting all evening. But the truth is, I really do want to see his face. I want to know what his eyes and his mouth are like. Are they just as dreamy and perfect as his back?

My heart's racing when I finally summon all my courage and glance at the group. Jess is wrong. He's not simply looking at me—he's turned my way, full frontal. The black fabric of his t-shirt is stretched across his chest, showing off his nearly perfect body. Or, at least, it looks perfect to me.

"Flirt," Jess orders, slapping my ass playfully.

"This is about to become a case of domestic abuse." I giggle, intercepting her hand before the dark prince in the leather jacket decides that she and I are an item and scratches us off his list.

"Some bimbo's going to claim him before you know it." Jess rolls her eyes, seemingly irritated.

The lights in the club go out before my brain can form another witty comeback. The crowd gasps.

"Ohmigod!" Jess grabs my elbow and yells like a maniac, "Pinch me, girl! Are we finally seeing fucking Black Rose?"

"Yes, we are." I nod, my eyes glued to the stage. And the dark prince is long forgotten.

2. AFTER

I force my eyelids open and stare through the blurry veil. The indistinct forms on the corner of my nightstand begin to take shape. There's a clock—an old one with the alarms on top, actual hands, and a pretty swirly silver finish. It's sitting by the lamp, and I'm wondering why it's there. I've been using my cell phone to check the time ever since my father bought it for me when I was fourteen.

The downstairs has been buzzing. People have been coming and going ever since I got home from the hospital. A couple of them may have been reporters—I heard my parents arguing with someone a few times—but for the most part, everything since the attack has been a huge cavern of distorted voices and unfamiliar faces.

Dakota is dead.

The thought blasts through my mind like a cannonball, obliterating any semblance of peace still left in me.

I try to focus to determine what's hiding behind the clock. After several seconds of fighting with my stubborn vision, I realize that it's pill bottles. I vaguely remember a doctor giving my mother prescriptions for me.

I move my hands, and my palms feel like they've been skinned.

Then when I try to take a deep breath, there's a strange burning in my chest that starts spreading to my throat, lungs, and stomach.

A tiny fraction of me, the part that's still processing the events at the club, wants to cry, but the rest of me is so numb that I can't even move a finger, let alone experience something as complex as a human emotion. Besides, it seems somewhat unnecessary since tears aren't going to bring Dakota back.

There's a knock on my door, and then I hear my mother. She sounds small and defeated, nothing like herself.

"Alana?" she calls out and waits.

Go away.

"Honey?" The door makes a squeaking noise when my mother steps inside, the faint aroma of cinnamon trailing behind her as she walks to my bed and carefully sits on the edge. The scent is a sweet, invisible hug, full of forgotten childhood memories that are happy and bright. I want to grab it and wrap it around me like a blanket, but my arms won't wake up.

"Did you get any sleep, sweetheart?" she asks, resting her hand on my shoulder.

I blink through the haze in my eyes. "Some." It's a lie. I don't know if I slept. My head is all sorts of messed up. My ears are still ringing.

"Mikah Bennett is here to see you," my mother says softly. "But if you're not feeling up for it, that's okay. Your father doesn't think it's a good idea that you two talk right now."

"What's Mikah doing here?"

"I believe he tried to text you and you didn't answer. He called the house several times. You don't have to talk to him if you don't want to."

A grim silence that's thick with anguish falls between us.

"Okay," my mother whispers after a few moments. "I'll tell him you're asleep." She gets to her feet and walks to the door, the sound of her careful footsteps thudding inside my head like a hammer.

"It's fine," I push the words out, my voice rusty and foreign. Parts of me still feel dead and I'm wondering if it's because I haven't moved since yesterday.

A sigh of relief flutters across the room. "You sure?" My mother pauses, perhaps waiting for me to reconfirm what I just said.

"It's fine, Mom," I murmur, bringing my bandaged hand to my face to rub my eyes, my fingers trembling above my cheek. I haven't looked at the damage since I got home from the hospital, but it feels like the glass is still lodged deep in my skin. However, unlike Dakota's injuries, my wounds will eventually go away.

"Please have him come up here. I'm a little dizzy," I mumble under my breath. A little is an understatement. It feels like one terrifying, never-ending freefall.

"Oh…I'm not sure Dad will approve of that, sweetheart…" she counters, her breathy voice cracking.

Something inside me snaps, and the bitter words that have been stacking up in my head start to form a long, ugly speech. The speech I've been preparing for my father for years. The only reason I hold it in is because it isn't meant for my mother, and besides, I'm too exhausted.

"Just tell him to come up, Mom," I repeat sternly, staring at the light blue curtains above my desk.

She slips out quietly, leaving me alone with my angry thoughts.

There's a shift in the air when a new set of footsteps enter the room. It's suddenly cold and uninviting, as if the temperature has dropped below zero.

I'm lying on my side with my left hand tucked between my cheek and my pillow when Mikah stops across from me and leans against my desk, arms folded at his chest, eyes bloodshot and vacant. I don't need a magnifying glass to see the fracture in him. It's written all over his uncharacteristically thin face that's covered with several days' worth of stubble. I wonder if he can see all the wreckage in me.

As Mikah's chest slowly rises and falls, accidental streaks of sunlight dance across the window behind him, flickering around the shape of his shoulders. His gaze moves to my nightstand and I can tell he's avoiding looking directly at me.

"You didn't return any of my texts or calls." His voice is rough and indifferent.

"I haven't checked my phone," I confess. *I haven't brushed my teeth or showered either. Because I couldn't force myself to do anything.* Must be all the sedatives my mother's been feeding me.

"The funeral's on Thursday."

Dreadful silence fills the room.

I swallow the lump in my throat and let his words sink in. "Okay."

When Mikah drops his shoulder, the bright afternoon light blinds me. Squinting, I lift my head off the pillow and try to sit up.

"You don't have to come," he rasps, staring at one of the posters—probably Black Rose—above my head. "But I think it would be...good. For everyone."

Funerals and good don't actually go together, but I understand what he's trying to say. He just didn't pick the right words. Although what are the right words that could possibly be said about someone's death? There are hardly ever any. Unless that person deserves it. Dakota didn't deserve it.

I swallow past the tightness in my throat and ask the question I'm dreading to hear the answer to, "Do you know how many people died?"

Mikah draws a deep, shaky breath. "Twenty-four."

A wave of nausea nearly knocks me over. "Oh." That's all that comes from my mouth.

The images in my head are suddenly so clear that I can almost smell and hear everything, and this unwelcome case of déjà vu makes me even sicker to my stomach. The burn in my chest ups its game and it feels like someone has shoved a flaming torch into my heart.

"Are you okay?" Mikah's eyes finally drift to me. They're vacant and sad, and it's obvious he doesn't really want to be here, because he has far more important things to do. Like burying his younger brother.

The space between us sears with agony. The desolation on his face is terrifying. It bleeds across my room, filling each corner until if feels as if there's no more air left to breathe.

Ignoring his question, I break eye contact and start plucking a stray thread from the sleeve of my oversized sweater. My fingers aren't cooperating because of the bandages, but I keep at it anyway.

Mikah and I were never what I'd call friends. I suppose I've been as much of a constant in his life as he's been in mine due to the fact that I dated his brother while they shared an apartment. But now, he's all I have left that ties me to Dakota, and I can't decide if I want him to stay in my life because he reminds me of everything good I once had...or if it'd be better to cut him loose. Better for everyone—me, him, my parents, his family. In a way, we're all an assembly of little reminders, shattered pieces of a life we're no longer going to live. Instead, we're going to exist in an ugly and wretched imitation.

"You know..." Mikah uncrosses his arms and rests one hand on my desk. Then he looks down for a second. "You have some stuff at the apartment." The tips of his tattoo that stick out from under the sleeve of his forest green jacket are dark and sharp against his olive skin. I wonder if he left it on because Dakota told him insane stories about my father or because it's freezing outside.

"Yeah, I know. I'll pick it up next week," I say. "Is that okay? Next week?"

Is it okay to come back to your place now that Dakota's gone?

"Yeah. Just text me first." He nods, running his palm across his forehead to tuck a stray piece of hair behind his ear.

There's a pause. Neither one of us knows what to say anymore and it's weird.

"Look." Mikah shoves both hands into the pockets of his jacket and steps closer. "I have to go. I've got things to do. Are you sure you're gonna be okay?"

His question surprises me. I'm not certain what defines okay anymore. That I'm alive and breathing? Sure. What about the fact that I can still smell the gunpowder and the blood every second of every day? Or that I can hear all these screams in my head, even in my sleep?

Does he hear them too?

"Are *you* going to be okay?" I whisper. I don't sound like myself at all.

Mikah takes a few moments to process my question. "I don't know." With his gaze trained on the door, his body language speaks volumes—he wants to get the hell out of here as soon as possible. "See you Thursday...maybe," he says and leaves my room without looking back.

I sit against the headboard of my bed for what seems like forever, staring at the wide-open door, listening to my parents' rumbles in the room across the hall.

"I don't want him to come anywhere near this house again!" my father says loudly. He doesn't bother to keep his thoughts to himself. He wants to be heard. "If she hadn't gotten involved with that other boy in the first place, she wouldn't have been in that bar on Saturday at all!"

It's a club, Dad, not a bar, I mentally correct him.

And I wasn't involved. *I was in love.*

<hr>

A gasp of surprise leaves my mother's mouth as I stagger into the kitchen. She stops whatever it is she was preoccupied with right before my arrival and rushes to help me.

"Mom, it's fine." I push her aside and drag myself across the room. My legs are two marshmallows, but her fussing drives me nuts, so I'm determined to make it to the table on my own. I don't understand why she hovers as if I'm still seven.

"Do you want a sandwich or do you want to wait for dinner?" Her voice is on the verge of breaking and I feel like I should be nicer, but the horror running through my brain makes it difficult and I already regret coming down.

"I think I'll just have coffee."

My mother ignores what I say and moves toward the fridge. "How about turkey deluxe?" She pulls the door open and inspects the shelves.

"Mom, it's okay. I'm not hungry," I say, this time a little louder. My pulse drumming against my eardrums jolts into a gallop.

"Do you want mustard or mayo?"

"Mom!" My frustration rises.

"What?" She swivels in my direction, and her eyes, big and full of stress, land on me.

"I don't want a sandwich, Mom!" The words come out from my throat in the form of an ugly cry and I realize my whole body's trembling.

"Okay, okay, okay." My mother runs up to me and draws me into a tight embrace, pulling my head against her chest. "It's okay, sweetheart. I'll make some coffee."

She holds me until my panic subsides, her hand stroking my tangled hair like she used to do when I was young. We don't move or talk and I don't hug her back, because I don't have the heart to give affection at the moment. I just sit there and stare at the wide-open fridge and its shelves stacked with dozens of packages and bags of produce, wondering why we need so much food.

My mind finally settles and I brave the question that I've been meaning to ask ever since Mikah left. "Mom, what day is it?"

"It's Monday," my mother says, and her arms drop down to her sides and she moves to the counter.

"I'm scheduled to work on Friday night."

"Sweetheart, you can't work like this. Dad already called the restaurant and told them you're taking a leave of absence." She flips the coffeemaker lid open and pulls the dirty filter out.

A strange mix of annoyance and defeat rolls through my stomach. "What? Why?"

My mother tosses the old grounds into the trash can under the sink and shifts her attention to me. "Dad and I believe it's best you take some time off."

"What do you mean time off? Jess and I are moving in together on the first. I need the money for a deposit."

She shakes her head. "You need to concentrate on your health right now. The apartment can wait."

"No, it can't!" Another tremor races through my body. "We signed a rental agreement."

"Alana, you're not moving anywhere until you get better."

I feel acid boiling inside my chest. My parents have decided my life without asking me.

What else is new?

The silence stretches between us like rubber as I watch my mother hovering over the coffeemaker.

"Oh! Sweetheart." She snaps her head to the side and gestures at the pile of mail sitting on the counter. "There's a package for you."

Pushing away my anger, I slip from the chair and cross the room.

"What is it?" my mother asks matter-of-factly as I carefully draw a padded envelope from the stack.

The paper feels crisp and fresh against my fingertips—I totally forgot about ordering it. "It's just a book," I mutter, pressing the package to my chest as if it's some prized possession. In a way, it is. Because it came from the past. It came from the time when Dakota was still alive.

"That's nice." My mother's voice hums as I settle in the chair and place the envelope in front of me.

I wake up in the middle of the night choking on my own saliva and panting. The book is next to me, still unopened. My pillow and sheets are wet, and I don't know if it's because I've been sweating or if something else happened. After the conversation with my mother, there's a raw, bitter aftertaste of defeat in my aching mind. My heart beats fast and loud; my pulse is skyrocketing, and I can hear it thrashing in my temples.

Twenty-four people.

I shove away the damp blanket and prop myself against the headboard, my eyes darting around the dark room, searching for something familiar, searching for something to latch on to, but there's nothing. Nothing except for the package I'm too scared to touch.

Bang! Bang! Bang!

Stay down! Don't move.

I can't seem to catch my breath. There's a scream stuck in my lungs and it desperately wants to come out.

She's bleeding. Get a paramedic here.

How many fingers do you see? Can you hear me, sweetie?

I pull my legs up to my chest and rock my body, wanting to stop the noise from getting into my head.

Is anyone still inside? I'm looking for my brother.

Sweetie, I need you to let me see your hands.

Up until now, the memories of the aftermath have been only a shapeless blur. I'm not sure why it's all coming back to me now, at four in the morning. I remember the police arriving and more gunshots. I remember the paramedics taking me outside. I remember sitting in the van while some woman in uniform is trying to talk to me, and I remember watching Mikah moving through the crowd outside the club. There's blood dripping down his cheek, but I don't think he's hurt. I think the blood is mine. He stops one of the officers and asks him questions, and I can tell by how fast his hands move that he's panicking. There's a short exchange and then they're gone.

Now I'm in the hospital, and my parents tell me Dakota was shot to death during the attack. That's all I get. No details. They don't tell me how many times he was shot or where he was standing when it happened or if it was an instant death or a slow one where he lay there, terrified, watching the horror around him.

I replay this moment in my head several times, wondering if I should have said or done something differently. Cried maybe. But I didn't. I just sat there in silence, my hands and my face bleeding. I sat there waiting to wake up, waiting to snap back into my normal life. But it never happened.

This is my normal now. Without Dakota.

And I don't like it a single bit, because it's empty and cold and it makes no sense. Things are just...gloomy and hopeless.

Minutes keep passing as I rock against the headboard, fighting for control over my own body and mind. After a while, the dread seizing up my chest finally begins to subside. My thoughts and memories are still a mess, and the noise inside my head doesn't quite want to go away, but my consciousness slowly breaks through the wall of terror, piece by piece. And when I'm finally able to move and process everything adequately, I walk to my desk and open my laptop.

I'm still not fully certain about this, but the avoidance is killing me. My parents haven't said a single word about the attack since our return from the hospital.

I sit in my chair, my heart sprinting, my fingers hovering above the keyboard. With my hands stitched up in multiple places, typing even three simple words proves to be a challenge. I wait a while before hitting the enter button, allowing my brain to prepare for the onslaught of information. My stomach twists into knots as the headlines finally fill up the screen of my laptop. Pushing regret and panic down, I click on the first article and start reading.

"Jealous Boyfriend Kills 24 People in Portland Club Shooting"

Gunman identified as 26-year-old Joseph Miller...

Hours prior, Miller shot his way into the Portland live music venue to look for his girlfriend, Andrea Coleman. He and Coleman had a disagreement over her going to a concert without his consent...

The neighbors describe couple as troubled...

When Miller arrived at The Crystal Room at about 10:25 pm, there were around 700 people inside the club...

Miller unleashed fire, killing 24 people and injuring over 200 rock concert attendees...

Coleman was a big Midnight Rust fan and could be seen at almost every show the band played in the Portland area...

Authorities say Miller acted out of jealousy. At this time, it's not clear where he obtained the weapon...

The lead singer of Midnight Rust, Dakota Bennett, who was recently named one of the most promising guitar players of 2019, is among the victims of the attack...

Drummer Luke Jamison suffered severe spinal injuries and has been hospitalized...

I swallow through the stiffness in my throat and shut my eyes to stop the text from floating. The panic is back and it's worse than ever because things are just plain wrong. There's a Joseph Miller Wikipedia page, but there's nothing when I search for Dakota's name.

3. BEFORE

Halfway through Black Rose's set, Jess makes a really bold move. She waves at one of the bohemian-looking guys without consulting with me. Two seconds later, all six pairs of eyes are glued to us like bees to a honeypot. Including those of the dark prince in the leather jacket. His gaze lingers on Jess briefly, then slides over to me. It's deep and unwavering and seems to make everyone else disappear, even the dozen or so bodies jumping to the wild beat between us. His eyes are crystal blue, like steel. The color I've always thought was just a myth.

My heart does something similar to a pique flip when the side of his mouth tilts up. I bite the inside of my cheek to try to prevent myself from grinning like a fool, but it's too late. My lips stretch into a smile without checking with my brain first. I imagine my face is probably the color of a ripe tomato, but thankfully, he can't tell since the only source of light in the club right now are the dancing spotlights.

We spend the rest of the show engaging in an intense staring competition. The kind of intense that makes my insides melt. And it's not even because he's been looking at me for very long; it's *how* he's been looking at me. He's been *studying* me like an art collector would study a canvas. It's almost as if he can see right through me. All my secrets, all my hidden desires, all my dreams. I feel like I should break eye contact because we're in the middle of a madhouse, surrounded by screaming fans, and I promised myself to have fun and enjoy the music. But instead, I take every bit of what he has to offer. I latch on to the faint smile and the slight nod of his head. I revel in all of his not-so-subtle signs of attention and stash them into my secret box at the very back of my imagination. For safekeeping. For later. For when I'm alone in my room.

His friend with the decent haircut interrupts him and the invisible connection between us is lost.

The music stops and the lights go out. People begin to cheer and stomp, demanding an encore.

"He's going to bore a hole in your head, girl!" Jess yells in my ear, slapping my shoulder. She's rocking the hot mess look. Her wet auburn curls are stuck to her neck and there are light traces of mascara under her eyes.

"You started it." I laugh, returning my attention to the stage.

My heart's still thump-thumping, and I'm not certain whether it's because I'm loving the show or because of the dark leather jacket prince who's staring at me like I'm some unknown form of extraterrestrial life.

When the first notes of the next song float through the jam-packed club, the crowd erupts. Screams of pleasure mix with the beats and lyrics, coursing through me like an invisible force. I love the feeling of freedom the music gives me—when I get lost in it entirely.

"Oh my fucking God!" Jess shrieks, pulling on the sleeve of my jacket. "He's going to jump!" Her eyes shine with excitement. She's like a firecracker, carefree and full of energy, and I'm loving that she's my best friend. Because without her, my life would be an absolute bore.

Devin Monroe, the lead singer of Black Rose, is rocking on his heels at the edge of the stage, microphone near his mouth, hooded eyes scanning the crowd. Being a part of this turbulent, massive experience is as breathtaking as it is frightening, something my father probably wouldn't approve of, but I honestly don't care. At least not at this moment.

Devin Monroe's body flies across the narrow pit as he launches himself from the stage to do a round of crowd-surfing. I'm being pushed and pulled in all directions, and for a second, I lose Jess. The adrenaline racing through my veins gives me an incredible feeling, one I don't get to experience often. Dozens of quivering hands follow the singer through the air like a herd of sheep led by a lion until security helps him to the ground and escorts him back to the stage, where he finishes the song.

My ears are still ringing long after the set ends. Jess insists on staying behind in case the band decides to come out for some photos. She elbows her way to the front and clings to the barricade next to a bunch of other super fans.

I'm sweaty and feel like I've been run over by a truck, and although the idea of a hot bath and a warm bed is wonderful, my sense of adventure prevails. The blue-eyed mystery man probably has a lot to do with that.

"I swear I'm never taking a shower again!" Jess squeals, ignoring the fact that half the club can probably hear her. Somehow, I believe that was her intention all along. She's one of the few chosen ones touched by Devin Monroe, and this will probably be in the Twittersphere for weeks to come.

"Eww." I try not to laugh while my eyes jump from one head in the room to another, searching for the prince in the leather jacket. Now that the high of the show is beginning to fade, images of him invade my mind. I've never had a guy look at me the way he did. *Like he was trying to communicate something to me.* But sadly, he's nowhere to be found. Neither is the rest of his group.

"Devin fucking Monroe touched me!" Jess's high-pitched squeal drowns out the thoughts in my head. "Devin fucking Monroe, Alana!"

The main floor is still packed as people patiently wait for the Black Rose guys to make an impromptu appearance.

"I was there. Remember?" I say, checking the time on my phone. My father's expecting me home by midnight, which is ridiculous, considering it's Friday.

"Did he touch you too?" Jess looks at me expectantly.

"I don't want to be on your Twitter," I warn her, scanning the main floor.

We watch the road crew breaking down the stage until it becomes obvious the band is taking the rest of the night off. The security guards start hustling everyone out into the buzzing lobby.

"You wanna stay over at my place tonight?" Jess asks.

"You know how my dad is." I roll my eyes. "He said to be home by midnight."

"You two really need to renegotiate."

"Let's get t-shirts." Ignoring her comment, I pull her in the direction of the merch booth.

"I'm serious. What are you? Thirteen?" Jess snickers as we go to the end of the line.

"Yeah, well." I blow out a heavy sigh, not sure how to explain to my best friend that trying to change my parents' viewpoint on partying late isn't an easy undertaking.

"I'm surprised your dad doesn't come to check on you when you sleep over at my place."

"Maybe he does." I shrug, laughing. The image of my father hiding in the bushes in front of Jess's house with binoculars amuses me to some degree. The only reason he ever lets me spend the night at my friend's house is because her father regularly donates to the church we attend. I'm not sure that actually qualifies Jess's dad to be a suitable chaperone, if not the opposite. The Tillers are gone a lot on business, including some of the weekends I spend at their place. But my father doesn't need to be aware of that.

"That would be totally creepy!" Jess agrees, her mouth twisting.

"I know."

"Soo," she drawls like she always does when things are about to steer into serious talk territory. "I found this one apartment downtown. The landlord said she can waive the credit check if my parents co-sign."

A little rush of unease flows through me. I haven't been able to bring up the moving out discussion to my parents. My father insists I live at home while I'm in college. Maybe because he wants to make sure his money doesn't go to waste.

It's sad he still doesn't trust me.

"I haven't looked for another job yet," I confess. A partial reason for my procrastination is that I like working at Anna's Pastry. I've been helping the owner, Mrs. Kaminski, ever since I was fifteen. My guess is that the only reason my father allowed me to work for her at such a young age is because she's also Polish. And while my pay is miniscule and my boss can be unreceptive to my Instagram and other social media marketing ideas, I feel happy there. The thought of leaving the bakery gives me anxiety.

"I told you to look when summer gets here," Jess scolds me. "No one's hiring in the middle of the holiday season. I fucking hate Christmas."

"What's wrong with Christmas?"

Unlike Jess, I haven't mastered saying the F-word outside the privacy of my room as well as she has. My biggest fear is that if I say it too often, it will one day slip out of my mouth in front of my father and he'll decide not to pay my tuition anymore.

"Sorry." She rolls her eyes dramatically and moves ahead as the line inches forward. "You know I respect your parents, but you need to get out of that house before your dad sends you to some convent because you're too fucking nice to tell him no or stand up to his bullshit."

Her words hang in the air, heavy and somewhat hurtful. They sting because that's what the truth does—it makes you feel really crappy, especially when it comes from your best friend.

"Just think about it, okay?" Jess goes on. "We'll be perfect room-mates. We can do something cool in the kitchen. Like a permanent set-up where we can take sick photos for your blog. Or we can do videos."

I don't respond. Instead, I let the idea settle in my mind. Moving downtown is a big deal. Jess and I have been dreaming of living together since we were kids. Will my father still be okay with me driving the Prius? Will he still pay my tuition? Will he still give me spending money?

"Do you know how to film and edit videos?" I ask quietly, my question dissolving into the post-show noise of the lobby.

"Girl, I'll figure it out. You just need to get on board. We can make you a whole cooking show. Martha Stewart 2.0 or Gordon Ramsay style, only prettier." Obviously, Jess likes to exaggerate everything.

"I'm not sure I want to do the whole Gordon Ramsay thing." I laugh.

"Don't worry. It's all minor details," she assures me. Then her attention is diverted when she glances down at the screen of her phone and opens the devious Twitter app to announce to the rest of the world that Devin Monroe touched her.

After we buy two limited edition Black Rose *Rough Stitches World Tour* tees, Jess pulls me aside to inspect our purchases. A couple of years ago, she was given the wrong size and by the time we noticed, the merch booth had already wrapped up.

"I have to make sure." She checks the labels and presses the shirt to her body.

"It looks good," I say, laughing at her OCD.

"Yes, it does." Jess nods, satisfied. "Come on." She hides the tee in her purse and motions for me to follow her to the exit.

The second I step outside, a sharp gust of icy wind slips under the collar of my thin suede jacket. Sometimes Oregon weather can be cruel, especially at the end of November. The days are still sunny and bearable, but the evenings are sadistically cold and not at all girls-night-out-friendly.

"You want to grab a milkshake?" Jess offers, holding on to my arm as we maneuver through everyone gathered in front of the club. The air is an odd mixture of cigarette smoke, sweat, and the barely-there fresh scent of the upcoming winter.

The idea of consuming something that's not heated to at least eighty degrees seems insane, and my common sense tells me not to agree to Jess's proposal, but trips to Patty's have been *our* thing since junior high and I've missed curfew before. Not many times but definitely a few. And mostly on purpose just to see my father's reaction. What's the worst that could happen? Another lecture?

"Sure," I say, zipping up my jacket before I turn into an icicle.

"Hey, you!" A man calls from the crowd. I'm not sure whether it's directed at Jess and me or someone else.

When I look up, I see the steroid diet guy in the ill-fitting leather pants—the one Jess wanted to set me up with—moving toward us. His eyebrow shoots up his forehead as he examines her from head to toe, a cocky smirk lingering on his lips.

Jess doesn't beat around the bush. Over-confident guys like this are her specialty. "Hey, yourself. What's going on?" She sounds sugary sweet with a pinch of dirty. Releasing my arm, she twirls her damp auburn curl around her index finger.

"I saw you inside. Looked like you were having fun." Steroid guy jerks his chin in the direction of the club entrance. His gaze shifts to me for a brief moment, then back to Jess.

"I saw you too," she purrs, turning up her flirt mode.

"My band's playing a show here with Eclectic Blue on the thirtieth." He lets his words sit between the three of us, probably thinking this is a great pickup line.

"Oh, nice! I like Eclectic Blue." Jess's tone pitches as it always does when she gets excited about something. "That's awesome. Is this you inviting us?"

"Exactly."

She goes straight for the kill. "They're VIP tickets, right?" Eagerness laces her voice.

"Sure. Does your friend here"—his eyes cut to me again before sliding to her again...*or to her breasts, to be more exact*—"want to come?"

"I talk," I call out, waiting for his reaction and wondering why Jess always has to get in with the worst guys ever who either try to grope me or pretend I'm invisible. Right now, it's the latter.

This doesn't faze him. "Cool." He draws his cell phone from the front pocket of his leather pants.

"What's your band's name?" Jess asks.

"Midnight Rust." Steroid guy smirks. "I'm Luke. My boys are over there." He waves at no one in particular somewhere behind him.

"Nice to meet you, Luke. I'm Jess." She turns to me and her eyes are the *be nice* kind of wide. "This is my friend, Alana."

I raise my hand slightly to greet Luke and smile. I doubt he sees my attempt. His eyes are pretty much glued to my friend's partially-exposed cleavage. Looking at her boobs makes me shiver. It's way too cold to be showing any skin.

As people swarm around the lot like ants, the invisible cloud of adrenaline that hangs low above our heads starts to dissipate.

My hair, still wet from the show, feels like icy globs of cement plastered to the back of my neck. The milkshake idea seems so absurd now.

I open my mouth to ask Jess for her car keys, but the words die on my lips because the prince in the leather jacket distracts me from the task at hand. He steps out from the crowd and positions himself next to his friend, facing me. His dazzling blue eyes search mine.

My body's frozen, but I can still feel the heat radiating from him. It's a different kind of warmth. A little dangerous, a little intimidating, and a little addicting. And it ignites a strange flutter-like sensation in my belly, similar to the one I felt during the show. *Is this how pheromones work?*

Up close, he's even more beautiful. He has an elegant face with a strong jaw and a cleft in his chin, high cheekbones, and wide-set eyes—all that, touched with a hint of softness. His skin's the color of milk and honey and I wonder if he's real. What if I'm dreaming. What if when I wake up, he's gone.

My heart beats faster when he tosses a smile at me—wide, all-consuming, and with dimples—pretty much knocking me off my feet.

For a second there, I actually forget I'm a sweaty ice pop.

"Hey," he says, ignoring the noise around us. His voice is a blend of rough and tender, and it washes over me like a warm, playful wave, flirty and tempting. Erasing all my surroundings.

"Hey." I return the greeting, not sure if he can hear me when my tongue stiffens. He doesn't need to, though. Because he looks at me as if he can read my mind, and I wonder if that's why he's smiling.

"Did you enjoy the show?" he asks without paying attention to Jess or Luke.

"Yes." I nod. "Did you?" My eyes drink in every detail of him slowly and hungrily. He's the kind of guy you'd see on Pinterest when you type "gothic fashion." He wears rings and a chain necklace and his boots have metal studs. I can tell he's put a lot of thought into his outfit.

"I did... I heard my buddy hooked you up with some tickets to see our show?" He gives Luke a pat on the back.

"Looks like it." I breathe out, thrusting my hands into the tiny pockets of my jacket. The cloud of condensation coming from my mouth floats lazily in the air between us. "So…" I drawl, letting the words sit on my tongue for a moment. "You're in a band."

"Yep." A head tilt. "And you like rock music."

"Yes."

"What's going on, DK?" Luke finally tears his eyes off Jess's boobs to acknowledge his friend's presence. "You got two extra tickets for the ladies?"

Watching them interact is fascinating. There's a lot of gesturing and almost no words, like it's some secret sign language only known among musicians.

"Sure." The blue-eyed prince returns his gaze to me. "You're coming, right?"

My heart screams and dances like a cheerleader. "Yes." I break eye contact and look at Jess. She's grinning at me from ear to ear.

"Cool. I'm Dakota. This fool right here"—he throws his arm over Luke's shoulder and draws him closer—"is our drummer."

"What's the name of your band again?" Jess asks.

"Midnight Rust," Luke responds, standing upright, tall and proud.

"How come I've never heard of you?"

"That's fixable, honeybun." He chuckles.

I cringe at the cheesy endearment.

Dakota smiles again and his gaze returns to me. "I didn't get your name."

"Alana," I mutter, drawing my right hand from my pocket to push away a strand of hair the wind has whipped across my face.

"Do you have a phone"—he pauses—"Alana?"

My name coming out of his mouth doesn't even sound like it belongs to me. He's turned it into something entirely different. Something sensual.

"Yes, I have a phone," I say, dumbstruck.

"I'll text you the show info in a few days when we sort everything out."

"Okay. Sure."

He keeps staring, his hand reaching out to me. The reflection of the colorful marquee lights dancing along with the blue in his eyes hypnotizes me.

"Oh." I give him my phone.

Get it together, Alana. You've been swooning over this guy all night. It's not the time to be spacing out when he's finally asking for your number.

Dakota punches his digits into my phone and hits the call button. *Very sneaky.* "Now you don't have any excuses," he says, returning it to me.

"I wasn't going to look for any," I respond quietly.

"I didn't think so." He smiles, but this time it's not a dimples-on-display, toothy grin. It's subtle and tender, meant for me only.

***

Jess drops me off at home at one thirty in the morning. I tiptoe through the living room while holding my breath, hoping my parents are fast asleep, but my father catches me in the hallway upstairs.

"Alana?" His voice is stern and annoyed. "I thought we agreed on midnight." He moves away from the doorway and flicks on the light.

"Jess and I went to Patty's after the show," I squeak out from my spot, my heart dropping to my stomach because I feel a little guilty for lying.

"Your mother and I worry." My father shakes his head, the lines around his eyes deepening.

"I'm not fourteen, Dad," I counter, expecting another reprimand, but none follows.

There's a moment of awkward silence that drags on for what seems like forever—something that's never happened between us before.

"Okay." He nods, his face calmer and softer. "Get some rest. We'll talk tomorrow."

"Aren't you going to ask me about the show?"

"Did you and Jess have fun?"

"Yes." I brave a small smile.

"Good." My father steps closer and kisses the top of my head. "Now get some sleep. Your mother's going to need some help at the shelter tomorrow."

After we say our goodnights, I go in my room, wrestle out of my sweaty clothes, and hurry into the shower.

Once I'm in my bed, the temptation to search for Dakota's band online overrides my desire to sleep, and I twist and turn for a good thirty minutes before giving in. A blend of excitement and panic rushes through me the second I see the band's name come up at the top of the Google search results. I click on the website and wait for it to upload, my mind reeling as my heart prances.

A large black and white photo fills the screen of my laptop. It's dark and intimate with the smeared faces effect, which only lessens my interest in the rest of the band members. I ignore them and shamelessly stare at Dakota until my eyes hurt. He's not-of-this-world mysterious. Black eyeliner, hair slicked back, and every curve of his face is sharp and well-defined as if it's been sculpted by Michelangelo himself. Seeing him when he looks like this makes me feel weird things. It makes me wonder if my father's right—if the devil truly has many forms and Dakota is one of them.

4. AFTER

The dress is uncomfortable and makes me feel like a plastic doll wrapped in sandpaper. My chest hurts and my head is heavy.

I've lost count of how many pills I've taken since last night because of my dread for this moment. I've been dreading seeing Dakota one last time. I've been dreading that the image of him dead will push all the happy images of us out of my memory.

"Are you feeling okay, honey?" my mother asks as we wander through the lobby of the funeral home, directionless. "You look pale." She sighs, gazing around.

My father's quiet and seems displeased. He was probably expecting a church setting.

I'm mostly just numb and sleepy from all the sedatives, and there's a light tremor flowing through me because I can't seem to find an exit sign. What if something happens? What if someone brings a gun?

We move through the crowd slowly, my mother tossing an occasional smile at the guests. Familiar faces swim around me like fish in a tank. On the opposite side of the room, I see Jess hovering over Luke, who's in a wheelchair. I see Blaze, the bass player, sipping on a beer near the window, but I don't see Mikah.

The main area of the inside of the funeral home is nothing like I thought it would be. It's spacious yet cozy with dome-shaped windows and maroon draperies. The soft chandelier light glitters across the bronze furniture, making the place look like some filthy rich guy's living room. There are plants, couches, and small tables around the perimeter, and a few rows of chairs are neatly lined up in the center. There are no religious symbols or anything hinting at Dakota's family favoring any church in particular, which is definitely a minus in my father's eyes. The only indication of this being a funeral is a casket set up at the front of the room next to a small podium.

I stare at it with my hands clutched into fists, wondering why I came. Wondering why Dakota needs all these flowers? He's dead. He doesn't care. He never liked flowers when he was alive. He liked cold beer, The Cure, and hummingbirds.

"I don't know if this was a good idea." My mother's frail whisper drags me out of my daze. She places her hand on my shoulder and gives it a light squeeze, and I realize that I must have started to doze off.

"Can I have a minute?" I turn to them and they both look miserable, with sad eyes and faces that are ravaged by worry.

"Sure, honey." My mother nods, her mouth slanting as I take a step back and begin walking toward the casket. The murmurs in the room mesh into one vibrating growl inside my head. I feel the violent thumps of my heart against my ribs throughout my every cell.

My feet falter and misbehave when I near the casket. There's just enough space between it and me to keep the body out of my line of vision when I come to a complete stop.

The fear of seeing something I won't be able to unsee trickles down my gut like boiling mercury. What if he's been hurt really badly? What if he doesn't look like himself? The thought of carrying this horror with me for the rest of my life scares me to death, even though I don't believe there's anything scarier than being in a room with a psycho who has a gun and wants to kill everyone.

Panic grips my throat and lungs when I finally move closer to the casket. My hip bones bump hard against the mahogany finish and my fingers fumble with the rough fabric of my black dress.

My eyes are blurry and I have to blink through the tears before the picture in front of me finally comes into focus. That's when the chill hits my bones.

Dakota's face is porcelain white and unfamiliar. He's still exquisitely beautiful in a dreadfully painful way, but he's not what I remember. He isn't breathing and he isn't smiling. The realization that he's actually dead and I'll never see him again after today hits me so hard that I have to grasp the edge of the casket to prevent myself from tumbling to the floor.

My head starts to spin and I stand like this, unmoving and quiet, for a very long time, ignoring the people in the room and the dull ache in my palms.

I take a deep, tremulous breath and reach into the casket. Then what comes out of my mouth is barely a whisper, more like a slur. "I'm sorry. I love you...I'm sorry."

I'm not sure what exactly I'm apologizing for when my fingers touch Dakota's. His skin is cool and lifeless and he feels like a piece of rubber. It's nothing like the way he felt before. Not even close. And it makes me mad that he can't give me a second of warmth.

"Hey." A soft voice echoes somewhere near my ear.

I shudder but don't let go of Dakota's hand.

"Alana." My name is called.

"Huh?" I turn my head and come face to face with Mikah. He's shaved, his hair is tied back, and he's wearing a suit, but his eyes are bloodshot and his cheeks are sunken. He's a wreck.

I wonder if he's been sleeping at all. I wonder if he's having nightmares too.

"Why don't I take you to your seat?" he says quietly, giving me a light pat on the shoulder.

"Did you notice there's no exit sign here?" I mouth at him.

"What?" Confusion flickers in his green eyes.

"There's no exit sign. There should be an exit sign..." I'm on the edge of panic.

"Let me take you to your seat," Mikah insists.

I shake my head and look back at Dakota, our hands still locked together. Mine, small and bandaged, and his, cold and unresponsive.

"Alana, come on." When Mikah moves closer, his breath fans

against my injured cheek and my skin, still tender from the glass cuts, stings with pain.

I don't react. My feet are planted in front of the casket like two oil drilling rigs, and my fingers are gripping Dakota's as if my life depends on it. It hurts, but I don't care.

"I'm sorry," I mutter as tears prick my eyes.

"Alana," Mikah repeats my name, seizing my wrist in an attempt to separate me from his brother. I don't let go. "I don't want to hurt you." His voice is stern. "Please. Do you think this is fucking easy for me?" He has no choice but to apply force to rip my hand away from Dakota's.

"I'm sorry," I mumble at nothing or no one in particular through the fresh coat of moisture in my eyes.

My mother comes to the rescue and takes me to our seats on the last row.

"Are you sure you want to stay, honey?" She fusses with my hair. "You still look really pale."

"I'm good." I push her hand away. "Don't touch it. It's fine."

"Sure. Okay." She does as I ask, wearing a defeated expression while my father stays unusually silent.

I slip back into the comfortable dark and shut off all my senses. My eyes are trained on the podium where people begin to speak, but I can't hear anything or make out any of their faces. Mikah's is also a blur. I watch him through an imaginary lens that makes everything look happier and I almost miss him crying. At the end of his eulogy, a single tear rolls down his cheek and instead of taking his seat, he hands his notes to his stepfather and leaves the room.

My teeth are chattering by the time I walk behind the building. Running outside without my coat in the middle of February isn't one of my best ideas, but the truth is, I'm so numb, I can barely feel anything.

Mikah's sitting on the edge of a massive concrete flower bed. It must have looked cozy and colorful during the summer, but right now, the soil is desiccated and covered with a blanket of dirty snow.

The gloomy, ominous clouds hang low above our heads, threatening yet another blizzard. This winter has been one of the longest and darkest I've ever seen, and I catch myself thinking that I desperately want it to end. Even if it would wipe out all the good memories. I just want to stop feeling broken.

Mikah's turned with his back to me, cigarette smoke floating around him like a halo.

The snow crunches under the weight of my suede shoes as I try to step quietly over to the flower bed, my hands clutched in front of me, my heart rate kicking up. There are thousands of words in my head, but none of them seem to be appropriate.

"Are you just gonna stand there?" Mikah rasps out after a while without looking at me. He brushes the traces of tears from his cheeks, tosses the last of his cigarette on the ground, and draws another from the pack that's sitting right next to him on the cement block.

"Can I have one?" I ask, blurting out the first thing that comes to mind.

"Since when do you smoke?" He chuckles, shifting to face me. His green eyes, still glistening from the tears, search mine.

"Since now." I shrug, shuffling my feet. My toes are completely frozen and my body has reached a point where moving only makes it more painful, but if someone decides to shoot at us, at least there's plenty of room to run. There are no walls and no missing exit signs.

Mikah rises to his feet and closes the space between us in three strides. "Here." He takes off his suit jacket, puts it over my shoulders, and hands me his cigarette. When his gaze catches mine, we stand motionless for a few moments, staring at each other, each of us probably wondering if the things we're feeling are any different. A strange type of connection exists when two people are grieving over the death of the same person. It's frightening and nerve-racking, yet it's like we have this invisible bond and understand each other without the need to speak.

I've never smoked in my life and I have no idea how to hold a cigarette and look natural, so I grab it across the middle with my thumb and my index finger, wondering which end goes into my mouth. Although I just saw Mikah smoking, my brain has completely lost it.

"The other way," he says, stepping back to get another one for himself.

"Okay," I mumble under my breath. I stick it between my lips but immediately remove it when the unpleasant taste of tobacco on my tongue causes my stomach to churn. My injured palm stings with the movement, but I try not to think about the pain.

"You dated a dude who was in a fucking rock band and he didn't teach you how to smoke, church girl?" Mikah rolls his eyes and flicks his lighter in front of my face.

Bringing the cigarette toward my mouth again, I pause. "He doesn't..." I trip over my words. "Didn't smoke." My heart feels heavy and swollen. All the little things about Dakota start to crowd my mind —the food he liked, the TV shows he watched, the bands he grew up listening to. It's terrifying to realize how much a person can integrate himself into your life in such a short period of time.

"Right." Mikah nods, averting his gaze. "It was a joke. You were supposed to laugh."

"Oh... Sorry."

Laugh? He wants me to laugh at Dakota's funeral?

The air between us shifts again and we're back to being distant and awkward.

I stare at the cigarette in my fingers while Mikah lights his. He inhales sharply, waits a few seconds, and then blows the smoke out through his mouth and nose, most of it hanging around me like a toxic veil.

"Isn't smoking bad for your voice?" I ask, studying his features. There's a tiny dimple on his left cheek and his eyes are big and wide, slightly slanted, like Dakota's. They normally have a hint of playfulness in them, but not today. Today they're miserable, with dark blue circles beneath them. It's as heartbreaking as it is fascinating to see so much of Dakota in Mikah, and it makes something inside me twinge and burn.

"Kinda." He gives me a one-shoulder shrug. "Not like I'm doing a lot of vocals, anyway. It's just backup. No one cares what I sound like."

"I do," I say breathlessly, for lack of a better response. There are other questions lingering on the tip of my tongue—not ones to ask today or tomorrow, but they're there.

Does this mean the band is over now that there's no singer?

Mikah brings his lighter toward me, so I place the cigarette between my lips again and he curls his hands around the end, lighting it carefully. "Just breathe in," he instructs. "And try not to burn yourself, all right?"

"All right." I gingerly hold it between my index and middle fingers since that seems to be the least painful position, and then I inhale. The thick smoke coats the inside of my mouth. It tastes bitter and clogs my throat.

"Take it into your lungs," Mikah says, slipping the lighter into the pocket of his slacks.

I start hacking and my chest feels like someone forced a bucket of ash into it. I have to pluck the cigarette out of my mouth before it drops to the ground.

Mikah shakes his head, amusement flickering in his eyes.

"How the hell do you get addicted to this?" I force through the cough.

"You get used to it." He snickers. His face lights up for a brief moment and the corners of his lips curl, which makes me feel somewhat content because, in a way, I just made him smile.

We stand motionless, facing each other, with our noses and cheeks red from the cold. He smokes slowly and elegantly while I'm choking and wheezing until a new set of voices drift toward us from around the corner. I don't bother hiding the cigarette, because it seems silly. After surviving a bullet rain, I reserve the right to have whatever bad habit my heart desires, and no one's going to stop me from trying things.

Not even my father.

"Hey, you two," Luke mutters, maneuvering his wheelchair around the piles of snow. Blaze follows him like a shadow, his face blank.

It's strange to see them wearing suits instead of their usual denim and leather, especially Luke. Right now, I'm missing his ill-fitting pants.

"You mind if we join the party?" His eyes shift between Mikah and me as if he needs our permission.

"Nah, man." Mikah tosses what's left of his cigarette on the ground. "Knock yourself out."

"Is Jess inside?" I ask, dropping my cigarette as well. We haven't spoken since The Crystal Room, which is weird because we usually talk every day.

"Yep." Luke draws a brand new bottle of Jack Daniels from the folds of his coat.

We form a small, quiet circle and stand like that for a few minutes, staring at the dirty snow beneath our feet.

"Fuck, man." Luke runs his palm over his face. "Fucking DK, man. I'm going to miss him." His voice cracks and I can hear him fighting a sob.

Mikah nods, drawing another cigarette from his pack. His gaze darts to me, but I wave it off because my mouth still tastes like an ashtray.

"Let me have one too?" Luke requests.

They smoke in silence while Blaze works on opening the bottle of Jack. He tosses the cap aside and says, "To DK. May he rest in peace."

"Yeah, man. Rest in peace," Luke adds with his cigarette hanging from the corner of his mouth.

Blaze drinks straight from the bottle and offers it to Mikah next.

The dark clouds drifting above our heads have grown bigger and heavier, and the sky now looks angry. A gust of cold air circles around me like a twister and bites the cuts on my cheek.

My gaze follows the bottle of Jack and lingers on Mikah's lips wrapped around the rim. He tips it up and takes a few swigs, his Adam's apple rolling up and down under his olive skin.

"You okay, Alana?" Luke calls to me, eyeing the bandages on my hands.

"Yeah," I breathe out.

Truth is, I don't know what I am right now. Half of me is numb and half of me is hurting while my brain tries to get used to the idea of Dakota being dead. It feels almost as if the last three months of my life were borrowed from some epic romance novel, and then the writer decided to go all Shakespeare on me and took my boyfriend away.

"You need anything, you let me know, right?" Luke motions to the space between us.

"Okay. Thanks," I tell him.

Mikah tears the bottle away from his lips and wipes the liquor dripping from the corner of his mouth with the back of his hand. His eyes seek mine and he offers me the Jack.

I'm too cold to move.

"It won't kill ya." Blaze sniffs, giving me the side-eye. His tone is low and bitter. Something tells me he'd rather not have me around right now.

I grab the bottle with both hands and bring it to my mouth; my gaze is trained on Mikah because out of everyone present, he seems to be the least intimidating. The liquor burns my throat and I seriously think about eating some snow, but the idea stays in my head. Instead, I drink some more and then give the bottle to Luke.

"Atta girl." Blaze chuckles. "I knew you had it in you, Cupcake Queen."

A small part of me wonders whether this has been my nickname for a while or he just came up with it, but most of me is frozen from the cold and wants to crawl into my bed and never leave it.

"Aren't you on antibiotics?" Mikah asks Luke.

"Fuck the antibiotics."

There's a long pause. The Jack makes another trip around our circle, and by the time it reaches me, there's almost nothing left. I end up drinking the last of it.

"Finished?" Blaze checks the bottle.

"Yeah." I clamp my lips together.

"Make a wish then, Cupcake Queen."

"Okay." I nod, my head starting to feel really fuzzy. "I think I'm drunk."

"You're all right. Let's go," Mikah says. "You're going to freeze to death."

I give the empty bottle to Blaze and follow Dakota's brother back inside. It's only when we reach the lobby that I realize I forgot about my wish.

There are no more speeches. People simply wander around—some look bored to death and some seem to be too busy trying out the snacks to care about the funeral—as if they're pretending to be sad. And some, like Dakota's parents, are distraught. The kind of distraught that makes your guts twist. It's not hard to tell fake politeness from true grief. They're as different as night and day.

I find the whole concept of a funeral, especially this one, overwhelming. It's a lot of sorrow in one place, and that upsets me even more, shredding the last of my calm.

I'm hiding on a couch in the corner, right near the exit. In case I need to run. My head is spinning and my mouth is dry, but the pain in my hands has dulled and I'm pretty sure it's because of the Jack Daniels.

I see Jess approaching me. She looks funny. She looks like two Jesses. Her dress is solid black and simple, like mine, and she hasn't gotten as crazy with the makeup as she usually does when we go out.

Her parents are here too, which is a bit of a surprise because they've been traveling all over the country lately. I've literally almost forgotten what they look like.

"Hey." She sits next to me and carefully takes my hand, as if it's fine china. "Are you okay?"

"I think your boyfriend got me drunk," I say, trying to hold in a hiccup while my gaze follows Mikah's silhouette as it moves through the crowd. He's shaking hands and accepting condolences, but there's this particularly odd hint of devastation in his eyes that no one else here has. Can anyone see it besides me?

Jess is quiet and I can almost feel whatever it is we've had between us since we were kids falling apart. I'm not sure why exactly. Because her boyfriend lived and mine didn't? That's not really a valid explanation, but there's nothing better I can think of right now. My mind's been taking a lot of trips to some parallel universe lately.

"Do you want to come over this week?" Jess asks, rubbing my shoulder. "We can bake something."

"I don't feel like baking," I confess. I don't feel like doing anything at all.

"We can watch some movies."

"Yeah. Movies are better." They don't usually require much thinking.

"Okay, so...do you want me to pick you up?"

"Text me tomorrow." I turn to her and withdraw my hand from hers.

"Sounds like a plan." She nods.

We sit in silence for a little while until I realize I haven't mentioned my discovery to anyone. So I tell her, my voice barely holding. "Did you know Joseph Miller has a Wikipedia page?"

"What?" She stares at me and looks dumbfounded, along with some other strange expression I can't read.

"He has his own Wikipedia page."

Jess blinks rapidly at me but doesn't say anything.

"All you have to do to get your own Wikipedia page is kill someone." My mouth twists in disgust, and I can feel rage filling every part of me from the inside. "Dakota doesn't have one."

"We can make him one," Jess offers placatingly.

"But that's not right!" My tone is now angry and high-pitched. "We shouldn't *have* to make him one! Don't you understand?"

"We'll make him one, okay?" she repeats, wrapping her arm around my shoulder.

I know it's supposed to feel better when your best friend hugs you, but it doesn't anymore.

5. BEFORE

We're in my room, sitting on top of my queen-size bed. Jess is trolling Midnight Rust YouTube videos while I try to finish up my essay on failure and success before getting ready for my shift at the bakery. But the truth is, my mind isn't in the mood for my studies or work.

All I've been thinking about this past week is Dakota. He texted me out of the blue on Wednesday when I was in class. It was just a simple "hey" and a microphone emoji, but it took me a whole day to come up with a fitting response because I've never been in a text message relationship with a guy before.

It's funny how you can barely know a person, but he'll still be the first thing you think about when you wake up in the morning. Without much effort, Dakota Bennett has planted himself into my life so deeply that it scares me.

"This song is life," Jess says as if on cue, rolling onto her side to face me. "I have no idea why we've never heard of these guys. They're so good."

I pluck the pencil I've been chewing on for the last hour from my mouth and set my notebook on the nightstand. Homework isn't happening today. Not with Jess spinning the same song over and over again and shoving her laptop at me every two seconds. Dakota's voice is way too distracting.

"Next weekend, you should wear that red crop top I gave you for your birthday," she suggests.

An image of my father chasing me with a jug of holy water comes to mind.

"You know what my mom said when she saw it?" I ask, laughing.

"You showed it to your mom?" Jess's eyes are full of horror. After my father almost kicked Jess out for giving me black nail polish with sparkles for my thirteenth birthday, we agreed to keep all her gifts private.

"She said it ended before it even began."

Jess moves the laptop aside and rolls onto her back, eyes trained on the ceiling and her face tense. "Your mom is so weird."

Her words bite a little. "What do you mean?"

"I mean..." She pulls her lower lip between her teeth and pauses. "Don't get me wrong. I have nothing against your dad. He's a solid dude, but he's got some loose screws. Why did your mom...marry him?"

Her question startles me, and not because it's sudden or inappropriate but because I've actually asked myself the same thing lately. A lot. Do people see my family the same way Jess sees it? A religious fanatic father ruling the household with an iron fist and a mother and daughter who follow him like sheep. Is this an accurate picture?

"Why does that make my mom weird?" I ask quietly.

Jess confirms my theory. "Your dad acts like he owns you both and she never says anything. You still have to lie to him about where you go."

The eerie silence that settles between us lasts for a good minute as I try to digest everything Jess just dumped on me. The YouTube video has come to an end, and now there's no more music and I'm missing the quiet storm of Dakota's voice.

"Just because he's paying your tuition doesn't mean he should tell you what to do." Jess reaches for the laptop and switches the browser windows. My eyes catch a collection of Midnight Rust photos on the screen.

"You're stalking the band now?" I ask, totally forgetting about my parents because there, in one of the shots, Dakota is shirtless. He's in the middle of the group, laughing, his face turned slightly away from the camera. It looks like a post-show cell phone photo with fans or friends. His hair's wet and his body glistens with sweat. The image is somewhat blurry, but that's a good thing. Seeing that much skin confuses me even more.

"I'm conducting a study." Jess giggles. "The drummer may have asked me out."

"No way!"

"Yes way!" She flips over onto her stomach and slides the laptop toward me.

Heat rises to my cheeks as I glance at the screen again. Something inside me twinges. A jealousy streak maybe, because in the photo, there's a ridiculously perfect girl next to Dakota—the kind who'd fit him better than me—with long platinum blond hair and a butterfly tattoo on her shoulder.

"Earth to Alana!" Jess waves her hand in front of my face.

"Do you think he's talking to me because he likes me or because he just wants to sleep with me?" I ask, tearing my gaze away from the laptop.

She studies me for a few seconds. "Both."

I stifle a groan, wondering if that's a joke. If it is, it's pretty cruel.

"I'm serious," Jess says as if she's reading my mind. "I'm gonna tell you something right now." She lifts her head off the pillow and props it up with her hand. "Guys always say they want a bad girl, because it makes them look cool. But they're all liars. What they want is a girl like you. A nice girl who hasn't been fucked by three dozen other dudes. They just don't say it out loud. Trust me, if he's texting you like crazy, it's because he wants all of you. Mind, body, and soul."

I roll my eyes. Parts of me feel warm, fuzzy, and a little uncomfortable. Jess isn't the kind of a friend who has a sensitivity filter. She's more of a brutal truth and ugly metaphors type of person.

"Those creative writing classes are really paying off," I say with a bit of sarcasm.

"Have you looked in the mirror lately?" Jess gives me a toothy grin.

"Don't know what you're talking about." I brush her off, minimizing the window with the band's photos.

"You are aware you're smoking hot, right?" Her eyebrow jumps up her forehead. "Like get-the-hell-out-of-here hot."

"And you're aware you aren't allowed to say the H-word in my house?" I grab one of the pillows and toss it at her.

She ducks and rolls to her back to avoid the impact. "Is your dad home?"

"I think so. Why?"

"Smoking, devil-melting-hell hot!" her voice booms through my room like thunder.

"My father's going to ban you from our house." I throw another pillow at her and we laugh until my cheeks begin to hurt.

"Do you know what you're baking for your Christmas post?" Jess changes the subject once we calm down.

"Red velvet cupcakes."

"We did those last year."

"No, they were Nutella cupcakes." I slide from the bed and go to my closet to grab my khakis and work shirt.

Jess closes the laptop and checks her phone. "Do you need a ride?"

"No. It's fine. I'll drive myself."

Who knows? Maybe these are my final weeks to use the Prius. Maybe my father won't let me have it after I move out.

I baked my first cupcake when I was fourteen. It was a simple vanilla one with buttercream frosting and sprinkles on top, and I was over the moon when my father ate the whole thing. Six months and twenty different recipes later, he drove me to Anna's Pastry to meet Mrs. Kaminski and find out if she needed help.

That's how I got my first job and how my blog started.

The thought of telling the woman who took a chance on me when I was a clueless teenager that I no longer want to work with her makes me feel guilty. Especially now, right before the holiday season when it's the busiest time of the year for the shop.

My phone pings in my pocket, jarring me back to reality, and I realize it's almost ten and I've only swept half of the dining room.

"Can you come in at two tomorrow, Alana?" Mrs. Kaminski yells from the back. She still has a bit of an accent. Unlike my father, whose parents immigrated to the States from Poland long before he was born, she came here as a grown woman in the nineties, along with her husband and kids. Her family has owned this bakery for over a decade.

"I have class until one," I say. "I'll do my best to be here by two."

My anxiety pushes me to sweep faster. I know the message that just came in is from Dakota. I spent a good portion of my shift searching for covert places to text him back. Freezer, restroom, three trips outside to the dumpster to take out the trash.

After finishing up the dining room floor and stocking the front for tomorrow morning, I finally summon enough courage to talk to Mrs. Kaminski. It's the end of the day and she's sitting in her tiny office, staring at the screen of the old computer that looks like it belongs in a nineties movie and has probably been here ever since the bakery opened.

"Mrs. Kaminski." I stop in the doorway and clear my throat. "Do you have a minute?"

She tears her gaze away from the spreadsheet and looks at me with her tired eyes. "Sure."

"I know this probably isn't a good time, but I believe I might be leaving in a few weeks."

She clutches her hands together and makes a sound that's a mixture of a sigh and a gasp.

"I can still work until after Christmas," I add, feeling like a total traitor and wanting to take everything back.

Mrs. Kaminski gives me a small smile, and the web of wrinkles around her eyes deepens. "I can't keep you here forever, dear. I wish I could, though." A quiet laugh escapes her throat. "You are a good girl and a great help. Whatever you decide to do next, I hope it works out for you."

Her words clatter around in my head like pieces of broken glass, cutting and stabbing.

"Thank you," I say, my hand reaching for my phone that's buzzing inside my pocket. "I'll see you tomorrow at two."

"Have a good night, Alana." She returns to her dinosaur of a computer.

I pull off my visor and rush outside, the back door slamming shut behind me as the soft beep of the alarm follows me to my car.

My phone feels hot and heavy in my palm and I take a moment to catch my breath before looking at all the unread texts from Dakota.

6. AFTER

I sit inside my car in the parking lot for what seems like an eternity, paralyzed with fear, studying the printout of the campus evacuation map and staring at the scars on my palms. The pain is now gone, and what's left is a strange pulling sensation. My coffee is lukewarm and tastes like expired milk with a shot of acid. I'm trying to remember whether I took my anti-anxiety medication this morning, because ever since I left my house, my breathing has been out of control, shallow and fast one second and loud and slow the next. I'm not entirely sure how I didn't get into an accident on the way here.

Jess and I never met up last weekend. It was partially my fault because I ignored her texts. On Wednesday, when I finally summoned enough courage to check my social media for the first time since the attack, I spent a good hour staring at the photo of Luke she posted on her Instagram from the hospital where he'd gone in for his second surgery.

There's a small fraction of me that's jealous of them, and I wonder if it's because I was always a bad person or because I've become one. Everything around me has changed. The attack divided my life into the light before and the dark after. There's nothing left in between. No grays or any other colors.

Maybe my mother's right about me needing more time off, or maybe her constant nagging has convinced me. My father even brought up an indefinite break over the weekend, which didn't sound like him at all. All my life, he's been hell-bent on making sure I have a college education. Why is he now against me going back to school?

After checking the evac map one last time and skimming through the long string of unread text messages on my phone, only to ignore every single one of them, I grab my backpack and get out of the car. My knees feel weak and my feet begin to quake.

You can do it, Alana. It's just a college campus.

I slam the door of my Prius shut, slide the keys into the side pocket of my backpack, and start walking. My heartbeat picks up and my stomach churns. There's bile coming up my throat. The fact that I'm about to enter a building with several thousand people inside and very few exits rattles me. The t-shirt underneath my jacket is damp from my sweat and the backpack feels like it's stuffed with bricks.

I haven't been anywhere since the night of the shooting except for the hospital and Dakota's funeral. My mother's been insisting that I see a grief counselor, but there were no appointments available last week, so she made one for me for tomorrow. She also won't stop talking about some local support group she's found online.

Coming to a complete stop in front of the main entrance of the building where my class is located, I evaluate the massive concrete steps. The heavy wooden doors swinging open and closed non-stop look morbid and menacing.

I stand like this, with my hands clutched around the straps of my backpack and my chest heaving, for a good minute, wondering if I should go home.

"Alana?" Someone taps my shoulder, yanking me back to the real world.

I jerk away and swivel toward the sound.

The person across from me is Mallory. If my memory serves me right, we have English and a couple of other classes together and she borrowed my notes once. Her eyes are wide with shock and she's looking at me as if the hole in my chest is visible.

"Hey," I mumble under my breath, my hand reaching out for my injured cheek.

"I'm sorry. I didn't mean to scare you." She gives me a sympathetic smile.

"You didn't." I shake my head.

"How are you?"

"Okay." *Considering my boyfriend got shot and killed a couple of weeks ago.*

"I-I'm so sorry to hear about Dakota," she stammers through her condolence.

"Thanks," I tell her, wondering if that was the right thing to say. I've never had anyone close to me die before. Are there any rules of etiquette regarding how to act in public after you bury someone you love? Although, technically, Mikah and his family buried Dakota. I was that girl at his funeral who tried to tear his hand off.

"Hey"—Mallory clears her throat—"if you need anything, let me know."

The number of times this phrase has been thrown at me since The Crystal Room is probably well above a hundred. I'm sick and tired of hearing the same exact words day after day. I should have a proper response handy, but my brain still struggles with the answer. I give her a small nod, and the silence between us becomes awkward.

"Call me or text me, all right?" She forces out another smile.

"Okay. Thank you," I say as I watch her hop up the steps and disappear into the building.

I don't remember how I make it to class. My mind blocks everything out and wanders off into some parallel universe where Dakota is still alive. I relentlessly push through the noisy crowd in the hallway, my hands clutching the straps of my backpack, my head low and my gaze trained on the floor. My damp t-shirt sticks to me. Thankfully, no one can see the sweat stains under my jacket.

Talking to more people is not part of the plan today. *Or ever.*

Once I'm inside the auditorium, instead of going to my usual seat in the front, I search for every means of escape and walk all the way to the back to take a lonely spot in the corner, near an emergency exit and away from the stares of other students. Some are nosy enough to turn around and look, but most don't bother. Maybe because The Crystal Room is now old news.

The chatter dies down and a quiet murmur takes its place when the professor finally enters the auditorium.

I drop my gaze to the brand new notebook in front of me and stare at the white pages. My brain tries to recreate the building evacuation plan, but I can't remember where exactly the crisis response boxes are. I know there are fifteen on this campus. There are also six emergency phones and seventeen AED locations. *Or is it sixteen?*

Concentrate, Alana. Concentrate.

My mind's having a hard time focusing on the lecture. I'm not entirely sure why I need to know what year John Locke was born or what his major works were about, but I still force myself to jot down some notes because I practiced holding a pencil all weekend and I don't want my efforts to go to waste. And because this is what college is for. Taking notes. Although mine are just a bunch of sentences that make very little sense, and I probably won't have any use for them. Ever.

A fire drill might be a better alternative, but we haven't had a single one since I started going to this college, and I'm certain that's not right. They need to be carried out at least twice a year.

We're fifteen minutes in when I hear the squeak of a door followed by heavy thuds. Someone is late to class, which is nothing unusual. Professor Pollock isn't that great at keeping his students interested. I suspect that by the end of the semester, there will be only five of us left. That's if *I* make it to the end of the semester. I've already missed quite a lot. Does this college have any special make-up rules for students who take time off after being gunned down? Is there some sort of excuse for people who've lost someone?

My eyes are still glued to my notebook when I hear a loud pop. I jerk in my seat, and my heart crashes into my ribcage. A chorus of whispers swirling around snap me out of it, and I realize what I heard was only a door slamming. But in my head, it sounded like something else. It sounded like a gunshot.

"Ms. Novak?" The professor moves in my direction.

"What?" My vision blurs and my hands shake.

"Are you okay, Ms. Novak?"

"Yes," I murmur, tossing my notebook and my pencil into my backpack.

The whispers that trail after me as I charge for the door grow louder. The noise is overwhelming and I almost want to stop and tell them to shut up, but instead, I rush outside as if the building is on fire. My feet carry me into the courtyard, where there are no walls and no people crowding me.

Where I can breathe and run if I have to.

There's a police car in our driveway when I return home. Something tells me my parents didn't expect me this early, because their faces are twisted with anxiety when they see me walking into the house.

"Ma'am." One of the officers gives me a light nod. The other one shows me a tight-lipped smile. The two of them, along with my parents, watch me take off my jacket as if I'm stripping and pole dancing in the middle of our living room.

"What's going on?" I look at my parents, then at the police. There's a heaviness inside my chest and I feel like I can't get enough air.

"We'll talk about it in a bit, sweetheart," my father says. His every-thing-is-okay face isn't that great; I can read through his bullshit perfectly. Something's going on and they just don't want to tell me. It sickens me that they think keeping stuff from me or keeping me away from things is going to make it better. Things are shit and they're not going to get better.

"Okay, fine," I snap, hurrying toward my room, my heart sputtering.

I hear my mother following me up the stairs. "Alana!" I can tell by her voice that she's on the verge of panic, and I wonder if she's going to unplug the router to stop me from checking the news. She's done it once before. Right after the funeral. I'm expecting the internet to go out at any second as I draw my laptop from my bag and set it on the bed. There's a knock on my door, and my mother's still talking. Only, her words don't reach me.

My eyes are trained on the screen, my chest caving. I feel all the air leaving my room at the sight of the headlines.

"New Details Emerge During Hearing Regarding Portland Nightclub Shooting Suspect"

"Miller's Attorney Insists on Psychiatric Evaluation"

"Judge Considers Trial Delay"

7. AFTER

I wake up in the middle of the night, trembling and wheezing. My sheets are wet from the cold sweat and my heart's plummeting into my gut.

I lie there, stupefied, eyes wide open, hands clutched to my chest, staring at the white ceiling and listening to the desolate howls of wind. The hemlocks right outside my window are thrashing wildly against each other and I can almost hear the branches crying. It's a sad, chilled- to-the-bone sound of hysteria. Like the sound of something unsuspecting being torn apart by something mighty and neither having any control over it. They're two forces, one doomed and one destined to demolish the other.

I'm trying to tell if it was the noise from the trees scraping against the glass or the dream I was having that woke me up. In my dream, Dakota was holding my hand and his palm was stone cold, just like at the funeral. His smile was wide and playful, but his eyes were empty and colorless.

I inhale through my nose and exhale slowly through my teeth in an attempt to calm myself down. My breaths are shallow and weak, and my t-shirt is uncomfortable and itchy against my skin.

After sitting in my own sweat for a good hour, I crawl out of bed and search for my phone.

This is a very bad idea, Alana, my common sense reminds me as I hide under the blanket and flip through my contact list, my heart racing as my thumb hovers above the screen. *Normal people sleep at this hour.*

It rings a few times, and then a tired voice answers, "Yeah?"

"Can't sleep," I blurt out, rocking back and forth on my bed with my knees tucked under my chin.

"Sorry." Mikah's whisper is barely there, and I can't tell whether he's been sleeping or he simply doesn't want to talk to me. The truth is, I didn't know who else to call. Jess has been taking sleeping pills to help her get through the nightmares, and trying to get her between ten at night and six in the morning is like trying to call the Bermuda Triangle.

"Did I wake you up?"

"No...not really." He pauses, his breathing on the line abnormally loud.

"Do you..." My tongue feels thick and useless in my mouth. Everything I was going to say has turned into a tangled ball of incoherent thoughts and I'm not sure how to untangle them to build a proper sentence.

"Do I what?" Mikah says.

The air around me becomes hot and heavy, and I push the blanket aside before I suffocate from lack of oxygen inside my makeshift hiding place. It's not like my parents are going to hear me, anyway. "Did you know"—I feel sick from the mere fact that I have to say his name—"Miller's attorney is going to insist on insanity?"

"I heard."

"You know what that means, right? They'll send him to some fucking hospital." This is probably the first time in my life that the F-word has left my mouth, but I'm so angry that I can't control the words pouring out of me.

"I know."

"It's not fair." I sound small and defeated.

"Life's not fucking fair, Alana."

I don't ever remember him calling me by my name and, in a way, it feels nice. It's nice to know I'm not just some girl his brother dated.

The mere idea that a person who shot twenty-four people in cold blood is going to get off on some stupid technicality makes me shake. I choke back my anxiety and change the subject before panic consumes me entirely. "Do you sleep at all?"

"Not much. You?"

"I can't. I keep having these dreams. Like I'm still there..." My voice cracks and I stop mid-sentence, wondering whether talking about Dakota right now is wise. *Whether talking about Dakota with Mikah is wise.*

"Smoke some weed," he offers, as if it's Tylenol we're talking about.

"Have you met my parents?"

Mikah ignores my question. "Do you still plan on picking up your stuff from the apartment?"

"Yes. I'm sorry. I forgot. I was supposed to text you."

"You were. Last week."

"Is Friday okay? Are you going to be home?"

"Friday's fine. In the afternoon. I've got boxes. Don't bring any."

"Okay. Thanks."

Silence.

I wait for Mikah to say something, but he doesn't.

"I'm sorry I called so late." I fall back on the damp pillow.

"You mean early?" A light chuckle.

"Right." I stare at the ceiling, nibbling on my bottom lip. "Is it okay...if I call you sometime...when I can't sleep?"

"It's fine." His voice softens and for a brief moment, it sounds a lot like Dakota's. "Get some rest. I'll see you Friday."

He ends the call before hearing my goodbye.

"See you Friday," I whisper to no one and toss the phone on the nightstand.

After staring at the dark for a good minute, I crawl out of my bed, turn on the light, and settle at the desk. The book has been sitting next to my pink organizer set for a while now, but I haven't had the heart to open the package yet. Something about reading it scares me. I don't think it's the bloodsucking monster factor. I think it's something else, something I'm going to find there I might not like. Or like too much. I may like the wicked grim as much as Mikah does.

Resting both hands on top of the envelope, I close my eyes and try to analyze the mess of my thoughts. They're horses on a racetrack, competing with each other inside my head.

I sit like this for a little while, until my mind slips into a long-awaited glimpse of tranquility. Opening my eyes, I grab a pair of scissors. My fingers are stiff and trembling as I begin to cut the side of the envelope. The bubble wrap scrunches lightly as I pull the book out of the package and scan the cover. It's blood red and black, and against the oak finish of my desk, the dark colors look ominous. Just like the title.

Dracula.

I've never read a horror novel, but I want to read this one. I don't know whether it's because Mikah recommended it to me or because it seems fitting to read horror when you live in one.

8. BEFORE

I'm regretting wearing the red top to the show, because the temperature outside is subzero, and the walk from Jess's car to the club reminds me of a walk through hell that's frozen over. My jacket and boots feel paper-thin and aren't much protection against the frosty wind. I'm well aware that beauty requires some sacrifices, but part of me wants to run back to Jess's car and cuddle in front of the heater. My body has never been subjected to this much torture simply to ensure that the boy in the band that my friend and I are going to see is thoroughly impressed.

Then we have to endure the cold for another ten minutes while the person working the Will Call window sorts out the backstage passes the guys left for us.

Once we're in the lobby, Jess calls Luke.

"You look fucking beautiful," she says proudly, sliding her phone into the back pocket of her skinny jeans.

"I feel like a chunk of ice." I bring my trembling hands to my mouth and blow some hot air to restart the circulation in my fingers.

"Sexy chunk of ice." Jess winks, waving her laminate pass in my face. "Let's go find backstage."

The fact that she always wears next to nothing in winter when she goes out and doesn't blink at the cold makes me wonder if she's human. Unless it's liquid helium running through her veins instead of blood.

Inside, the dominant color of everyone's clothes is black. There's denim, spikes, leather, and tons of tats, some of them with what my father would call "blasphemous" designs. Which brings me to what I've wondered half my life—whether he's really my father, because I personally find all these "unacceptable" things oddly fascinating.

I find people who aren't afraid to be who they want to be interesting. Even if they don't meet my father's unreasonable standards.

The main floor is packed. The music blaring from the speakers is gravelly with overwhelming lyrics. I hear the ominous words *dark, midnight,* and *blood* that stir something in me. Not in an unpleasant way, because the melody is still beautiful. Chilling but beautiful. Much like some of the Midnight Rust songs on YouTube. These words somehow resonate with me and with my feelings.

We meet Luke next to a narrow door near the side of the stage. He's dressed in solid black, his blond hair slicked back. His cheeks are pink and his eyes are wide as they roam around the room. He looks tipsy. The bouncer's gaze ping-pongs between Jess and me and our IDs for a very long time before he finally hands us two yellow wristbands.

The backstage area is a dark maze of endless hallways full of equipment and half-naked bodies—girls in spider web tees and tights, guys in spandex and leather. I feel like a teddy bear who accidentally got shipped into an adult toy store by mistake.

Luke's head is gliding above the heads of everyone in front of us as he leads the way. He's tall, loud, and a little drunk, and everyone seems to want to talk to him.

We reach the end of the hallway and get ushered into a small, stuffy dressing room. The smell of alcohol, cheap perfume, and cigarette smoke crawls up my nostrils as Jess pulls me into the cluster of people.

She has this amazing gift to instantly blend in anywhere, be it the rock'n'roll scene or an academic seminar. I just stand next to her, unmoving, smiling at everyone as I look around the room for Dakota, suddenly feeling nervous about not fitting in. My gaze slides from one person to another until it reaches an opening among the bodies.

There, in a tiny space between the studded jacket of a guy with a mohawk and the skin-tight top of a girl with purple hair, is a man who looks a lot like Dakota, although a bit older. I'm thinking he may be one of the guys from the band photos or videos, but I've been too starstruck to pay attention to anyone but the lead singer.

He's sitting on a bench in the corner. Alone. Or at least, that's what it appears he wants to be, because he's not participating in any of the conversations. There's a guitar on his lap and his palms are resting protectively on the body of the instrument as if she's an antique. He's wearing a Lost Boys t-shirt, and patches of ink cover his long, sculpted arms. He's somewhat magnificent in his solitude, and the curiosity dancing in his eyes when his gaze catches mine sends a light chill up my spine.

"Hey, you!" The velvety voice that comes at me from the crowd belongs to Dakota. He reaches out to grab my shoulder and pulls me away from the center of the gathering.

"You made it." His fingers, soft and warm, are still pressed against my skin, and despite my father preaching so much about how immoral it is to let guys like Dakota touch me the way I'm being touched right now, I don't think it's sinful. My father probably got the Bible all wrong.

If anything, it's amazing and sizzling and makes me tingle all over.

"Yes." I nod, my lips stretching into a silly smile. My eyes can't get enough of him. His stage persona is sophisticated yet dark and enigmatic with a touch of wicked.

"You want something to drink?" he asks.

"Ummm." My eyes dart around the room, scanning everyone's wristbands. Not a single person is wearing a yellow one besides Jess and me. "Water's fine."

"Sure." Dakota leans forward, his mouth near my ear. "I'm glad you came." His breath, hot and heavy against my temple, trickles down my neck like an invisible feather, leaving a trail of goose bumps. His earthy smell entraps me in a sensual daze, the kind I don't want to escape from. The kind that's dirty, erotic even.

The fact that these forbidden thoughts creep into my mind staggers me.

If this is what my father considers a fast track to hell, I'm buying a one-way ticket and taking Dakota with me.

The pre-show chaos around me is strangely exciting. I've never been backstage before and I'm wondering if the stories about drugs and strippers are only stories, because, despite the abundance of drinks, no one here is snorting anything or having sex.

Jess and Luke look awfully cozy and Dakota had to step away for a second. I'm in the middle of the room surrounded by people I don't know, feeling uneasy. A bottle of water in my hand screams "minor."

"You look lost, new girl," a rough voice calls from behind me. I spin on my heels and come face to face with the guitar guy I saw earlier on the bench.

"I am," I agree, trying not to be too obvious while I stare, but he's the kind of guy you'd stare at against your will. Dark and mysterious with long midnight black hair, emerald green eyes full of secrets, and intricate ink designs on his arms that must have tons of stories behind them. He's the kind of guy my dad would call a "sinner."

"I've never seen you before," the stranger says, his face emotionless.

"It's my first time here," I explain, and the plastic bottle crackles between my fingers.

"I see. Well, all right. Have fun." He gives me a curt nod, his eyes sizing me up one last time as he prepares to retreat.

That's when Dakota's smile enters my line of vision.

Standing side by side, they look almost identical, and now I have no doubt they're related. Jess may have mentioned something when she trolled the band's YouTube channel, but I probably missed that part. They have the same facial features, the same hair color, and the same body build. The same yet different. Like two sides of the same coin. Maybe even like Jekyll and Hyde from what I can tell by their demeanors, although that might be a stretch, because I don't know either one well enough.

"I see you already met my brother." Dakota confirms my theory, his gaze shifting from his *brother* to me and back before he shows me a dimple-dazzling smile that makes my heart dance. "Mikah, this is Alana. Alana. This is my brother, Mikah."

"Hi," I say meekly, wondering how upset my father would be if he knew I was backstage with the band. I'm also wondering why he infiltrates my thoughts at the most inappropriate moments, like right now.

"Cool." Mikah's sounds indifferent. He turns to Dakota and gives him a light pat on the back. "I'll see you on stage, kid." Then he disappears into the crowd.

As Mikah leaves, I sense a shift in the air between them. Awkward tension maybe or perhaps it's something else?

"Don't pay attention to him. He doesn't like people much," Dakota explains, laughing.

"Okay." I shake off the unsettling feeling and try not to let the odd encounter with his brother get to me.

The lights dim and a wave of excited whispers rush through the club. Jess grabs my hand and pulls me toward the stage. Luke got us spots at the mixing board area, but Jess insists on getting the full rock'n'roll experience. According to her, watching a show from the sidelines is a waste of a good time. She gets high on being in the middle of the chaos. Sometimes I think that for her, rubbing against sweaty people is like crack is for junkies. I don't try to stop her. We get as close to the front rows as the rabid fans let us. There are a lot of girls our age in the crowd, which, for some reason, ignites a tiny spark of jealousy in me.

Dakota's band may be a bit more popular than I thought.

Jess finds us a spot that's free of obstructions and we wait for the set to begin. Anticipation fills every part of me as I gaze up to the stage and drink in the shimmering dark. When Luke's silhouette lingers beside the mountain of amplifiers, everyone cheers. He walks over to his drum kit and sends a few tipsy smiles to the girls propped against the edge of the stage. There's no pit here tonight like during the Black Rose show. The setting's more intimate. I suspect the lack of massive props is because Midnight Rust isn't a headliner, but I can tell a lot of people came specifically to see Dakota, because half the audience is wearing his band's merch and the other half is sporting Eclectic Blue t-shirts.

My heart gallops as people push from behind to get closer to the music the moment the rest of the band comes out on stage.

Dakota looks so collected, as if he were born for this. His hooded glance flutters over the crowd as he moves to the beat in front of the microphone. He doesn't move a lot, just enough to get the audience going. Every word and every smile has a purpose. He strums the chords on his guitar slowly and gracefully, letting the haunting melody float through the club as the clouds of white fog that trickle across the stage grow thicker and begin to spill into the crowd.

I watch him with sick fascination as his words slowly ravage my walls. He's exactly the kind of guy my father has always warned me about. Sinfully beautiful and addictive. His deep voice burns and tingles inside my chest like a fireball, and I find it hard to contain my emotions. I avoid looking at Mikah at all costs, but my eyes betray me during his guitar solo. He's not one of those show-off players who likes to get creative or draw attention to his portion of the song. He's modest in his presence. I can't quite read his body language, but his face says it all. He runs through the riff effortlessly with his eyes closed and his head tossed back.

My chest expands from the onslaught of sounds, and I tear my gaze away from his hands to look at Dakota again.

Together, they're psychedelic.

I'm standing in the middle of the alley, watching the guys load up the last of their gear and waiting for Jess to come out.

The tips of my nose and fingers are frozen solid, and the mist that's falling over the city feels cold and miserable against my face.

Dakota rounds the van, says something to Luke, and heads over to me. His hair's still damp and he blows hot air into his fist to get his hands warm. "Did you like the show?" His eyes search mine.

Like is an understatement. I've never seen a band like Midnight Rust before. I've never thought songs about death could be this beautiful. I have questions. Tons of them. I want to know why Dakota's so obsessed with such dark subject matter, and I want to know how he and Mikah write music together and what their process is like. But I realize asking about his brother might be a bit out of left field. That's why I push those thoughts back.

"I loved it," I say dreamily, rubbing my palms together. My inner fangirl is going crazy right now.

"Do you want to go see a movie sometime?"

His question makes everything inside me quake. Not counting the pre-show dressing room small talk and non-stop text messaging, we barely know each other. Without a doubt, my father's going to say no to this, but that doesn't make me want to tell Dakota yes any less.

I inhale sharply and the cold air stings my lungs as my mind goes through all one hundred and ten scenarios of how to avoid a lengthy conversation about boys and their intentions with my father.

"I'll let you pick the movie?" Dakota tilts his head, his eyes pretty much pleading with me. They're devastatingly beautiful and expressive and hard to resist. In the corner of his left one, there's still a tiny black smudge of eyeliner that he was probably in too much of a hurry to remove, and I want to reach out and wipe it off.

"Sure." I nod, my hands clutched into a ball in front of my chest. "I'll go."

"Awesome." The grin that spreads across his lips gives me goose bumps. I just saw a whole lot of girls throwing themselves at him during the show and he chooses to ask *me* out.

"Hey, DK!" Mikah's gravelly voice comes at us from the van. "Are you done?"

Whistles echo across the alley.

Dakota glances over his shoulder. "I have to go. I'll text you later?"

"Okay." My mind is reeling and my heart's in total overdrive. *What have you gotten yourself into, Alana?*

I have to remind myself to breathe as I watch him rush back to the van. The sound of his boots thudding against the frozen pavement pounds in my ears until the roar of the engine cuts it off.

After Jess drops me off at home and I've taken a shower and added a few more photos of Christmas cupcakes to my Pinterest board, I find myself going to the Midnight Rust website again.

I'm not sure exactly why, but I flip through the band photos again, this time studying each one differently, taking my time to compare Dakota and Mikah. Their eyes, their cheeks, their lips. I wonder how they make music together—what it's like for them as brothers to be in the same band. I wonder what it would be like to have a sibling of my own. Would it be like being friends with Jess or would there be more fights and disagreements and parents favoring one over the other? Then I wonder how my father will react when I tell him about going to the movies with Dakota.

9. AFTER

I ring the bell once and listen to it echo on the opposite side of the door. My heart beats like a drum. This is the first time since Dakota died that I've come here, and as my right foot taps out a wicked dance on the welcome mat, the feeling of doom and desolation that's taken over my mind forms a toxic cloud above me.

I hear footsteps approaching, and then the lock snaps and the door swings wide open. Mikah's wearing a black t-shirt and a pair of faded jeans, and his body takes up almost the whole doorframe. His hair's tied back and his face looks even thinner than it did the last time I saw him—at the funeral.

His eyes stare into mine unblinkingly for a few seconds, as if he's trying to remember why I'm here.

"Hi," I breathe out, clasping my hands together in front of me. "I came to pick up my stuff."

"Oh. Yeah, okay." He steps to the side to let me in, and his gaze drops to the floor. "I said to text me."

"Sorry, I forgot," I confess, walking past him into the living room. My chest tightens at the sight of the bare walls and the boxes. "Are you moving out?"

"Can't afford it on my own." Mikah shuts the front door.

We both know this is only half the truth.

"Did you already find a new place?" I shove my fists into the pockets of my coat for no particular reason. Maybe it's the scars or maybe it's because I'm not sure what to do with my hands. My gaze darts around and lands on the black guitar case in the corner.

"Still looking."

The silence that stretches between us becomes sour and awkward and ominous.

"You know where the room is." Mikah gestures at the hallway.

"Okay, thanks," I mumble, my heart still hammering, my palms suddenly damp and my vision blurred. The way my body reacts to everything now is exhausting. It's in a state of constant fear with every muscle so tense that it physically hurts.

Taking a deep breath, I shuffle my feet in the direction of Dakota's room. My hand is shaky and doesn't feel like mine at all when I push the door open. I almost expect him to be sitting on his bed cross-legged with his laptop in front of him and wearing a silly grin.

Instead, there are several large boxes stacked in the corner near the nightstand. The bed is untouched and the closet is wide open. Some of the posters that used to decorate the walls are rolled into a neat pile on top of the desk. There's a visible layer of dust covering all the surfaces.

When I lift my head and stare at the empty ceiling, a sense of hollowness spreads through me like wildfire, filling my every cell with endless agony. At this moment, my brain finally realizes that he's gone and he's not coming back. My heart doesn't get it, though.

My heart's still a raw wound and wants to stay in denial indefinitely. Because denial is comfortable.

After a few minutes of being frozen in place and breathing the stuffy air, I cross the room, fumble with the jammed window lock, and slide the bottom pane open. The frosty breeze creeping inside ruffles the posters on the nightstand and the tattered corners of Dakota's notebooks he used for jotting down song ideas.

After getting my things out of the drawers, I pull one of his leather jackets from the closet and try it on in front of the mirror. Its sleeves are way too long and with the way it sits so heavy across my shoulders like a suit of armor, I'm wondering how he wore it.

I stand there, staring at my reflection, and my mind begins drifting off, getting lost in the memories of Dakota and me.

When the sound of Mikah's footsteps thumping along the hallway yanks me out of my daze, I'm sitting in the middle of the room with my knees buried in the carpet as I organize some of Dakota's clothes that I pulled from the closet.

"You don't need to do any of that," Mikah says, walking into the room. There's a plastic container in his hand and he moves past me to shut the window.

I jump from the loud slam of the pane against the sill. Sudden noises have been bothering me a lot lately. At night, I lie wide-awake, listening to the sounds of trees outside or an occasional car passing by, sometimes wondering whether one of these days I'll hear a gunshot.

"It's okay. I don't mind helping," I counter.

"I want my mom to look through it before I pack it."

"Oh... Okay." I rest my hand on the pile of t-shirts I already folded. They're soft against my scars and smell like Dakota.

"Look, I have to take some of the stuff to storage, so..." Mikah clears his throat and sets the container next to me. "If you're about done, I gotta leave before they close."

"Sure. I just need to pack these few things." I push myself off the floor and get to my feet.

"Looks good on you, church girl," Mikah says, his gaze sliding over the jacket. "A little big, but you're totally rocking it."

"Thanks." My fingers fumble with the lapel.

"You want to keep it?"

"Yeah."

"It's yours."

"Thanks." I feel like this is too much to ask, but I still do as I motion toward the ceiling. "What about the hummingbirds?"

"Our mom took them," Mikah mutters.

We go back to the living room where he's already set several boxes near the door. I'm still wearing Dakota's jacket, and my coat and purse are sitting on top of the plastic container I put all my other things into.

The thought of going home sends a feeling of dread down my spine.

"I really don't mind helping you," I say meekly, the hard container pressed against my chest. "I promise I won't say a word."

Mikah's face softens. "Sure. Can you take some of these boxes to my truck? Just the small ones."

"Yeah. Should I leave mine here or put it in my car?"

"Whatever you want is fine. I'm going to get some clothes on. My keys are on the kitchen table."

While Mikah's getting ready, I carry my things to my car, and then I haul two more boxes from the apartment to his truck.

The drive to storage is mostly quiet, except for the music blaring from the speakers. It's dark, sad, and unfamiliar, and I wonder what the name of the band is because I don't believe Dakota ever played it for me. However, my mouth won't open to articulate the question.

When we get to the unit, we stack everything up inside in grim silence. Mikah spends a good hour rearranging all of the boxes to make sure there's enough room, and I mainly just watch him because he's not that great with instructions. Occasionally, he asks me to hand him something, but that's as far as our interaction goes.

The sun has gone down when we arrive back at the apartment. We get out of the truck and Mikah pats his pocket to find his cigarettes. He looks tired, his face devoid of any emotions. Sometimes I wonder how he can hide them so well. I know he feels as much as I do, if not more. He was there when it happened and he cried at Dakota's funeral. But for the most part, he's like a rock. Cold and unbreachable. And I want to know how he does it, how he manages to block out every little thing that terrifies me.

I'm trying to decide between leaving him alone or asking if he needs more help with packing when he holds out the pack of Marlboros.

"You want one?" His eyes slide to my face.

"Ummm..." I stare up at him. "Sure." My fingers take them from him and pull out a single cigarette.

"You need instructions again?" he asks blandly.

"I think I can manage."

He draws the lighter from his pocket and lights our cigarettes.

I take a careful drag of mine and let the smoke coat my mouth and throat little by little.

"Don't waste my fucking cigarette, church girl," Mikah says, inhaling deeply.

"I'm not," I whisper.

He pushes the smoke out and it floats from his mouth in the shape of ragged circles.

"Is that the nickname you guys had for me?" I ask, looking at the red streaks of sunset splashing across the dimming sky.

"No."

"Then why are you calling me a church girl?"

"What do you want me to call you?"

His question is unexpected. Not that I anticipated an apology or anything. He's not that kind of a guy. "What did Dakota call me?"

"I don't know. He didn't talk about you."

Somehow, I don't believe him.

Mikah takes another drag and looks away, his gaze wandering off into the twilight distance. "Why do you want to know what he called you? Didn't you two spend like twenty-four hours a day together?"

This sounds a lot like a reprimand. "Because the time we had wasn't enough," I say, my voice cold. "Because I miss him."

Mikah stares down at me through the cloud of smoke. "Do you fucking think I don't miss him?"

"Then why don't you want to talk about him?"

"What for? He's dead."

The words float in the air, ugly and sad, soiling the last of the calm between us. It feels almost like if we don't say them out loud, Dakota might somehow come back.

"I'm sorry." I toss the cigarette on the ground and grind it into a patch of dirty snow with the heel of my boot.

"Look." Mikah tilts his head, his expression still serious but not as unkind. "I'm not a fucking therapist. If you want to talk about this shit that happened or my brother, talk to your counselor. If you want to talk about other stuff—not related to those two things—it's fine. I just can't take any more drama on right now."

"Okay. Do you not want me to call you then?"

"That's not what I said."

"I understand."

He finishes off his cigarette and locks the truck. "I have some beer. Do you want to hang out for a bit?"

"Sure."

<hr>

We sit in the living room on opposite sides of the coffee table. Mikah's on the couch, surrounded by boxes. I'm in a chair, still wearing Dakota's leather jacket and slowly getting used to its weight on my shoulders. The table creates the illusion of a barrier between us.

The music in the background sounds a lot like something Dakota would listen to. Soft and a bit sad. The cold bottle of beer feels foreign between my palms, and it tastes like crap. Not as bad as Jack Daniels, because it doesn't burn as much, but not as great as pineapple juice.

I contemplate whether I should tell Mikah about my Bram Stoker classic quest but decide against it. I don't want to look stupid by bringing up a book I'm not done with yet and have him criticize me for it. Instead, I choose an easy topic.

"I'm thinking of trying to bake a cheesecake for my blog."

"Have you baked one before?" Mikah asks, taking a swig of his beer.

He probably doesn't care about my blog or what my hobbies are, but since Dakota and the attack are off limits, I'm not sure what else to talk to him about.

"No. But I can bake cupcakes and carrot cake and red velvet cake and..." My tongue sticks to my palate.

Truth is, I have little interest in blogging right now. I haven't posted anything on my Instagram in weeks either, not since before The Crystal Room. My parents insisted I needed to stay away from the internet and social media after I had a panic attack. Finding out about a mass murderer getting a trial delay will do that to you, but what do they know, right? They weren't there.

"I see." Mikah's eyes slide over to me.

I take a small sip of my beer and pick at the thin plastic label coating the bottle. My gaze locks on Mikah's and I stare at him for a while, wondering why he invited me in.

We drink in silence, although I know it's probably best to leave since this hangout doesn't seem to be going as planned.

"Do you want another one?" Mikah asks as soon as his beer is empty. He rises to his feet and maneuvers around the boxes and into the kitchen.

I look at my bottle. There's still some left, but I say yes anyway.

The alcohol takes effect somewhere in the middle of my monologue on how to make a perfect cheesecake. I've never made one myself, but a girl can dream, right? My head's suddenly woozy, my body feels like it's fallen apart inside Dakota's jacket, and I'm having a hard time moving my hands.

"I think I'm drunk," I announce, shifting in my chair.

"You've had one beer." Mikah cocks an eyebrow at me as if I spoke to him in French.

"I don't really drink."

"I can see that."

"I'm kind of sleepy," I confess.

"Knock yourself out." He gets up and disappears down the hallway, the sound of his heavy footsteps growing softer and softer. He didn't just desert me here, did he?

I'm too dizzy to get up from the chair, so I keep sitting with my beer in my hands and my eyes closed until Mikah comes back a few minutes later with a blanket.

"Just sleep it off, okay?" He grabs the bottle from me and sets it on the coffee table.

I nod. My vision is blurred and my mind's fuzzy, and I realize for the first time since the attack—I don't feel like something bad is about to happen to me. Maybe it's the beer or maybe it's this place or maybe it's Mikah, but it's nice not to be scared for once.

I'm not sure exactly what time it is when I wake up, but I know it's very late. Past my curfew kind of late. It's that one hour in the middle of the night when everything goes still, when there's no traffic and no dogs barking, and if someone breathes somewhere inside the building, you know.

The blanket is on the floor. It must have fallen while I was asleep. The living room is dark and cold, and the apartment has an odd vibe— a blend of messy memories and uncertain future.

"Mikah?" I call from the chair, but for some reason, my voice is shot. His name comes out in a ragged whisper. My head's still a little fuzzy and the tips of my fingers tingle from lack of circulation when I try to move.

The quiet, barely-there music that I hear drifting through the darkness of the apartment seems bizarre at this hour.

Sitting up, I study the shadows in the living room and strain to hear the chords. My breath is stuck somewhere between my lungs and my throat. It's both calm and electrifying and sounds nothing like Mikah. I continue to listen until the music stops.

My bladder is what finally gives me the nudge to get up. Wrestling off Dakota's jacket, I stand and make my way down the hallway. The door to Mikah's bedroom is slightly ajar and light seeps through the narrow crack.

Inching forward, I peek inside and see Mikah perched on a chair with his acoustic guitar on his lap. He's staring at the screen of his desktop computer, and I recognize the Pro Tools interface.

Some of the things I learned when I used to watch Dakota work on the band's demos sort of stuck. Like what pedals are for, or what brands of amplifiers are best, or what Pro Tools is. They're small pieces of information you tend to pick up when you spend all your time with a musician.

Mikah tears his gaze away from the computer and plucks at the strings of his guitar, humming some words I can't make out. Seeing him sing makes me shiver all over, and I lose my balance and fall against the door, pushing it open. I grab at the handle to close it, but Mikah's already noticed me.

He stops playing and spins in his chair. "Are you still drunk?"

"No." I shake my head, looking around. He's taken the painting and most of the posters down, and what's left is bare walls and the essentials. His bookshelf is gone too. "Did you write that?" I gesture at the guitar, moving toward his bed to sit down.

"It's just some demos." He shrugs, his green eyes following me.

"You have a really nice voice."

Mikah doesn't respond. He drops his gaze to his guitar and fingers the strings. The melody filling the room is painfully familiar.

I watch him mess around with the chords with the same fascination with which I used to watch Dakota. During the shows, Dakota was always the one to perform the acoustic parts. At the last rehearsal before The Crystal Room performance, they played an acoustic song that they'd written together, but for some reason, it never made it into the final setlist. Hearing Mikah perform it without the shadow of Dakota's voice is strange.

The music abruptly comes to an end and Mikah sets his guitar aside and rises to his feet. "Are you hungry?" he asks, stretching.

"What do you have?"

"I don't know. Tacos, I think."

"Tacos are fine."

We eat in the kitchen in silence. The food tastes like rubber dipped in hot sauce, but it does the job.

When I get back home at six in the morning, my father's already up for work. I was hoping he'd still be asleep, but it's one of those weird Saturday mornings. Perhaps there was a messed-up shipment or someone called in sick.

"Your mother and I didn't sleep all night." My father vocalizes his displeasure with a combination of anger and disappointment as soon as he sees me walking into the living room. "The least you can do is pick up the phone."

"I was helping Mikah move some stuff to storage."

"I don't believe it's a good idea for you two to talk."

"Why not?"

My father sighs, and his tone softens. "Because you need to concentrate on yourself right now. Your school, your health, your future. You missed your therapy session yesterday."

"I rescheduled it," I counter. "I didn't feel well."

"That's why you need to be consistent with your treatment, Alana. To get better. If you keep skipping, it won't help."

"I'm not skipping."

"Why couldn't Mikah find someone else to help him?" He's almost pleading with his eyes and I notice that the net of wrinkles around them seems to have grown bigger. I wonder how much of that is my doing. "Why does it have to be you? And what are you wearing?"

I look down at my hands, my gaze sliding up to my chest and shoulders. I realize my coat is still in the trunk of my car along with the rest of my stuff I picked up from the apartment and I'm wearing Dakota's jacket. "I'm tired, Dad. Can we talk later?"

"Yes, when I get home," my father says, moving closer. He kisses the top of my head like he always does. "Get some rest now."

I watch him leave and then drag my feet up the stairs and into my room with the intention of sleeping, but sleep never comes.

After fighting my racing thoughts for a little while, I get back to reading *Dracula*.

10. AFTER

On Sunday, I decide to skip church.

Asking for things from a random, obviously deaf man in a robe who already took everything precious from me is stupid. It's not like my prayers are going to make him turn back time, press the replay button, and erase the attack or place Dakota and me somewhere safe. This stuff only happens in books and on TV. Real life is ridiculously cruel.

My parents aren't happy about my decision not to participate in our sacred family tradition, but, surprisingly, they let it slide. Probably because being around me has become a living hell. Or maybe they believe I'm going to embarrass them again by sneaking out to get drunk, like I did at Dakota's funeral.

There are no fights or lengthy conversations, just a quick, unexpected okay from my father.

I leave the house around eleven when my parents are still at church. The drive to the grocery store is short. It's only a half-mile down the street and around the corner, and I feel really good about this trip. But right when my Prius pulls into the parking lot, bits of dread begin to trickle into my stomach. There's a huge crowd near the entrance and the thought of going inside gives me goose bumps.

I look for a spot away from the chaos, park my car, and decide to wait. At quarter to one when both of my legs are asleep and my back is developing a deep ache from sitting in one position for so long, I grab my purse and fish out my phone.

He probably doesn't care about your baking, Alana. Just leave him alone.

After a brief hesitation, I open my messages and text Mikah.

I'm going to try making a cheesecake today. Do you want me to bring you some?

My prediction is correct. He doesn't respond nor does he read my message. Maybe he will later when he's not busy or maybe it'll be by mistake. Maybe there's another Alana he's seeing and he'll confuse me with her and accidentally look at my text instead.

I wait some more, but eventually, the rumble in my stomach and lack of circulation force me out of my car. The outside air is deceivingly pleasant. Blotches of dirty ice scattered around the parking lot have almost melted, and although the wind is merciless, crawling up my sleeves and under my collar like an evil spider, biting and chomping, when the sun touches my face, the fusion of warm and chilly feels nice against my skin.

I rush into the store with my purse slung over my shoulder and my hands thrust into my pockets. However, panic seizes me as soon as my feet step inside. My gaze drops to the tiled floor and I stop for a second, trying to remember where the baking supplies are, but my mind draws a blank. My anxiety is now in full force, laughing at me. Why did I think I could do this?

"Do you need any help?" someone calls from off to the side.

I lift my head and see a store clerk in front of me. He's my height and is probably about my age. He's pale and freckled, and his nametag reads "Jarrod."

"I need baking supplies," I mumble, trying to keep my heart rate under control, even though that doesn't seem possible at the moment.

"Aisle seven." The clerk motions at the area I'm supposed to be headed to. He has a nice smile. He seems polite and honest and doesn't look like someone who would start shooting at people out of jealousy.

"Thanks." My fists in my pockets tighten because I don't want him to see me shaking.

My phone buzzes in my purse when I'm in the middle of aisle

seven, staring at the bags of flour. We have some at home, but I'm not sure it's the kind that will work for a cheesecake.

I tear my gaze away from the shelves to check my texts and I see a message from Mikah.

i'm out of town maybe next time good luck

The heaviness of defeat pushes hard against my chest. My vision blurs and I narrow my eyes to try to bring the bags of flour back into focus, but instead, they turn into shapeless, floating blobs. The faint sound of footsteps behind me comes out of nowhere. I spin around and look at the empty aisle and the shelves stacked with food, my pulse racing. The air feels hot and sour.

Bang! Bang! Bang!

Stay down! Don't move.

I drop to my knees, my purse falling off my shoulder as my phone clatters across the tiled floor. Heat burns my chest.

On the opposite side of the aisle, I hear more footsteps and agitated voices.

"Are you okay?"

"Do you want me to call 911?"

"This is Thomas's kid!"

"Are you Alana? Can you hear me?"

A pair of strong hands pull me off the floor, but my legs don't cooperate. My thoughts are hazy and my body doesn't feel like my own.

"Let me call her parents," a man says from somewhere nearby.

I want to tell these people I'm okay and there's no need to bother my father and mother, because if they find out I freaked out at the grocery store, they'll never let me go back to work at Toro Bravo. But when I try to articulate the words, nothing but shallow breaths come out of my mouth.

The light inside the room is unusually twenty-karat-diamond bright. I don't remember it being this blinding the last time I was here. Although everything, including the memories of my latest hospital visit, is a bit fuzzy.

My mother's worried voice drifts at me from the other side of the room and I attempt to lift my head off the pillow, but all my vision snags on is the top of my father's gray head. The dizziness drags me back down a second later.

As I lie there, squinting and wheezing, my mind spins with endless questions. Then when the doctor finally exits the room, my mother gives me her undivided attention.

"Sweetheart." She grasps my hand carefully to make sure the IV needle in my vein doesn't move. Her meek smile tells me the news I'm about to receive isn't great. "The doctor wants to keep you overnight to run some more tests."

"Why?" There's a lump in my throat and I can't get rid of it no matter how many times I swallow.

"Because you had a panic attack at the grocery store, Alana," my mother says, leaning closer. Her eyes skim over my face. They're sad and confused with a dash of fear. "How can we let you leave the house? What if you get sick when you're driving?"

"I won't," I slur through the fog in my head, knowing all too well that I don't sound very convincing right now.

She looks up at my father, perhaps waiting for some show of support, but he doesn't say anything. His heavy footsteps move in the direction of the door and disappear into the hallway.

What remains is hot, lingering silence that drags on for an eternity, until my mother's desperate sigh slices through it like a knife.

In a way, I'm glad I'm this broken and we don't have to pretend anymore that I'm still my father's little girl. Living the life he designed for me was exhausting.

11. BEFORE

My heart thunders wildly as I make my way through Jess's front yard. The air outside is frosty and full of fine, swirling snowflakes that land on my face and thaw instantly.

There's a solid black classic Mustang with tinted windows parked by the curb, and somehow, I have no doubt it belongs to Dakota—he doesn't strike me as a Prius or a Toyota guy. It's a car for people who live a different lifestyle. A little fast and a little dangerous. Safety and reliability are not their concern. Adventure is.

As if on cue, the driver's side door swings open and Dakota steps out. He's wearing a black coat, a black sweater, jeans, and a pair of black military style boots with metal studs.

"Hey." His velvety voice fills the snowy air between us, melting the cold.

"Hey," I respond, trying to discern whether my father could somehow see past the long hair and the earring and accept the fact that I like a guy who's in a band.

I told my parents I was going to spend the evening studying with Jess and would probably be home late. They bought it. Like they always do.

"You look nice," Dakota says, rushing to open the door for me.

"Thank you. You look nice too," I mumble under my breath, my cheeks burning despite the cold.

Who the hell tells a guy he looks nice, Alana?

"Thanks." Dakota laughs. "Took me all afternoon to get this whole makeup thing right."

Our eyes meet briefly as I step into the warm car, and a fuzzy sensation fills my stomach. Do guys even do these things nowadays? Like holding a door?

"Ha ha." A small giggle bubbles up my throat as I get comfortable in my seat.

"Do you like The Cure?" Dakota asks, fumbling with some of the CDs stacked behind the visor above his head.

"Sure." I take a second to study the interior of his car. It's clean and smells like sandalwood. There's a small dreamcatcher ornament hanging from the rearview mirror and more CDs loosely stacked in the center console.

I'm still not certain whether we're on a date or not. The word hasn't been said yet, but we've been texting each other like crazy all week, and this, whatever's going on between us, feels natural and real.

Come to think of it, my life started to transform the minute we met. Last Monday, after my classes ended, I finally got up enough courage to drop off the job applications I'd downloaded online over the weekend, and one of the restaurants called me for an interview. Of course, there's still the talk-with-the-parents issue. My father's not going to be happy. But that seems insignificant at the moment.

The leather squeaks under my weight as I turn to look for the seatbelt buckle.

"Here." Dakota shifts to help me, and our hands collide. Tingles run across my skin.

"Thanks." My breath comes out in a quiet pant.

"Are you good?" He pulls back, but his fingers linger on mine, probably longer than they should.

"Yes. Thank you."

"You don't have to thank me every time I ask a question." He laughs softly as he hits the stereo play button and then music fills the car.

The second half of the movie is a complete blur. Dakota's holding my hand, and it's so distracting that my heart sprints as if it's desperate to make it into the *Guinness World Records*.

By the time the credits are rolling on the gigantic screen, even the tips of my ears are steaming hot.

"Are you hungry? Do you want to grab something to eat?" Dakota offers when we're in the lobby.

I stare down at my phone and contemplate whether texting my mom to tell her I'm staying over at Jess's would be too last minute and too suspicious, but my mouth has a mind of its own. "Sure, but I have to be up really early."

"I guess a trip to Seattle on a private jet's gonna have to wait then." He smirks. "How about some milkshakes from Patty's?"

"Are you kidding me?" Excitement bursts through me like a dozen small fireworks. "I love Patty's milkshakes." What amazes me isn't even the fact that he put me, dinner, and a private jet in one sentence. It's the fact that he actually knows a place I like.

"Right. It's the only diner in Portland open after ten." Dakota's laughter, lively and deep, fills my head, and I wonder how the light and the dark coexist in him without disturbing each other.

Outside, a layer of fine snow has already dusted the ground, the trees, and the cars. The city looks like a magical ice kingdom. The snowflakes squeak faintly under the weight of our boots as we make our way to Dakota's car. He reaches for my hand and his long fingers slip between mine.

"Is this a date?" My voice comes out as a strained whisper.

Dakota slows his pace and turns to face me, our hands still linked together. "Do you want this to be a date?" he asks, tilting his head to the side. The streetlight shimmering at us from above flickers across the skin on his cheek.

"Yeah," I breathe out. "I do."

"Then it's a date," he mouths at me as his grasp on my hand tightens.

When we arrive at Patty's, the snow is coming down hard. It's covered every single thing outside, including a homeless man seated near the entrance. I don't know his name, but I've seen him here before a few times during the summer.

We walk into the diner and after we grab a table, I wait for Dakota to get our order.

I'm a bit curious if anyone working here is going to notice who I'm here with. This is our—my and Jess's—spot, and this is the first time she hasn't been present for the milkshake tradition.

"Strawberry." Dakota sets my cup in front of me and slides onto the bench across the table. His forehead and his coat are now covered with tiny rivulets of water.

"Chocolate chip cookie?" I ask, studying the brown swirls of crumbs in his milkshake.

"Wanna try?" He wiggles his eyebrows at me, nibbling on the straw.

"I don't really like chocolate," I murmur as my gaze diverts to the foggy window. The tiny white flakes outside are still hard at work.

"How can you not like chocolate?" Dakota laughs. "Are you even human?"

"I think so." I search through my purse and fish out a ten-dollar bill. "Can you excuse me for a second?"

"Do you want something else? I'll get it." His eyes dart to the cash in my hand.

"No. It's okay. Can you wait here?"

"Sure," he answers.

"Be right back."

After I buy a hot dog and a large order of fries, I go outside and give the food to the homeless man.

Dakota's motionless in his seat, his eyes following me through the dining room as I make my way back to our table. The silence between us lasts for a good minute. He's probably waiting for an explanation and it takes me a little while to come up with one.

"My parents..." I hesitate and the words disappear from my lips. *Give generously to them and do so without a grudging heart...*

Dakota bites the tip of his straw and waits; his gaze is a blend of softness and intensity.

"My parents do some volunteer work at the church we go to," I explain, pushing my hair, which is damp from the melting snowflakes, away from my flushed face.

He plucks the straw from his mouth, scoots his milkshake to the side, and lays his hand on the table in front of me.

I dig some coins out of the pocket of my coat and place them in his palm. I'm not sure why. He makes me do irrational things.

"Silly." Dakota smiles, glancing at the quarters then back at me. "I just wanted to hold your hand."

"Oh." A low gasp leaves my mouth and my cheeks burn. "Okay. You can." I slip my fingers in between his.

"So... What else do you do besides feeding homeless and going to rock concerts?"

"I bake cupcakes. What do you do besides singing and playing guitar?"

"I'm an event coordinator at Cascade Locks."

"That sounds like fun."

"Baking sounds like fun too."

Talking to Dakota is so easy. I had no idea it could be like this with a man.

The car comes to a complete stop and I shift in my seat nervously. The sweet taste of Patty's milkshake is still on my tongue.

"Thanks." Dakota turns to face me. "I had a really great time."

"Me too." I nod, unfastening my seatbelt. My palms are sweating again and my heart's beating a bit faster. I blame it on all the hand holding at the movie and the diner.

"Can I see you tomorrow?" he asks quietly, his eyes drilling into mine.

My brain scrambles to fathom his request. I need a moment to process what he's said.

"Tomorrow?" I murmur finally, locking my hands on my lap when they begin to shake. This is going way too fast. And no, I don't hate it.

"I can't. I need to finish some assignments for Monday." The words die on my lips. I just turned down a guy in favor of my college studies. Jess would kill me.

"So when?" Dakota unfastens his seatbelt and moves closer to me.

Our faces are now only a fraction of an inch apart and his heat is consuming me like a black hole.

"Thursday?" I say. "I'm free next Thursday."

"You're going to make me wait that long?" The right corner of his lips curves up and his dimple makes an appearance.

Here comes the lame excuse. "I have finals next week," I explain, wondering if it's a deal breaker. Maybe he doesn't like me enough after all.

We fall back into silence, but Dakota never stops looking into my eyes. He studies me carefully, then slides his hand up my shoulder and tucks a lock of my hair behind my ear.

My heart jumps into my throat when his mouth gets closer to mine. I'm convinced he's going to kiss me any second now, and although I desperately want to taste him, I'm also terrified because all the lectures my father has given me about evil men wanting to take my virtue are now imploding inside my head. I squeeze my eyes shut and try to push away the irrelevant thoughts that are ruining the moment.

"I guess I don't have a choice, do I?" Dakota's velvety voice caresses my cheek.

"No, but...you can still text me," I mumble.

"You bet." His whisper makes me shiver all over.

I'm sitting there with my eyes closed and my cheeks burning when his lips brush against mine. They're warm and soft and feel just as heavenly as a bite of a vanilla cupcake.

I don't dare move—I'm scared of doing something wrong. His lips grow firm, moving slowly and carefully at first, and then they're a little demanding, making my head spin. When his breath washes over my tongue, our gasps become one. It's the most intimate I've ever felt with someone in my entire life.

Dakota pulls away and mutters in my ear, "Have you even been kissed before, Alana?"

I'm not sure whether I should be offended or flattered, but one thing's for sure, the reason he asked me this question is because he already has an idea of what kind of a girl I am and my answer is simply going to verify it.

"Not like this," I confess, my voice rough due to the way my heart's thumping. The two times I got roped into stupid games at the high school parties Jess and I sneaked into don't count. Those weren't kisses. Those were stupid dares I don't really care to remember.

This, right now, *this* was a real kiss. It was mind-blowing and sensual, and I hope my inexperience wasn't too disappointing. I hope Thursday is still happening.

"Where did you come from?" Dakota laughs quietly against my cheek, his fingers brushing across my chin.

"I don't know... The moon?" I come back with a joke.

"Thursday can't come soon enough," he utters and then kisses me again, his tongue slipping into my mouth and finding mine. His strokes are slow and gentle and it makes my stomach tingle with pleasure. I don't believe I've experienced anything this carnally delicate before.

Our lips and tongues explore each other leisurely for a very long time and I enjoy every second of it—every lick, every moan, every pull. I'm not ready for it to end when Dakota finally breaks us apart, but we're both out of breath and it's late.

"I'll text you tomorrow," he says, his fingers moving into my hair, pushing some of it away from my flushed face.

"Okay." My eyes can't get enough of him. The fact that I won't see him for six days is driving me nuts. "Thank you for the movie and the milkshake." Now I'm blabbering.

"Anytime."

I step out of the car and rush to the front door, my heart hammering. The purr of the engine behind me tempts me to look back at Dakota one last time. So once I'm on the porch, I spin around and wave at him like crazy. He's behind the wheel with the passenger window down, and although the space between us is filled with millions of twirling snowflakes, I can still see him smiling. And the things that smile does to me are insane.

12. AFTER

My heart thrashes wildly as I try to absorb my surroundings. The street's full of guys sporting their lightweight jackets and girls showing off their spring wardrobes. The snow has melted and the sunny, warm weather has taken control of the city. I'm occupying a small table on the patio right next to the trash can, which is considered the worst place to sit, but there was no other spot available when I arrived, except for a booth inside.

My mother insisted on me taking another week off from college, so I missed more tests and deadlines. And while a portion of me feels guilty, the rest of me has already given up on this semester. The truth is, I'm probably going to keep attending classes merely to have an excuse to get out of the house, because being around my parents has become dreadful.

In front of me on the table is a blank notebook that's supposed to be my diary. My therapist suggested it a couple of sessions ago as a way to "deal with my repressed emotions," but I haven't been able to formulate a single thought worth writing down. Most of the time, it's just one word. *Dakota.*

And I don't want his name next to bad things I'm trying to get rid of that are bound to eventually spill out of me, so I never write it down. I just let it stay in my head because that's where he belongs. With me. Not on paper.

Jess is already thirty minutes late, and her excuse is that Luke's doctor's appointment is running behind schedule, which has me wondering if I should just text her and tell her not to come. Glancing at my phone for the tenth time, I flip through the recent messages and pause when my finger reaches Mikah's name. We haven't spoken in over a week and I feel like he's deliberately avoiding me. My message with an offer to help him move still reads "delivered."

Jess shows up when I'm in the middle of a heated debate with myself over whether or not texting Mikah again is a good idea. I can't understand my need to hear back from him. It's not like we were ever the best of friends. Sure, we shared a few moments. We had some drinks and smoked a couple of cigarettes together. That's hardly any sort of relationship, but there's this restless part of me that wants to know he's okay, that he's eating and sleeping. Because he's the only living thing that still somehow connects me to Dakota and I worry about him. Being in the dark and not getting responses frustrates me.

It takes Jess some maneuvering to get to our table. "You look really good," she says, glancing around, probably in search of a better spot.

"You too," I say, studying her new hair. She's cut it short and dyed it a wild shade of red, which makes her look like a flaming torch dipped in glitter. It's a nice change. Bold and radical. Something I could probably use right now, but I'm too chicken.

After a few seconds of examining the crowd and glancing through the window into the coffee shop, Jess settles on the bench across from me. She places her oversized Gucci bag on the table next to my empty notebook and asks, "How are you doing?"

That's not the question I was expecting from her. And the tone she uses makes it sound more like a manufactured phrase similar to the one you hear when you call technical support and they have no idea how to help you. *We understand your frustration.* No, they don't. Just like Jess probably isn't prepared to hear how I'm *really* doing.

"Your hair is great," I say.

"Luke loves it." She smiles, but it doesn't reach her eyes.

Anxiety courses through me like an electromagnetic wave. "You can rock anything." I try to shake off the impending dread of this lunch business going sour.

"Thanks."

There's a long pause. I can't think of anything else to talk about, and it's weird because we used to talk for hours. There's something in her gaze that wasn't there before. Anger maybe. I can't quite put my finger on it. It's not just the hair. She's different. Everything I loved about my friend has faded, giving way to a new version of Jess.

I choke back my concern and choose to disregard the obvious change. "How's Luke?"

"He has another surgery next week."

"What are the doctor's saying?"

I'm not entirely sure I want to know. The rumors are that Luke might not be able to play drums again because of his spinal cord injuries, but it's the polite thing to ask. Or at least I think it is. Especially when your best friend is dating the guy.

"We'll see after the surgery." Jess gives me a small smile, then changes the subject. "Did you order already?"

"Not yet. Do you know what you want?"

"Not really. To be honest with you, I ate a couple of hours ago."

I'm not sure what to say to that. Actually, I'm not sure anymore why she wanted to meet for lunch. It was her idea, not mine. And I wasn't the one who was very unfashionably late. It almost feels like she's just trying to squeeze me in.

"Look, I'm sorry." Jess reaches for my hand. "I know I'm a shitty friend. I haven't called. It's just that I've been so busy with Luke and all."

"I understand. It's okay."

"You should come to the meet-up," she says, releasing her grasp on my hand.

I silently watch Jess dig through the contents of her designer bag. My stomach roils at the sight of the brochure she lays on the table in front of me. My mother's been driving me mad with her support group ideas, as if my weekly sessions with the therapist aren't enough. Besides, I'm not convinced they're helping. They just frustrate me more. Kind of like the empty diary.

"I believe this could help you deal." Jess smiles gently.

I look down at the blocks of text and notice her name printed in red at the bottom of the page.

The dread gushing through me explodes inside my chest like a grenade.

My best friend is organizing weekly meetings for the survivors of the attack while I'm waiting for a guy I'm not even supposed to think about to return my text.

How pathetic am I?

My voice is low and sounds strained because the rock in my throat makes it hard to speak up, but I push through it. "What do you do when you get together?"

"We talk about our experience," Jess explains.

Her jaw begins to quiver and her eyes glisten with tears. For the first time since the attack, I'm seeing my best friend almost losing it. And I hate to say it, but I almost *want* her to fall apart, because I'm tired of being the only one who's weak.

Jess wipes her cheeks with the heel of her hand and draws a deep breath through her teeth to calm down. "This is lame," she says, putting her brave face back on.

The noise of the street looming around us is too loud and too distracting and my thoughts begin to trip over one another, turning my mind into melting jello.

"It's not." I shake my head. "You have the right to be broken whenever you feel like it."

"I don't want to be broken."

"But we are."

My words float in the air between us like an invisible cloud of toxic waste.

"We all are," I repeat quietly. "You, me, Luke. Mikah, Blaze."

"We don't have to be, Alana," Jess counters, grabbing my hand. "We can't let grief and fear rule our lives. We have to take charge and fight through it."

She sounds too radical, almost maniacal. She's nothing like the Jess I used to know who only cared about makeup and outfits. My brain understands everything that's being said, but my heart's stuck somewhere between the night of the Black Rose show and the day I nearly ripped Dakota's hand off his dead body. It's almost as if I'm trapped in that time—it's a strange feeling that comes and goes, but I'm not sure if I want it to dwindle away. Perhaps not just yet.

"Will you come?" Jess presses.

"Sure." I nod.

"Great. I'll text you the details tonight." She smiles victoriously.

Tino picks up on the first ring.

"Thank you for calling Toro Bravo. How can I assist you today?" His tone is the definition of cheery and it makes me a little uncomfortable because that's what I'm supposed to sound like too, but I don't know if I have it in me anymore.

"Hey, Tino. This is Alana," I say with my eyes trained on the steering wheel of my Prius. I'm still in the parking lot, my mind replaying the conversation with Jess.

"Alana." His voice drops to a disappointed mutter. "How are you?" Dishes clank in the background.

"I'm good. I just wanted to see if Angelo's in." I already left three messages with the restaurant manager over the course of the past ten days, but the answer I get every time I call is always the same. *He's not available.*

"Let me check." Click. The line goes dead. He didn't even care to turn on the hold music.

I inhale deeply and try to relax, but my heart's catapulting into my throat. All my doubts are swarming inside me like a tornado. What are the chances the restaurant will give me my shifts again? They probably have tons of applications to choose from.

The line clicks again and I hear Angelo speaking, "Alana, how are you?"

"I'm good. I called last week..." My breathing becomes shallow and I realize I'm hyperventilating.

"Yes. I received your message. I'm sorry I didn't have a chance to return your call. It's been a busy week."

"I understand." My cheeks feel flaming hot. "I just wanted to let you know I'm doing better and I'm ready to go back to work, and if you want to put me on the schedule next week or even this weekend, I'm good to go." I don't sound like myself, probably because I'm trying too hard; I hope he doesn't pick up on it.

Angelo clears his throat. "Alana." Pause. "I think it's best you take some more time off."

His words slice right through me.

"I'm fine. I don't need more time off," I counter.

"We already hired someone. I'm sorry."

A wave of despair crashes into me. I can't lose this job. I need it. "Do you want me to fill out another application?"

"Alana. I really am sorry, but a month is a very long time. I'm running a business. I can't afford for an employee to be taking a leave of absence for this long. I wish you good luck and take care of yourself."

The line disconnects.

I'm not sure what exactly I'm feeling right now—annoyance, anger, or disappointment, or maybe all of those things, but it hurts.

———

It's three in the morning, and I'm tired of tossing and turning in my bed. My mind's racing a thousand miles a second, and all my thoughts are alternating between Angelo pretty much telling me he fired me a month ago but was too busy to call and my unread message to Mikah.

I shove the blanket aside and sit up, my eyes darting to the night-stand where I left my phone. Rational Alana knows there are no messages waiting for her, but impatient Alana, the one who's anxious to talk to someone other than her parents, checks anyway.

He said it was okay to call him if I couldn't sleep. And we've already established he's a night person.

When Mikah's voice on the line finally slices through the darkness of my room, my heart does a small, happy flip.

"Hey," he mutters.

"Can't sleep," I say meekly, waiting for him to pick up the conversation, but he responds with silence and it's depressing. It makes me wonder if calling him this late is a good idea. Maybe it's all in my head and he doesn't want to be friends with me. Maybe he's trying to move on, to leave all the reminders of the past behind, and my texts keep dragging him down.

Mikah breaks the silence. "How did the cheesecake turn out?" His voice has that soft-around-the-edges tone to it that Dakota's used to have when he drank.

"It didn't," I say, pulling the blanket over my legs.

"How come?"

"It just didn't work out." I have no intention of telling him I freaked out in the middle of the grocery store. Besides, what are the chances he hasn't already heard about it? Half the neighborhood was there when my parents arrived. I'm surprised it wasn't on the news, but it wouldn't have been, because Joseph Miller's name has been claiming all the headlines.

I feel a tiny rush of panic flowing through my stomach. It always happens when I think of the attack or anything related to it.

"Well, that's a bummer," Mikah says into the phone.

"It's no big deal." I sigh. My brain's working overtime. I have questions about *Dracula*, but thinking about telling him I bought the book he recommended to me feels weird since I never bought anything Dakota mentioned. I don't know why I did it. Maybe deep down, I hoped to find answers inside the novel. "Can I ask you something?"

"Sure," Mikah agrees.

"Why do you think Stoker wrote *Dracula* in the form of diary entries if it's a fiction novel?"

"I thought you never read it."

"I started, but it's hard to follow. I believe it would make more sense if it wasn't a bunch of records thrown together."

"I don't think you get the whole point of literary fiction." The change in Mikah's tone tells me he's getting frustrated with my questions.

"Yes, I do. I remember what you told me—it's a time capsule. It reflects the state of society at a given period of time and doesn't change based on present day society or expectations. We read tons of the Victorian era authors in high school. I get the idea of what he was trying to do."

"Then why did you ask?"

"Because this is a fantasy book."

"What's wrong with fantasy being written in the form of diary entries?"

"It makes the reading experience less pleasant," I confess.

"No one's making you read it."

"You told me to." I laugh a little, wondering if he remembers. "You said it was the best horror novel I'd ever read."

"It is."

"I expected it to be scarier."

"You know when they say read, you don't just read the words. You read between the lines."

He sounds patronizing and I don't want to argue anymore, so I change the subject. "Did you finish moving?"

"Almost."

"Do you need any help?" The truth is, I want to see his new place. I wonder how different it is from the old apartment. I wonder if he's put up the posters Dakota collected.

"You already asked me that."

Oh, so he did see my text. "I know, but I just wanted to make sure."

"I'm good."

I hear him walking around, his muffled footsteps echoing on the line. There's a faint click of a beer cap clattering against the kitchen counter and the slam of the refrigerator door.

"Do you talk to Luke at all?" I tread lightly, imagining him standing in the kitchen with the bottle glued to his lips and taking a swig. "He has another surgery next week."

Mikah ignores my comments. "Look, I'm tired. I've been up since six this morning. I'm going to hit the sack. Talk later, all right?"

"Sure," I whisper, my heart sprinting as I dread what usually comes after we talk. It's a strange, empty feeling. A withdrawal of sorts. I suppose addicts experience something similar when they get cut off.

My shaky voice must give away my anxiety, because Mikah's tone softens. "Hey, Cupcake Queen," he says. "Take it easy, okay?"

"Okay." I swallow past the growing lump in my throat.

"I'm serious. Don't fucking let this shit define you and your life. You're too fucking good."

My messy emotions swell in my chest. Mikah's never said anything this nice to me before, and the way he pronounces *good* makes me shiver all over. It sounds a lot like the way Dakota used to say it, dragging the vowel a little.

"I'm not." I battle the onslaught of memories. My words come out slurred. "I'm not sure what I am anymore. I'm just so tired of everything. I'm tired of being scared all the time."

My gaze stills on the wall as I wait for Mikah to say something, but the silence that fills the line seems to go on forever, until he finally murmurs, "I'll talk to you later."

"Okay, good nig—"

Mikah hangs up before I finish the sentence.

13. BEFORE

My father's face screws up in displeasure. "When were you going to tell us?"

"I'm telling you now." My heart's racing despite the meditation session I had earlier in my room to prepare for this conversation.

"I don't want my daughter to wait tables in some seedy bar!"

"It's not a bar. It's an upscale restaurant, Dad! Why do you always have to twist everything I say?"

My mother lets out a long, slow sigh but stays on the sidelines like she always does when things between the three of us become heated.

The air in the living room is thick with rage and I already know bringing up the move at this moment is a bad idea. My father can only handle disobedience in small doses.

"What was wrong with the job at the bakery?" he asks, placing both hands on his hips. "Has Mrs. Kaminski treated you wrong? She's a nice lady and the pay's great. Besides, what's going to happen to this blog of yours?"

"Dad"—I roll my eyes at the ceiling—"I don't need to work at the bakery to have a baking blog. I want to try something different."

"Does it have to be downtown?" His eyebrows pull together as a sign of concern. "College should be your first priority right now."

"I have a 3.7 GPA! My last final is in two days and I'm starting at Toro Bravo after Christmas. It's vacation time. It's perfect. Can't you see?"

"I don't like the idea of you working in a place like that."

I drop my gaze to the floor and try to breathe, but my heart's doing a crazy dance and I realize the move-out-to-downtown portion of the talk isn't going to happen today or anytime soon, for that matter.

One thing at a time, Alana.

"Why don't we all sleep on it and discuss this again over the weekend?" My mother tries to defuse the situation, but it's clearly not working, because my father's face only gets redder and unhappier.

"I'm spending Friday night at Jess's," I say firmly. "We're baking cupcakes and working on the Christmas post for my blog."

"Waitressing isn't good enough for a girl like you," my father sputters, looking at me like I've just committed a crime, which wouldn't be far from the truth if he knew about that kiss with Dakota and the dirty thoughts constantly filling my mind.

"Whatever." I roll my eyes and head back to my room.

"Young lady!" My father's stern voice follows me up the stairs. "You need to watch your manners."

I shut the door, ready to sulk in silence, but a new text message from Dakota that must have come in when I was trying to reason with my parents sends my heart into overdrive.

my friend's band has a show at Mississippi Studios on friday night. i have an extra ticket. do you want to go with me?

I reread the message at least ten more times, trying to figure out whether he wants to keep the Thursday dinner plans and see me the day after or scratch the dinner and only see me on Friday. I feel a rush of panic rolling through me. All the what-ifs suddenly make my head hurt. I sit on the edge of my bed and stare at the phone for a while before finally sending him a response.

Sure. What about Thursday?

thursday i'm taking u out

An odd mix of relief and bliss washes over me.

Yes, I'd love to go with you on Friday.

A kiss emoji pops up on my screen.

I dial Jess and tell her about the change of plans.

She takes the news better than expected. "What band are you seeing?"

"He didn't tell me. He just asked if I wanted to go with him. Mississippi Studios."

"I'm going to ask Luke who's playing," Jess says.

"Okay, so are we moving the cupcakes to Saturday?"

"Yes, Saturday's good. But not too early."

"Okay. Thank you."

"And when you get here, be ready to give me details, girl. Details," she requests before ending the call.

14. AFTER

I look at the photo attached to Mikah's message and type in a *Yes*.

The reply comes in almost instantly, which is so unlike him. Very random and unexpected, considering the last time we spoke, he pretty much hung up on me.

K i'll drop it off in a bit

I'm thinking that he moved a couple of weeks ago and he's just now discovering my toothbrush? Who the hell returns a used toothbrush anyway?

But I don't say anything. Instead, I send him a thumbs-up emoji and try to concentrate on my philosophy assignment. However, the idea of him coming by gives me goose bumps, and I don't quite understand why. In a way, that scares me because the only other person who ever gave me goose bumps was Dakota.

Spring break has passed by so fast that I've barely had a chance to catch up on all my assignments I was given extensions on due to extenuating circumstances. As expected, April has been unkind and gloomy. There have been some really warm days and some really rainy ones, and this week's weather still seems bipolar. I wonder if it's this moody because she's a woman. Because that's how we are—we can't always control our emotions. They seem to go from one extreme to another. Kind of like me going from zero to ten at the sight of Mikah's text. It's strange and exhausting.

This morning was sunny, but the afternoon has brought more clouds, and the constant change of scenery outside my window is giving me whiplash. That's my excuse for not getting philosophy done. And for not answering countless texts from Jess with invites to the meet-up she organized for the Crystal Room attack survivors.

Mikah's truck roars into our driveway at around six. My father has just gotten home from work and my mother's in the middle of making her famous chicken casserole.

I rush downstairs in my sweats and tee. Parts of me tingle with anticipation and parts of me are a little nervous because I haven't seen Mikah in several weeks and I wonder if he's changed. His Instagram has been dead ever since the attack. The last post was a selfie of him, Dakota, and Blaze before the show. Every time I look up his account, that's the photo I see.

"Who is it?" My father asks as I hurry past him to the front door. He takes off his jacket and slings it over his forearm, his tired eyes following me.

"Mikah," I say casually, putting on my sneakers and slipping out onto the porch without giving him further explanation.

The warm wind whips my hair against my cheeks, so I pull it back and tie it into a bun.

Mikah steps out of his truck and gives me a nod, a mask of indifference on his face. His thumbs are tucked into the front pockets of his jeans and he's wearing a Ramones t-shirt.

"Hey," I say, walking up to him.

"Hey yourself," he mutters, his eyes locking on mine.

"You didn't have to drive all the way here. I could have stopped by and picked it up." *And checked out your new place.*

"It's not a big deal. I was going to be in the area anyway."

"Business or pleasure?"

"Both."

He grabs a small box from the truck and hands it to me. "These were all in the bathroom."

I look down at the contents and realize that they're indeed my things—toothbrush, deodorant, and dental floss.

"Thanks."

"Sure." He gets a pack of cigarettes and a lighter from the front pocket of his jacket. "How's Mission Cheesecake? Still happening?"

"It's on hold," I say, pressing the box to my chest. The blog in general is on hold. I haven't had any desire to bake or cook ever since my freak-out incident. My parents barely let me go to college. My mother once offered to drive me herself.

"I see."

My eyes follow as Mikah pulls a cigarette from the pack. He sticks it into the corner of his mouth and flicks the lighter several times in an attempt to battle the stubborn wind.

I watch him smoking with fascination. He makes it look like he's having sex. I truly don't know why my mind makes this comparison, but I can't think of anything else that could give a person such satisfaction. Although I remember seeing a very similar expression on Dakota's face every time we were together.

And I miss that a lot. I miss making someone smile. I miss the feeling of being needed. I miss it so much it hurts.

Mikah withdraws the cigarette from his mouth, his gaze on me. His eyes glimmer in the sun like Dakota's used to, but they aren't like the ocean. Instead, they're like the forest, with tiny flecks of gold scattered throughout the emerald green. I don't know why I've never noticed it before now. Maybe because I've never seen him in bright daylight.

He holds out his cigarette, offering it to me, and I stare at him for a few seconds, my heart hammering. Sharing things is an intimate gesture. You don't share with just anyone. You only share with people you trust.

I tear my right hand from the box with my toiletries and take the cigarette. It's warm and familiar against my skin, like an old friend.

"Are you going to look at it until Christmas?" Mikah asks, his voice jarring me back to reality. The left side of his mouth curls up, revealing a dimple.

"No." I shake my head and slip the cigarette between my lips, my eyes trained on the burning tip. The smoke licks against my tongue and throat. It's thick and bitter and stings a little, and I wonder if it's what Mikah tastes like.

"Yeah, okay." A soft chuckle drifts at me.

I glance up at him and inhale deeply, our gazes tangling together in a wild dance.

The nicotine buzz crashes into me suddenly, making me dizzy, and for a second, I feel like I'm flying. Apparently, Mikah can tell, because he moves closer to take the box away from me and sets it on the hood of his truck.

"That hit me pretty hard." I remove the cigarette from my mouth and exhale slowly, watching the smoke.

"Yeah, when you first start..."

The slam of a door startles me, and my heart drops to my stomach. Mikah's eyes shift from me to my house and I hear my father's footsteps as he thunders down the driveway.

"What is this?!" he screams, his tone laced with anger and disappointment.

I turn around, still holding the cigarette.

"You need to leave, young man!" my father fumes. "I don't want to see you anywhere near my daughter again! Do you understand?"

Mikah doesn't flinch. His face is stone cold, his gaze unwavering.

"Stop it, Dad," I say, trying to keep my cool. "Your blood pressure will jump again."

"Go inside." He moves closer and snatches the cigarette from me, his hand striking mine in the process.

"I'm not going anywhere." My voice is raised, my temper on the brink of detonating. The high of the nicotine is gone and what's left is frustration and a sore wrist.

"Yes, you are! And you"—my father motions at Mikah—"you're leaving immediately!"

"No, he's not!" I stomp my foot, rage and annoyance pulsing

through me. "You can't *fucking* tell me what to do!" This is the first time I've ever cursed in front of my father.

The moment his palm slaps across my cheek, the tears hit my eyes. I gasp and grab my burning face as my heart jolts.

"Yes, I can and I will because you're my responsibility!" he yells, saliva spraying from his mouth. "Because you live under my roof, Alana!"

His words swarm around me like an entire bee colony, buzzing and stinging.

"Then why won't you let me move out?"

"So you can shack up with some jobless lowlife and party your life away? You're not well enough to go to the grocery store on your own, let alone handle a job and an apartment!"

Acid rises in my throat.

Mikah steps closer and grips my shoulder. "You didn't have to hit her." He sounds abnormally calm when he speaks to my father.

I stand there with my hands over my face, my scarred skin rough on my cheeks and my chin. I can feel every ridge, every little bump. My side vision catches the neighbors' porch. They're watching us like we're Sunday night HBO, their jaws hanging open.

"Come on." Ignoring my father's threats, Mikah presses his palm against my back and nudges me in the direction of the truck.

I'm so dazed over the fact my father just smacked me that I blindly follow his lead and slide into the passenger seat—there's no way I'm going home. My head still in my hands and my father's voice striking inside my head like a hammer, I lower my gaze to the floor and notice the box with my toothbrush.

Mikah leans over to fish out my seatbelt, his long body stretching across me. I hear the click of the buckle and the engine roaring to life, and when I look up, I see my mother rushing out onto the porch, her features twisted with shock. She shouts my name and waves at us nervously as Mikah backs out of the driveway.

I'm not familiar with the neighborhood Mikah's truck is taking us through. The sun, low on the horizon, flickers from behind the roofs of the bungalows we're passing, and the narrow street twists like a snake, making my stomach queasy.

"You good?" Mikah asks, turning down the music a bit. It's one of the earlier Type O Negative albums, which I don't mind at all. On the contrary. Dakota used to play it for me and I loved it. The songs match my mood perfectly.

"Yes." I nod and turn to look at Mikah. His eyes are set on the road and he has this apathetic expression on his face that says *I don't give a shit*, but I know it's just a disguise. If he didn't care, he wouldn't have said anything to my father.

"What chapter are you on?" He throws a quick glance at me and I swear there's a glint of genuine curiosity in his gaze.

That's when I realize he's talking about the book. "I'm almost done."

"You're the slowest reader I've ever met." He chuckles.

"Well…" I say with a sigh. "It's not the type of book I'd normally pick."

"Well, you're not the type of a girl who'd pick this book."

"What's that supposed to mean?"

"You're a *Jane Eyre* type girl."

"Really? Stereotyping much?"

"I'm not stereotyping. You bake cupcakes for fun. You loved *Jane Eyre*."

"So just because you're a guy, you're the only one who's allowed to be into overly complex and incoherent horror books?"

"You probably enjoyed *Wuthering Heights* too. Women dig that shit."

"Are you done figuring me out?" I huff, crossing my arms on my chest.

Mikah's tone softens and I wonder if he's guessed why I decided to read a book I'd otherwise never pick. "Are you done figuring *me* out?"

I ponder for a minute before confessing, "I want to understand your fascination with the undead."

There's a long pause. Then Mikah's half-hysterical, half-amused laughter cuts through the music.

"What did I say?" I ask, looking at him.

"You know you're fucking weird." He shakes his head.

"How am I weird?"

"You tell me what you think when you finish the book, okay?" Mikah says a few moments later.

I nod silently.

"Hey"—he clears his throat—"what's this about you and the grocery store?"

"Nothing." I turn up the music.

"Come on." His hand intercepts mine and he lowers the volume again, his fingers lingering on my knuckles longer than necessary. "I'm serious. What happened?"

I swallow past the tightness and give him the watered-down version of events. "I got sick at the store."

"How sick?"

"Oh gosh, you're not making this easy!" I cry out. "It's already embarrassing."

"Well, if you tell me what happened, I'll stop asking."

"I freaked out. The doctor said they were hallucinations."

There's a long pause.

"What did you see?" Mikah finally asks, his gaze briefly shifting to me and then to the road.

"I didn't *see* anything." My voice drops to a whisper.

"So what was it?"

A wave of anxiety flows through me and I feel bile burning the back of my throat. "I heard it."

"What did you hear?"

I turn my head and stare at him. The lines of his face are a lot like Dakota's but a bit sharper. "I heard the gunshots."

His Adam's apple moves slowly as he swallows.

"It was stupid." I look away, and my foot begins to tap against the floor mat. "My parents made a big deal out of nothing."

Mikah lowers the windows, draws two cigarettes from his pocket, and hands me one. The expression on his face is a little of everything. Serious, sad, and haunted. It's like the don't-care mask has melted away. He's lost a lot of weight since the last time I saw him and his cheekbones have become more pronounced. I wonder what else is different. Is he sleeping any better? Does he like his new place? Does he still work at the same shop?

Mikah motions at the cup-holder-turned-mini-storage space. "Light me up, huh?"

"Sure." I grab the lighter. My hands are trembling along with the truck and it takes me three attempts to get his cigarette going before I light mine.

We smoke in silence with the wind and the smoke doing the tango inside the car. Nicotine owns me completely. It's an odd, unfamiliar rush. A lot like adrenaline but more addictive. It's relaxing. It takes the edge off. It makes all my worries seem insignificant.

"You're getting the hang of it, aren't ya, church girl?" Mikah lets out a small laugh when I make an attempt to blow smoke rings.

"How do you do it?" I ask, watching the shapeless puffs coming out of my mouth.

"Takes practice." He smirks.

"You need to stop calling me church girl."

"But I like it."

"Why?"

"I don't know." He takes another long drag. "It's as close as I can get to God."

"Why do you want to get close to him? He's a selfish asshole." Anger drips from my words. "He took your brother, but he's letting some murderer live." I know we're not supposed to talk about either of those things, but I have this strange need to voice my opinion in front of him because Dakota wasn't just my boyfriend; he was his brother too. And pretending that he never existed bothers me. "Joseph Miller killed twenty-four people in cold blood and he has his own Wikipedia page!"

Mikah tosses his cigarette out the window. "I don't want you saying his name."

"Do you want me saying Dakota's name?" Tears pool in my eyes.

"We had a deal. I can't hang out with you if you're going to bring my brother into this every time we see each other."

It sounds weird coming out of his mouth. The seeing each other part.

"Why?" I ask.

He doesn't respond.

Frustration simmers beneath my skin. "Why, Mikah?" I can't stand this secrecy anymore. Trying to figure out the way his brain works is like trying to solve an ancient riddle, but at the same time, he's created some sort of connection between us. We hang out, we talk, we discuss Bram Stoker's writing. It makes no sense why he wouldn't talk about his brother.

Mikah dodges my question. "I was going to stop by a friend's house. You wanna tag along?"

"Yeah. Sure." I nervously wipe my tears with the heel of my left hand.

"You're going to burn my car." Mikah grabs the cigarette from me. "Tissues are in there." He motions at the glove compartment.

I turn up the music, flip the sun visor to get to the mirror, and clean up my face.

"Whose house is this?" I ask, staring up at the property hiding behind a thick line of trees and untrimmed bushes.

"A friend of mine," Mikah mutters as we get out of the truck.

I'm wearing his Black Sabbath hoodie that he fished out from the back seat, and I know it's not making me look like any less of a wreck, but the thought of going home sends shivers down my spine. It's both funny and sad that I would rather have strangers laugh at my ridiculous outfit than be anywhere near my father right now.

My mind craves something different. A change of scenery maybe. A break from the dull numbness my life has become.

I'm glad my cell phone isn't with me so that I don't have to stress over the endless calls from my parents. We've already established I'm a shitty daughter. Listening to their lectures is not going to change that fact.

"Are you good?" Mikah asks, glancing at me over his shoulder as we walk up to the house.

My anxiety kicks in at the sound of loud music inside.

"Yeah." I nod, thrusting my fists into the pockets of his hoodie. They're huge, probably big enough to fit a watermelon, which makes me feel even smaller than I already am next to Mikah.

"You sure?" He rings the doorbell several times as his gaze lingers on me.

Dread gushes through me like blood from an open carotid artery. "Yeah. I'm fine," I lie.

"All right." He breaks eye contact and stares at his phone.

The minute the door opens, wild laughter wrapped in the smell of burnt pizza and weed drifts from inside. The guy meeting us has a buzz cut, a lot of tats, and a toothpick hanging from the corner of his mouth. He doesn't strike me as someone Mikah would be friends with.

"What's up, Bennett?" He looks from Mikah to me. Then he and Mikah perform one of those strange manly greetings that consists of a bunch of different hand movements that seem rehearsed, and I wonder how long it took them to learn all that stuff.

Mikah turns to me and makes a brief introduction. "Alana. Eddie."

"Hey, how are you doing?" Eddie steps to the side to let us in, the toothpick traveling from one side of his mouth to the other. His eyes slide from my face to my chest, which makes me wonder if he only allows girls who meet certain criteria into his house.

"Hey." I don't bother to smile—he doesn't seem like he cares much about manners.

My goal right now is not to freak out on his porch, because I'm not sure I want to go in. There are too many people inside.

"Jackson upstairs?" Mikah asks, ushering me into the house.

"Yep," Eddie answers, slamming the door shut.

My heart drops to my stomach when I hear the click of the lock behind me. My fists in the pockets of the hoodie tighten and my knees suddenly become weak.

The onslaught of people and music sends my mind into overdrive. I freeze in the middle of the living room and take in my surroundings while Mikah talks to one of the guys. Dim lights moving across the faces and surfaces make my head spin. I narrow my eyes to bring the fuzzy images into focus, but they don't seem to want to cooperate.

"You sure you're okay?" Mikah's breath fans against my ear.

"Huh?" I turn to the sound of his voice and meet his gaze. His eyes sparkle green, and when the light streaks lick his cheeks, it reminds me of the first Midnight Rust show.

"You want a glass of water or a drink?"

"I wouldn't mind a drink," I say, trying to calm my heart rate.

"Okay." His long fingers wrap around mine. "Come on."

I've never held his hand before, and the feel of his calloused skin against mine makes every cell in me burn an enigmatic fire.

I follow behind him with my eyes trained on his inked arm, my heart still doing pirouettes. We walk into the kitchen and he goes straight for the fridge while I brave a couple of smiles at a group gathered around the table.

I glance from one face to the next, evaluating each person. Everyone here is a potential shooter because large crowds attract people with guns, and this house is one huge party.

As I'm examining the room to determine the best way out in case of emergency, *she* invades my line of vision. Her hair is sparkling white, like the first snow, and I recognize her from a photo and also a party that I went to with Dakota where she showed up with Mikah. Girls like her are hard to miss. They don't blend in like I do. They want to stand out.

"Hey, babe." She throws her arm around Mikah's neck while he's putting together our drinks. Her lips touch his cheek and he leans into the kiss. I can't help but wonder if they sleep together, because the intimacy between them is obvious. Jealous Alana wants to tell her to stop touching him, but Alana who still has some common sense left decides against it.

When Snow White is done mauling Mikah, her gaze shifts to me. "Hey." She doesn't tell me her name.

"Hey." I don't give her mine either.

No introduction follows.

Mikah hands me one of the plastic cups and says, "I'll be back in a second."

Everything happens so fast that my brain doesn't have time to process his words. When I finally realize he's leaving me for the blonde, they've already disappeared.

———

I've never been big on parties, but the ones I went to with Dakota consisted mostly of the music scene crowd. This place is different. It's a girls-in-bras, guys-with-dreads kingdom of anarchy, a free zone for anyone who wants to get high or drink themselves into a stupor without a care about the quality of their music. Weed is everywhere. Its smell clings to my skin like pond scum. By the time I make it back to the living room to look for Mikah, I've already had three different guys offer me a joint and a girl ask me if I have an extra Tampax.

"Hey!" someone calls out as I maneuver around the large group gathered near the pool table. "Cupcake Queen?"

I swivel toward the sound and notice a familiar face. I can't remember his name, but I've seen him backstage with Midnight Rust a couple of times. He has a silly drunk grin and he doesn't strike me as a guy who'd open gunfire on a band because his girlfriend is a fan.

"Cupcake queen, right? DK's girl?" He pulls me into a one-arm hug because his other hand is occupied with a bottle of beer. "What the fuck are you doing here? I thought you didn't do parties. Aren't you like a Mormon or something?" His words are garbled.

My chest tightens at the mention of Dakota, so the stupid religious commentary doesn't seem important. "I'm sorry, I don't remember your name," I say honestly.

"I'm Zeke." He hits himself in the chest. "I went to high school with DK. Is Mikah here?"

"Yes." I nod, nervously looking around the room.

"Tell him I said hi."

"I will."

Zeke nudges me in the direction of the pool table. "You smoke weed?"

"Not really." I shake my head, watching him set his drink aside and pull a bag out of his pocket.

While he rolls a joint, I scan the room. The faces surrounding me are unfamiliar. They have glazed eyes and disinterested expressions, and I'm glad no one cares I'm wearing sweats.

"This is some good shit," Zeke says, handing me the joint. "You need to try it."

"I don't—"

A girl with purple hair interrupts me, "It'll make you feel good."

"Yeah. Try it," another voice to my right slurs.

I stick the joint between my lips and Zeke lights it up. The moment smoke fills my lungs, a massive cough spasm attacks me. Tears prick my eyes.

I hear a storm of laughter and giggles.

"Easy, Cupcake Queen." Zeke slaps my back as I hack out the smoke. "Go slow or it'll hit you really hard."

I sip on the drink Mikah made me to sooth my throat and smoke some more of the joint, this time following Zeke's advice and pacing myself.

My head begins to spin, but I don't believe the weed is working. By the time I've finished the joint and the drink, I feel like crap. Sleepy, dizzy, and tired crap. The faces in front of me are now dancing smears and the queasiness in my stomach has returned.

I tug on the sleeve of Zeke's flannel shirt. "I don't feel very well. I think I need to lie down."

He hooks his arm through mine and leads me away from the pool table, his double exposure grin flashing at me as we move through the living room crowd.

People are everywhere—on the couches, in the corners, leaning against the walls. The music and the barrage of voices begin to close in on me. Then comes a loud pop.

Bang!

My heart trips in my chest.

More noise.

Bang!

"Zeke!" I jerk my arm away from his and spin around. The low thud of my pulse pounding in my head hurts my eardrums, and my voice doesn't sound like mine at all, more like it's been run through a voice generator. "Zeke?" I hear a strange buzzing.

"You lost, beautiful?" someone calls out. His squinty eyes glide over me and he scrunches his crooked nose.

I force my tongue to move. "Have you seen Mikah?"

"Huh?" His mouth forms a perfect "O" and a gust of alcohol-drenched breath strokes my cheeks.

"Have you seen Mikah?"

"Who?"

"Mikah?" My lips feel numb. Am I saying his name correctly or does he go by a pseudonym in this house?

The perfect O guy with the mousy eyes disappears and I drive through the crowd in the direction of the hallway. Hallways mean bedrooms. Bedrooms mean beds. Beds mean sleep.

The floorboards beneath my feet begin to shift, and my body feels heavier with each step as my heart hammers.

I stop, pressing my back against the wall, and stare at a yellow glow coming at me through the doorway of the room across from me. There, above a row of candles, stands Dakota. The eyeliner and stage-ready-hair Dakota. In his leather jacket and a tight black tee.

My heart flips and I feel goose bumps rising on my arms. He's hauntingly beautiful, just like the first time I saw him.

I push myself off the wall and step into the room, my eyes skimming over the flickering candles lined up on top of a cabinet.

Sadness and disappointment roll through me. He's not real. It's just a photo. A cutout from a big promotional Midnight Rust poster.

"Weren't you one of his girls?" a deep male voice booms behind me.

I rub at my eyes and look around. I'm in a den and there are people here. Smoking. Drinking. Laughing.

"Virgin Mary." Some girl's drunk giggle drifts from the opposite side of the room.

Anger courses through me. I walk over to the poster, grab the bottom corner, and pull it off the wall. The sound of ripping paper and a candleholder rolling across the floor fills the room.

"What the fuck are you doing?" Someone's hand grips my shoulder in an attempt to drag me away.

"Don't touch me!" I shake him off and turn around.

In front of me is Snow White, and I immediately wonder where the hell she and Mikah have been. Her stare is cold and angry. She's holding a drink in one hand and her other is squeezed into a fist. "You're not the only girl he ever dated."

I'm trembling with rage and defeat, drowning under the weight of her words.

"Just because he died when he was with you doesn't mean shit. I gave him four years! I was there for him when he was at his lowest, and then you came along and snatched him away." Her voice pitches. "You know what you are? A three-month crash course in how to deflower a virgin."

Laughter erupts around the room.

"Fuck you, whore!" I cry out, fighting angry tears. No one speaks that way about Dakota and me! No one!

"Cat fight!" someone yells.

I've never hit anyone in my entire life, but the sudden urge to destroy pushes me over the edge. I jump at her, fast and determined, and the liquid splashing across my face stalls me only for a brief second.

"Fucking amateur." She laughs, tossing her empty cup to the floor.

I throw my body at her, fists flying. My hair's in the way and I can't see anything, but I hit whatever is in my way until a pair of strong hands grab me.

"Stop it," Mikah says, pulling me away from Snow White.

"Let me go!" I scream, clawing at his forearms, my legs kicking.

"Fucking stop it already!" He drags me out of the room like a rag doll.

In the hallway, I'm propped against the wall, his rough hands on my shoulders, keeping me in place.

"Calm the fuck down, okay?!" There's moisture in my eyes, so I can't make out his face, but I can smell his familiar Marlboro scent.

"Let me go," I whimper, but parts of me have already given up. I'm too drunk and too dizzy with rage to fight against his hold.

Amused laughter inside the den only feeds my insecurities more. I'm not sure what to believe at this point.

My chest caves and every beat of my heart slams into my eardrums like a mallet.

Mikah lifts up my chin with his fingers and looks into my eyes. "Are you high?"

I attempt to catch my breath and I shake my head.

"Did you take something?"

My fuming consciousness is madly flipping through everything that just happened and I slur the first thing that comes to mind, "Your friend Zeke says hello."

I hear a heavy sigh. Mikah's face finally begins to swim into focus. He's mad at me. I can tell by the way the area above the bridge of his nose is twisted.

"I'm sorry about your hoodie," I say, fiddling with the sticky, wet fabric that's plastered to my chest.

"You'll buy me another one," Mikah mumbles, his hold on me loosening.

"I think I need to pee. Do you know where the bathroom is?"

"Are you going to behave?"

"Yes. Scout's honor." I attempt a pitiful imitation of a salute, and I think I hear Mikah chuckle.

He removes his hand from me and takes a step back. "Can you walk?"

"I think so." I move away from the wall and sway from side to side like a willow tree.

"Don't ever take any shit from people you don't know. You understand?"

I nod, tossing my arm in the air. "Lead the way, captain."

They say the eyes are the windows to the soul, so my soul must be some hazy, drunk and high bitch because that's exactly what I see when I look in the bathroom mirror.

My breaths are fast and shallow and my heartbeat is all over the place, and no matter how hard I try to convince myself that everything

Snow White said about Dakota was just a product of her imagination, the doubt still eats at me like acid.

I question his every word, his every text, his every touch. I question all the times we were together and it's the worst feeling ever. Were *we* just a lie?

A light tap on the door jars me back to reality.

"Alana?" Mikah calls. It's the third time in the past ten minutes, and I'm wondering if he's been waiting outside all along. "Are you okay?"

I've taken off the hoodie, and my white tee has a huge red stain on the front that sticks to my skin uncomfortably. I'm not sure what kind of drink it was, but it smells like her—like cheap floozy.

More knocking. "If you're sick, you need to tell me."

Sick is probably not the right word. More like shocked and disappointed. Terrified too. Drawing a deep, shaky breath, I go to the door and unlock it. The fast beat of the music crawls into the bathroom along with the stench of body odor and weed, causing my stomach to churn.

"Can I come in?" Mikah asks from behind the door. I never pegged him for a guy who'd ask permission, but I suppose both Bennett brothers are not what they seem.

The problem is, as much as I want to be left alone right now, I still like him around because he's my only connection to Dakota and I'm too scared to lose this bond—no matter how weak it is. "Yes. It's fine," I say.

Mikah squeezes himself into the bathroom and shuts the door, his eyes inspecting me as if I'm under a microscope.

There are too many things on my mind, and I don't know what to ask him first. "Whose idea was Cupcake Queen?"

Ignoring my question, he walks over to one of the high cabinets in the corner and examines its shelves.

"Whose idea was it? Yours or his?"

"Does it matter?" Mikah growls, digging through the stack of towels.

"Yes, it does. Because, apparently, I'm the Cupcake Queen Virgin Mary. No one even fucking knows my name!" I throw both hands in the air, wrath burning my cheeks and my chest. "It's like I was some conquest for him!"

Mikah turns to me, and his face is beginning to blur and spin. "Do you have to be so dramatic?"

"I'm not being dramatic." My voice is like a psychopath on a ledge, ready to jump off and start screaming. "How would you feel if someone told you that your relationship with the person who you thought was your everything was a lie?"

"You know what?" Mikah moves closer, his index finger pointing at my nose. "You're a fucking spoiled brat who's used to people catering to her every need." His eyes shoot right through my heart. "Life's a piece of shit, Alana. An ugly, unfair piece of shit. Get used to it."

The intensity of his gaze heats every part of me, but I choke down the stupid tears because I need to prove him wrong. "I don't want to get used to it."

Tossing his head back, he covers his eyes with the heels of his palms and takes a deep breath.

We stand still, facing each other, the air around us is thick with tranquil rage.

Mikah breaks the silence. "I'm not trying to take sides. This isn't easy for me." He draws his hands away from his face. "I asked you for one thing—not to bring more shit into my life—and you keep dragging my brother into every conversation." He sounds calm and reserved, but his eyes are fuming.

The lump in my throat grows bigger. "I'm sorry." I swallow past the thickness, pushing it down to my chest. My gaze drops to my wet tee and I absentmindedly pluck at the fabric stretched over my bra.

Mikah goes to the cabinet and rummages through the shelves again.

"Here." He turns around and hands me a t-shirt.

I stare at it for a few seconds, trying to figure out who it belongs to.

"It's clean." Mikah rolls his eyes impatiently.

"Are you sure?"

"Would you rather keep wearing liquor and someone else's saliva?"

"You always do that." I grab the shirt from him and smell it just to make sure.

"I always do what?"

"You always find a way to make me feel stupid."

His brow arches in silent skepticism. "You're not stupid."

I bite the inside of my cheek and reevaluate what I just said. Maybe stupid isn't the right word. More like irrelevant and unimportant, but my mind's a bit of a mess right now. My hands are shaking and my heart's racing. The liquor-stained t-shirt is unpleasantly itchy against my skin, and I want it off because the thought of Snow White's saliva being on me is now burning a hole in my brain. Or maybe the weed is finally kicking in or I shouldn't have drunk alcohol. The doctor said it's a big no-no with my medication.

"I never said you were stupid," Mikah repeats, his gaze lingering on mine. There's a dash of annoyance in his tone.

"But you're thinking it." I feel another wave of anxiety rushing through me. I have to set the clean t-shirt on the counter before it slips from my trembling hands.

"How the fuck do you know what I'm thinking?"

"I just do."

"How?" He stares at me as if I owe him a winning lottery ticket.

"It's written all over your face," I slur, tugging on the bottom of my tee.

"You're making these assumptions based on what?"

"See, you're doing it again." I turn around and attempt to pull the dirty t-shirt over my head, but my hair gets in the way. Who would have thought weed could make you feel this disoriented? Or was it the drink he mixed for me before he took off with the evil bitch?

"A little help here?" I squeal through the wet fabric that's stretched over my face. My elbows are stuck.

I feel goose bumps rising on my neck when Mikah's fingers brush over my skin.

My shoulder jerks. "Ticklish."

"Don't move," he growls, his hands going to my hair to untangle it.

"Can't breathe."

"Don't fucking move," he orders, rearranging my arms. "It's not helping."

"Okay. Thank you... Sorry." My mouth won't stay shut.

After some maneuvering and hair pulling—I'm convinced some of it definitely unnecessary—Mikah finally manages to free me of the dirty t-shirt. He tosses it in the sink and when he hands me one of the towels from the shelf, it appears that he's fighting to avoid looking at me, which is so unlike him. He's the challenge-accepted, I'll-look-if-I-want kind of guy. Or at least he was five minutes ago. It doesn't really hit me until after I'm finished cleaning the liquor residue off me that I'm not wearing anything except my bra.

I suppose this makes us even. I also suppose this should be awkward, and in a way, it is, but in another way, it's not. My mind hasn't decided yet how exactly I feel about it. For the most part, I'm just numb and mad. The anger's still there, deep inside, simmering, and the questions are still needing answers.

"Do you want me to take you home?" Mikah asks.

I grab the clean t-shirt and slip it over my head. It definitely doesn't belong to a girl, because it can fit two of me and smells like laundry detergent and tobacco-scented cologne.

"I don't want to go home." I run my palms over the fabric and press it flat against my stomach. Thankfully, my sweats and bra didn't suffer from the liquor assault.

"Do you want me to take you to your friend's house?" Mikah's gaze shifts to my face.

"Can I go with you?" I ask, my voice barely above a whisper. Maybe, if I'm lucky, he didn't hear me and we can forget this embarrassing moment.

"Look"—he shakes his head—"I'm not your babysitter."

I blink through the mist gathering in my eyes. "Why don't you like me?" My heart's sick and restless when I realize I have nowhere to go.

"I never said that," he mutters. His dark, tumultuous eyes stare into mine as if he's trying to hypnotize me.

My brain carefully assesses each word. The strange things I'm thinking right now would have never gotten into my head if I were sober. Part of me understands that, but I still act on it. Moving forward, I reach out and touch Mikah's cheek. His rough stubble grazes my fingertips as I run them down the line of his jaw. He feels a lot like Dakota and it terrifies me. It terrifies me because I don't want him to.

"Alana," Mikah rasps out my name. His palm covers my knuckles, but he doesn't remove my hand from his chin. We stand like this for a few seconds, dumbfounded, staring at each other like we can't figure out what to do or say next.

A little spark in my chest becomes a blazing fire under his endless gaze.

I inch forward and press my lips to his, my heart leaping.

There's a long, excruciating pause, our bodies so still, you'd think we stopped breathing. My every cell revels in this small taste of him. He's mint and Marlboros with a bit of salt, and my mouth burns raw against his.

I feel a soft, low gasp rumbling in his chest before his large hands cup my face and his tongue parts my lips.

Then we turn into a mess of moans and breaths. Our bodies clash together and he pushes me against the counter, roughly pressing his hard length against me. I don't know how to respond to his force except with more force. Dakota never touched me like this. He never let his hands wander over my body without permission. He took his time and we did it slowly.

There's no taking our time now. We're as far from gentle as we can possibly be and everything I do is pure instinct, a hunch of how I should react to this madness. Our tongues are too busy exploring each other's mouths, our hands too busy seizing and grasping, for me to think about it. Kissing Mikah is like being in the middle of a storm. It almost hurts physically.

He lifts me onto the counter without breaking the kiss. Then his palms grip my ass and he pulls me toward the edge, his trim, hard body sliding between my legs. He's a little bigger than Dakota and my hands hungrily roam over him, studying the contours of his chest.

It's a disturbing yet equally wonderful sensation to be so lost in another man. Suddenly, the dead parts of me have woken up and I feel *everything*. Every heartbeat, every touch, every moan.

Mikah tears his mouth from mine, and his lips slip down to my neck and kiss it greedily, the tip of his tongue tracing over my pulsing vein. Our breathing is so loud that it drowns out the sound of the music booming on the opposite side of the door. The world doesn't exist right now. It's just me and him and this kiss, probably the dirtiest one in my entire life.

Every inch of my skin burns with strange desire as I melt against him, feeling like I can't get enough. My fingers move behind his head to remove the band from his hair. But when I tangle my hands in its thickness the way I used to do with Dakota, my heart trips in my chest, the guilt hitting me hard.

"Mikah," I murmur. "Mikah."

His lips leave my neck and his eyes seek mine.

"I'm sorry." I press my palm against his pec and apply pressure.

He steps back just enough to let me slide down from the counter. My head is spinning, and everything that just happened between us finally settles into my brain.

I cover my mouth with my hand and move to the door with no intention to leave. I just need space, and this is as far as I can get in a fifty-square-foot room.

There are no words, but there's more guilt and there's shame, and it all feels like a betrayal.

"Can you just take me home?" I ask quietly.

"Yeah." His voice is low and rough, but no matter how much he tries to mask it with indifference, I can still sense all the emotions dripping from him.

It's drizzling outside when Mikah and I leave his friend's house. We don't speak about what happened in the bathroom. Actually, we don't speak at all. Not a single word is uttered after the moment he agrees to take me home.

We climb into his truck silently and he starts the engine while I fumble with my seatbelt. My mouth still burns from the kiss and my heart's sputtering, but the high of whatever Zeke gave me is wearing off and all the questions I had earlier about Dakota's ex-girlfriend are now roaring inside my head like a stadium full of people.

"Did you sleep with her?" I ask Mikah brazenly, my voice shaking.

His gaze is set on the road and he's doing a great job of ignoring me.

I refuse to give up. I need answers. "Are you not talking to me now?"

"What's there to talk about?" Mikah growls, tightening his grip around the steering wheel. The tic in his jaw doesn't escape my sight.

"Everything." My chest clamps with horror just remembering the words that were said at the house. "Did he even like me? Was all this a game to him?" I don't want to be some bet.

"We had lives before you," Mikah snaps. "You're not the fucking center of the universe, Alana. There were other people. There were friends."

The truck picks up speed and the drizzle begins to hit the windshield with full force.

"He doesn't even have his own Wikipedia page!" I cry out, fighting the tears collecting in my eyes. My head's a mess of thoughts. I'm not sure if I'm upset over Dakota dating someone before he met me, or the possibility of us being a lie, or the fact that he's not important enough to have his own Wikipedia page. Or maybe I'm upset because I feel guilty for kissing his brother. *For liking kissing his brother.*

"He doesn't need a Wikipedia page!" Mikah says angrily.

"Joseph Miller doesn't need one either!" I ball my hands into fists. Saying the name out loud sickens me. "Yet people made him one anyway. Why can't you make one for your brother?" I'm trembling. "Why do you keep pretending like nothing happened?"

"Twenty-three years. That's what happened," he growls, not taking his gaze off the road. "Have you ever seen someone you've known all your life with two bullet holes in his chest?! Right. That's what I thought. You came to his funeral to see him cleaned up and dressed up."

A wave of nausea washes over me... I wish Mikah wouldn't have said that. Every single word is like a kick to my gut and I crumble in my seat under the heaviness of his despair.

The image he plants in my mind throws me back into a state of terror, back to the night at The Crystal Room. It hits me so hard and deep that the hurt in my chest begins to expand, spreading through me like a cancer, wrecking and damaging every cell.

My cheek, the one I injured during the attack, begins to prickle and my stomach coils. The smell of blood and gunpowder clogs my throat.

"When you see what I've seen, then we'll talk!" Mikah's heated, irate voice slices me open.

I can't breathe and I can't think straight. I can't stop trembling, and being this close to him right now is too much. *Everything is too much.* I feel like I'm drowning in a senseless ocean of ruin and desolation. Drowning without Dakota. All I want is to be someplace else. Someplace that's not here.

I hear a click in the back of my head after I mindlessly reach for the seatbelt.

"What the fuck are you doing?" Mikah growls, his hand clutching my shoulder.

The squeal of the brakes cuts through the music. The truck jerks, sending me forward, and my head hits the dash. A dull pain spreads across my forehead, but I'm too dazed to pay attention to it. My fingers pull on the handle, and the door of the truck swings open, letting a sheet of drizzle in.

I breathe in deep and hoist myself from the seat. The air filling my lungs is almost too heavy as I tumble out and my feet hit the muddy ground.

The field in front of me spreads out as far as my teary eyes can see.

"Alana!" Mikah's voice penetrates the darkness. His booted footsteps slosh behind me as I start running. My sneakers fall through the mud. I'm not sure where I'm headed, but it's somewhere downhill, because it feels like I'm falling into an abyss of rain and grime. All I really want is to be as far from this hurt as I possibly can. My breathing is heavy, my heart's racing along with my mind. Mikah's yelling shatters against the noise of the traffic behind me and I push through the pain in my knees and move faster. Every muscle in my body draws tight and my lungs hurt from the lack of air. The wind bites my face, blurring my eyes and I can't tell where I am anymore. It feels a lot like a circle of horror. A trap full of smells, screams, and bodies.

Bang! Bang!

The mud slurps and splashes under my sneakers, and the wet grass slaps against my ankles.

"Alana!" he calls my name again.

Bang! Bang!

"Alana! Stop!"

Bang! Bang!

"Alana!"

My pulse beats madly against my eardrums, and my heart's on the verge of bursting into a million bloody pieces when I trip over something hard. I fly forward, and when I land on my hands, my scarred palms hitting the ground first, mud splashes across my chin and lips.

"Alana!" Mikah shouts.

I don't want to see him right now. I don't want to see anyone. I'm tired of trying to fit in. I'm tired of trying to reassemble the parts of me that don't want to be put back in place, because some of those parts are dead and don't work well with the ones that are still alive. There's a piece of me that just wants to die, and I can't tell if it's a side effect of the anti-depressants or what my therapist calls survivor's guilt. I just know I want all this to stop. I *need* all this to stop.

It's too much. Too much to feel all at once.

"Alana!" Mikah's voice closes in on me like a hunting dog on a fox.

I spit out the mud and as I'm pushing myself up, he slams against me and I lose my balance. We fall down and roll across the grass, our arms and legs twisted, our breaths heavy and loud, yet I don't feel anything except rage. I fight him relentlessly, tossing my fists at him because in this moment, he deserves it, but then he gets me flat on my back.

Mikah moves up my body and his face invades my line of sight. I throw a hard punch, not sure where it lands, and he grabs my wrists and presses them into the ground, his weight holding me still. We're now a furious, panting mess and this—the filth and the dark—suits us because I don't know how else to describe what's going on between us.

"If you want to leap from a moving car, you don't fucking do it while I'm driving," Mikah growls, the line above the bridge of his nose deepening. "Do you understand?"

My lips are shut tight, and I jerk beneath him.

"Do you understand?" he repeats, his eyes drilling into me. They're big and livid, the emerald green consumed by black.

My clothes are cold and wet against my skin, and the consequences of my jump are starting to come down on me hard and fast. In the form of physical pain. My muscles are aching; my lungs and my chest burn.

"Do you?" Mikah drills.

I jerk again, but his thigh presses against mine, pushing me deeper into the mud.

We still for a few seconds, our bodies strained and our faces a gasp apart as we stare at each other. It almost feels like a competition, but I have no idea what we're competing for.

Swallowing past the lump in my throat, I push the words out, "I understand."

The line on Mikah's forehead relaxes. He lets out a sigh of relief and his breath fans against my dirty cheeks. "Don't ever fucking do that again. You scared the shit out of me."

I have no idea what to say to him. I'm still mad. He never answered my questions. I just lie there motionless and completely wrecked and watch the faint shadows moving across his face.

"Don't do that again, okay?" Mikah repeats, his tone unusually soft. He releases my wrists and after he pushes himself up, he sits next to me in the grass.

I want to get up, but my emotions are still running rampant and I'm too sore to move. Each bone and muscle screams with agony, but the worst pain is in my left ankle.

Mikah's quiet, his face tense with concern.

"I believe I sprained my ankle," I say through the small puffs of air coming out of my mouth.

"Let me take a look." Mikah slides across the grass and examines my leg. "I don't see any swelling." He rises to his feet and pulls me off the ground. I stagger and wince as I grab on to his shoulder.

"Can you walk at all?"

"I'm not sure," I confess, holding on to him for dear life. The pain pulsing through my leg is excruciating and I'm scared to put weight on it.

"Okay." He slips one arm under my knee, supporting my back with the other, and scoops me up. "You're washing my truck, Cupcake Queen." His voice vibrates against my temple. "Deal?"

"Deal," I mumble, throwing my hands around his neck.

"My truck's up the hill. Try not to kill us, all right?" he jokes as we head that way.

The little chime above my head jingles briskly as I pull the door of the artisan coffee shop open and take in the interior. There are at least three dozen people inside, talking and smiling. I catch the soft sounds of laughter, but it's not the drunk, crazy brawl you'd hear at a bar or on campus after midterms. This crowd is different. All of these people were at The Crystal Room during the last Midnight Rust show.

I notice Luke and Blaze at a small table near the window as a few glances are aimed in my direction.

Jess steps out from a group gathered near the jukebox and waves at me, a wide smile lighting up her face.

I give her a quick wave back and then I limp to meet her halfway as my gaze jumps from one exit sign to another. I can't imagine why she chose this place—its layout isn't the best. There are only two doors, and the large wooden tables scattered throughout are going to make it hard to get out if someone decides to open fire.

I heard the owner of the coffee shop lost his niece during the attack and volunteered to host the meet-ups here, but in my mind, I'd rather it be in the park. Anywhere with more room to run.

"I'm so happy you made it." Jess beams. She holds out both hands to greet me and pulls me toward a table with snacks. "You have to meet Ashley and Reese."

These names don't ring a bell, but I nod in agreement.

"What happened?" Jess motions at my ankle.

"I sprained it. It's nothing serious." I don't feel like elaborating with a bunch of strangers listening to our conversation, so I quickly change the subject. "Is there coffee?" I scan a row of muffins laid out in front of me.

We chat for a bit and Jess introduces me to some of the people, including Ashley and Reese, who are our age. There are a lot of familiar faces, and although I don't know who they lost or if they were hurt as badly as Luke, their sadness gets to me. In a way, this meeting reminds me of Dakota's funeral. A lot of misery and mixed emotions stuffed into one tiny place and I don't feel like I belong here, because I can't stomach seeing Luke still in a wheelchair. I can't stomach seeing my best friend pretending that she's stronger than ever. She's not. None of us are. Deep down, we're all cut up and twisted, but no one talks about it. The only talk I hear is about moving on.

The meeting's extremely casual. There's no call to order or round-table discussion. Everyone's gladly sharing their progress while I'm spending most of my time checking my phone and wondering when Mikah's going to text me back.

The night of the kiss, as I choose to call it—because I'm not sure how else to define that particular moment in my life—after Mikah drove me to the ER, he took the liberty of contacting my parents. I was pissed at him when my father barged in like a speeding locomotive, freaking out and fuming. It was awkward watching the two of them engage in a silent staring competition after what had transpired earlier in my driveway. After Mikah left the hospital, I was convinced he'd never talk to me again after my car freak-out, but he messaged me a few days later, asking about my leg.

Our texting spree revolved mostly around a discussion of *Dracula* and other horror books he deems worthy of reading, as if the night of the kiss was forgotten, but each time Mikah's name lit up the screen of my phone, it made me think about the exquisite feel of his lips on mine.

Someone's hand touches my shoulder, jarring me back to reality.

"Do you want to share your story?" Reese asks.

"Oh." I glance over at the group and say meekly, "Maybe next time."

She nods and steps away.

There's a rumble near the jukebox. When the soft sounds of an acoustic guitar pour from the speakers, my heart leaps to my throat. I haven't been able to bring myself to listen to any Midnight Rust songs yet. The mere idea of hearing Dakota's voice sends chills down my spine.

Dread seizes my chest, pushing me to my feet. I can't decide whether I should say something or just charge for the exit. My mind desperately tries to block the melody. These lyrics have different meaning now. They're too much.

Outside, the air is heavy with a lukewarm mist and it feels like I'm breathing through cheesecloth. There's a tiny portion of my brain that's dying for some nicotine.

"Hey," Jess calls. The slam of the door cuts off the jingle. "Are you okay?" She moves closer and concern skates across her face.

"Do you have a cigarette?" I mumble, balling my shaking hands into fists.

"Huh?" Her eyebrows pull together.

That's right. Jess doesn't smoke. I knew that. I have no idea why I asked. There's not much logic to anything I've been doing lately. "Never mind. Sorry."

"What's going on, Alana?" she whispers.

"I don't feel like I'm doing this right," I confess. "It's like there's no light at the end of the tunnel."

"There's always light. You just have to keep walking toward it."

"You say that like it's eventually going to stop hurting."

"Of course it won't; but it *will* get better," Jess says, her tone calm and reassuring.

I draw a deep breath. My gaze flicks to hers and we stare at each other for a few seconds.

She breaks the silence. "Are you talking to Mikah?" That's very out of the blue.

"Sometimes," I say, glancing down at the scars on my palms.

"He moved, right?"

"Uh huh."

"I'm a bit worried. He hasn't been returning any of Luke's calls."

"Really?" To me this is news. I was under the impression that Mikah has only been keeping his distance with me.

"Is he doing okay?"

I'm not sure how he's doing. He's cold and unapproachable unless we discuss literature. He doesn't want to share his real feelings with me. He doesn't want to talk about Dakota or anything that happened that night, and worry and fear for him and for us—whatever *we* may be now—gnaws at my gut.

"If I tell you something, can you keep it a secret?" I say softly, palming my cheeks, which feel like they're on fire.

"You're seriously asking me this?" Jess rolls her eyes. "Of course."

I scan the sidewalk and the street to make sure no one can hear me when I let these words out into the universe. "We kissed."

The expression on Jess's face is one of horror. "You and Mikah?" Her jaw snaps shut and her eyes widen.

I nod, swallowing past the throbbing lump in my throat as I hug myself.

"Are you serious? When?"

"Last week."

"And you're just telling me about this right now?" She sounds offended. "I'm your best friend."

"I know. I'm sorry. I needed some time. We had a few drinks and it just happened, and now I can't stop thinking about it."

"Crap." Her shoulders sag.

"Please don't tell Luke," I plead.

"I won't," she reassures me.

We fall back into a moment of depressing silence and I almost regret my confession.

"Is there something going on between you two?" Jess asks quietly, her voice laced with concern. Her gaze narrows on my face.

"I don't know."

"Girl..." she pauses for a second as if searching for the right thing to say, but I can tell she's struggling with the idea of Mikah and me kissing as much as I am. "Just be careful."

"What do you mean?" I don't understand what she's trying to tell me.

Jess moves closer and whispers, "Just because they look alike doesn't mean one can replace the other."

I want to scream at her for saying this out loud, but at the same time, she makes me question my real motives behind the kiss.

"Look, I'm not saying that's what you're doing." She touches my shoulder. "But don't go there if you don't mean it. It'd be shitty to do that to him and to yourself."

I nod in acknowledgment and force a small smile.

Jess and I talk for a while longer, until Blaze comes out to grab her. I don't go back inside. Instead, I say my goodbyes and head to my car and call Mikah.

He answers almost instantly. "How's your leg?"

"It's better. I drove today." I don't tell him where exactly I drove.

"You still owe me a car wash, remember?"

"Yes, I do."

I wait for him to say something else while my brain paints a very vivid picture of us kissing. My stomach squeezes and my heart rate begins to escalate. *No, I'm not trying to replace Dakota.*

"You ever read Stephen King?" Mikah asks.

"I tried reading *Carrie*. It's a bit creepy for my taste."

I hear a soft laugh. "You asked for horror recommendations. Try *Salem's Lot*."

"Do you not care about my sleep at all?" I joke.

"Of course I do." He pauses. "I gotta go. I'll text you tomorrow."

The line disconnects before I get to respond.

16. BEFORE

Apparently, the whole Mississippi Studios trip is a group thing.

"Luke's picking me up in twenty minutes," Jess announces as soon as I arrive at her house.

"Luke's coming over here?" My jaw hangs open.

"Yeah. We're going too."

I was under the impression tonight's date would be just Dakota and me. But my bigger problem is explaining to Luke why I "live" with Jess.

Now that I've gotten a taste of Dakota, I can't stop thinking about us and I'm scared to mess it up. Yesterday, he took me to a nice restaurant. It was a real date with candles and delicious food, and it felt surreal, almost like at the movies. We kissed until my lips went numb in front of the Tillers' house when he dropped me off. Ah, the perks of having parents who are obsessed with traveling.

"Can you help me with my hair?" Jess yanks me out of my daydream. "And I need some details, remember?"

"What details?" I follow her into the bathroom.

"About last night. You didn't even stay to hang out after he dropped you off."

"You were snoring like an elephant." I laugh.

"I don't snore." She shakes her head.

"Yes, you do. I'll record it next time."

Then Jess does what she always does in cases like this—abruptly changes the subject. "Come on. Spill it."

Dakota's Mustang pulls into the Tillers' driveway at quarter to six, when I've already relived yesterday's date in my mind four times.

The temperature outside has dropped dramatically since last night, and I rush to the car like a marathon runner, praying to God that Luke's running late and doesn't see us.

When we arrive at Mississippi Studios, Blaze and Dakota's friends are already waiting for us in the lobby. The bouncer checks our IDs and uses a black marker to draw a huge cross on my wrist.

The venue is dark and has just enough lighting to allow us not to trip over other people. The narrow balcony encircling the floor of the main room is packed, and the dozens of yellow globes and Christmas lights hanging from the high ceiling give the place a festive, homey vibe. It's nothing like the club where we saw the Black Rose and Midnight Rust shows. This is intimate and people seem to know each other well, because Dakota keeps getting stopped every two seconds on our way to the bar.

"Are you hungry? Do you want anything?" he asks as we push through the chattering crowd to get to the bartender.

"Just water," I say, untying my scarf.

My phone pings when we get to the end of the line at the bar, and when I draw it from my pocket, I see a text message from Jess.

THERE'S NO COAT CHECK HERE!

I smile at her OCD. Tonight isn't one of those *beauty requires sacrifices* nights, but she's hard to convince otherwise.

The line inches forward and we move closer to the bar.

"DK! Hey!" I hear someone calling Dakota's name and he spins toward the sound. There's some handshaking, back patting, and a brief introduction. The guy's a little older and his name is Eric. He looks to be in his mid-thirties and he's wearing a whole lot of jewelry. But not the dark and simple kind that Dakota likes. His are flashy gold and he talks loud. If not for his clothes, you'd think he's a politician or one of those guys who writes books on self-help and then travels the world to give lectures.

When the bartender finally gets our order, Eric slaps a hundred-dollar bill on the counter and tells us the drinks are on him.

"Thanks, man. The next one's on me." Dakota grabs his beer and my water and we step away from the bar. Eric catches up with us as soon as he gets his change.

"There's a rumor that Brighthouse is going to pull the plug on their Seattle residency," he says matter-of-factly. "I can get you that slot."

Dakota tears his beer away from his mouth and I feel his grip tightening around my hand. I have no idea what Eric is talking about, but I sense it's important, because Dakota's eyes take on a spark. I've seen that glow before. On stage. "When?"

"February." Eric's gaze slides to my water and then back to Dakota's face. "Consider it before the offer expires. It's a hot slot. Going to get booked fast."

"Can I have a couple of days? Wanna talk to the guys."

Something inside me begins to tick when I see Mikah's head floating in our direction. I didn't think he'd be here. His hands are thrust into the pockets of his jacket, his eyes darting among the three of us. Skipping the formalities, he inserts himself between Eric and me, and the tension in the air is undeniable.

"How you doing, big man?" Eric extends his hand for a shake.

Keeping his hands in his pockets, Mikah growls out, "All right." But it's drowned out by all the noise.

I feel bad. I don't know why. Maybe because whatever Eric's talking about is important to Dakota, and Mikah's being an ass.

The crowd begins to cheer and people move onto the balcony to grab their spots.

"Call me, DK!" Eric shouts over the music.

Dakota gives him a thumbs-up and nudges me in the direction of our group.

"We should do it," Blaze says, twisting his straw. "I'm fucking done playing the same venues over and over again.

"I concur." Luke nods, and his hand slips under the table and rests casually on Jess's thigh.

Our group's occupying the largest booth at the very back of the noisiest downtown restaurant I've ever been to. The glow of the Christmas lights gives the place a more intimate vibe, despite the rowdy crowd. Most of the people here are drunk, loud, and entertaining to watch. My father would probably have a heart attack if he knew where I really was. He still thinks I'm with Jess baking Christmas cupcakes for my holiday blog post.

Dakota's arm is curled around my shoulder and he's using his free hand to pick up french fries from the plate in front of him.

"You know what I think." Mikah shrugs, the dull expression on his face speaking volumes. He's sitting on the end next to the aisle, sliding his steak around the plate with his fork, and I'm wondering if he's ever a people person.

There's another guy and a girl with us at the table. They're Luke's friends, but their names are a bit muddy because I've been introduced to so many people tonight that my brain is over capacity to remember everyone at this point.

The band we saw earlier was amazing. I loved every second of it and I loved sharing all those moments with Dakota. But now that the high of the show is gone, the discussion at the table takes on a serious tone.

"The shit that happened with Coral War was blown out of proportion," Blaze says, looking up from his straw. "They never had an offer in the first place. Jimmy's just a douche who can't play."

Luke snorts out a laugh. "Did you see his last interview?" His voice goes from low to high. "We're the future of alternative rock."

Laughter erupts around the table.

"Who the hell cares what Jimmy says?" Mikah growls, shoving his plate aside. "He's old news. Eric is fucking sketchy. No band he's ever managed has gotten a record deal."

"Because he's never managed a decent band," Dakota counters.

"Because no decent band wants to deal with someone like him."

"We don't sign anything."

"It doesn't matter. Word gets around."

Their voices mesh into one and the tension rising at the table becomes uncomfortable.

"Can we talk about this tomorrow?" Luke cuts in.

"Yeah," Blaze agrees. "Let's sleep on it."

Annoyance creeps over Mikah's face and he doesn't respond. He just takes a swig of his beer, stands up, and heads for the exit.

I watch him with my heart in my throat as he navigates his way through the crowded dining room, not bothering to look back.

"Dude needs an attitude adjustment," one of Luke's friends snorts out.

"Don't talk shit about my brother," Dakota says, his words floating across the table, heavy with threat.

There's a pause. Everyone falls into short silence before the conversation is steered in a different direction.

"Do you want to go with me to Blaze's Christmas party?" Dakota asks quietly, his mouth near my ear.

"When? On Christmas Day?" I ask in disbelief.

"Yeah. That's why it's called a Christmas party." Dakota laughs against my cheek.

In my mind, Christmas has always been a religious holiday and Blaze doesn't strike me as someone who goes to church or prays. If anything, he reminds me of Satan's illegitimate son who's been kicked out of hell for bad behavior. He's got piercings and tats and he wears a whole lot of jewelry with skulls. Or "offensive imagery," as my father would say.

"Like *party* party?" I ask Dakota quietly. *With drinks and games and people acting silly?*

"Yeah, like *party* party." He presses his face into my hair and breathes me in slowly, a gesture so intimate—and in public. An insecure part of me still wonders why he's with me when there's an abundance of girls who can easily give him what most guys like Dakota—good-looking and spoiled—usually want.

"I have a thing with my parents on Christmas."

"You can't skip it?" Dakota laughs. It's a quiet laugh for me only.

"No."

I'm convinced he's become just as addicted to me as I am to him, because he keeps trying to find ways to see me more often.

"You have some free days next week, don't you?" Dakota says into my hair.

"I have to help my parents with some stuff, but yes, I do," I whisper against his coat.

After dinner is over and everyone's headed home, we go to Dakota's car and sit in the parking lot with the heater running. He rubs his palms together to warm them up and turns to face me. His cheeks are a light shade of pink and his blue eyes are dead serious. "Can I ask you something?"

"Sure." My heart stills. I'm so used to his jokes and smiles and I'm wondering if I did something or if maybe he's upset with Mikah. Mikah's behavior earlier in the restaurant threw me off.

"Why did you have me pick you up from Jess's place?"

The question hanging between us isn't what I expected to hear.

Dakota's gaze, intense and unsmiling, demands clarification.

I draw a deep breath through my teeth and bite the inside of my cheek. The hot, stuffy air coats my lungs. Lying to my parents about where I spend my weekends and lying to him about where I live probably earned me a spot in hell a long time ago.

"Hey." Dakota's tone softens. "You know you can talk to me about things, right?" His fingers move into my hair and he cups the back of my head.

"I just..." I let out a loud, heavy sigh, not sure what he's thinking. "My parents are a bit...overprotective."

"Overprotective?" He draws his eyebrows together. "Of what? Me?"

"No." I shake my head, trying to come up with an answer that will make sense.

"Then what? You're not sixteen, are you?" He laughs a little. "Because I don't know any sixteen-year-olds getting accepted to college."

"No." A giggle bursts out of me. "If I were sixteen, you'd be dead."

"I see." He pulls away, but his eyes never leave mine.

There's a long pause.

I break the silence. "My father believes boys will somehow undermine my education." I'm not sure if my explanation is good enough. "He's Catholic," I add, but I don't say that I am, because the truth is, I don't even know anymore. I don't know if I'm what my father thinks a good Catholic girl should be. I feel misplaced in my own house sometimes.

Dakota rests his head against the headrest and stares up at the roof of his car. "So you don't want him to know you're seeing someone, or you don't want him to know you're seeing someone like me?"

"Maybe both," I mutter, fumbling with the bottom of my coat. The ridiculousness of my response doesn't hit me until he shoots me another question.

"So I'm not good enough to be your boyfriend." His voice drops to a whisper. "Is that what it is?"

"No. That's not what I meant!" The words tumble out of me in the form of a cry and I can sense the crack between us growing bigger with each second.

"Then why don't you want your parents to know you're seeing someone? I'm not some homeless guy without an education. I have a job and I have a place of my own. I believe I'm doing okay so far."

I need a few moments to let everything Dakota just said settle in. "I got a full ride to a college I didn't really like, and my father agreed to pay for the college I wanted to go to instead, under the condition I don't move out."

Dakota's quiet. His Adam's apple rolls under his skin as his face stays indifferent for what seems like an eternity, and I swear I would trade one of my kidneys right now to know what he's thinking.

Does he not want to see me anymore?

"Jess and I are looking for a place downtown," I mumble under my breath. "I got a job at Toro Bravo. I start after Christmas."

Dakota straightens up in his seat, his eyes drifting back to my face. "You're getting a job and an apartment so you can keep seeing me?" His voice grows deep.

My stomach is in tight knots. "Yes."

"What about the tuition?"

"Not sure yet." I shrug. There's a part of me that hopes my father isn't completely insane and won't stop paying for college just because I move out, but there's also a part of me that isn't sure what to think or what to do anymore.

"Do you plan on keeping me a secret from your parents for the rest of your life?" The corner of his lips curve upward and his features soften.

I don't know whether it's his smile or the "rest of your life" part, but comforting warmth instantly fills my chest. "No. I won't."

"You're going to have to tell them eventually"—he leans closer and whispers against my face—"Moonchild."

His hand slides to the back of my neck, and a trail of goose bumps run down my spine. His touch sets my entire body on fire. "I know. I will when the time is right. I plan on doing it after the semester ends. I have to have some leverage at the very least. My GPA should be good enough." I grin at him.

"Why are you so goddamn irresistible, even when you're ashamed of me?" Dakota's lips press against mine.

"I'm not ashamed of you." My breath blends with his and it's such an exquisite feeling, such a rush.

"Do you want to see my place?" he murmurs, kissing the corner of my mouth.

I freeze. This is the first time since we started seeing each other openly that Dakota's asked me to come to his apartment, and his question stirs a whole lot of mixed feelings in me. Jess says that when a guy invites a girl over, it means he's dead set on sex, and I'm not sure I'm ready just yet. I've been thinking about it a lot lately, but we haven't done anything except for kissing and holding hands.

"I'll take you home if you're tired." Dakota's tone changes when he notices my hesitation.

"I don't mind *seeing* your place," I say, biting the inside of my cheek. "I just can't stay over."

"I'm not asking you to stay over." He pauses. "I just wanted to show you my apartment. It's normal for people who are together to know things about each other."

"We're together?" I drawl, invisible droplets of pleasure spreading through me.

"Yes." He nods and leans back in his seat. "I believe we are. I want us to be."

"Okay. Let's go."

I stand in the middle of the large open-concept living room, staring at the walls of posters with my mouth agape. There's The Cure, HIM, Siouxsie and the Banshees, and more bands I'm not familiar with. A gasp is stuck in my throat and my fingers are clutching the top button of my coat, which I've been meaning to take off, but my fascination with the interior has hindered my motor skills.

Turns out, Dakota's apartment is only ten minutes away from downtown. It's on the top floor of one of the newer buildings in the Northwest District, and I'm wondering how an event coordinator can afford a place like this.

They say every home has its scent. Dakota's smells just like him. Old leather and wild sandalwood. It's a strange blend of music and masculinity that makes me want to know more about him, makes me want to know everything there is.

"Are all these from the printed magazines?" I motion at the posters.

"Most are." Dakota steps closer and helps me with my coat. "I've been collecting all these since I was a kid. They add up over the years." A smirk tugs the corner of his mouth.

"I can see that."

"Let me show you the rest." He places his hand on the small of my back and ushers me in the direction of the long, dark hallway. My heart beats a little faster and I feel my body stiffening under his touch. *Is this the part where he's going to insist on sex?*

Dakota slows down and flicks one of the switches on the panel we pass. Bright light spills at me from the ceiling and, somehow, I no longer feel as terrified as I did two seconds ago.

"This is the bathroom," he explains, gesturing at the door to the left. "This is my room." He points at the one to the right.

The third door at the end of the hallway remains unnamed.

We stand still and silent, staring at each other, our faces a hair's breadth apart. My mind's rushing through all the possible outcomes of my agreeing to come here tonight.

"Do you want something to drink?" Dakota finally asks, lessening the growing tension.

I think it's highly doubtful he's brought me here for a glass of water. "No thanks. Can I see your room?" I sound both shy and needy.

"Sure." He nods. His eyes twinkle like tiny blue stars, and his smile is wide and stunning. He motions for me to follow him.

I'm not sure what to expect when I enter Dakota's room. I've only seen two bedrooms in my entire life besides mine—my parents' and Jess's, which don't count.

I hear a soft click and one of the lamps that looks like a lantern glows blue.

This place belongs to a man. A man obsessed with all things dark. It's modest in décor, except for the countless posters hanging on the walls—one of Black Rose included—heavy draperies on the windows, and guitar gear occupying one of the corners. Music has touched every crack and crevice here and planted itself into this space indefinitely.

My eyes dart from one item to another, studying each detail carefully, like in a museum exhibit. There's a black lamp in the shape of a dragon that sits on the nightstand with a set of candles around it and a Toscano bookcase stuffed with CDs and vinyls.

The predominant colors are black and blue. Even the bedding is navy, and I'm wondering if there's any difference between his sheets and mine. I'm also wondering if I'm ever going to sleep in this bed. I'm wondering so many things that it makes my head spin a little.

"What are these?" I point at the small figures hanging from the ceiling.

"Oh." Dakota gets a gleam in his eyes. "Watch this." He returns to the switch panel and the dozen tiny birds flicker above my head.

"What are they?" I gasp, my eyes wide with shock.

"Hummingbirds." He smiles.

"They're beautiful." My gaze returns to his.

"They fucking are," Dakota agrees. There's a pause. "I'm sorry. I'm not very good at keeping my stuff organized," he confesses as I move to the center of the room, but I don't notice anything out of place.

"It's okay." A trace of a smile stretches across my lips, and I'm a bit unsure what to do next. My throat starts closing up and my palms gets sweaty. "I changed my mind. Can I have some water?" I say timidly, going over to his desk.

"Of course." He walks out of the room, leaving the door slightly ajar. The sound of his footsteps echoing down the hallway grows faint and then disappears.

There's a strange flutter-like sensation building in my belly because he's trusted me to be by myself in his personal space with all his quirks and secrets out in the open. It's almost like looking inside his head, which is both exciting and terrifying, considering the dark nature of his music.

I'm surprised when I hear someone else in the living room talking to Dakota, their tone low and indifferent—Dakota never said anything about having a roommate. I freeze in my spot and listen to the hushed whispers as they travel through the apartment, arguing with each other.

When the noises reach the end of the hallway, I realize it's Mikah.

"...you never fucking listen to me, DK." His rough voice crawls into the bedroom through the narrow crack between the door and the frame. "Eric's bad news. He's going to screw us all over."

"But at least I'm fucking doing something," Dakota comes back, his tone bitter. "I'm not going to sit and wait for some shitty label to get to my demo tape."

"Fine. Do whatever you want." His heavy, booted footsteps thumping along the hallway vanish behind the door that slams shut.

Dakota enters the room a few seconds later. He tries to mask his uneasiness with a smile, but it looks forced and doesn't reach his eyes.

"Is everything okay?" I ask quietly, fumbling with the hem of my sweater.

"Yeah. Just band stuff." He hands me a glass of water.

"You and your brother live together?"

Dakota nods, moving closer. "Yep." His palms slide up my shoulders and linger on my neck. The warmth of his skin against mine is divine. "Don't worry about him. He's a major dick sometimes, but he keeps to himself."

I've never had anyone say "dick" in front of me, and I feel heat creeping up my cheeks, even if it was used in a context totally unrelated to sex.

It doesn't bother me. It makes me wonder what other foul words Dakota knows and how and when he's going to say them to me.

"Do you want to show me your collection?" I ask, motioning toward the shelf.

"You bet."

We hang out in Dakota's room until three in the morning, listening to music and staring at his hummingbirds while talking about his band and my baking blog.

He drops me off at Jess's shortly before four, and we spend another thirty minutes in front of her house kissing like tomorrow's the end of the world.

17. AFTER

"I know you're upset and I know you don't think this is going to help you feel better, but it will. Trust me." Jess purses her lips together and waits for my answer.

I'm not sure how I feel about her idea yet or if there's much of my best friend left in her. The person sitting across from me isn't the same girl who gave me black nail polish for my thirteenth birthday. She's a new version of Jess who's developed a bunch of crazy ideas over the course of the past few weeks.

The sight of Joseph Miller's name slapped all over the printouts she's laid on my bed makes my stomach churn.

I swallow back the nausea and look at her. "This won't make any difference. His attorney won't stop pushing for insanity just because a bunch of people with homemade posters show up in front of the court-room." My gaze flicks to my nightstand where my phone is. Mikah and I are supposed to meet up later. The official story is the car wash I owe him. I don't know what the unofficial one is. He didn't return my texts for a while, so I have no idea what's going on with us at the moment.

"Yes, it will," Jess counters. "Our voices need to be heard. Yours, mine, Ashley's, Luke's." There's a wild spark in her eyes I've never seen before. She's changed a lot since the attack. We all have. I'm just not certain I like what she's becoming. Although I'm not one to be passing judgement. My life is like a train slowly going off the tracks. I'm struggling with keeping my grades just above the fail mark. I'm constantly rescheduling my therapy sessions. I never went to another meet-up. But the worst thing of all is that I believe I might be developing some very conflicting feelings for the older brother of my dead boyfriend.

"Is Blaze going?" I ask, shaking off my anxiety.

"Yes." Jess picks up some of the printouts and tosses them back in the folder. "Are you still talking to Mikah?"

"Yes."

"You should tell him to come too."

"He won't."

"His brother got shot and he won't support the cause?" Her words cut through the air like a hacksaw, each one causing something inside me to snap.

"Look, he hasn't told me anything... I just know he won't." My voice cracks. "He won't even talk to me about Dakota."

I expect Jess to bring up the kiss, but she doesn't respond. I watch her scoop up the rest of the printouts without saying a word.

When she's finished, she sets her folder aside and says, "Do you know what I dream about sometimes?"

"What?"

"I dream about putting a lot of bullets through Joseph Miller." Her gaze locks on mine. "Twenty-four. Where it hurts the most, but it's not immediately lethal. And then I would watch him slowly bleed to death."

I feel my eyes growing wider as acid rises in the back of my throat.

"Don't tell me you've never thought about it?" she whispers, her words floating in the air like ash.

"I don't know," I mutter.

"Well, maybe you should." She stands up and grabs her folder. "If we all just keep quiet and suffer in silence, nothing's going to change."

"What do you want to change? They're all dead!" My voice shakes and I start to feel dizzy and sick.

"People like him deserve to die, Alana. It's only fair that there's a death penalty in every state."

I can't tell if Jess has really changed that much or if she's just delusional, but politics would normally be the last thing she'd discuss. The old Jess couldn't tell the difference between republicans and democrats.

Our goodbye is cold and I sit on my bed for a few minutes, processing everything she just said until another wave of nausea sends me running to the bathroom where I drop to my knees in front of the toilet and throw up.

***

I pull into a guest parking spot and double check Mikah's text for the apartment number.

It's an older complex hiding behind a line of trees. The courtyard isn't very big, but it's full of flowers, and the smell of spring blooming feels pleasant and refreshing. After the strange conversation with Jess earlier today, I need something like this—something new and uncorrupted by the events of this winter.

Mikah's apartment is on the second floor, and when he answers my knock at the door, his greeting is quick with a touch of coldness. He's wearing a t-shirt, a pair of faded jeans, and an old tattered leather jacket I've never seen on him. Maybe it's one he only wears to wash cars.

"Hi." I look past his shoulder and notice a huge poster of The Cure on the living room wall.

"Wanna check it out before we go?" Mikah steps aside to let me in.

"I'd love to."

It's small with hardly any furniture and a stack of unopened boxes in the corner. It has a weird vibe—it doesn't feel like a place where someone would want to settle down.

"How's the ankle, Cupcake Queen? You ready for some physical labor?" Mikah breaks the silence as I study the shelves with his book collection and CDs. Some of those CDs used to sit in Dakota's room.

"Do you still have his vinyls?" I ask.

There's a pause and it dawns on me. I'm still expected to honor our initial agreement. Dakota and the night of the attack are the things we're not going to talk about.

"I'm sorry," I say softly.

"Are you wearing that?" Mikah motions at me, changing the subject. "You know you're going to get wet, right?"

"It's fine. They're not new," I explain. I've got tons of jeans and shirts. Besides, they're just clothes.

Once we get downstairs, Mikah leads me to the back of the building where the tenants' vehicles are neatly lined up in several rows. The moment I see the glimmering of the sun on the hood of Dakota's Mustang, all the memories made in that car creep up on me. My feet stop moving and I freeze in the middle of the parking lot.

Mikah turns around, his gaze locked on mine.

"I thought we were going to wash *your* car." The words come out of my mouth in shallow breaths and dissolve in the warm April air like a drop of paint in a jar of water.

Mikah ignores my question. "Are you coming or what?"

I swallow the bitter lump in my throat and quietly follow him to the car.

The car wash we end up taking the Mustang to is down the street from the apartment complex. It's a self-service one and it's empty.

I'm not exactly sure why Mikah asked me to come, but I'm really glad he did. I've been a nervous wreck during this past week since we didn't talk. I've replayed our kiss in my head a million times in an attempt to recreate that strange feeling I had the second our lips got a taste of each other. It was guilt wrapped in something new and exhilarating and I've wanted to experience it again.

"Have you ever washed a car before?" Mikah asks as we get out of the Mustang.

"I've helped my dad."

"All right, then you're not totally useless."

"You're underestimating my skills. I'm a woman of many talents."

"We'll see." He pats his pockets and pulls out two cigarettes. One for me and one for him.

We smoke in silence, staring at the car. Mikah's puffing neat rings into the warm air that mix with the messy clouds I'm blowing out. There's something brewing between us, and although I can't put my finger on it, I can sense the shift. He wouldn't have texted me for no reason. Not after what happened.

"Are you selling it?" I ask carefully, motioning at the car.

"No."

"I'm glad."

He responds with a low grunt and more smoke.

"Jess came over today."

"Okay." He seems uninterested in my friend.

"Did you know she runs a weekly support group for...everyone who was at The Crystal Room that night?" I'm not sure how to word what I'm trying to say. "She asked me about you. You haven't been returning Luke's calls."

"I haven't had time."

Somehow, I don't believe he's telling the truth.

"She's just worried."

"Why's she worried about me?"

I decide not to bring up the rally Jess mentioned. I don't want to stain this moment with the filth that comes with the name of the person who's the reason we're all so fucked up right now. "She's worried about everyone."

"I'm fine." Mikah goes to the trash can and puts out his cigarette. "Are you ready?"

I may have lied a little. I've never helped my father wash his car. Things like this have never been required of me. My chores are mostly dishwashing and helping around the kitchen. The self-service car wash is a whole new level of knowledge for me, but Mikah's presence makes me want to say what I wish I could do or what I think he wants to hear.

As usual, he's stingy with his instructions and it makes me look like a blind kitten tossed into the lake. Except my eyes can see. And they stare at him shamelessly as he moves around the car, spreading the soapsuds with a big yellow sponge.

The wet front of his t-shirt stretches across his pecs and I feel warmth gathering in my chest and stomach.

"Are you going to just stand there?" Mikah calls after a while, wiping the sweat off his forehead with his forearm. "Can you put some more coins in?"

"Sure, but I don't have any."

He rolls his eyes and motions to the back pocket of his jeans like it's the most obvious thing. Not in my world. My mother and father were very vocal about male body parts during *the talk*. The only man I'd ever touched was Dakota...until the night of the drunk kiss. My sneakers slurp against the wet asphalt as I walk over to grab the change. My hand hesitantly flutters near Mikah's pocket and I slip my fingers into it, trying my best not to touch anything but the money.

His heat filters through me like oxygen, filling every cell with an unexpected buzz.

"Is it only quarters?" I draw my hand away from his behind and stare at the coins in my palm.

"Yes. Fill it up, Cupcake Queen."

Ignoring the fever taking over me, I hurry to the pay station and add more time.

After Mikah's finished polishing the Mustang, he rolls it into the parking lot and we take another cigarette break.

"You're a fucking weirdo." He looks at me long and hard, half-suspicion and half-amusement in his gaze. "I thought you said you knew how to wash a car. What is it with you and withholding the truth, huh?"

I like him like this—cocky and full of himself. His crooked one-sided grin makes my heart swell. If only I could be silly and clumsy for him every second of every day just to keep him smiling.

Before I can answer him, the purr of another engine echoes across the parking lot. I glance over my shoulder and watch as a white Corolla pulls into a spot on the opposite side of the lot. Disappointment hits me like a punch. I was hoping no one would show up here until we left. I liked just the two of us with no intruders.

The nicotine rushing through my veins is hard at work, battling the approaching anxiety, but I'm not sure it's enough. I turn back to Mikah and stick the cigarette between my lips to finish the last of it.

Mikah's t-shirt is soaking wet and his hair has fallen out of its band and lies messily across his shoulders.

"Hello. How are you?" a male voice calls from behind me. My guess is that it's the Toyota driver. I spin toward the sound and see a man walking in our direction. He's small and looks to be somewhere in his late thirties, and something tells me he's not here to wash his car.

"Yeah?" Mikah tilts his head and taps his cigarette lightly to ash it.

"I'm C.J. Barnes." The man slips his hand into the front pocket of his jacket, pulls out what looks like a business card, and hands it to Mikah. "I write for *Portland Sunrise*." He pauses to give us a second to process the information. "I just wanted to say I'm very sorry about your loss. The magazine is putting together an editorial about the families of The Crystal Room victims, and I'm working on a story on your brother and was wondering if you were open to speak to me."

From condolences to business in less than a second.

I see the life draining from Mikah's face, along with his good mood. He tosses the cigarette on the ground and motions for me to get in the car. I do as he says, heading to the Mustang and quietly slipping into the passenger seat. My anxiety returns and starts to invade my mind.

The man continues, "I really am sorry and I understand how you feel, but if you could just hear me out..."

Mikah jerks the driver's side door open. "Were you there?" His tone is void of emotion.

"No. I wasn't," the reporter responds.

"Then don't tell me you understand what it's like to see people you know die right in front of you and not be able to do anything about it."

He gets into the car and slams the door shut. His anger fills the air.

I want to say something to make Mikah feel better, but the words in my head are all wrong and twisted, so instead, I just rest my hand on his wet shoulder.

He thrusts the key into the ignition and the engine roars to life.

Then we drive back to his place in silence.

I'm sitting at the kitchen table and on my second beer when Mikah comes out from the shower. He's changed into a pair of jeans and a clean t-shirt and his mood has improved a little.

We order some Chinese takeout and I seriously consider asking him to let me sleep on his couch. Even if it means spending the night in a place where I shouldn't be wanting to spend the night.

It's partially the alcohol talking, but for the most part, it's the need to change something in my life. There's also my parents. They haven't made these past two weeks easy.

Mikah grabs a beer from the fridge and pulls up a chair. His eyes seek mine and he pops the cap without looking at it. I'm sure he's done it so many times that he can do it in his sleep.

"Are we going to talk about the kiss?" I ask in a nervous whisper.

His jaw clenches. "Why?"

"You know why." A rush of panic courses through me. It's a perfect catch-22 situation he's put me in. We can't talk about Dakota, and talking about the kiss without talking about Dakota isn't happening.

"Look, there's nothing to talk about, okay?" He shakes his head as if it was just some friendly peck on the cheek, and I'm wondering if he's lying and he's been thinking about it too. However, I don't know how to ask about it without making a fool of myself. What if it didn't mean anything to him? I'm not sure if it should mean anything to me either, but somehow, it does. It means a whole lot.

"What do you mean there's nothing to talk about?" I ask, pushing down a wave of defeat.

"You had some drinks. I did too. It was an accident." Mikah pauses.

My heart trips. "Okay."

"It's better if it's this way, Alana." He sets his beer aside. "I might be leaving for a while and I wanted you to hear it from me."

Panic settles in my stomach. All I do is nod.

"I sent my demo tape to a small indie label in Seattle last year and they reached out to me a couple of weeks ago. They want to meet and possibly set up some acoustic shows for summer and I want to do it. I *need* to do it."

I feel like he just punched me in the gut. There's a scream forming in my lungs and tears prick the back of my eyes.

"How long will you be gone?" I ask, trying to keep my emotions under control. My gaze slides to the unopened boxes in the living room.

"I don't know."

"But...why now?" The truth is, I want to know why so soon? Or why is he leaving at all when I'm here? This sudden move makes no sense.

"Because people like me don't get a lot of opportunities, Alana."

"But what about me?" My question comes out in the form of a pathetic whimper. The beer's finally talking.

His tone softens. "I'm not leaving you. You can still text me or call me at three in the morning." I see a hint of a smile.

"It's not the same."

He takes a deep breath and runs his palms over his wet hair. "I'm not doing this for me. I'm doing this for both of us. For me and for him. This wasn't just my dream. This was his dream too and his music deserves to be heard. All the songs he wrote but never got the chance to sing. They *need* to be heard."

The words rattle inside my head, bitter and despondent. I know they're supposed to sound hopeful, but to me, they're just sad. "Why are you telling me all this?" I choke back the tears.

He leans forward and stares at me unblinkingly for a few moments. "I'm telling you this because I care about you, Alana."

My heart's beating frantically, as if it's trying to punch its way out of my chest. His hands lie flat on the tabletop and a desperate part of me expects for him to reach out to me, but he doesn't.

"What am I going to do when you leave?" My voice is rough and low, and my mouth is dry. I'm turning into a blabbering mess again.

"What did you do before me?"

It's a simple and straightforward question, but I can't seem to dig the answer out from the chaos my mind has become. Right now, I can't remember anything before him. It's like the attack has suddenly erased everything that my life was before Joseph Miller walked into The Crystal Room with a gun and started shooting, and it scares me.

When no response follows, Mikah takes a swig of his beer and asks, "Do you want to watch a movie or something?" It's random and doesn't feel like him, and I wonder if he's just trying to soften the blow.

"Is this you throwing me a pity party?" I laugh through a curtain of tears.

"It's either that or you can help me rob a bank." A smirk tilts the side of his mouth.

I'm in shock because, apparently, Mikah Bennett has a sense of humor.

We settle on the couch in the living room, our bodies close but not touching. It's weird being next to him and doing something so normal, although the images on the screen soon turn into colorful blobs and the noises around me become muffled.

My eyes close and my brain shuts down. My head dropping onto his shoulder is the last thing I remember before falling asleep.

18. BEFORE

My phone pings in my pocket when I'm pouring a bowl of soup for the woman on the opposite side of the catering table. She's small and wears an old, tattered coat that has so many holes it would hardly protect from the cold anymore. A twisted expression on her cracked lips vaguely resembles a smile, but her eyes are vacant, void of all emotion.

Whenever my parents brought me along to help with their volunteer work when I was a child, I asked myself several questions quite often. Why do some people choose to live under a bridge and starve to death? What makes them stop trying? Why do they give up on life? Life is a precious gift we only get to live once. There are no rewind and erase buttons. There's just play.

When I was fourteen, I witnessed a homeless man stab himself in the chest with a fork at one of the volunteer functions my parents had helped organize.

I stopped asking myself those questions on that day.

The same way I recently stopped asking myself why my father believes some guy with a cross who we've never seen is going to give him a permanent spot in Paradise in exchange for following some absurd rules from an ancient book that hasn't been edited or revised in over two thousand years.

My mother's standing next to me, fumbling with the dishes and talking to one of her friends from church. The hum of the dining room drowns out their hushed voices and I can only hear bits and pieces of the conversation. Not that it matters. I find it odd that they choose to discuss which nail salon offers a better pedicure while serving the homeless. It seems somewhat inappropriate in front of the people who can't afford basic things like food or clothes.

The air inside is stale, and the unmistakable stench of body odor mixed with the smell of mashed potatoes and beans makes my stomach queasy. There's a small Christmas tree set up in the corner near the entrance, and long strings of Christmas lights and ornaments are hanging from the ceiling. This place has a weird vibe. It's like a glass jar filled with water and oil that's forced together—a sight that's disturbingly striking.

I hand the bowl to the woman and smile at her since that's what I've been taught all my life. To smile at the less fortunate because even a minor gesture makes a difference.

The woman grabs the bowl and gives me a curt nod instead of a thank you, which is pretty common. Some of these people have lost the ability to express their gratitude in the same way most of us do.

As soon as she steps aside, I retrieve my phone from my pocket and skim through the messages Jess has been bombarding me with all day. She and her family are spending the holidays at some fancy ski resort in Colorado.

Truth be told, it's not her texts I've been wanting to read, though. It's Dakota's since we've only seen each other twice over the course of the last two weeks. The first time was when he showed up on campus, unannounced, after my English final with flowers and a cake, which I'm sure was all Jess's doing. The second was the day before Midnight Rust got flown to San Francisco for a last-minute private gig their new manager set the band up with.

That night, we went to Patty's to grab some hot dogs and milkshakes and Dakota picked me up and dropped me off at home instead of Jess's. I expected my parents to question me about it, but they were out until very late and didn't see me coming and going in a strange and, as my dad would say, "devious-looking" car.

I'm still flipping through the countless photos of mountains Jess has sent me when a faint shuffling off to the side lets me know someone is near. I lift my gaze and evaluate the young man standing on the other side of the table. He moves closer when he sees me looking. The hood of his sweatshirt is pulled up and hangs low on his forehead, hiding his face. His hands are shoved into the pockets of worn-out jeans that look to be at least five sizes too big, and I wonder whether this is all the weight he's lost since he became homeless or if these clothes even belong to him.

Hiding my phone away, I smile at him.

"Hey, Moonchild," he rasps, pushing the hood off his face slightly.

My heart jumps into my throat. "Dakota?" I whisper, looking over my shoulder. Thankfully, my mother isn't around. "Are you crazy? My parents are here." God forbid my father sees us talking.

"I know. I'm sorry, but I had to give you your Christmas present." A teasing smirk tilts the corner of his mouth.

"I thought you were at Blaze's party."

"I'll go check it out later." He rocks back on his heels, his gaze holding mine. "Meet me behind the building in ten minutes?"

"Okay. Sure." Sudden heat spreads through me like a raging wildfire. My cheeks burn at the mere idea of sneaking out to see my boyfriend right under my parents' noses. I despise it yet love it so much, it's almost disturbing. As much as I want to keep Dakota a secret to shield him from the inevitable family drama, I desperately want my father and mother to accept him for all that he is, for all the stained-with-dark beauty he carries inside him.

"Are the mashed potatoes any good?" Dakota asks, glancing at the table.

"Are you hungry? I'll bring you a serving," I say quietly. "Just go before you get me in trouble. Okay?"

"See you in ten minutes, Moonchild," he mouths at me, pulling his face back under the hood. His eyes dart impatiently from me to the empty space between us as if he's wondering what it's going to take for him to erase the distance.

I hurry to make him a plate before my mother returns, and then I leave through the kitchen.

Outside, the air is crisp and fresh, and my lungs are desperate for a much-needed cleanse. The sky's heavy with clouds that threaten to unleash yet another snowfall. Come to think of it, Portland hasn't seen a winter with this much attitude in a while.

"Hey." Dakota's soft voice drifts from around the corner. He's waiting for me in the alley. The bottoms of his jeans are buried in the snow beneath his boots.

I rush over to him with a plate full of food, my coat undone and my knitted pom pom beanie forgotten inside.

"Where's your hat, silly?" Dakota asks, placing his hands over my ears. "You'll get sick."

"No, I won't," I counter, trying to catch my breath. The cold air stings the bare skin on my face and my neck.

"Yeah, you will." He grabs the plate from me and sets it on the step of the fire escape.

"Are you insane? My parents are going to kill me if they see you like this. They'll believe I'm dating a homeless guy. Where did you get all these clothes?" I fist the thick fabric of his sweatshirt, thinking how he can rock almost any look without much effort.

"They're mine." Dakota chuckles. "Didn't I tell you I used to weight three hundred pounds? It's the keto diet."

"Liar." I slap his chest.

"You should have seen me last year." He snorts out a laugh.

"Nonsense."

"Nah, I just needed to make sure I had on a good disguise. Come here." He leans forward and presses his lips to mine, his hair brushing against my cheeks.

The flutter inside my stomach starts spreading throughout my body, filling me with blissful warmth. Kissing Dakota is like breathing. It's become an essential part of my life. I need him just as much as I need air, and I can't stand when we're not together.

"I don't have your present with me," I say against his mouth, wrapping my arms around his torso. "I didn't know you were going to ambush me here. I'll give it to you next time I see you."

"You didn't have to get me anything," Dakota husks in my ear, drawing a little black box with a tiny red ribbon from the pocket of his oversized sweatshirt.

"I wanted to." My heart beats a bit faster when I take the present in my hands. The velvet finish feels smooth and warm against my freezing fingers.

"Come on. Are you going to look at it until we both turn into popsicles?" Dakota laughs, and the sound of his voice, deep, dark, and beautiful—like all of his songs—makes me shiver all over.

I twist the box in my hands and when I pop it open, my heart jumps. Inside, there's a silver necklace with a tiny pendant in the shape of a hummingbird.

"Do you like it?" Dakota asks, his tone tentative.

"Oh my gosh! I love it!" I exclaim, running my fingers over it. "It's so tiny." My gaze jumps between his face and the necklace.

"It's handmade."

"It's beautiful! Thank you so much." I'm out of breath as my excitement skyrockets.

No one has ever given me anything this exquisite and intimate, and I'm not sure how to react. "My present sucks compared to yours." I look at his gift again before closing the box.

"I can guarantee you it doesn't." Dakota wraps his arms around me and pulls me into a hug, and I rest my head against his chest.

"Yes, it does," I squeal into his oversized sweatshirt.

"You know why I'm positive it doesn't?" he asks. "Because you're my present."

My heartbeat accelerates.

"Are you doing anything next Thursday?"

"No. Why?"

"I have the day off. I want to take you somewhere."

"Thursday's good," I respond.

"When are you starting the new job?"

"Next Friday. I'm still helping at the bakery. Just a couple more days until the Christmas craze is over."

"Okay, don't make any plans for Thursday, Moonchild."

The warmth of his body blends with mine and we stand like that—motionless and cuddled together in silence—for a very long time, and I almost wish my mother and father would find us already so we wouldn't have to hide anymore. *So I wouldn't have to hide him anymore.*

19. AFTER

My pulse is pounding against my eardrums so hard that I can barely hear the noise of the crowd. Jess is in front of me, pushing Luke's wheelchair through the screaming chaos. She's wearing a pair of black slacks and a black jacket. I catch an occasional "excuse us" as we barrel toward the crowd control barrier.

My mind's a fuzzy mess, and I still don't know what I'm doing here and why exactly I agreed to come. My therapist insisted I shouldn't get involved in any of this when I brought it up during my last session, but I couldn't ignore the anger that's been gnawing in my gut anymore. It's because of everything. The diary that doesn't want to get filled with words, my parents who don't understand me, Mikah leaving me behind.

This seemed like the right place to go. However, now that I'm here surrounded by hundreds of raging fanatics, I'm not so sure. Maybe I should have gone to class instead. Maybe I should be trying to get a passing grade.

My gaze darts from one person to another, inspecting their hands and bags.

What if someone has a gun? How ironic would that be?

Unfamiliar voices fill me with impending dread and fear.

"Hey!" A tap on my shoulder causes a rush of panic to wash through me.

I turn toward the sound and a blurred face gradually swims into focus. She's my age and has a small ragged scar directly above her collarbone peeking from under the strap of her blue tee.

"Hey! I'm Ashley Clayton," the girl says with rigor in her tone, as if I'm supposed to know that name. She grabs my forearm. "You're Alana Novak, right? You dated Dakota Bennett?"

I swallow past the lump in my throat and nod.

"Joseph Miller killed my sister," Ashley says with a straight face, but her eyes take on a dark, vengeful spark. Although she looks familiar, I don't remember where I've seen her—on the news, inside the club the night of the attack, or maybe at the survivors' meet-up Jess organized—that's it! Jess briefly introduced me to her at the meet-up. What baffles me, though, is that Ashley's talking about her sister's death like it's a pair of shoes she forgot in the changing room of a department store.

"I'm sorry to hear that," I mutter, pulling my arm away.

"You did the right thing!" she screams over the noise. "This has to stop! These fucking pigs hiding behind closed doors and making laws need to hear what we have to say!"

Her words pound at me like a sledgehammer. I can feel her frustration and anger, yet I can't seem to let more of it in. I already have enough of my own.

"I have to go find my friend," I say, taking a step back. I stumble on someone's boots and a few jumbled apologies leave my mouth.

"How many more?!" an irate voice yells out ahead of me. People start picking up the chant and it begins to spread through the maddened crowd like wildfire. Posters fly high above the heads of the protesters.

I bounce between the screaming bodies like a ping-pong ball, fighting for air. My heart thunders and my stomach roils.

Bang! Bang!

Get down!

My feet trip and I fall forward, but someone's hands catch me before I hit the ground.

"You okay?" the man asks, his eyes seeking mine.

"I'm fine. Thank you," I mumble, straightening up. My head's spinning and all I want is to get out of here and go home.

There's no more anger left. Just frustration and terror.

I walk until the crowd begins to thin out, my heart racing, my vision impaired. The air around me is thick with fury and wrath, and the sun beaming above my head is painfully bright. After crossing the street, I lean against the trunk of the nearest tree, close my eyes, and try to breathe through the wave of panic.

My phone buzzes and I fish it out of my pocket. My first thought is that I hope it's Mikah, even though he hasn't texted me in over a week, but it's Jess.

Where are you?

Squinting to stop the text from floating across the screen, I stare at the letters for a few moments. My mind struggles with the idea of going back into the raging mess. Crowds aren't safe. Crowds attract people with guns.

I return the phone to my pocket and look down at my sneakers, trying to think of an explanation for why Mikah hasn't responded to any of my messages. Things seemed okay the morning after the movie night. I slept on his couch and he made me coffee before I left. But three days later, we're back to square one where he ignores me until the invisible switch in his brain flips and he decides he wants to hang out, and I don't know if I can take it anymore.

"Alana?" I hear my name called.

"C.J." The man puts on a small smile and moves closer. "C.J. Barnes." There's a business card in his hand. "We met a couple of weeks ago. At the car wash."

I blink away the mist in my eyes and sift through my foggy memories.

"I know this is very difficult for you." He steps forward, his head blocking the sun. "But I was hoping you'd be open to speaking to me."

"Have you been following me all this time?" I ask, studying his face. He doesn't look like a shooter. He doesn't look like he could harm a fly. Somehow, he doesn't look like a reporter either. He looks more like a failed writer turned college professor.

"It's my job," C.J. explains, shoving his card at me. "Your parents wouldn't take my calls."

Shock grips me. "You called my parents?"

"Look"—he clears his throat—"I know you must hate me for ambushing you and Mikah Bennett at the car wash, but this story I'm working on is important. Victims' voices need to be heard too."

"We're not victims," I say, staring at his business card. *We're fucked up products of a fucked up society.*

"Survivors," he corrects himself, but I'm already seriously doubting his people skills and his qualifications.

"Why should I talk to you?" I ask, taking his card.

"Because Dakota Bennett deserves a story more than Joseph Miller does."

His words storm through me like a hurricane. Part of me wants to say yes, but the rest of me—the portion that's so attached to Mikah— understands it's not my place to decide what Dakota deserves. He has a family and if they don't want his name in the newspapers and online, I don't have the right to talk about him either.

C.J. draws a pack of cigarettes from the front pocket of his jacket and when he offers me one, I take it.

"Think about it, Alana," he says, handing me his lighter.

"Have you had anyone else come forward?"

"A couple of people." He nods.

I break eye contact with him and stare at the sea of posters being held in the air and trembling against the blue backdrop of the Oregon sky. Six months ago, my biggest problem was figuring out how to tell my parents about Dakota. But now, it all seems so trivial.

I light my cigarette and inhale the thick smoke into my lungs. Nicotine hits me instantly and flows through my veins like fresh blood, filling me with a high calm. I know it'll last for only a few minutes, but a few minutes is better than nothing.

"Can you write Wikipedia page content?" I ask, pushing the smoke out.

C.J. nods again.

"Can I have another one?" I motion at my cigarette.

"Sure." He hands me the pack and the lighter. "Keep it."

"Thanks."

"Call me when you're ready." C.J. shows me a sympathetic smile and steps back to leave.

"I'm not making any promises."

He raises his hand to wave goodbye and disappears into the crowd.

I put in my earbuds and set my phone and an empty cup next to me on the bench. Both of my parents are still at work and I don't believe they'll somehow find out I'm about to smoke a cigarette in our backyard unless they've installed security cameras to spy on me.

The anxiety rocking through me starts to ease up after I take a drag. I turn up the music and inhale the smoke as deeply as my lungs will allow. This is the first time since the attack I've listened to Dakota sing and it feels heavenly. His voice is a fine blend of tender and rough and it washes through me like water, filling me with the memories and sensations I've almost forgotten.

I close my eyes and tilt my head up toward the sun, its warmth caressing my skin like a mother would her child. Somewhere amidst all this darkness and chaos, there's a glimpse of the peace I'm trying to catch. I need it to last me at least a few days. At least until the madness of the hearing stops popping up at me from every internet page.

The song is on the second chorus when I feel an earbud falling out of my ear and the music suddenly disappears.

"I'm not going to repeat myself," my father says, holding out his hand in front of me. "If I see you smoking again, I'm sending you to a rehabilitation center." His eyes burn with annoyance.

"It's not cocaine, Dad," I mutter, grabbing at my earbud that's dangling over my chest. "It's just a cigarette."

"You need to stop this nonsense, young lady." His hand jerks impatiently near my face.

"If you hit me again, I'll go to the police." I jump up from the bench, grabbing my phone, the cigarette still in my hands. The hurt begins to choke me.

"I'm tired of putting up with your behavior," my father says, his tone flat.

"What behavior?" I toss both hands in the air, my eyes are filling with moisture.

"You're skipping your therapy sessions and you're not taking your medications as instructed. You're out at night with some questionable characters! I have no idea where you are and what you're doing and who you're doing it with"—he pauses for a second to catch his breath —"like some slut! I didn't raise you to sleep around!"

His words are like razor blades, cutting me into thousands of pieces.

"Guess what, Dad?" I throw the cigarette on the ground. "People fuck before they get married. They fuck until they're tired of each other and then they fuck someone else until they meet the one person they think they won't get tired of fucking for the rest of their lives."

My father's face twists with shock, his jaw hanging open.

"And you know what else?" I say, swallowing the emotions that clog my throat. "You're not going to hell for that. You know why? Because this is hell. We live in fucking hell already."

I don't hear or see anything on my way back into the house. My heart's beating itself into oblivion and my mind is a black hole.

I don't remember how I ended up in front of Mikah's apartment. I left my house hours ago and drove around town aimlessly until my rage became desperation and the bitter aftertaste of defeat lessened. Now the tears are gone and what remains is just the fog in my brain.

I ring the doorbell several times and concentrate on the chirping of the crickets in an attempt to block out the noise in the apartment. What if Mikah's home but doesn't want to see me? If that's the case, then I'd rather not hear him.

The sound of his footsteps breaks through the haze in my head and stirs something inside me.

There's surprise on his face when the door opens. It's one of those rare times I've seen him show emotion. His broad frame fills the width of the entrance and the fresh scent of his aftershave sneaks up my nose.

"I'm sorry. I know I should have called, but you weren't answering my texts," I say, clenching my fists, and I almost expect rejection.

"I was out of town. Went to see family," he mutters, his eyes running up and down my body.

"Can I come in?"

"Yeah, sure."

He steps aside and I brush past him into the living room, my gaze darting to the mountain of boxes. The idea of him leaving burns my heart.

The door slams behind me and Mikah goes into the kitchen. He grabs two beers from the fridge and brings me one, as if he's just read my mind and knows I feel like shit.

"Thanks," I say, walking over to the window. The view isn't the best —just the tips of the bushes crowding the ground floor of the building and the dark, star-studded sky, but it's different from the one at my house, so it's a nice change.

"Did you hear the defense is asking for more time to review the evidence?" I ask, taking a small sip of my beer. It tingles and bites against my tongue.

"I heard."

"Don't you think it's funny how the law works?"

Mikah doesn't respond.

"It takes less than ten minutes to take the lives of twenty-four people, but it takes months to get the killer to trial."

The silence that fills the room is toxic and goes on for a while. Even the crickets decide to take a break.

"The system's fucked up, Alana." I hear Mikah behind me as he moves closer and his heat wraps me into a strange, buzzing embrace. He reaches for the window over my shoulder to slide it open and sets a pack of cigarettes and an ashtray on the ledge.

I don't dare move, because I'm scared if I do, it'll disturb the fragile balance between us. I revel in his forbidden warmth like a child who's eaten stolen candy.

Mikah lights up our cigarettes and leans to the side. He rests his elbow against the window frame and slowly blows the smoke into the air outside.

"Do you ever think about doing something to unfuck it up?" I ask, tapping my cigarette lightly against the edge of the ashtray.

"Like what?" He brings his beer to his mouth and takes a swig.

"I don't know." I'm wondering if Jess has ever tried to rope him into protesting, but the question never comes up because it doesn't feel right.

"There's nothing I can do to make things different." A sad smile touches Mikah's lips. "I'm not a fucking magician. I don't want this hate to consume me. I don't want anger and rage to rule my life, because I don't want to waste however much life I have left."

I let out a deep sigh. My gaze drops to the bottle of beer I'm holding and I realize I'm starting to feel dizzy. I haven't eaten anything since breakfast and all it's taken for the alcohol to get to me is a couple of sips. The weird thing is that I like this sensation of dullness taking over my body. There's no worry anymore. It's temporary, but it's still nice.

I finish my cigarette and light another one. Mikah does the same. After we're done with the first round, he gets us two more beers from the fridge. Talking seems useless at this point, so there's very little of it. No matter what we say, things are still messed up and we're still hurting.

Instead, I just watch Mikah. I study the lines of his face and length of his hair, the curves of his arms, and the ink scattered over his olive skin. Looking at him does funny things to my insides, but I blame it mostly on the alcohol.

"Did he ever tell you how I fucked up his hair when he was seven?" Mikah asks out of the blue and my heart stills. This is the first time he's brought up Dakota, and I hang on every word.

"Yes. He did." I nod, tightening my grip around the beer bottle.

"Did he ever tell you about the Legos?"

I shake my head. "No. I don't think so."

"He caught pneumonia once when he was five..." Mikah's voice falters. "He stayed in the hospital for several days and my parents bought him a bunch of toys. After he got discharged, they didn't bring any of them home. They left everything at the hospital."

"Why?"

"My mother said it was a nice thing to do for the other kids. She didn't believe we needed more toys." His gaze lingers on me for a second and then jumps back to the dark sky. "I was pissed at her and at him." A pause. "So…a few months later, our grandmother gave him a huge Lego set for his sixth birthday. You know what I did?"

An odd flutter fills my stomach. "No. What did you do?"

"I stole it from him and I buried it in the backyard. I was a vengeful motherfucker with a grudge."

"Did he ever find the Legos?"

"My parents found the box later that fall."

"Were you always a mean brother?" Emotions begin to jam my chest. The image of a young Dakota crying over his missing Legos burns bright in my mind.

"We were mean to each other sometimes," Mikah confirms, rubbing his eyes with the back of his hand. "When our mother favored him, I attacked. We fought a lot. We were always competing, but I never let anyone else make fun of him. I attacked other kids when they called him out. Except for the hair incident. I got mad because our mother chose to go see his school play instead of taking us to the fair like she'd promised. It felt like all our plans always revolved around his schedule and I wanted to hurt him for it. It was only that once, and I felt like shit after doing it, but I never told anyone. Not until now."

I swallow hard and set my bottle on the ledge because my head is spinning.

"When you're a kid, everything is simple. One minute you hate and the next you love. There's no middle ground." Mikah chuckles softly, sipping on his beer. "I felt both of those things toward my parents. You know what I never felt?"

"What?"

"I never felt like I belonged… But I did with my brother. I felt like I belonged with him when we made music." Mikah runs his palm over his cheek and I realize he's crying. My restless heart jolts into a sprint.

Seeing him defeated makes me want to take all the pain from him, but I have no idea how.

My hands reach for his cheeks, cupping his face, and my lips seek out his mouth. The kiss is chaste and friendly. Or at least, that's what my drunk brain tells me. But that's enough to ignite the small spark that's been lingering between us all evening.

I hear a low rumble in his chest as his hands slip around my waist and rest on my ass to draw me closer. His need is deep and he's not holding anything back. Our bodies hot with want, our lips taunt each other, and the sound of our moans splinter off into the warm night and fill the kitchen. His tongue stroking mine is demanding and fierce and his hands roaming my skin are blatant and grabby.

I don't know how we make it to the bedroom. It seems like a very long, very hot trip that consists of multiple make-out sessions against every single wall in the apartment. When we finally stumble into his room, I'm a wheezing mess and my panties are soaked. I'm not sure why—we haven't even gotten to third base yet, but my body begs for him to take me.

Mikah reaches for the hem of my t-shirt and pulls it over my head, his eyes darting to my breasts. He drops his face and kisses them through the lace of my bra as my fingers move through his hair. As we plummet onto his bed in a panting frenzy, Mikah's on top of me, kissing down my neck as our bodies move together. He's heavy and hot, and his hips rolling against the pulsating area between my legs in a perfect rhythm tease me with the promise of something wild.

His fingers fumble with my zipper and he rids me of my jeans and panties within seconds. When he pushes himself off the bed and starts undressing, my heart staggers like a hopeless drunk as I watch him wrestling off the rest of his clothes.

The dark shadow of his silhouette hovering above me and his scent —smoke and cologne—shatters all my defenses. He's lean and fit and his ink artwork is so magnificent that looking at him pushes me over the edge.

I scoot away from the edge of the bed and Mikah lowers himself back on top of me and helps me to take off my bra. We kiss and touch each other with a sense of crazed urgency, as if we need to get it over with before we realize what we're doing is wrong. I know it is, but I can't help it. *I like the way he makes me feel.*

My stomach spasms with need as Mikah kisses his way down to my breasts and takes my nipple into his mouth, his tongue moving in slow, magical circles. I release a deep moan and fist his hair, my mind slipping into unhinged insanity.

My pulsing center aches with want. I tremble all over as Mikah's mouth moves farther down my body and his lips lightly stroke my skin. They are greedy and ravenous. I'm so high on his touch that I lose track of everything he's doing to me.

"Turn around," Mikah growls against my stomach, pushing himself up.

My heart slams into my chest. I've never done it like this before.

We're a mess of pants and moans as he repositions me.

"Are you on the pill?" His voice rumbles through me and I realize I'm on my knees, my hands grasping the headboard, and he's behind me.

"No." I say nervously. A pool of wetness gathers between my legs.

Mikah doesn't say anything. His hands cover my ass and he runs his calloused palms up my back, leaving a trail of goose bumps in the wake of his touch. His fingers sink into my hair and he tugs on it gently, just enough for a wave of tingles to run across my scalp, but I'm not sure what's expected of me. I'm too drunk to think straight.

Mikah moves closer, his heat coaxing me into sweet madness. He slips his hand between my legs, and when he begins to massage my swollen clit, the rush is incredible. Tossing my head back, I close my eyes and let the sensation take over my brain.

"You're so fucking wet," Mikah whispers against my neck, pushing his finger inside me. "Don't tell me you've never thought about us fucking."

A startled gasp rushes out of me. He's a dirty talker and I like it. I like hearing these filthy words. They're honest, unrestrained and unfiltered.

My breaths are loud and shallow and I'm burning all over when Mikah slides a second finger into me. He pumps them in and out wildly, almost taking me to the brink of something I don't believe I've experienced before, and I wonder if this is what everyone raves about when they talk about sex. I wonder if this is what real pleasure is like. The feel of Mikah's hardness behind me is terrifying because I have no idea what he's going to do next, but my body loves it. My every nerve throbs when he withdraws his fingers from me.

The tip of his tongue licks a wet trail across my shoulder and he grabs at my hips, positioning himself at my entrance. Then he slams into me deep and fast, and I'm overcome with dull, delicious pain as my insides struggle to accommodate his size. My hands squeeze the headboard, and the sound that leaves my mouth is a combination of a scream and a whimper.

"Fuck." I hear him curse in my ear while his mouth grazes my temple. He palms my breasts and thrusts harder, the bed squeaking under the pressure of his movements. I writhe beneath his weight, my vision blurring.

Mikah groans against my cheek and rocks steadily, his sweat dripping across my back as his breaths blend with mine. Hurt, anger, and want roll through my stomach all at once, forming into a throbbing ball of impassioned yet lewd hunger that fills my every cell.

"Have you thought about me?" Mikah grunts, his body crashing into mine. His hips grind against my ass as his damp chest rubs against me. "Tell me. I know you have," he presses. "I know you've been fantasizing about me fucking you. That's why you call me at three in the morning."

I respond with a loud moan.

"And you were already so fucking wet from just thinking about this, weren't you?"

I don't know what to say. His words make me question our phone conversations, but I'm too drunk to give an answer and he's too wound up to pursue the conversation. So instead, we continue to fuck.

It's a long, loud, and dirty act, and Mikah rides me like a madman until I can't handle any more. He reaches around to pinch my clit and that's all it takes. I come hard, my arms and legs quivering as my head spins. I've never felt anything this powerful during sex. All of my emotions that've been stuffed in a small box somewhere deep inside me discharge in the form of a desperate scream of release. He shudders against me and after he pulls out, I feel hot fluid searing across my back.

"Don't move," he rasps into my hair, reaching toward the nightstand. Moments later, when something soft slips over my skin, I realize it's only a tissue.

We both fall onto the damp sheets afterward. There's no hugging or kissing. No guilt talk and no discussing what just happened.

There's just silence. Deafening and excruciating silence.

I wake to the smell of freshly brewed coffee and cigarette smoke. My body's sore and my mouth is dry. A light breeze dancing across the room touches my face with featherlike gentleness.

I force my eyelids open and see Mikah's silhouette drawn against the dark clouds floating outside the open window. He's wearing nothing but his boxers and there's a cigarette dangling from his mouth. His straight hair falls over his shoulders in messy cascades, and the sight of him makes my stomach coil with desire. However, when pieces of memories from last night begin to fit together, guilt with a pinch of horror and shame is the first feeling that washes through me.

I swallow past the tightness in my throat and push myself up, hands scrambling for the sheet to cover my nakedness.

Mikah turns to me, and when he holds out a mug of coffee, I scoot to the edge of the bed and grab it from him, telling him, "Thanks," and taking a much-needed sip.

"You sleep okay?" he asks, his tone flat.

I give him a quiet, "Mm hmm," but I'm too dazed by the fact that I had sex with my dead boyfriend's brother to have any sort of conversation right now. It's all coming down on me so hard that I'm not sure coffee alone is going to help.

Mikah steps back to the window and continues smoking his cigarette.

The silence between us drags on for a good minute and I use this time wisely—I consume as much caffeine as I can to get my confused brain going.

I expect more than just a random question about my sleep, but after a while, I realize that this is just as awkward for Mikah as it is for me. First, he wanted to keep his distance. Then he tried to get me to confess I'd fantasized about him. Which is he today? Detached or interested?

Fighting off my anxiety, I motion at his cigarette. "Can I have one?" My heart rate begins to pick up its pace.

"Sure." He tips his head.

I set my coffee on the nightstand and walk over to the window with the sheet wrapped around me. Mikah pulls a cigarette from the pack sitting on the ledge and moves closer to me, positioning himself behind me. Although we're not touching, I can feel his breath dancing across the back of my neck.

I find this calm his presence brings bizarre because Dakota made me feel this way too, which bugs me.

Mikah brings his hand to my mouth and slips the cigarette between my lips. The heat of his body blends with the heat of mine, and I get lost in my own thoughts until the flick of the lighter snaps me out of it.

I inhale the smoke slowly and let it seep into my lungs as Mikah's fingers move through my hair, carefully pushing some of it aside. Then his lips touch my neck. "Any progress with *Salem's Lot*?" His whisper trembles against my artery and I feel like I'm going to explode.

"What's up with this fascination with vampires?" I ask, trying to keep my voice steady as I push some smoke out.

Instead of responding, his mouth stretches and he nips at my skin playfully.

I bite back a giggle when he hits a ticklish spot.

"Do you not want immortality?" he says with a funny accent.

A faint smile touches my lips. I've never seen this side of him and I want more. "I started it, but I believe I need to read something a little lighter right now."

Mikah removes his teeth from my neck. "Sorry, I'm not familiar with any rom-coms."

"Don't worry. You don't strike me as the type."

The pause destroys the moment of ease and we continue to smoke in silence.

"Do you know what time it is?" I ask, putting out my cigarette.

"Around eight," he mumbles against my ear.

"I have to get to class."

"I have to go to work," he responds as his hands rest on my hips and he kisses me one last time on the cheek.

My anxiety makes a comeback when I'm trying to clean up in Mikah's bathroom. I'm not sure if it's the coffee or something else, but the tremor that takes over me messes with my attempt to fix my bedroom hair, and I have to set down his brush on the counter and breathe through it. That's what my therapist told me to do, anyway. After a few minutes of pointless inhaling and exhaling, I decide to see if Mikah has anything I can take. I'm convinced at this point that even Advil is better than nothing.

I peek into one of the cabinets, and there, on a small shelf, are a lot of pill bottles. Some are anti-depressants like mine, and some are ones I'm not familiar with. Perhaps Mikah's having nightmares too. I grab one of the bottles with my shaking hand and read the label. It doesn't sound familiar, so I put it back. I find the ones I've been prescribed and shove two pills into my mouth.

A knock on the door interrupts me. "You all right?" Mikah asks.

"I'll be right out," I say, returning the pills to where they were.

When I'm finished in the bathroom, we get ready in relative silence with very few words exchanged between us.

Mikah stops me when I'm on my way out. "I'll be gone for a few days." He reaches for my face and tucks a loose strand of hair behind my ear. "I'm going to Seattle."

"Okay." I have the urge to kiss him before I leave, but something— maybe guilt or maybe the leftovers of my common sense—stops me.

Instead, I just say goodbye.

Campus is a blur.

Everything Mikah did to me last night pours into my mind from the confines of my secret drunk-and-repressed-memories box during philosophy. It's all I think about until I get back home. I think about his calloused hands and his firm lips on me. I think about how raw he sounds when he comes, how his sweaty skin sizzles against mine, and how dirty and sinful and full of betrayal we were. I'm reliving every second of us while the professor is giving a lecture and the onslaught of feelings makes me so dizzy that I can barely think straight.

It's a strange zombie-like mode with my body and my brain functioning separately. As if they're two different entities with different desires and driven by different motives. One is still hurting and missing Dakota, and the other desperately wants to get lost in what Mikah has to offer.

I know it's shameful and wrong to long for something we shouldn't have done in the first place, but I can't stop thinking about it. The need and confusion simmer deep in my veins.

On the way home, I stop by the liquor store to buy a pack of Marlboros. Then I smoke three of them in the parking lot, one after another, because I'm not sure how else to calm my brain down before seeing my father after what happened yesterday. He'd already left when I stopped by this morning to change before class. The thought of going to Jess's instead crosses my mind, but her death penalty obsession scares me. She's already sent me a bunch of hurtful texts because I left the rally yesterday, calling me a traitor and a bad friend. Facing her this soon after my renegade retreat seems worse than facing my parents.

When I get home, my mother is busy with dinner prep and my father's car is missing from our driveway, which is a huge relief. Finally, the stars have aligned in my favor. Even if it's just for one evening.

I saunter into the kitchen and pour myself a glass of juice.

"How was school?" My mother puts on a friendly smile and I'm wondering if my father told her about the fight we had yesterday. I can't tell if she's on my side or if she's decided to play the pretend everything's okay game because, in her mind, I'm hopeless.

"Fine." I give her a one-shoulder shrug.

"Are you ready for finals?" She grabs the celery root and chops off the leafy ends.

"I think so." I nod, watching her face relax.

If there's one thing my mother's great at, it's cooking. I'm convinced her mind wanders off into a parallel universe when she's preparing our meals, sort of like the way my mind checks out when I bake something. Or used to...since I haven't baked anything in several months. I miss the feeling of accomplishment I get when I create something. Even if it's just a cupcake.

"Mom?" I try to sound small and needy because I really want her to hear me this time.

"Yes, sweetie?" She stops cutting.

"Can you help me with a cheesecake?"

"Oh." The ease on her face turns to surprise. "Sure."

"Can we go to the store right now?"

My mother sets the knife aside and looks at the digital clock on the microwave. "How about tomorrow?" There's hesitation in her tone, and I'm sure it has something to do with all the food sitting on the table in front of her that she's planning to turn into a five-course dinner.

"I really want to go right now."

I'm not sure if she understands, but I pray she does.

My mother grabs a paper towel to wipe off her hands. "Yes... Let's go right now. Let me just put this chicken away and we'll go."

The next morning, I wake up to the sound of rain hitting against my window. The soreness between my legs is almost gone, but my mind's still reeling from sex with Mikah.

I roll over to the side and grab my phone, hoping to find a message from him. Instead, there's one from Jess.

It's almost nine and hearing my parents' hushed voices coming from downstairs seems odd because my father's usually not home at this hour. Unless something's happened.

My mother and I were up all night creating the perfect cheesecake, and for the first time since the attack, baking felt good. At the moment, though, my feelings are more of a mixed bag, mainly due to the silence on Mikah's part. But I decide to give him the benefit of the doubt. After all, he's in Seattle on business.

Shaking off my concern, I glance back at my phone and click on the message from Jess. It's a link to a Wikipedia page. *Dakota's* Wikipedia page. At the very bottom, there's a note indicating the most recent edit was made last night at nine thirty.

20. BEFORE

"Close your eyes," Dakota whispers in my ear, resting his chin on my shoulder. His hot breath tickles the side of my face and a whole field of goose bumps rise on my neck.

I do as he says and let the rumble of the waterfall raging in front of us take over my senses. It's magnificent and resilient. Wanting to stay alive, even in this weather. Even in this kingdom of snow and ice where everything else around is frozen solid and dead until the return of spring.

I find it really strange that in the entire eighteen plus years of my life, I haven't seen Multnomah Falls in winter. During the summer, with the forest sparkling green and the sky clear and sunny, yes. Multiple times. But not in December. And I never would have thought of it if Dakota hadn't brought me.

"Listen." He tightens his grip around my waist, pressing his broad chest against my back. The sound of his voice, smoky and soft, blending with the roar of the water is lullaby beautiful.

"What am I listening to?" I ask, clutching his wrists for support. The weakness in my knees has become sort of permanent when he's around.

"Just listen," he rasps, the length of his body gently pushing me forward until my stomach hits the icy railing of the bridge we're standing on.

I gasp and snap my eyes open, my poor heart plummeting to my stomach at the sight of the swirling water below my feet.

Dakota laughs. "I'm not dropping you, silly." His lips slide across my cheek. "Don't you trust me by now?"

"I know... I'm just..." I sound meek because I can't quite find the right words to express everything that I'm feeling. With him, it's all been like an endless flight through the sky, scary and fascinating, and I'm wondering if there's a crash approaching or if this is what it's going to be like for as long as we're together.

Today I let him pick me up from my place instead of Jess's because my parents had already left for a day trip to Vancouver to see some of my mother's friends.

"You have to give it some time before it speaks to you," Dakota says mysteriously, brushing his cheek against mine.

"Should I do it again?" I ask, watching the water tumbling down the cliff.

"Yes, do it again. And no peeking or cheating this time." He presses me against the railing a bit harder.

"Okay." I shut my eyes and rest my head against the crook of his neck.

The noise of the waterfall begins to slowly consume me. At first, it's just a clamor inside my head and the stinging-cold drizzle touching my cheeks. Tiny and a little unkind to my skin, each drop razorblade crisp. A reminder of how fragile and how insignificant we are. And how dominating winter can be.

Dakota's hands linked with mine feel hot against my chest. There's something exceptionally sincere about the way he hugs me. Lustful yet caring. Bigger than just affection. Bigger than us. Bigger than the world. I think if he were to ask me to jump with him right now, I probably would because no one has ever made me feel so complete and happy. This single moment of true joy that some people don't ever get to experience is probably worth the sacrifice. Worth dying for.

"Are you cold?" Dakota says quietly after a while. His voice is smooth as velvet and I'm wondering if the legends got it wrong and sirens are actually not females, because my boyfriend might very well be one. Not only does he sing beautifully, but he also has the rare ability to turn me into jello with the snap of a finger.

"No." I shake my head, relaxing against him with my eyes still closed.

He brushes his hand over the tip of my nose. "You're going to turn into a snowflake any second now, Moonchild."

"Then you'll have to carry me to the car." I giggle, my breath melting into his palm. Despite our multiple layers of warm winter clothes, the curves of our bodies fit perfectly together. As if we were made for each other. And I can't help but wonder how he'd feel against me naked.

The rumble of the water is still thumping in my ears when my eyes drift open.

"Then I guess I'll have to." Dakota spins me to face him and lifts me off the ground.

Squealing, I grasp the fabric of his coat as he throws me over his shoulder. "You're going to drop me!" My heart flips along with my body.

"I would never." He wraps his arms around my thighs to keep me in place and picks up the pace. My feet dangle in the air helplessly and I pray to God we make it to safety without falling into the water.

The deep snow crunches beneath Dakota's boots as he rockets toward the end of the bridge and takes a narrow trail that will lead us back to the parking lot. We're at a fork in the path when his foot catches on some debris hidden under the snow. He loses his balance and we summersault down the hill like rag dolls.

The next thing I know, I'm on the ground, face up. A blurry tree branch hanging above obstructs my nearly perfect view of the gray winter sky.

There's a noise off to the side and I shift my gaze to see Dakota's tousled hair drawn against a crystal curtain of white trees. He crawls over to me and pushes my messy locks away from my cheeks.

"Are you okay?" he asks in almost a whisper.

My ears and my head are freezing cold and I realize I must have lost my hat during the fall. "I think so."

"Are you sure?" His mouth enters my line of vision.

I watch him fumbling with the scarf tangled around my neck, my heart beating like a drum. There's a shooting pain in my left hip that's spreading to my stomach and knee.

"Dakota?" I mumble under my breath, reaching for his shoulder.

"Mmm?" He stops messing with my clothes, his eyes locking on mine, and it feels like time stops along with us. It stands still and waits for me to finish forming the sentence.

"Do you have a bucket list?" My voice is little and rough.

"Everyone has a bucket list." The corners of his lips perk up.

"Is there a spot for me on your bucket list?" I ask.

"I have a spot for you in my life." He brushes his knuckles against my cheek. "Am I on your bucket list?"

"Yes. As a matter of fact, you're all over it." I inhale sharply, still trying to catch my breath because my silly heart won't stop assaulting my ribcage.

"I'm listening." He quirks a brow.

"I've never kissed anyone while lying in a pile of snow."

Dakota laughs. "As you wish, Moonchild." His lips come crashing down on mine like a tsunami. He slides his hand to the back of my head, lifting it up from the ground, and we kiss madly until there's no more air left and we're both panting and shaking from the cold. I think if I were to pick my own death, dying like this, in his arms, wouldn't be such a bad way to go.

"We better get out of here before you catch pneumonia," Dakota says against my mouth, and then he helps me to my feet.

"I'm working on my bucket list, remember?" I giggle, brushing off the snow. My hip and my shoulders are sore and I can bet my whole bakery paycheck I've got at least a dozen bruises.

"Hey." He tightens his grip on my hand and draws me closer. Our bodies collide and his arms trap me in a warm hug. "What other things are on that list?" he asks quietly, his gaze holding mine.

"I'll tell you later." I bite the inside of my cheek and my face feels hot all of a sudden as my stomach growls.

"Tell me now." He pouts.

"I'll tell you after pizza. How about that?"

"Look at how sly you are." He cradles my head and kisses my lips gently. "Let's go look for your hat and then get some pizza."

On the way back to Dakota's place, we pick up a large deluxe pizza with a side of buffalo wings and pasta.

We have dinner in his room on the bed with the hummingbirds flickering above our heads and the food and a mountain of napkins laid out in front of us like we're having a slumber party. The music that's playing in the background is unfamiliar and I make a mental note to ask Dakota what band it is.

The truth is, I've never had a bed dinner before in my life. My parents always taught me to behave like a lady while at the table, to keep my shoulders straight, and to use the appropriate silverware. If they were to see me right now with cheese dripping down my chin, they'd probably disown me.

Dakota sits across from me, his back resting against the headboard of the bed and his fingers tapping against his thigh to the beat of the song. He's changed into a clean t-shirt and a pair of loose jeans with a rip in the knee. His hair is tied into a bun, so his face is free from obstruction, perfect for me to stare at. The huge pizza box between us is getting emptier every second. I'm on my third piece and my stomach is still asking for more while the rational area of my brain tells me to stop before I pop like a balloon or get too big for my jeans.

"Okay, pizza's done. So about your bucket list..." Dakota says, his blue gaze darting between the pizza box and my face. His fingers freeze.

My jaw stops moving and the heat rises to my cheeks. "You're impossible," I mumble with my mouth still full of cheese and pepperoni.

He gets to his knees and leans over, placing his hands on either side of the box. "You said we could discuss your list after pizza." His eyes, blue and arresting, look right through me.

"I'm not done eating," I reply with a smile, sending the rest of the slice into my mouth.

"Yes, you are." He gathers all the napkins and plates together, shuts the pizza box, and sets everything on the floor next to the bed.

I swallow the pizza lump in my throat and try not to panic over my greasy fingers.

Dakota moves closer, pushing me down gently until my back presses into the firm mattress. "You're stalling, Moonchild," he whispers against my cheek, and the weight and length of him on top of me feels dangerously pleasant.

"My hands are filthy," I whimper, trying to keep them off the sheets as his hips grind against mine.

"Are they?" He smirks, grabbing my left wrist.

"Yes." My voice grows soft. "I don't want your bed to smell like pepperoni." He's right. I'm stalling, because that's not really what I should be saying, but my brain cells refuse to cooperate.

Dakota brings my hand to his mouth and brushes his tongue from the bottom of my index finger to the very tip. The warmth that pulses through my stomach spreads to the tender, throbbing area between my legs. My heart beats like a little hammer, my muscles turning to liquid.

"It won't," he reassures me, and his broad chest expands against mine. His breathing becomes heavier and parts of his body harden as we move fluidly together, my legs and arms entangled with his.

I almost forget there's still leftover cheese on my fingers when Dakota's mouth comes down on mine, transforming us into a fervent clash of lips and tongues and a mess of panting and moaning.

We kiss wildly until the pounding of footsteps outside in the hallway reminds us we're not alone in the apartment.

Dakota playfully groans into the blanket, but I hear a dash of irritation in the sound.

We lie still for a few minutes, listening to slamming and banging in the living room. Our clothes are twisted and our bodies molded into a huge, warm human ball.

"Sorry," he rasps against my collarbone, his lips still on my skin. "Sometimes my brother can be an inconsiderate asshole."

"It's okay." I laugh a little, wondering if we were too loud and Mikah heard us. My fingers move into Dakota's hair and I wrap the silky strands around them.

"Didn't you say you had filthy hands?" he purrs into my chest.

"Didn't you say you didn't care?" I giggle at him.

The noise comes into the hallway and grows louder, then disappears into Mikah's room.

"I don't. But you need to help me wash this pizza off now."

I can feel his lips stretching into a smile against my skin, his smoldering breath sliding across my neck, caressing and teasing.

"How about we clean your room first," I say, gently pushing him to the side. Reluctantly, he rolls to his back and watches me pick up the leftovers of our dinner from the floor, his eyes dark and hooded, hands tucked behind his head.

"You don't have to do that." His voice meshes with the music playing in the background. "I'll take it to the kitchen later."

"I don't want to accidentally step on the food. There are people starving...you know," I say, trying not to sound too patronizing.

"You know you're too fucking good for me, Moonchild," he husks, his gaze following me out into the hallway.

I bite back a grin and head to the kitchen to put away our leftovers. The rest of the apartment is dark and has finally grown silent, so I quietly search the cabinets for some storage containers. Then the sound of footsteps behind me catches me off guard when I'm in the middle of rearranging the beers inside the fridge to make room for the food.

I jerk my hand away from the drinks and swivel around to see who it is. Mikah stands next to the kitchen table, shirtless. The annoyance on his face is more than evident. He cocks an eyebrow at me and moves closer.

"I'm sorry. I didn't touch anything...valuable." There's panic in my tone and I'm not making any sense because my eyes are too busy trying to avoid looking at him. All that skin makes me uncomfortable. Tats or not, he's half-naked and I've never been this close to a shirtless guy before. Not even Dakota.

Mikah doesn't respond. He walks over to the fridge and positions himself next to me, trapping me between his body and the door. His hand reaches out for a beer, and the curve of his bicep flashes right in front of my face.

"There's some pizza and buffalo wings," I say meekly. "Do you want any?"

He steps to the side and pulls out one of the drawers, his gaze dropping to the contents.

The silence between us drags on and becomes awkward as I watch him pop the cap with the bottle opener. My heart beats faster than usual. It's like a little bird, thump-thumping against my ribs ferociously.

"Is it from Escape?" Mikah breaks the silence.

"What?"

"The pizza?" He takes a swig from the bottle and motions at the container sitting on the kitchen table. "Is it from Escape from New York?" His green eyes are dead set on me.

"Oh." My breath comes out in the form of nervous gasps. "Yes."

He nods and then his lips wrap around the rim of the bottle again.

"Do you want me to warm it up?" I ask, averting my gaze.

"Nah." He shakes his head. "I know how to use a microwave."

"Okay. Sure. I'll just leave it here then," I whisper, running my sweaty palms over my jeans.

"Sure." Another nod.

I rush back to Dakota's room like my feet are on fire. He's sitting on his bed cross-legged, and in front of him, there's a stack of CDs and the organizer case I bought him for Christmas.

"I thought you snuck out and called an Uber." He laughs as I shut the door.

"Is it okay if your brother has the rest of the pizza?" I ask in a low voice, trying to pace my heartbeat. "I told him he could."

"Yeah. It's fine." Dakota shrugs, his eyes searching mine. He tosses the CD he's holding to the side and motions for me to come over. There's something childlike in the way he longs for my affection and it makes me wonder if he's really twenty-three. His hunger is not purely sexual; it's a bizarre blend of both carnal and platonic, and it makes me shiver all over.

I go to the bed, slide the CDs out of the way, and sit next to him.

"Are you okay?" he asks, touching my cheek.

I have to think about it for a second. The question that comes out of my mouth seems somewhat irrelevant. "Is he always like this?"

"Who? Mikah?"

"Yes. Why is he so..." I pause to look for the right word. *Pissed off and brooding.* "Unhappy."

"Don't worry about him. He's all right."

I fall back on the mattress and lock my gaze on the ceiling design. "How is it to grow up with a sibling?"

"I can't compare it to growing up without one. It's always been me and my brother." Dakota lies down next to me, the heat of his body crawling along my thigh and shoulder.

"Did you fight a lot when you were kids?"

"Sometimes."

"Jess and I never fight."

"That's 'cause she didn't put food coloring in your shampoo." Dakota snorts out a laugh.

"What? Your brother did that?" I gasp.

"Yep."

"But that's a girl's prank."

"I know, right? I had blue in my hair for a week. All the kids at school made fun of me."

"How old were you?"

"Seven. Mikah was nine. Our mom was so pissed that she sent him away to his dad's for a week." Dakota pauses.

"Do you and your brother have different fathers?" I ask carefully, wondering if this is the real reason behind the tension I sense between them sometimes. Although I didn't notice it when I saw them together on stage. At that moment, they were at peace.

"Yes, but...his old man is...out of the picture now."

"How do you mean?"

"He didn't stick around. Got married, moved to a different state. Mikah doesn't talk much to him. It's just my mom and my dad now."

I feel it's time to change the subject. "How do you come up with your song ideas?"

Dakota rolls onto his side and rests his hand on my stomach. His large palm feels as if it's burning a hole in my t-shirt. "I don't know.

How do you come up with your cupcake ideas?" he murmurs against my cheek.

"Pinterest."

"Maybe I should try that."

"What? Pinterest for your song ideas?"

"Yeah."

"Why are your songs so...sad?"

"Why do you think they're sad?" He props his head on his palm to see my face better.

"They just feel sad because they're all about dying," I confess. "Not that they aren't beautiful. They really are."

"You think my songs are beautiful?"

"Yes."

"You know what I think?"

"What?"

Dakota leans forward and brushes his lips against mine, his hand sliding across my rib cage to cup my breast. "I think you're beautiful."

I don't do anything to stop him. I let him touch me because I like how it feels. Sinful, dirty, and wonderful.

We lie next to each other like this for a little while, his fingers tracing circles across my ribcage and around my collarbone as I watch the hummingbirds.

"When Mikah and I were in high school," Dakota says in a hushed voice after a few minutes, "our mom took us to a park in Washington. She's a bit of a nature freak and she knows all these secret spots tourists never find. So if you drive north maybe an hour and a half from Seattle and exit near the creek, there's a trail that takes you to a small grassy area in the middle of the forest with a huge hummingbird statue. It's carved from wood and I believe it's been standing there for decades, maybe centuries. It's so old. I don't have a clue how my mom knew about it, but she took us there to see it and it was freaking awesome."

"Who do you think made it?"

"Not sure. People who lived there..." Dakota rolls onto his side and brings his face close to mine. "I want to take you there one day. It was so peaceful and we just sat for an afternoon and listened to the trees talking. It was awesome."

"I'd love to go there with you sometime," I say.

"We will." Dakota smiles and continues talking about the day he spent there with his mom and brother.

The part of me that's falling for him fast and hard is contemplating staying over, but the other part of me, sensible and reserved, realizes that if he doesn't drive me home right now, before my parents get back from Vancouver, we might end up getting caught by my father. Which is not something I want to happen today. Today's been too perfect.

My heart jumps into my throat when I see the downstairs lights in our house beaming bright from all the way down the street.

"Can you just drop me off here?" I ask Dakota in a panic.

"You're not walking at night alone." He throws a glance of disapproval at me and steps on the gas. His car is insanely loud and doesn't belong in this neighborhood. The worst part is that I already know that even if my father is fast asleep, a mad roar like this will wake him up.

The Mustang crawls down the snow white street like a locomotive through the wilderness of Antarctica. It's late and most of the neighborhood is dark. When we pull into my driveway, Dakota puts the gear in neutral and turns down the music.

"Thank you for today," he turns to me and whispers.

There's a war raging inside me. I want to kiss him goodbye badly, but I'm also scared my father might be watching us, and a lengthy lecture about my virtue is not something I want to hear tonight...or ever.

"I loved it. Thank you for taking me," I say breathlessly, unfastening my seatbelt. "And thank you for the pizza."

Dakota leans over and slides his hand to the back of my neck to pull me in for a kiss. I don't want to put on a late night show for my parents, but he's too hard to resist. Every bone in my body longs for him physically and emotionally, and I wish I felt more certain that my mother and father and all my friends would accept him for all his quirks.

Our lips crash together and mesh into one hot and relentless slow dance. The kind that owns you completely.

"I'll miss you," Dakota says against my mouth as we break the kiss.

"I'll miss you too." The words just come out. I don't think about whether they're right or too soon. It's how I feel and I say it.

"All right, get some rest. I'll text you tomorrow."

I slip out of the car and rush to the front door. He waits until I make it inside before pulling out of the driveway.

"Alana?" My mother's voice drifts at me when she steps out of the kitchen as I'm on my way upstairs.

"Hey." I muster up a smile.

"Who's the young man?" she asks, her eyes studying me carefully, probably looking for clues I've done something wrong.

"Ummm...just someone I met." I do my best to sound indifferent, but I don't believe staying calm while talking about Dakota is possible in my universe.

"In college?"

"No." I shake my head.

"Is it something we should discuss with your father?"

"It's late, Mom," I groan out. "He just dropped me off. Can we not make a big deal out of it?"

"I'm not making a big deal out of it, but if you're going to see him again, I think it would be good if we discuss this all together."

My frustration grows so huge that I want to bang my head against the wall. "Who I see isn't your decision to make, Mom. You either have to accept it or not." My voice cracks and deep down, I feel bad for saying it out loud to her.

"Get some rest. We'll talk tomorrow." She offers me a tired smile.

I don't ask her about the trip to Vancouver. I charge for my room before my father makes an appearance.

21. AFTER

I have no idea what's happened between Mikah and me.

I'm convinced he has his own time measuring system. A few days has turned into weeks, two groggy late-night phone calls and stingy texts that stopped coming in five days ago. That's after he fucked me until I passed out.

My father's right. All guys want is sex. Maybe God took Dakota because he was different. Because he was too good for this life.

"Alana? What a nice surprise to see you here." Mrs. Kaminski's voice jars me back to reality.

I'm sitting at the corner table in Anna's Pastry's dining room, my phone on my lap, my new portfolio my mother helped me pick out the other day next to me on the bench. The speech I've been preparing all week is a little jumbled inside my head right now and I almost regret not writing it down, but reading it off a note would probably lessen my chances of convincing Mrs. Kaminski my ideas are solid.

Lifting my gaze from the lifeless screen of my phone, I make an attempt to smile. "Hey." Waiting for Mikah to return my text is like waiting for hell to freeze over.

"How have you been?" Mrs. Kaminski settles across from me.

"I'm good. I appreciate you taking the time to see me." My gaze darts to the crowd lining up in front of the register. The new girl is older and seems to be catching on quickly.

You'd wonder what could possibly go wrong at a place that sells mostly cake. At a burger place, people always find plenty of reasons to complain. The meat turns out to be undercooked *after* they've finished their sandwich. Even I know it's just an old trick to get a freebie. Bakery clients aren't any better. Wrong color frosting. Wrong size sprinkles. Box shape doesn't match the shape of the cake. Dog got sick after eating the leftovers. All these things seemed like the end of the world to me when my biggest worry was getting an A. But now, these complaints feel contrived and silly, and a C is more than enough.

"Of course." Mrs. Kaminski smiles a warm smile. "Are you hungry? How about a vanilla éclair?" She remembers the smallest details, like my obsession with French pastry.

"No, it's okay. I already ate."

The truth is, I'm too nervous. My stomach is queasy and my heart's flatlining. I'm not certain whether it's because Mikah has been ignoring me for over five days or because Mrs. Kaminski might not want to give me my old job back.

"I thought you found another job?" Mrs. Kaminski asks once we get down to the business of why I'm here. "Your father said you were working in some fancy restaurant downtown." She looks at me long and hard.

"I was, but I had to take a leave of absence and they let me go," I confess, setting my portfolio on the table. "I have some ideas for the bakery." My heart rate picks up and the words in my head begin to trip one over the other. "And I really want to return to work."

The printouts in my shaking hands rustle as I lay them out on the table in front of Mrs. Kaminski. "There's a lot of cool stuff we can do... Like a blog...or rebrand the Instagram account... You haven't been posting any stories at all. We can go live from the kitchen too..." My mouth is dry and I'm starting to forget the rest of the speech.

"Hmm..." Mrs. Kaminski's gaze darts from me to the mess on the table that's supposed to look like a business presentation. She picks up one of the printouts and her face tenses. "Why don't you tell me about the blog, and then we can talk about the stories and the rest of your ideas and see what we can do, huh? How does that sound?"

"Sure." I set my portfolio aside, my heart dancing.

I'm not sure if Mrs. Kaminski agrees to hear my thoughts on how to rebrand her store because she feels sorry for me or because she's genuinely interested, but thirty minutes later when I leave the bakery, I have my old job back.

Mikah's text must have come in while I was in the middle of my nerve-racking business meeting with Mrs. Kaminski, because I don't see it until I get to my car. It's his favorite three-letter word "hey" and a blushing emoji, which makes me think something's wrong with him. Blushing emojis are not his thing.

A light flutter wrapped in panic rolls through my stomach as I dial his number. The spoiled brat in me is pissed at him for not returning my texts, but the girl who's struggling to grasp the true nature of the confusing feelings she has for her boyfriend's brother is ready to jump with joy and scream his name. Five days of radio silence is overkill.

"What's up?" His voice is rough, but it stirs me up anyway, making every cell in my body buzz.

So it's no surprise that my brain short-circuits. "You didn't say anything about my cheesecake." I blurt out the first thing that comes to mind, because I don't want to sound pathetic and go straight to accusations.

"I haven't tried it. How am I supposed to know if it's any good?" Typical Mikah response. "Maybe you took that picture off whatchamacallit?" He pauses for a second to look for a word. "Pinterest?"

I feel my lips stretching into a smile. "No. My mom and I made it."

"Well"—he clears his throat—"you've got a great eye. You take nice pictures of cakes."

"Is that all you have to say about my cheesecake?"

"I can't say more unless you bake one for me."

The memories crash at me all at once. Sometimes I don't get how he and Dakota could be so different yet so alike. I wonder if they ever noticed how they mirrored each other's words, actions, and thoughts. It's both fascinating and scary. And it hurts a little because it reminds me of our loss.

"Maybe one day," I say, trying to get my emotions under control.

Mikah doesn't respond. The tension between us grows thicker, and I use my fresh rush of courage to ask him the question that's been spinning in my head for five days now. "Why didn't you text me back?"

His response is cryptic and a lot like a punch in the gut. "I was busy."

"Are you still in Seattle?"

"I came home two days ago."

My heart sinks to my stomach. *He's only telling me this now?* "Do you want to grab some food?"

There's a long pause, the purpose of which I don't understand. Is this his way of telling me we need more time apart? Am I too naive to see that what happened between us was just drunk, mindless sex?

"Not like a date or anything…" I say. My voice drops to a whisper. "Sure."

"Do you want to meet at Patty's?" As soon as I say the words, I almost want to take them back. That's where Dakota and I went to eat on our first date, and asking Mikah to meet me there feels a lot like cheating.

"That's fine," he mutters. "I'll meet you there at nine."

"Okay. See you at nine."

The tiny part of me that's still upset at Mikah for not telling me earlier that he was back in Portland expects him to blow off dinner at Patty's, but he's already there when I arrive at quarter to nine.

I recognize the lines of his silhouette through the glimmering glass as I make my way toward the entrance. He's staring at nothing in particular and he seems at ease. Just another guy grabbing some food. You wouldn't think that three months ago, he was one of the seven hundred people gunned down in a Portland nightclub by a jealous psycho. No, scratch that. A psycho gets to slide on an insanity plea. Joseph Miller isn't allowed to be mentally ill.

The view of the crowd packing the diner sends shivers down my spine, and I have to stop briefly to calm my stupid heart. Campus has become easier, although I've been finding myself tuning out during classes lately, and places I haven't been to since before the attack still make me nervous. *People make me nervous.*

Everyone is a potential shooter and there's no way of knowing otherwise. Any place, any time.

There's a brilliant idea forming inside my head as I evaluate the faces of the patrons. Maybe installing metal detectors can eliminate the possibility of someone sneaking a gun into Patty's?

After a few seconds of sifting through my racing thoughts, I walk into the diner and make my way to the far side where Mikah's sitting, away from the clatter surrounding the checkout area.

"Hey," he mutters as I slide onto the bench across from him.

"Hey." My chest expands from the sudden onslaught of emotions. I'm uncomfortable, confused, and a bit scared because I don't know how to look at Mikah anymore without imagining him naked and doing all sorts of dirty things to me. It might have something to do with the fact that I don't fully regret it. Guilt plagues me, but I don't have the need to undo what we've done. Truth is, I liked it. Being with Mikah made me feel alive.

Our eyes meet and his penetrating gaze holds mine for what seems like an eternity.

I never really thought of it until right now, but the way you see a man after you have sex with him is always different from how you see him if he's a friend. This change of perception with Dakota was gradual but effortless because I always knew I wanted more than a platonic relationship with him. After our first time, being with him felt simply like adding a little something to the already existing palette of what he was.

With Mikah, it's nothing like that. It's like being on a ship in the middle of the ocean and coming across an iceberg. Only a small fraction of him is on the surface, and seeing the rest is only possible if you jump. Dive into the freezing cold water and die a slow excruciating death while observing all of the beauty that's hidden away.

That's what looking at Mikah feels like at the moment, and I'm terrified that eventually this will hurt even more than it's been hurting since the night we let ourselves loose.

"How was Seattle?" I ask, grabbing a napkin from the dispenser so that I can occupy my hands with something. I wonder if he's seen the Wikipedia page. Jess told me Blaze and Luke were the ones who made it.

"It was okay." Mikah shrugs, sticking his fork into the pile of mashed potatoes on his plate. "How's college?"

"My finals are starting next week." I shift on the bench restlessly. I can't keep my eyes off of him, and the bad thing is that they might be looking for some sort of a hint that our sex wasn't just a drunken incident. *I don't want it to be*, and that terrifies me.

Mikah stares right back. His gaze holds mine like a dynamic rope would hold a mountain climber. "Break a leg."

"Thanks." I flip the napkin and fold it in half. "I'm going to be working at the bakery again."

"Oh yeah?"

"I'm actually pretty excited. The owner liked some of my ideas."

"That's good."

Then there's an awkward pause and I'm grasping at straws, trying to think of anything to keep the conversation afloat.

"Did you read *The Witching Hour*?"

"It's on my list. Do you plan on finishing up *Salem's Lot*?"

"Maybe after finals."

This is where I run out of small talk ideas. Besides gothic literature, there are other questions gnawing away at my brain, and the need to get them out pushes me over the edge. "I didn't think you wanted to see me anymore." My voice drops to a whisper, dissolving into the clatter of the busy dining room.

Mikah stares at me for a few seconds before breaking eye contact. "I just needed some time to figure things out." His hand slides across the table and he nudges the edge of mine with his fingertips.

I still in my spot. My head begins to spin and my pulse pounds heavily in my ears. "Something's going on between us," I say quietly.

"Something is," Mikah agrees, his hand unmoving as his eyes flick back to me, leisurely taking me in, and his Adam's apple rolls slowly beneath his skin.

We sit like this for what seems like forever, looking at each other, our gazes dancing.

"Are you hungry?" he asks after a while. "Do you want something?"

"Sure." I nod since my brain can't think of anything better to say. I'm still processing. My heart beats madly against my chest and the sweat is already hard at work under the fabric of my tee.

I hear the muffled sound of a text message alert coming from my purse. Mikah leans back to draw his phone from the front pocket of his jeans. We both stare at our phones and then at each other.

"Is that Jess?" I ask, wondering if he received the same group invite I just did.

"Yeah."

"She should really stop this mass texting thing."

Jess has been doing it a lot. Come Monday morning, you can always expect a short letter from her with updates on the Miller case or Luke's health. Wednesdays are usually reserved for the meet-up info. Today it's an invite to a show Blaze is putting together to raise money for some charity.

"Right." Mikah rolls his eyes and puts his phone away.

"Will you go?"

"I think I'll be out of town."

I'm convinced the distance he's created between himself and the rest of the guys in the band is because he misses Dakota, but it could also be that he's simply moved on while no one else has.

We walk out of the diner at around ten. The air is warm and fresh and smells like summer. Seeing a small group of kids crowding the entrance of Patty's reminds me of my own high school days when Jess and I used to come here on Fridays to get our milkshake fix and stare at some of the boys on the football team. Well, mostly, she was the one who stared.

We stroll to my car. Mikah's right behind me, his heat breaking through the warmth of the night and licking my skin through the damp fabric of my tee.

When we reach my Prius that's parked at the very back of the lot—away from the noise—Mikah leans against it and offers me a cigarette.

I take it like a hopeless junkie.

We haven't talked about what's going on between us. Acknowledging the fact isn't enough. On one hand, I blame Jess and her spammy text for sidetracking us, but on the other, I blame my fear of being rejected.

Mikah flicks his lighter and lights his cigarette.

It's sick how much I love watching him smoke. There's something lucidly genuine in the way he welcomes nicotine. He inhales slowly, his broad chest rising and falling. Then his face relaxes and his gaze burns against mine like a thousand fires.

"Did you read *Wuthering Heights*?" I ask. I know my question is random, but books are always the safe topic with him.

"In high school." Mikah nods.

"I take it you didn't like it?"

"It wasn't my favorite."

"It wasn't mine either."

Mikah tilts his head and stares at me for a while. "Seems like it would have been your type of book."

"It was depressing," I confess.

"Then why are you reading everything I tell you to read? It's all depressing."

"Why are *you* reading depressing?"

Mikah looks up to the sky and pushes the smoke out. "Life is depressing." His gaze darts back to me and he hands me the lighter. "People are shit, Alana." His voice lacks its raw edge. It's soft with a touch of sad. "They're mean and judgmental."

"Fuck them," I say, my hands shaking when I try to light my cigarette.

"Look at you, church girl." Mikah chuckles. He moves closer to me. "You're evolving." A sudden gust of wind rips the clouds of smoke that are floating between us apart, and the lack of a barrier causes my anxiety to kick up a notch.

"Shut up." I roll my eyes and flick the stubborn lighter again and again, swallowing past the growing tightness in my throat. My thumb's already sore and my brain is craving the nicotine fix badly.

Mikah takes the lighter from me.

"I always knew you had it in you," he says in a ragged whisper. "I felt it the moment I saw you." He puts his cigarette between his lips again and brings its tip to mine, the length of his body filling my view.

I close my eyes and inhale carefully until my cigarette is lit. The smoke does a wicked dance inside my lungs, soothing me with its magic power, taking all my worries away. It's a strange kind of high. Dark and liberating. The kind of high people like my father don't understand.

Mikah draws his cigarette from his mouth and drops his head to my ear. "You were a little rabbit tossed to a pack of wolves and you stood there and ate us up as if we were vanilla ice cream." His lips, hot and disturbingly tempting, linger at my temple. "And you don't fuck like a Virgin Mary."

My heart does a double flip. I exhale the thick smoke through my nose and pull my cigarette away for a second to catch my breath. Then Mikah's hand slips under my chin to lift it up and he covers my mouth with his. It's a dirty and wet Marlboro kiss with a touch of starvation and shame. It makes my head spin and my knees weaken. His tongue strokes against mine slowly, each lick deliberate and breathtaking, as our lips move at a perfect pace.

Although I'm not ready for it to end, guilt drives me to break the kiss. I don't want to scrap my memories of the places I've been to with Dakota by making new memories with his brother. It's too much like betrayal.

Mikah takes a step back and slips his cigarette into his mouth, his green eyes never leaving mine.

"I don't want to be a rabbit," I rasp out, my voice shot from the lack of oxygen, as the Virgin Mary comment burns like a torch inside my head.

"You're not." Mikah shakes his head. "Not anymore."

"Who am I then?"

"You tell me. I'm not a mind reader."

I let his words settle in. He's a fusion of hot and cold and I lose myself whenever I look at him.

"Life's too fucking short, Alana," Mikah mutters, smoke seeping from his nostrils. "Figure it out before it's too late." He turns around and starts walking toward his truck that's parked on the opposite side of the lot.

I'm too confused to stop him. I just stand there and watch.

I sit in my Prius in our driveway and stare at the check engine light on the dashboard. It came on sometime today but didn't really hit me until now.

My lips still burn from the kiss with Mikah, and the conversation we had earlier at Patty's is on repeat in my mind. This thing between us hasn't been resolved. On the contrary, it's a lot more complicated after today.

There's a light on in the garage and I'm surprised to see my father up this late, going through boxes he hasn't touched in over a decade.

"What are you doing?" I ask, stepping inside.

"Just cleaning up," my father says, not bothering to look at me.

We haven't been on the best of terms lately. Not since the day I poured my speech full of fucks on him...and I'm starting to believe that he's given up on the idea of trying to make me into someone I'm not.

"It's midnight, Dad." My eyes dart to the open boxes in the corner and I recognize some of my old toys.

"You should at least use gum," he growls, inspecting the contents in front of him. "You reek of cigarettes. One day they'll kill you."

"Cigarettes don't kill people," I murmur. "People with guns do."

My father straightens and finally looks at me. His eyes are tired and he's aged a lot since February. He looks worn out in this dim yellow light. I'm just now noticing how much gray he has in his hair and how deep the web of wrinkles around his eyes and mouth have gotten and it's unnerving.

"You haven't been to church in a while."

"I don't feel like God—if he exists—hears me," I tell him honestly.

"God hears everyone..."

"Dad, I'm not sure if you understand this, but not everyone is like you. Just because I'm your daughter doesn't mean my brain works the same way yours does. I have my own desires and I want to make my own mistakes so that I can learn from them. I want to create my own experiences, and all you do is try to convince me that your beliefs are the right ones when actually, there are no right beliefs. I want you to stop trying to make some imaginary person out of me. I want you to accept me for who I am."

My father doesn't respond. He shoves his hands into the pockets of his khakis and thinks for a while. There's both confusion and anger in his eyes.

"Just because I don't agree with you on something doesn't mean we can't still be a family." My tone takes on a high pitch because I have this stupid need for him to hear me at least this once while I'm in control of my own emotions and not a raging, screaming mess.

"I failed you," he says quietly. "I've only ever wanted what's best for you."

"Why do you believe you failed me? Because my GPA is below 4.0? A piece of paper doesn't define a person. And that's all it is—a piece of paper."

"Because I couldn't save you from the horrible things you've seen..." He gives me a sad smile, his voice shaky.

I avert my gaze and look past him at the shelf with his toolboxes. It's probably the first time in months we've spoken to each other like two adults, without yelling, and I'm scared to say something wrong because I really don't want this to turn into another fight.

"It's not in your power, Dad." A sigh leaves my mouth, and the heaviness in my chest pushes hard against my heart. "You can't stop bad things from happening just because you pray. Look at me?" I shift my gaze back to him. "Look at me and tell me you truly believe God allowed someone I loved to be killed for a reason?"

We stare at each other for a while, the silence between us thicker than mud. I'm baffled my father doesn't come up with an answer because he always has a line from the Bible to throw at me.

"That's what I thought," I say. "The world is a shitty place full of shitty people, and I don't want to waste whatever time I have left asking for forgiveness or things I may never get. I want to live it to the fullest."

My father's face tenses, but he still doesn't contradict me.

"I'm going to bed," I say, turning to head home, but I come to a stop when I remember about my car. "The check engine light came on in the Prius."

"We'll take it to the shop." My father nods.

"Thanks. Goodnight."

I don't know what exactly pushes me to call Mikah when I get to my room. Maybe the Virgin Mary comment. But I dial his number twice and I sit there and listen to his voicemail recording, breathing into the phone like a teenage stalker and not saying anything, because I have no idea what to say.

22. BEFORE

"Dad?" I stop in the doorway of my father's study and wait for his reaction. He's hunched over in front of his computer, his eyes jumping across the blocks of text on the screen. "Do you have a minute?" My throat feels itchy and I want to fast-forward the upcoming conversation to the moment in the future where we peacefully agree on my moving out.

My father motions for me to come over, his gaze sliding to me from above the frames of his readers as he looks up from the screen.

I stop in the middle of the room and force a smile. My mind's going a thousand miles a second and the speech I've been practicing all week is now becoming a jumbled mess in my head.

"Everything okay, sweetheart?"

"Yes. I just wanted to talk about something," I say, pulling up a chair.

"Okay." My father takes off his glasses and sets them on the desk next to the old family photo in which I'm probably no older than six or seven.

"One of the girls at the restaurant is leaving." I begin strategically pressing the right buttons. "And I asked to pick up some of her morning shifts."

"Good. I don't like you driving downtown at night." My father's mood seems to lighten. He's never gotten over my switching jobs without his permission.

"There are also a couple of shifts I want to pick up during the week. They're early mornings and they work well with my class schedule…" My voice starts failing me.

"I believe three days a week is more than enough, Alana."

My heartbeat pounds in my ears like a hammer and my breath hitches, so I just come out with it because my anxiety level is off the charts. "Jess found an apartment not far from campus and she asked me to move in with her."

"The answer is no," my father says unblinkingly, his face twisting with discontent.

"I'm not twelve." My hands on my lap are clutched together in a tight ball, and my fingers are going numb from the lack of circulation. "I'm an adult. I can take care of myself. I'm not moving out to have a place to do drugs or drink if that's what you were thinking."

He ignores me and changes the subject. "I'd like to meet this young man who's been picking you up all week."

I swallow the lump in my throat. My plan was to ease my father into the fact that I'm seeing someone. I've purposely had Dakota pick me up and drop me off at the appropriate times, but the truth is, we've barely gotten to spend any time together since our trip to the waterfall. He worked at the resort all weekend, including New Year's night, and then went out of town with Mikah for two days to see family up north.

"What does he do?" my father's voice booms through the room.

"He works."

"What kind of work?"

"He's an event coordinator at the resort in Cascade Locks."

"How old is he?" My father frowns.

"Twenty-three."

There's a long, excruciating pause.

"You need to get your priorities straight, Alana. You're a freshman. Your college costs me a fortune. I don't want you to have any distractions while you're working on your diploma."

His words cut through me like a knife. "Dad!" I jump to my feet, my body shaking. "Listen to yourself! I'm not one of your charity cases or your master plans. I'm your daughter. I'm a human being with my own needs and feelings. Don't you understand?"

My voice is loud and doesn't sound like my own. Anger and frustration have taken control over my brain and there's no stopping me now.

My father rises to his feet and his expression changes from blank to authoritative. "You need to calm down."

"I don't want to calm down. I want you to understand that you can't plan my life for me. I can see whomever I want and live wherever I want."

"I'm trying to give you a future."

"You're suffocating me! That's what you're doing." I want to throw some more of my opinions into the mix, but my mother joins the conversation.

"Sweetheart, I believe you're overreacting." She stands in the doorway, her eyes darting between me and my father, and I feel the air literally leaving my lungs.

"Fine." I grit my teeth, emotions jamming my throat. "I'm going to move out anyway. You don't have to pay my tuition if you don't want to."

The silence that fills the room is heavy and asphyxiating. Parts of me are still reeling and still want to do battle, but the lack of understanding from my parents is disheartening. It's like talking to a wall.

I leave the study without saying a word, my parents' hushed tones following me upstairs until the slam of the door cuts them off. My room suddenly seems too small, the things that are in it foreign. They belong to a person my parents wish me to be, not the person I truly am.

After a few minutes of pointless pacing, I lock myself in the bathroom and call Dakota.

His voice on the line is like a breath of fresh air. "Hey. How'd it go?"

"It went really bad," I confess, not hiding my irritation. "They said no."

I hear a sigh, and then comes *the* question. "Are you at least going to tell him you're seeing me?"

My response is a frustrated stutter. "Y-yes... I was trying to have a conversation with him, but he kept asking all these stupid questions, like where you work and how old you are."

Dakota laughs. "I'd probably ask the same questions if I were him. He's just concerned."

"Are you siding with my father now?"

"No. I'm just trying to put myself in his shoes and be objective here. I want to be with you, but I don't want us to keep sneaking around. It's fucking lame. I just want everyone, including your parents, to be okay with us. No matter how weird of a couple we may be."

"We *are* weird, aren't we?" I whisper, and my lips stretch into a smile. I press my back against the door and sit on the floor. "Why are you so perfect?"

"Trust me, I'm not. You haven't seen my bad side yet," he rasps. His voice is deep and low and sends shivers down my spine.

"Maybe I want to."

"I know you do. I *want* you to."

There's a moment of quiet, and it's so peaceful in my mind, so clear, despite the fact that my parents are probably downstairs looking online for some convent to ship me off to.

"Can I ask you something?" I finally brave the question I've been wondering about, mostly because asking it face to face terrifies me.

"Sure."

"Why did you ask me out?"

"What do you mean *why*?"

"I mean...I'm not the type of girl you'd normally date. You know, I bake cupcakes for fun."

"What do cupcakes have to do with us?"

"You know what I mean."

"No. I don't."

I blow out a sigh. "You know what they call girls like me."

"I really don't. You're overthinking it, beautiful."

I feel heat rushing to my cheeks. He's never called me *beautiful* before. "Are you going to answer my question?"

"Are you going to ask the right one?"

"I'm asking you. I just want to know what a guy like you sees in a girl like me. I'm not doubting us. I just need to know because I want to understand how we work. Because I don't know how to explain it to my parents so that they can understand it too."

There's a pause.

"Remember the night we met?" Dakota says quietly. "I watched you during the set. You weren't just enjoying the music. You were the music. Your face was bliss. Not a care in the world. And I wanted to know you and now that I do, I think you're beautiful. Take-my-fucking-breath-away beautiful. All of you. The cupcakes included."

My heart swells with emotions. "You haven't even tried any yet."

"That's because you've never baked for me."

"I will when Jess and I get a place."

"You can bake at my place."

"I don't want to invade your kitchen." What I mean to say is, I don't want Mikah prowling around me all grumpy and slurping on his beer while I'm preparing my specialty dish for my boyfriend.

"I'm serious. My brother is going to be out of town next weekend. We can organize a whole bakefest if you want."

I snort out a laugh. "A bakefest sounds good."

"Then it's a deal."

"Deal. I work Friday and Saturday, though."

"Are you working Sunday?"

"No."

"Then it's set. We're baking on Sunday. Are you feeling better now?"

"Yes."

"Cool. I have to get some stuff done. I'll text you later."

After we say our goodbyes, I head to my room and begin my online cupcake recipe research.

23. AFTER

I'm going to make macarons today after work. You're welcome to stop by the bakery if you want to try some.

I reread my text again just to be sure there are no grammar mistakes or I don't sound too pushy, because lately, Mikah hasn't been very friendly. Although he probably doesn't care about grammar and punctuation. He hasn't even read my last text from two days ago.

"Alana?" Mrs. Kaminski's voice drifts at me from the front as soon as I hit the send button. The loud chatter coming from the dining room is my cue to get back to my duties.

The job at the bakery has been great. Now that the semester's over and I officially passed all my classes and no longer have a cloud of my father's wrath looming over me, I can concentrate on something that interests me. Like blogging, baking, and social media.

Last week, Mrs. Kaminski and I finished working on the new look of the store's website, and for the first time in months, I felt really good. It felt like I finally accomplished something without fucking it up in the process. She also agreed to let me try baking some of her signature cakes here at the store after closing, under the condition that I get enough content for Anna's Pastry's website and Instagram account without burning down the place in the process. I've been staying at work late almost every day since last Sunday, preparing and photographing cakes I couldn't have done otherwise, simply because I don't own half the equipment Mrs. Kaminski does. The oven itself is state-of-the-art. My mother would never be able to afford one like we have at the bakery, and even if she could, she wouldn't buy it just to tickle my fancy.

A response from Mikah comes at around six when we're in the middle of the dinner rush. I don't have the willpower to wait for things to calm down, so I excuse myself and run to the bathroom to check my phone.

Locking myself in a stall, I read the message at least three times, my heart jumping around in my chest.

r u going to be alone?

A smile stretches my lips. We haven't seen each other in a few weeks, not since we met at Patty's and our attempt to clear the air ended up only complicating everything. And while the distance has been sort of good for me because I had fewer distractions during finals, I've found myself thinking about Mikah even more often. We've chatted a few times on the phone—the usual late-night calls that always happen after nightmares—but I've realized that's not enough anymore. The needy side of me misses him. A lot. Misses his Marlboro scent and his crooked smile.

After a few minutes of staring at the text, I type a response.

Yes, it's just me.

The answer comes instantly.

what time?

My heart leaps into my throat.

11:30

Ok, i'll stop by. address?

I spend the rest of my shift in a daze with a stupid grin on my face and my stomach full of butterflies. I've never invited someone to the bakery after-hours, and it feels a lot like I'm committing a crime. A pleasant kind of crime but still a crime because even Dakota has never been here.

Mrs. Kaminski leaves shortly before eleven, after helping me prep some of the ingredients for the macarons. I blast through the dining floor with the broom like a tornado, my legs bumping into every single table and fixture. It's probably the fastest I've ever closed up on my own. The idea of Mikah watching me bake makes me both anxious and excited. I rush to the bathroom right after cleanup to fix my falling-out-of-the-bun hair and put on some more eyeshadow.

At quarter till midnight, when I've separated all the egg whites and there's still no sign of Mikah, I decide to text him.

Are you on your way?

My heart's racing as I hit send and put the phone down on the table next to me so that I can see an incoming text.

At twelve thirty, there's still no answer and my message remains unread. Panic and disappointment rattle my chest. Fighting tears, I pipe the mixture onto the tray, tap it, and while it sits before going into the oven, I move on to the cream.

Two hours and five dozen perfect macarons later, the lack of response from Mikah feels like the end of the world. It shouldn't, because, obviously, the sex was just what I've thought from the beginning, drunk and meaningless. A mistake. But my stupid heart doesn't get it. *He acknowledged the fact that there's an* us! *Taking it back without asking me is wrong.*

I finish snapping the photos, clean up, pack a few macarons for my parents, and close the store. Outside, it smells like rain, and the sky is black and starless. Just like it always is before Portland gets hit with a thunderstorm.

After smoking two cigarettes, one after another, I slip into my Prius and attempt to get it running, but all it responds with is a buzzing sound.

My father's car pulls up to Anna's Pastry twenty minutes later, the bright headlights of his Subaru Outback slicing through the fresh mist like a hot knife through butter.

I'm on my sixth Midnight Rust song, and my body is half-shivering and half-numb because the resentment from being stood up has morphed into the worst kind of ache.

It was just sex, Alana, I tell myself as I watch my father step out of his car. Drunk sex that meant nothing to Mikah. A *fuck*. That's what he called it.

I reach out for my phone and pause the music. Listening to the guy whose guts I'm currently hating play a guitar seems absurd. Even if he *is* extremely good. Apparently, I'm a masochist.

My father's wearing a pajama shirt under his jacket, and his face, which looks sleepy and fatigued, gives away his irritation. A small part of me—the responsible daughter—feels like crap for waking him up in the middle of the night, but mostly, I'm shocked and confused by Mikah's behavior. Does he have a list where he separates the girls he sleeps with into fucks-like-a-Virgin-Mary category or not?

My father taps on the windshield, snapping me out of my angry daze.

"How long will this be going on for?" he asks when I get out of the Prius. "Do you have to stay at work this late every night?"

"It's just a short-term project, Dad," I explain, rubbing my eyes.

"Are you getting paid for doing this?"

"Yes. I am."

"I really don't like you being here on your own at this hour." My father shakes his head. He'd probably throw a fit if I wasn't spending my nights at the bakery, but I suppose, in his mind, making cakes at three in the morning is better than *slutting* around in broad daylight.

In a way, I agree with him. This isn't the safest neighborhood, but for some reason, I've never felt scared inside the bakery. At least, not when I'm alone. Being alone is better than being surrounded by hundreds of people whose thoughts you can't read. Croissants aren't going to pick up a gun and shoot, because croissants aren't jealous creatures.

"I baked some macarons," I tell my father, ignoring his last comment.

And he, in turn, ignores mine. "Let's take a look." He motions for me to move away and slips behind the wheel, his eyes scanning the dashboard. "I don't understand. We just took it to the shop three weeks ago."

"Maybe they should give us a refund." I shrug, watching my father turn the key and listen to the sputtering sounds coming from my Prius.

He checks under the hood next, his face puzzled. "I'll call a tow truck to take it to the shop again first thing in the morning."

"Okay." I nod, ducking inside to grab my things and my macarons.

I fish out my so-called diary full of useless doodles from the bottom of my bag and tear out an empty page to leave a note on the windshield for Mrs. Kaminski that the Prius is broken down.

My father's waiting for me patiently, his hands thrust into the pockets of his jacket as a light drizzle sprinkles across his gray hair. He double checks all four doors once I lock the car, and we silently load into his Subaru.

The awkwardness between us is depressing.

"I believe you should make some adjustments to your schedule. This is too late to be baking, Alana," my father expresses his concern again. He's like a broken record.

The anger coursing through me becomes annoyance. My fingers fiddle with the handles of the paper bag I stuffed with macarons. "I can't do this when the store is open. I can only do it after hours."

"What if something happens? What if someone tries to break in?"

"Dad." I mask my anxiety with a nervous laugh. "What's there to steal? Butter and sprinkles?"

He lets out a heavy sigh, his gaze shifting back to the steering wheel.

"Do you want to try some?" I ask, shoving the paper bag at him.

"Not right now." His head jerks and he reaches out for the gear shifter, ignoring my three hours of labor.

Tears of frustration begin to pool in my eyes and I try to choke down my emotions. The last thing I want to do is cry in front of my father, but every little feeling I've been harboring since February, including my conflicting opinions about Mikah, God, and the death penalty, transforms into this loud, stupid wail that comes out of my lungs like a rocket. My hands are still clutching the bag with the macarons and my eyes are a watery mess.

"Alana?" I feel my father's hand on my shoulder. "What's wrong?"

I shake my head.

"Alana?" His pained voice echoes through my throbbing head.

"This is the first time I've baked macarons," I whimper between my sobs, sounding whiney and small. "And no one even wants to try them. No one."

"What are you talking about?" My father's face is a trembling smear in front of me.

"Do you know how hard it is to make perfect macarons, Dad?" I ask, not bothering to wipe away the tears.

"I know. I know, sweetheart." He nods, pulling me into an embrace. "I'm sure they're delicious. I'll have some at home. I promise."

We sit like this—with me crying against my father's chest and hugging the bag of macarons I made for Mikah—for a very long time. Until there are no more tears left.

When I wake up at around noon, my face is swollen from all the crying, my head's hurting, and my throat's sore. The rain beating against the window has hidden the sun and sprinkled the dark sky with messy clusters of raggedy clouds.

I settle at my desk, open my laptop, and read through the latest updates on the Miller case. There's still no trial date, which doesn't surprise me at all. It feels more like a reality show now. There's an article about his girlfriend's dog. There's an article about his neighbor's arrest. There's also a detailed article about how much evidence has been gathered and analyzed, and I don't understand any of it. I don't understand why so many hearings are necessary to determine whether a man who killed twenty-four people is fit to stand trial.

When panic from the sudden flashbacks starts clogging my lungs, I shut my laptop and scramble for my phone.

There's a text from Mikah waiting for me. It came in a couple of hours ago when I was still asleep.

im sorry i didn't make it last night

No explanation.

I stare at the message for a good minute, my stupid heart beating madly. The jerk doesn't deserve my tears or my attention, but something inside me pushes me to send him a response.

Okay

Downstairs in the kitchen, there's a note on the fridge from my father about the Prius being at the shop, and the macarons I baked yesterday are organized neatly on a plate. My mother must have done it before leaving for work. After counting them, I determine my parents ate at least three, and this fact instantly brightens my mood.

By the time I finish my breakfast and get back to my room, another message from Mikah has popped onto the screen of my phone.

im really sorry i don't want 2 leave like this don't be mad

But I am. I'm mad at him for making me wait all night, and I'm mad at him for making me believe the sex between us meant something.

Apparently, to him, it didn't.

24. BEFORE

I'm not sure why exactly I insisted on going to this boring—to say the least—party. I guess I was partly jealous, partly curious and couldn't wait until the weekend to see Dakota. The idea of baking at his place was so raw and real that it began to haunt my dreams, and I just wanted to speed up the time to be with him. I spent all day Tuesday looking for new recipes online and picked up some food coloring for the frosting. However, one thought of my boyfriend spending his Wednesday night in a house full of pretty drunk girls with no inhibitions while I'm putting together a new Pinterest board drove me nuts. That's why I asked him if I could come.

He didn't mind. On the contrary, he seemed excited.

Now, I'm regretting it. My pink top is like a sore spot in a sea of black, and I'm probably the only person in the entire house who doesn't have a drink or a cigarette. I swear I can feel people laughing at me behind my back.

Dakota's on his second beer as we navigate through the maze of rooms in search of the guy who organized this whole thing. Apparently, he's someone useful to be friends with. At least, that's what I gathered from what Dakota told me on the way here.

"Yo, DK!" Someone shouts over the music. "Long time no see."

Dakota swivels toward the noise, his hand still linked with mine.

A tall guy in a Metallica t-shirt disengages from the crowd and inches forward to give my boyfriend a hug. It's a manly embrace with lots of back patting involved.

When they break apart, Dakota draws me closer and makes an introduction. "This is my girl, Alana."

"Nice to meet you." The Metallica guy extends his hand. "I'm Andy. *Mi casa es su casa*, if you know what I mean?" A smirk tilts the side of his mouth. "You keeping my boy straight?"

I don't get what exactly he means by keeping Dakota *straight*, but I think it's a good thing, so I smile and shake his hand.

"Let's get you some real drinks, okay?" He motions for us to follow him toward the kitchen, where we're handed two shots.

The music playing in the background is heavy, my-ears-are-about-to-bleed kind of heavy. It blends with the voices in the crowd perfectly. The whole house feels like one big quaking box filled with thick clouds of vapor, sweat, and the sharp stench of weed, which worries me because my father will definitely catch the smell.

I've never seen Dakota drunk until tonight. The good thing is that he's a happy drunk. Funny and easygoing and absolutely adorable with his dimples on display and his charisma in full swing. The bad thing is that he's not going to be able to drive me home now. Or drive at all, for that matter. Or even walk steadily.

I'm contemplating asking Jess to come and get us when Andy hands me another shot.

"I'm good. Thanks." I shake my head as my palm tightens around the glass he gave me thirty minutes ago. It's hot against my skin, and my knuckles hurt from holding it for so long, but I don't want people to look at me strangely because I don't have anything in my hand. Or more strangely than they already are, probably wondering how the heck I ended up with Dakota Bennett in the first place.

As if sensing my discomfort, he draws me closer and mutters against my temple, "You don't have to drink anything you don't want to." The sharp smell of alcohol on his breath crawls up my nostrils and almost knocks me off my feet.

I nod.

"I'll make you a cocktail. Come on." He grabs my hand and we barrel through the room toward the minibar no one's tending. It's just a bunch of people buzzing around like bees, looking dazed by the elaborate set-up. My guess is that these people aren't used to mixing their own drinks.

"It's okay. I'm fine." I try to reason with him since I'm not confident in his bartending skills. Not when he's like this, at least.

Dakota pushes his way in and scans the contents laid out before him. "Do you like pineapple?" He turns around and elbows a guy to his left to make more room for me.

I shoot an apologetic smile at the poor dude and step closer. Dakota snakes his arm around my frame and thrusts me into the tiny spot in front of the bar, the length and weight of his body holding me in place and separating me from the madness of the room.

"I'm not that thirsty," I squeal, my eyes darting around the counter that's filled with bottles of all shapes and sizes.

"I'm not trying to get you drunk," Dakota whispers in my ear, grabbing a clean glass from the stack. His voice is a low slur. "I'm not that kind of guy. If I want something from you, I'll tell you when I'm sober." He moves against me subtly. There aren't many layers between us right now, and I can feel every muscle, every breath, and every indecent thought running through his head at the moment. And sadly, I love it. I love that he's this obsessed in public. They say in wine lies the truth. The fact he still feels the same about me when he's drunk makes me happy. In a way, it proves he's not courting me only for my body, although we haven't even gotten to that part yet.

"Who's going to drive me home?" I ask quietly as I watch him toss a few pieces of ice into the glass.

"Don't worry about it. I'll call my brother."

"What about you?" Getting in a car with Mikah is the last thing I want to do.

Ignoring my question, Dakota grabs a small can and waves it in front of my face. "You like pineapple?"

"Yes. Pineapple's fine."

He shakes the juice, pops the lid open, and pours the contents into the glass with ice. I almost expect him to miss and spill it all over the counter, but he doesn't.

"Don't worry. I'll make sure you get home safe." His tone is soft around the edges. He hands me the glass and kisses the back of my head.

"DK? What the hell are you doing here?" a rough female voice calls out of nowhere.

I tear my gaze from my drink and see a girl on the opposite side of the bar. She's tall and fit, has tons of tats on her arms and neck, and her hair is wild. Acid blue. Long and styled to perfection.

"Hey! What's up, dude?" Dakota moves behind me, his body sliding against mine.

I don't dare move.

"I didn't think you'd be here. How are you?" The girl's eyes shift to me, and she flashes me a huge smile. "Hi. I'm Casey."

"Alana." I nod, feeling conflicted and slightly jealous. Of course my boyfriend knows other girls. They're his friends. I just haven't figured out how to deal with it yet. I've never dated a rock singer before.

Dakota wraps his arms around me and presses his cheek to mine for a second. "That's my girl." Sensing he's going overboard with all the mushiness in front of his friend, I make a mental note to start watching his alcohol intake and possibly attempt to stop him from drinking.

"He's an adorable drunk." Casey winks at me. "Just make sure he doesn't mix liquor with beer or you'll have to call the National Guard."

"Is he that bad?" I laugh a little, feeling at ease now.

"He thinks he's Superman when he mixes."

"Are you two talking about me?" Dakota asks, tightening his grip on me.

"We are," Casey says, grabbing a clean glass. "Make sure you behave."

We chat some more, mainly about Casey's band. Apparently, she and Dakota used to have a side project together but couldn't commit to it seriously. Then some people express their displeasure with us blocking the bar, so we move to the living room.

Dakota's in the middle of telling Casey about his upcoming Seattle tour dates when I see Mikah.

He emerges from the crowd, tall and impressive, his face tense and serious. There's a girl with him. I've seen her before—pretty blonde with a butterfly tattoo. She was in one of the photos Jess and I dug up on the internet when we were stalking the band online.

I wait for them to approach Dakota and me, but they walk past the bar and head toward the stairs, completely ignoring us.

In the living room, we're on the tenth round of tequila-pong. Thankfully, my boyfriend has great aim and hasn't been consuming as much as some of his opponents. I'm getting a little nervous, however, because it's late and somehow, we still haven't solved the problem of transportation.

There's a short break and we all go into the kitchen to get some more tequila and snacks. I haven't seen Mikah since he came in, and I'm wondering if he's gone for the night and if he's spending it with the blond girl. These things shouldn't bother me—his life is his business— but for some reason, my mind is curious.

Loud noises roll into the house as someone crashes the front door open. I hear heavy footsteps traveling through the room and someone yelling over the music.

"DK!" A voice calls out. "Get your ass in here. Your brother..." The last part of the sentence gets cut off by another crash and a chain of gasps.

Suddenly, an attack of panic trundles through my body. Dakota tosses his glass on the floor and charges outside, Casey and others trailing after him like a colony of ants.

My heart hammers madly as I follow after them. I don't know what exactly caused the riot, and by the time I make it to the porch, there's nothing to look at except for Mikah and Dakota. They're standing in the middle of the lawn, both visibly distraught, surrounded by the rest of the party. Dakota slaps him lightly on the cheek and wraps his hand around Mikah's neck. It's not a pissed off kind of smack; it's the brotherly tough love kind that's usually used when someone needs to be brought back to their senses.

The crowd's buzzing, despite the cold. The freezing air stings against my skin badly, but I'm too freaked out to go inside and look for my coat.

"Come on!" Andy throws both hands in the air and starts hustling everyone away. "Show's over."

"Fuck you!" a voice shouts. "Fucking cunt!"

I hear some gasps and giggles.

"It's just a misunderstanding," Andy counters.

"Misunderstanding my ass!"

I hop down the stairs and push through the crowd to get to Dakota. The profanity exchange heats up, and now there are at least five different people yelling and all I really want is to get out of here before something else happens.

A while later, we're in a car outside Andy's house. Mikah's in the back seat, apparently very drunk. Dakota's sitting quietly behind the steering wheel, his hands choking it.

The silence between the three of us is awkward. Mostly because they know what happened and don't want to share. The only thing I overheard as we were leaving is that Mikah got into a fight.

"I'll drive," I say, my voice shaky but determined.

"It's all right. I'm good." Dakota straightens up.

"You're too drunk to drive," I insist, holding out my open palm for the keys.

"I'm not. I swear." He touches the tip of his nose with his index finger. Casey's right; my boyfriend's a cute drunk with the mentality of a four-year-old, and the silly grin that doesn't want to come off his face makes me feel weird things. I just want to cuddle and sing him a song. Although I'm a horrible singer.

Mikah stirs in the back. "He's lying. His ass is fucking lightweight."

I ignore the remark because I only have enough patience for one overconfident child right now.

"I swear I'm good." Dakota spins in his seat looking for the seatbelt.

Last attempt. "I'm not going if you're driving."

"Oh, come on!" He slams both hands against the wheel like a little kid who's not getting the candy he wants.

"I'm serious. You've had a lot to drink and I don't want us to crash. I'll drive."

"This is a manual."

"I've driven a manual before."

He looks at me unblinkingly, as if I just told him I was from Jupiter. His mouth slants slightly.

"And she scores!" Mikah attempts to whistle, but what comes out of his mouth sounds more like a combination of wheezing and spitting.

"My father taught me how to drive in a manual," I explain.

Dakota blows out a sigh of defeat and places his key in my palm.

After we switch seats, I turn on the overhead light and study the gears for a minute. The truth is, I'm not very good with manual because the extent of my knowledge doesn't go beyond my driving lessons at the age of sixteen, but letting Dakota drive would be worse.

"Could you pass by McDonald's drive-thru?" Mikah requests from the back as I slip the key into the ignition. The engine roars to life and the car jerks.

Dakota's face twists in anguish.

"Can you please put your seatbelt on?" I try to get him occupied with something because his panic is distracting me.

"Hey!" Mikah calls out again. "Can you pass by McDonald's?"

"Okay, sure," I answer mechanically. My brain feels a bit overwhelmed at the moment, and I just want him to stop bugging me.

I'm not sure how what was supposed to be a quick drive-thru detour turned into a full-on late-night parking lot dinner. It's hard to say whose idea it was—Mikah's or Dakota's—because they pretty much ganged up on me, and in order to stop them from whining, I had to honor their wishes.

The sounds of chewing, slurping, and wrappers crinkling inside the car deafen my poor ears as I watch them polishing off their Quarter Pounders as if they haven't been fed in weeks. I wonder if this is the effect of the alcohol or if they're always like this when they're together.

"If I find one crumb, you're taking it to the car wash." Dakota thrusts his head between the seats and warns Mikah. His voice is still soft, but the food has sobered him up some.

"Fuck you," his brother responds, undeterred.

"You know what, asshole..." Dakota tears a piece of his sandwich wrapper and tosses it at Mikah. "Eat this."

The sound of drunken throaty laughter fills the back of the car.

I twist in my seat and see Dakota trying to rub something off the front of his coat. The sandwich in his hand begins to fall apart.

"Let me have it." I slide my fries into the paper bag and motion for him to give me the rest of his food before it ends up on the floor.

He complies and exchanges the sandwich for the stack of napkins I hand him.

"She's too fucking good for you, little brother," Mikah mumbles under his breath.

I ignore his remark.

"Go to hell." Dakota brushes him off and slides back to his seat. There's a huge ketchup stain on his coat and he looks confused and tired.

"Are we done?" I ask, drawing a deep breath through my teeth. "It's late and I still have to figure out how to get home."

"I'll take you. Don't worry," Dakota mutters, placing the paper bag containing what's left of his sandwich and my fries on his lap.

"You're just going to make a mess again." I catch his hand and pull it away from the food.

"She's feisty too." Mikah snorts out a laugh and makes a growling sound.

Annoyance rattles in my chest. I swivel in my seat and shoot him an angry look, but his gaze clashes with mine, stirring something in me. Something hot and heavy in the pit of my stomach. "Can you just be quiet while I'm driving?" I demand, shaking off the panic.

"What did I say?" He shrugs. His eyes, which are still locked on mine, darken. I try to figure out what happened to all the emotions that just bled out of him thirty seconds ago. Does he hate me that much?

"Just shut your fucking mouth, okay?" Dakota says, his tone frosty. He pats his pockets and retrieves a piece of gum.

The air in the car turns dense. I can sense the shift between them again. It's hanging over us like a case of bricks, ready to crash on us any second now.

"Fuck, you two," Mikah says in a low voice as I buckle up. I'm not certain he even meant for these words to come out. Maybe they were supposed to stay in his head and he's just too drunk to understand he's not thinking it.

The rest of the drive is less tense but silent.

By the time we get to the apartment, Mikah's passed out and we have to drag him out of the car. Not that Dakota's motor skills are completely restored, but at least he can still stand on his feet. It takes us a good minute to figure out how exactly to distribute two hundred pounds of dead weight between the two of us.

I'm out of breath when we finally reach the top of the stairs. Mikah's arm, which is thrown over my shoulder, feels like a cement block.

"I'll hold him and you unlock the door," Dakota instructs, rearranging his brother's body. "It's the blue key."

Once I'm inside, I reach out for a switch on the wall and flick it on. The soft yellow light from the lonely floor lamp spills through the living room.

There's a low thud when Mikah's boots hit the threshold as Dakota drags him into the apartment. He shuts the door with his foot and staggers into the hallway, panting and wheezing. There's more rumbling, followed by a series of incoherent slurs that sound a lot like Mikah.

Without bothering to turn on the rest of the lights, I quietly follow them down the dark hallway as they shuffle into Mikah's room. I feel kind of weird going in, because it seems wrong. Not the invasion of privacy kind of wrong. Just inappropriate since this is the room of the guy whose brother I'm dating. But I'm too exhausted to listen to my common sense. All I really want is to go home.

After some maneuvering, Dakota arranges Mikah on the bed and descends to his knees to take off his boots. I stand in the doorway and watch him with fascination as thin lines of light from a streetlamp spill through the blinds and linger across his back. Despite the ridiculous fight in the car, he still tends to his brother as if it's the most normal thing to do when your sibling isn't able to take care of himself. I've never seen this absolutely selfless side of him and I adore him more with each passing second. The fact that my parents might not see any of this beauty in Dakota because of their prejudice and tendency to judge a person by his appearance, his hobbies, and his education level troubles me.

Mikah produces a groan and jerks his leg. "What the fuck are you doing, DK?"

Dakota grabs Mikah's ankle and finally frees his foot of his heavy-duty boot. "Going to film homemade porn. I hear dudes with long hair are a big thing this year."

I press my lips together and try not to smile, but there's a mad laugh stuck in my throat.

"Fuck off, DK," Mikah slurs and attempts to lift his head off the pillow.

"Relax. I'm just messing with you. No one's going to watch you snore like a train."

"I think the food was bad." He blows out a heavy sigh.

"Are you going to puke?" Dakota stops messing with the second boot and sits back.

"I don't know. I'm fucking drunk. Did that piece of shit ever tell you anything?"

"Don't worry about it."

"I'm serious. Did he ever tell you anything? He's spreading fucking rumors. I can bet you a hundred bucks we lost the summer residency gig because of him."

I'm not sure what exactly the conversation is about anymore. I stand in my spot and don't dare to interrupt, like one wrong move might somehow destroy this tender moment between them. Instead, my eyes sweep over the interior of Mikah's room. He's really not good at keeping his private space clean or organized. There's stuff everywhere. Clothes, guitar picks, magazines, tools. It's like a little testosterone showroom. There are fewer bands posters on the wall than Dakota has, but there's a huge abstract painting hanging over his bed and a small shelf with a few dozen books, the titles of which I can't make out. Somehow, I didn't peg him as the reading type.

"I'm telling you the food was shit." Mikah exhales slowly.

Dakota glances at me over his shoulder as if I have a solution. My brain struggles to think of something less extreme than taking him to the ER. It might be all the excessive alcohol and they'll end up with the huge hospital bill because of a false alarm. "Maybe we can put a trash can next to his bed," I offer.

Dakota nods, still on the floor with Mikah's boot next to him. "There's an extra one in the closet by the bathroom."

"Sure." I step through the doorway and check the closet, and then I run to the kitchen to grab some plastic bags and paper towels. All of this in the dark because the only source of light in the apartment is the floor lamp in the living room, and I'm too dazed to worry about switches and other minor details. When I return to Mikah's room, Dakota's managed to get the second boot off. He rises to his feet and moves them out of the way while I stuff the bags into the trash can and set it next to the bed.

"I think he's good." Dakota reaches for my hand and pulls me aside gently.

"You sure it's okay to leave him alone?" I glance at Mikah. My voice drops to a whisper. "What if he chokes on his own vomit? I read about it online. People die like that."

"He'll be okay." Dakota shakes his head, a hint of a smile tugging the side of his mouth. "He'll sleep it off and be like new in the morning."

"You're positive?" For some reason, a tiny part of me is concerned when it shouldn't be.

"She's a keeper...that one," Mikah mumbles, his eyes closed. "If you fuck it up, little brother, I will whoop your ass myself."

I don't understand why, out of all things, he chooses to talk about me. In a way, it bugs me, but I don't say anything.

Dakota and I walk out of the room in silence. He shuts the door carefully and turns around to face me. His eyes search mine and he inches forward to close the space separating us. His body, strong and solid, gently pushes me against the wall. He slips his hand under my coat and glides his palm up the curve of my waist. Goose bumps pucker my flesh and I feel a pool of heat gathering between my legs. My cheeks begin to burn; my breathing becomes unsteady.

A faint stream of light drifting into the hallway from the living room touches only a small portion of Dakota's face, leaving the rest in the darkness.

"I'm glad you came," he says quietly, his lips teasing my temple. "I know it was a little disappointing toward the end." A light chuckle leaves his mouth, his hot, velvety breath spreading across my skin.

"It's fine. It wasn't that bad."

Dakota slides his hand to my neck and tangles his fingers in my hair. "I really want you to stay tonight." He presses against me, molding me to the wall. It's a pleasant kind of force. Right on the edge of dangerous, where I can feel all of him—hard in all the hidden places.

My heart slams into my ribcage. I open my mouth, but nothing comes out because there's a battle going on inside my head. Although I want to say yes, my logical side knows it's a bad idea.

Sensing my panic, he pulls back a bit and his face softens. "You don't have to say yes. I just wanted you to know I'd like that... I'd like to spend tonight and every other night after that with you... Because you're perfect."

He's not making much sense and I wonder if it's because he's drunk or because he just doesn't care to filter his thoughts, but every single word is like kryptonite for me. All my walls are down and he's broken through my defenses.

"I'm not perfect," I mutter, my voice shaking.

"You're perfect for me," he counters, and his lips spread into a smile. "And I'm falling for you so fucking hard. I've never felt this way with anyone else."

Swallowing nervously, I reach out for his face and brush my fingers over the cleft in his chin. He's stunning. Like an antique work of art. I want to dive into his eyes and bathe in his generous warmth.

"I think I may be falling for you too." My whisper is barely there because I'm not sure if what I'm saying is the right thing. This—expressing my feelings for a man—is uncharted territory for me. He and I seem like we're an eternity apart. When I think of myself five years from now, I imagine a different version of Alana. Educated and refined. Someone who Dakota would probably like much more. What he sees in me with my eighteen years of life inexperience is a mystery to me. I feel like my attempt at navigating through adulthood is similar to a child's attempt at learning how to walk.

We still briefly, and the air between us begins to vibrate.

Dakota brings his mouth to mine and kisses me on my lips slowly and carefully. His taste, mint with a pinch of liquor, is like sin. A cocktail of light and dark, making me drunk in my own way. His tongue does despicable things to mine, and I want him to keep kissing me like this until the world—with its prejudice and obstacles all around us—melts away.

When we're both out of breath, we break apart, our hands and eyes lingering on each other, touching and memorizing.

"You still want to go home?" Dakota asks, running his fingers through my hair.

"I don't, but I should," I confess.

"Okay." He nods. "Let me get us an Uber."

"You don't have to go with me."

"I'm not letting you go alone," he insists, fishing his phone from the pocket of his coat.

On the way to my house, we sit in the back of the car, holding hands and staring at each other. There are no words. They don't seem necessary. It's so peaceful with him that I don't think he's real. I think I'm dreaming and one day, I'm going to wake up and he'll be gone. And I'm dreading that moment like I'm dreading the end of the world.

The smell of coffee and cinnamon wakes me up at around ten, but the fear of my parents' wrath keeps me in bed for another hour. When I got home early this morning, my mother was on the couch asleep. She must have waited up for me all night.

It's almost eleven when I finally show up in the kitchen in my pajamas. My mother's unloading the dishwasher and my father's finishing up a late breakfast. There's a blanket of snow draping everything in the yard.

I drag my feet straight to the coffee maker. My head's still throbbing from everything that happened last night at the party and later at Dakota's place. Half of me is ecstatic, but the other half is in shock.

My father breaks the silence, clearing his throat and pushing his plate aside. "I believe we need to talk about this young man you've been seeing, Alana."

I grab an empty cup from the cupboard and dump some sugar in it.

"Sweetheart," my mother chimes in, "Your father's right. I think we should discuss this."

My heart begins to race. I clench my jaw and pour the last of the coffee into my cup.

"Alana?" she calls my name again.

Squeezing my eyes shut, I pinch the bridge of my nose and block out the outside world as I spend a few seconds attempting to streamline my incoherent thoughts.

"You came home last night at two in the morning, smelling like marijuana." My mother sighs.

"People at the party smoked it." I grab my cup, go to the table, and take a seat across from my father."

He looks at me as if he's deciding what would be a better punishment—setting me on fire or kicking me out. "I don't like that you're always out late with him."

The smell of coffee creeps up my nostrils as I bring the cup to my mouth and take a small sip to get my brain going. The effect is almost instantaneous.

"Are you and Jess trying to move in together so that you can invite guys over?" my mother questions me.

"No, Mom!" I toss my head back and cover my face with my palms. Thick as mud heaviness pushes against my chest. Yes, I plan on having

Dakota over when I move out. No, I don't plan on turning my new apartment into a brothel, but for some reason, my parents can't understand that. In their minds, the world is black and white, and I'm not sure how to make them understand that that's not exactly correct.

"Are you two having sex?" My father cuts right to the chase.

I draw my hands away from my face and take another sip of my coffee before going back to the conversation.

"I don't want you shacking up God knows where with some guy who's going to leave you three weeks later. That's not the way I raised you." His face reddens, his eyes burning with suspicion.

"Can I talk now?" I ask, doing my best to sound calm. My heart's still racing in fear and I begin to sweat.

My father takes a deep breath and nods curtly.

"His name is Dakota Bennett," I say, grasping my coffee cup. "He's in a band and you need to accept that fact, Dad. I already know what you're going to say, but before you share your opinion with me, maybe it's best you meet him."

There's a moment of silence.

"Does he smoke or drink?" My mother starts shooting off questions from her appropriate-boyfriend-for-Alana list.

"Does he go to church?" My father asks next.

"No... I don't know." I'm confused about who to answer first. They're like a bad cop and good cop combination, only both are bad in my case.

"What do you mean you don't know?" My father huffs, his suspicion growing.

"We haven't talked about it."

"Why not?"

"Because I don't think it's that important." My voice pitches and I start to lose it.

"Yes, it is. What if he's some Satan worshipper?"

A strained laugh escapes my mouth. "I assure you he's not."

"How do you know?"

"Dad, please." I draw a deep breath. "He treats me really well and he doesn't mind meeting you, but you need to understand that I like him and I'm going to keep seeing him, regardless of whether you like him or not. You need to accept that fact and let me figure it out for myself."

My mother is silent.

My father rubs his forehead and says, "Fine, but we're not discussing any move until I meet him."

25. AFTER

I've been questioning my decision-making ability a great deal lately.

Dark places with lots of people are a trigger. They freak me out. Why I thought going to the charity event Blaze and Jess organized was smart, I have no idea. I'm a sweaty mess, looking over my shoulder every two seconds to make sure no one who comes through the main entrance is carrying any firearms. There are several security guards circling the venue and a few more outside, but it doesn't make me feel any safer. The crowd's growing by the minute, and what was supposed to be an intimate gathering is now turning into the main downtown event of the weekend.

The small table for two I've been ushered to is surrounded by yelling people, and I have no idea who Jess paired me up to sit with, but they're not here yet. My phone is charcoal-hot in my palm because I'm still waiting to hear back from Mikah. The last message I sent him last night is still unread, which is typical and not something I normally get upset about. At least not anymore. I've been doing my best to keep my distance ever since he stood me up and didn't bother to offer an explanation. Although today feels different because it's his last day in Portland, and even though I want to see him before he leaves for Seattle, my pride won't let me mention it.

"Are you good, hon?" Jess's voice drifts at me from somewhere. Her fruity perfume fills the stuffy air around me as she steps out of the human mass to check on me.

"Yes. I'm good." I motion at my glass of water that Blaze spiced up with some vodka a little while ago to help with my anxiety since my pills haven't been doing shit. But the truth is, I'm freaking out.

"Okay, text me if you need anything?" Jess touches my shoulder and waves at Luke, who's maneuvering through the crowd in his wheelchair. He has a new look—buzzed all his hair off and got a neck tattoo. It's somewhat sickening to watch them being a cute couple since the ass grabbing and the vulgar kissing is their thing now. Maybe they're doing it because tonight there's press here or maybe they're just happy that they're both alive and don't give a fuck what everyone else thinks.

I catch myself on the thought that I want that too. I want someone to look at me the way he looks at her... The same way Dakota used to look at me. *I want Mikah to look at me like that now.*

The show begins at around seven. I have to fight off my panic all through the first song because the lack of light inside the venue terrifies me. My gaze jumps nervously from one person to another, looking for a gun. My heart's galloping like a horse on a racetrack and my lungs are out of air before the band finishes up their performance.

I don't remember how exactly I end up outside. My pulse pounds heavy in my ears and the haze has taken over my brain again. All I saw was a whole lot of blurriness as I barreled through all the people in the direction of the exit sign. My hands pushed against the heavy door and I stumbled out into a sheet of fine drizzle that feels wonderfully cool on my skin.

"Hey, Cupcake Queen? Is that you?" someone calls out from off to the side.

I turn toward the sound and see a familiar face hovering near the entrance. He's propping the wall up with his back and there's a cigarette in his mouth.

"I'm sorry. I don't remember your name." I shuffle my feet and look around. We're in the alley alone.

"Zeke," he says. "You were at Jackson's house a couple of months ago."

"Right." I nod. That was the night Mikah and I kissed. My memories of that particular moment are still a little impaired due to my being drunk and high, but I remember enough to know I liked Mikah's lips on mine and I'd love a do-over. Even if every time this thought comes to mind, it's basically the equivalent of me stabbing Dakota in the back. Yes, he's dead, but it still feels exactly like that.

"What are you doing here?" I ask Zeke, trying to shake off my anxiety.

"Just paying my respects." He sucks on his cigarette hard and his cheeks cave in for a second. "How are you holding up, Cupcake Queen?"

"Okay." I shrug. "Life sucks."

"Tell me about it. Fucking politicians. Milking this shit." Zeke lifts his hand in the air and rearranges his fingers into a gun. "If it was up to me, I'd just put a fucking bullet through his head. Boom." He jerks his hand and blows at the imaginary smoke coming from his index finger. "Game over. Motherfucker dead."

His eyes find mine. "You okay, queen?"

I blink at him rapidly as a cold shiver runs through my body.

"You want a hit?" Zeke pushes himself off the wall and moves closer. His face drops to mine and the smell of weed crawls up my nose. "You having a panic attack or something? You want me to call someone?"

I swallow past the chunk of lead in my throat and shake my head. "No. It's okay."

"You sure you don't want a hit? It helps with anxiety."

"Umm...Yeah. Okay," I agree, mainly because the buzz from the vodka is dumbing down my common sense.

We step under the awning to hide from the drizzle, and Zeke pulls out another joint from his pocket for me and lights it up. I smoke it carefully, without looking at him, while he asks me some random questions. They aren't personal and his company is better than being inside, but we get interrupted before our joints are done. The doors swing wide open and a group of people pour into the alley.

"Hey, Zeke!" I hear someone yell behind me and my spine stiffens.

A few girls walk up to us. My guess is that they're here because of the free weed.

There's an exchange of hellos and hugs. I watch them all swoon over Zeke from the corner of my eye, minding my own business until platinum blond hair swims into my line of vision.

She sees me too but doesn't say anything. When Zeke hands her a joint, she sticks it between her bright red lips and flicks the lighter. I stand in the middle of all the activity, surrounded by the chatter, my heart rate kicking up again and my head spinning.

"Didn't you date DK?" one of the other girls asks, giggling. "You had a pretty Instagram with cupcakes, right?" More giggling.

I blink at her through the cloud of smoke, unsure of why she finds it funny.

"She asked you a question, Virgin Mary," Snow White hisses, her hard gaze shifting to my face.

Annoyance courses through me, but I don't let it show. I can't. Not in front of these people. My tone is flat. "Fuck you." I toss the last of the joint on the wet asphalt.

"I wouldn't say fuck if I were you." She lets out a sinister laugh. The kind you'd hear in a high school hallway. Perhaps she didn't get the memo that this isn't a teenage soap opera. "Or your daddy might find out."

"Are you the one who's going to tell him?" I deadpan, trying my best not to let my emotions get the best of me. Although Jess always said I wasn't the type to pretend. "Snitch."

Whispers around us die down. I hear Zeke's coughing.

"I might." A wicked smirk touches her lips. "I might tell him you're slumming it with both brothers too."

My anger rises and heat floods my veins. I'm not sure whether she saw something when we were at Jackson's house or it's just her jealousy speaking and she knows nothing, but the words hurt me and I want to hurt her too.

"Dakota is dead." My voice begins to shake as I speak, and the tension between us spikes. "Stop talking about him like he's still your boyfriend. He's not. He's fucking gone and he's not coming back!"

I choke down the tears of anger filling my eyes and rush inside to hide. The combination of vodka and weed running through my system is making me dizzy, and my feet are beginning to feel like two bricks. They're dragging me down to the floor and I have to stop and lean against a wall to catch my breath, but the music rumbling through my head is too loud.

I need to get out of here.

The weed really kicks in when I'm in my car driving. Unlike last time, it hits me super hard. Hopping bunnies kind of hard, where my body and my brain seem to have traveled to two different dimensions. My head is a centrifuge, rotating and spinning, and I can feel the gray matter bouncing against the walls of my skull while I hear myself chanting non-stop, "God, please don't let me crash... God, please don't let me crash."

My foot on the gas pedal feels too light and I'm convinced that without the right amount of pressure, I'll drive into a ditch or a wall. Basically, I'm too stoned to pull over. Parts of me understand this is all the vodka and the weed's fault, but my brain is so fried that I can't perform a task as simple as using the brake pedal to stop the car. Instead, I just keep driving until my hands become numb from holding the steering wheel.

I'm not clear on how or why I end up in front of Mikah's place. Some of my memories between when I left the charity thing and now are missing, but by the time I make it to his apartment, the effects of the weed have worn off a little. My head's still spinning, but my body is somewhat my own again, and I force it up the stairs using whatever strength is left in me.

My phone's in my car, but I don't even care if Mikah ever texted me back—I just need to see him one last time before he goes away. Things between us are still unresolved and we never talked about the sex or Dakota. We actually never talked about anything.

I ring the doorbell a few times and wait. I struggle to stand up straight, and my arms feel like they've been dipped in mercury.

Mikah opens the door and drags his gaze along the length of my body, stopping in the vicinity of my face.

"Were you just going to leave like this?" I toss my heavy as hell hands in the air and peek into his apartment. There's nothing inside except the couch and dozens of boxes.

"Are you high?" Mikah's eyes follow me as I saunter into the living room.

My blood is roaring in my ears as I turn around to face him. "Maybe."

He shuts the door, his gaze cutting back to me. "You can't just show up here whenever you feel like it, Alana."

"Why not? Do you have something to hide?"

He doesn't respond.

"Do you have something to hide?" My voice pitches as I approach him.

"I'm packing." He completely brushes off my question and shakes his head lightly.

"You fucking stood me up and I hate you!" I'm failing to keep a grip on my anger, and all the hurt I've been hiding inside for so long just pours out of me.

"I said I was sorry," he tells me, the mask of indifference never leaving his face.

"Are you sorry you slept with me too?"

The air around us turns thick. Mikah doesn't break eye contact. His jaw clenches and his face takes on a pained expression.

"Answer me," I demand, staring at him unblinkingly. My palm slams into his chest, but I must not hit him hard enough, because he doesn't move an inch.

"I'm not sorry we had sex, Alana," he murmurs. "I just don't think we should keep seeing each other. Like, as friends or otherwise. Not right now."

The words shock me. I feel the floor beneath me shifting. "Why?"

"*Why?!*" Mikah snaps and his eyes widen. "Because you only call or text when you need to feel like you're with *him*! Not with me! Never with me!"

My heart clenches.

"I'm not a fucking substitute. I have feelings. And if you're too blind to see past your perfect nose, then I don't want this"—he motions between us—"to keep going."

Everything he's saying slowly settles into my mind. "How am I supposed to know all these things if you never want to talk about it?!"

At this point, we're both screaming, our voices booming through the apartment like thunder.

"You never want to talk about it either!" Mikah's face pinches in frustration. "All you want to talk about is him!"

"We have to talk about him first!"

"Why? He's fucking dead!"

Tears pool in my eyes and Mikah's silhouette becomes a blur. "Because I don't have anyone else to talk to." My hand reaches for his chest and I'm not sure if I want to hurt him again or simply touch him. There's this stupid part of me that desperately wants his warmth, but I can't see or feel anything. My head's heavy and my heartbeat pulsing in my temples drowns out the rest of the noise.

Mikah's hand catches mine. "You can't just show up here and ask me to pretend I'm him for a few hours and then go on with your day. It doesn't work like that. It's all or nothing."

"I'm not asking you to pretend."

"You are."

"I'm not."

"Yes. You are. You're a fucking weirdo. You don't even see it when you do that shit."

Hearing this from him is like a punch in the gut, but I'm so pissed off and frustrated that I just tell him, "Fine!" I jerk my hand out of his grip and bolt for the door. "Go to hell!" The curtain of tears in my eyes makes everything inside the apartment look fuzzy, and I trip over a box on the way out.

I hear Mikah's footsteps thumping behind me as my fingers curl around the door handle. I jerk it open with every intention to leave, but he catches up with me. His palm slaps against the door and it bangs shut. He presses his chest to my back, his weight pushing me forward. Panic shoots down my spine like a lightning bolt. My breaths are loud and shallow, and I'm convinced that whatever Zeke gave me wasn't weed, because it's not relaxing at all. On the contrary, every part of me burns with annoyance and anger.

"You wanna talk?" Mikah's hand slides to my hip. His low voice is hoarse and uneven.

"Do you wanna know what I feel?" he continues.

I hold my breath; my heart's stuck in my throat.

"Do you want to know what it's like to always be second best, Alana?" His warm mouth lingers at my ear. "Do you remember that night you baked cupcakes in our apartment and I came home early?"

Panic crawls under my skin and into every single bone of my body. I close my eyes and press my cheek against the door in an attempt to hold in the scream that's forming in my lungs.

"I heard you that night." His whisper slides down my neck and strokes my shoulder. "I heard you with him and I wanted it to be me instead. For once, I wanted to be first because I was tired of him getting all the firsts. I wished he'd never been born, and now that he's dead, I wish it was me."

My heart drops to my stomach, all my emotions running rampant.

"I wish *I* was dead instead of him. For you." Mikah's fingers move into my hair and his mouth touches my cheek. "I would die for you...if that would make you happy again." His body draws tense.

Silent tears roll down my face as I swallow past the rock in my throat. His words are like knives, slicing right through my heart.

"Is that what you wanted to hear?" Mikah's lips feather across my skin.

That is absolutely *not* what I wanted to hear.

His heart drums inside his chest and feeling its low, hard thumps against my back is terrifying. It reminds me of us on the floor at The Crystal Room.

"Is that what you wanted to hear?" Mikah repeats quietly.

I spin around to face him, my chest aching from the assault of emotions. "You're sick," I say, unsure if that's what I really mean, but I don't know what else to call him. I don't know what else to call someone who wishes his own brother would have never been born. He tossed that idea into the universe and now Dakota's dead. "I hate you."

"Do you think I don't hate myself?" Mikah's gaze locks on mine.

The line on his forehead deepens. "Do you think I don't hate myself for wanting him gone? Do you think I don't hate myself for wanting his girlfriend?"

Heat hits my cheeks. I've been waiting for him to admit his feelings for me for what seems like an eternity, but this isn't how I imagined it. The urge to inflict some sort of pain on him for doing the same to me pushes me over the edge, and I slap him across the face.

Mikah doesn't react. "You think I don't want him back? He's my fucking blood." His voice grows loud. "No one wanted me. Ever. I was supposed to be dead. Not him."

My mind is in overdrive. Mikah's confession is suffocating me and I can't look at him right now. I have to turn everything over in my head once it has cleared.

"I need to leave," I force the words out and jerk the door handle. "I need to leave…"

He moves out of the way and I slip onto the staircase without looking at him or saying another word. The misty cool air stings my lungs, and my cheeks burn as my feet carry me to my car. I reach for my face, anticipating to feel glass and blood, but it's just rain and tears, and then I realize I'm not at The Crystal Room anymore and there's no one here with me.

It's almost four in the morning when I pull into the Tillers' driveway. My knuckles ache from clutching the steering wheel for so long and my breathing is out of control. The trees surrounding the house are trembling under the onslaught of the pouring rain, and the street looks a lot like a scene from one of those eighties slasher movies Dakota used to make me watch. I never understood why exactly he liked them, but I used any opportunity to cuddle with him. Being in his arms felt nice. *So did being in Mikah's.*

I shut off the engine and sink back into my seat to analyze every single minute I've spent with Mikah. I don't want to believe he truly wished Dakota gone. We say things we don't mean in the heat of the moment. Just like I told him I hated him earlier, but I don't. I don't, because his torment is a part of me. What I actually want is to make him feel better. To make him stop hurting.

I scrutinize every word and every touch, looking for signs I should have noticed before, but there aren't any. The fact that my need for him hasn't faltered scares me.

I scramble for my phone to dial Jess. I only noticed her pissed-off messages hours after I ran off from Mikah's place.

The line rings a few times and goes to her voicemail.

Closing my eyes, I try to breathe through another wave of panic.

A tiny fraction of me still questions Mikah's words, but the rest of me wants to erase tonight and get a do-over. A do-over where I'm not a high, raging bitch and where we're not saying the things we don't mean. Too bad real life doesn't work that way. There's no rewind option upon request.

The phone in my hand buzzes and I realize the call is from Jess. A strange feeling of relief floods me.

"Do you know what time it is?" she asks in a gravelly voice.

"Late."

"Exactly."

"I'm sorry I left without telling you."

"You didn't have to come if you didn't want to. I'm not forcing you to do anything."

"I really need to talk to someone." I whimper through small gasps.

"What's going on?" Panic drills through her tone.

"I don't know." I push down my anxiety.

"Where are you?"

"I'm outside your house."

"Okay. I'll be right there."

Jess's silhouette emerges from the door a short time later. She rushes to the Prius and slips in the passenger side. We sit quietly for several seconds.

I'm not sure where to begin. I just know I can't keep it in me anymore, because this secret and all the chaos that comes with it is asphyxiating. "I slept with Mikah."

Jess's face turns from annoyed to surprised. The shock slowly fills the air inside the car and we fall back into a spell of uncomfortable silence.

"You're not kidding, are you?" she finally asks. There's anguish in her voice.

"I think I have feelings for him." "Like" isn't the word I'd use, because at this moment, what I feel for Mikah is a mix of everything.

"What about him?" Jess's eyes sweep over my face. "Is it mutual?"

"Yes."

She sighs. "How long has this been going on?"

"We started talking after the funeral, and somewhere along the way, it just became more. Now I can't figure out how to stop feeling what I'm feeling for him. He drives me crazy because he never talks about Dakota or about what happened, and I keep forgiving him because I can't stomach my life without him anymore," I confess. "I just don't think we're right for each other."

"Why not?"

"My shoulders sag. "It's wrong."

"Do you want to be with him?" Jess questions, her tone softening.

I never imagined Mikah and me being more than what we are right now. I can't even figure out a name for us.

"I just want to stop feeling afraid, and being with him terrifies me."

"Why?"

"Because people are going to talk."

"Is that what you're scared of?" Jess turns to face me.

"I dated his brother."

"He's gone now. He would have wanted you to be happy. I know if I were to die, I'd want Luke to have someone who'd care about him. I believe you should do what makes you happy and not what people expect of you. If Mikah makes you happy, then you need to tell him that. I'll never judge you for your choices, whatever they are. Others probably will, which is fine. We're all going to turn into ash or dust one day, anyway. Those who judge and those who don't."

My stomach heaves and I swallow past the tightness filling my throat. "Do you think about it...about why we're here and others aren't?"

"Every single day."

My heart begins to pound. "Do you feel guilty?"

"Sometimes. Do you?"

"Yes. I don't understand why I'm alive and Dakota isn't."

I don't understand why God—if he even exists—did this. He ripped out twenty-four lives like they were unwanted weeds polluting a potato field.

"Come here." Jess leans forward and throws her hands around my neck to pull me into a hug. "Go home and get some sleep. We can talk about it tomorrow if you want."

Our embrace is long and reminds me of a time when things were simple. Before The Crystal Room. Before Dakota.

We say our goodbyes and Jess hurries back inside.

After a few long minutes of chasing my thoughts, I text Mikah. I need closure.

Tell me you didn't mean what you said about your brother.

Then I drive home.

My parents are fast asleep when I stumble into the house. They haven't been waiting up for me lately like they used to. Mostly because of the baking blog project, not because of any newly-found trust in me and my actions.

My soaked shoes leave a wet trail all across the living room and on the stairs as I make my way up to my room. I don't remember changing into my pajamas, but I do remember looking for Dakota's leather jacket in my closet. I remember falling asleep with it and my phone in my hand and waking up to an empty screen hours later.

My message to Mikah is still unread when I finally return to my senses at around two in the afternoon. My head is less fuzzy, and although my body's sore, at least it feels like my own.

A rush of panic hits me when I realize my shift at the bakery is about to begin. I hurry downstairs to start a fresh pot of coffee, and then I take a quick shower and dress in my work clothes. My Prius is still in our driveway with the dry mud splatters around its bumper and hood, but the sky has cleared a little and the rain has stopped.

I don't remember much of my shift at the bakery. It's just another workday full of complaints, screaming kids, and parents ready to have a nervous breakdown. By the time we close up, my head's a mess. Mikah hasn't bothered to read my text and the taste of defeat is beyond bitter. When I get in my car, I fish out the business card C.J. Barnes gave me a few weeks ago and dial his number.

"This is Alana Novak," I say in a shaky voice. "Are you still working on the story about Dakota Bennett?"

"Still am," he responds.

"I don't mind meeting."

"Sounds great. How about tomorrow?"

"Tomorrow's fine."

26. BEFORE

My parents never question where I'm going if they see me taking my camera and my folder with printouts from Pinterest. It's almost always a sign I'm headed to Jess's to bake something for my blog, which is considered a non-threatening activity.

Today, my father looks puzzled when instead of Jess's Nissan, there's a black 1969 Mustang waiting for me in the driveway. The blizzard last night added at least an inch or two of snow to the existing layer, turning our street into an all-white crystal realm, and Dakota's car is like a UFO that's landed in front of our house—not fitting in with this quiet, fantasy-like neighborhood. Its polished-to-perfection black body glimmers in the bright afternoon sunlight that's rare for this time of year, right outside our living room window.

My mother's in the kitchen, still in her church dress, unloading the dishwasher. The clanking of pots and silverware and the hum of the radio follows me to the front door.

"I'm going to Dakota's," I inform them, checking my bag again to make sure I have my notebook with the new recipes. "I'll be back late. Don't wait up."

My father straightens in his recliner and raises an eyebrow in question. Apparently, the talk we had on Thursday morning didn't make much of a difference.

"He's going to help me with my blog post," I say. "I'm trying six different frostings."

"What about dinner? Your mother's making a casserole."

"I'm fine, Dad. I've had mom's casserole a thousand times before." I force a smile. My mother's an amazing cook, but I already forfeited my sleep in order to make my parents happy by going to church with them. Even though getting up at eight in the morning after working a third shift isn't fun at all.

The sound of the doorbell rumbles through the downstairs.

My mother steps out of the kitchen and my father rises to his feet. In order to avoid a lengthy interrogation, I didn't promise them anything elaborate like an official dinner with Dakota, but the fact that my parents will only have two minutes to form their opinions about him makes me nervous.

When I swing the door open, Dakota stands tall and solid on our porch in his black coat, his silhouette drawn sharp against the white curtain of fine snow swirling in the air. He's wearing a beanie and his hair hangs messily over his cheeks.

"Hello." My father steps closer, eyeing up and down Dakota's body.

"Hi, Dakota." My mother follows my dad's lead and walks over to get a better look at my boyfriend.

"Hi." Dakota shows a dimpled smile to my parents. "Nice to meet you." He steps through the doorway and extends his hand, which my father shakes energetically.

I take advantage of the awkward pause that's so atypical for my parents and carry both of my bags out to the porch. Dakota follows me and grabs the bigger one, hoisting it over his shoulder.

"Alana says you're in a band?" My mother strikes up a conversation.

"Yes." Dakota tips his chin. "My brother and I have been playing together since middle school."

"What kind of music do you play?"

"It's a blend of melodic and gothic rock."

"Do you tour?" My father takes over.

"Locally. Yes."

"I see." He puts his hands in his pockets. "My daughter says you work at Cascade Locks."

"Yes sir. I do. Music doesn't pay my bills. Yet. Gotta make sure there's always some leverage while you're pursuing your dreams."

"Right. Good thinking. Always have a backup plan."

When my parents are done with the questions, we say our good-byes and load into Dakota's car.

My heart's still on edge, so I take a second to catch my breath and process everything while Dakota starts the engine.

"I think it went well." Dakota's words interrupt my thoughts, and he glances at me.

"I think so too," I agree, my gaze holding his. The cold air colors his cheeks, and the snowflakes on top of his beanie and across his shoulders are starting to melt away. He looks tempting and I can't help myself. I lean over and press my lips to his. It's a glimpse of a kiss, quick and innocent, not meant for my parents. Although they probably can't see anything through the snow, anyway.

"Are you ready for my baking lesson?" I ask, sitting back up in my seat.

"Hell yeah." He nods, and a grin spreads across his face.

We sit in Dakota's kitchen, tired and sweaty. My printouts from Pinterest are covering all the surfaces that aren't occupied by pans and trays with my creations. There are tons of dirty dishes to be cleaned, but after four hours of teaching my boyfriend how to make perfect cupcakes, I'm feeling exhausted. I blame my dying spirit mostly on my lack of sleep and two super busy shifts at Toro Bravo this weekend. Being in training sucks.

Dakota's playing around with my camera and he looks adorable in his black HIM t-shirt with white patches of flour in his hair and on his face.

"I think this one's the money shot," he says, handing me my Nikon.

I look at the preview of the image with a trained eye and give him my verdict. "This isn't the best angle."

"Why not? Look at all that frosting." He rises from his chair and stretches his body over the table to see it from my point of view.

"Yes, but it's not just about the frosting. You want to make sure you get the entire structure since it's a three-tier cupcake stand," I explain. "People need to be able to see all of it in the photo."

"Okay, cupcake master. Whatever you say." A smirk touches the corner of his mouth.

"It's basic marketing."

"Really?"

"I've been doing this for a while." I smile at him. "You never know. Maybe one day I'll open my own bakery."

"Allow me." He takes the camera from me and fiddles with the settings. Then he says, "Come here," and pulls me into a hug.

"What are you doing?" I ask, watching him thrust my Nikon into the air.

"Taking a selfie." He angles the camera so that the lens is facing us and presses the shutter release button a few times.

When he's finished, we flip through the photos together. They're funny—our faces are scrunched up and we both have messy hair—but I love them.

"I think you'd make a great baker." Dakota aims a mysterious smile at me, putting the camera aside. "A very hot one too."

Heat rushes to my cheeks. His compliments stir things inside me. "I may need some help."

"I might know a guy who'd want the job if he fails to get a record deal."

"Maybe I'll take him up on his offer." My voice trails off and my mind snaps back into the vicious circle of what my life actually is. Not my imaginary life where I bake cupcakes for a living and Dakota plays stadiums but where I'm just a freshman and he's just a guy who's doing his best to get his local band signed with any small label ready to take a chance on his music.

"Did you already find a place to stay in Seattle?" I ask.

"Mikah knows a couple of people in the area."

"Are you excited?"

"I'm fucking high." Dakota laughs, settling into his chair. "It's a thousand-person-capacity venue. I know it'll be half-empty during our set, but it's way better exposure than we get here." His eyes take on a spark as he continues to explain why these February Seattle dates are so important for Midnight Rust. Apparently, Eric, the band's new manager, has some connections that could lead to a record deal. Some things are still in the air, but they're booking additional dates outside of Portland for almost every weekend in February and March.

It's breathtaking to watch him talk about plans for the band, even though it makes me feel left behind.

"I'm not going to see you at all when you get a deal." I sigh. There'll be a gazillion girls chasing him if he becomes famous and, somehow, I don't doubt that he will. He's too good for a local club. Too talented. Too beautiful. A visionary.

"You will. I'll take you with me."

My brain latches on to his words like they're a lifeline. Going on tour with him sounds terrifyingly romantic—in a rock'n'roll kind of way. "My parents will never let me."

Dakota leans back in his chair and studies my face. "Why don't they trust you?"

His question hangs in the air. I take a few moments to consider my answer, but there's not one that would really explain exactly how my family operates.

"Maybe they're scared I'm not mature enough to make life decisions," I mutter.

"I don't believe that's true. You're with me. That's the best decision you've ever made." A cocky smile touches his lips. I like how charmingly full of himself he can be sometimes. "I also think you're more mature than most girls your age."

"How do you know?"

"I've dated some." He pauses.

My curiosity's piqued. I want to know things I probably have no business knowing, simply because it concerns him, and everything that concerns him, intrigues me. "Have there been many?"

"It doesn't matter." Dakota shakes his head, getting to his feet and reaching out for me.

"Why not?" I retort.

"Because now I'm with you." He pulls me up from my chair and snakes his arms around my waist. "And I don't want this—us—to ever end."

Heat surges between my legs and my knees weaken. I put my hands behind his neck and study the patches of flour dusting his left cheek.

Dakota pulls me closer and brushes a stray hair off my forehead. His lips linger on my mouth, taunting me. Taking it slow, we savor each stroke of our tongues, each exchange of breath.

This level of intimacy between us—where his every moan echoes mine—is out of this world unbelievable. All-consuming and magical.

"I think we need a break from cooking," Dakota rasps against my mouth, his fingers fumbling with the ties of my apron around my back.

"What about the dishes?" I rub my thumb over the flour spot on his cheek.

"The dishes can wait." He smirks, dragging his lips down the side of my face. "You've got some flour on you too." His mouth moves to my neck and he kisses it gently, pushing me against the counter. I hear the clanking of dishes behind me as he tries to rid me of my apron.

The feel of his body pressed to mine drives me crazy, every inch of him sizzling hot. All I've fantasized about the last three days is our first time. Imagining and wondering what it would feel like to be with him.

"I want to make love to you," he whispers in my ear, cradling my head.

My heart stills and my legs quiver. I'm not sure what to say to that except yes, but I can't quite manage to articulate it correctly. All that comes out is a strained gasp.

"I've wanted to since the very first time I saw you," Dakota confesses. "I've wondered how you'd feel." He moves his palm along my side and down to my hip bone, tugging on the bottom of my shirt that's tucked into my skinny jeans. "I've wondered how you'd taste, and I've wondered how you'd sound when I'm inside you."

I swallow past the lump in my throat as my head starts to spin.

"Have you ever wondered about me?" Dakota asks. "How I'd feel?"

"Yes." I nod, running my hands over his shoulders and chest. "I have. I've wondered a lot."

He slips his arms around me to cup my ass, and when he lifts me up, I wrap my legs around him like it's the most natural thing to do. There's an ache deep inside me, an ache he creates in me every time we touch, and I want to make it stop.

"You're so fucking beautiful. You have no idea." His voice burns with temptation. "You're so fucking perfect. I don't know how I got so goddamned lucky."

He spins around and maneuvers us through the kitchen and down the hall into his bedroom. Our entwined bodies tumble onto his bed and we kiss until there's no more air in our lungs. His hands and his lips are everywhere—on my face, on my chest, on my stomach. The feel of him on top of me, exquisitely heavy and dominant, makes me tingle with anticipation.

I run my fingers down to his stomach and when I pull on the edge of his t-shirt, he breaks away from me and sits back, straddling my hips. His gaze slides down to the place where our bodies connect, the tip of his tongue tracing his lips.

"I want to see you," I say, moving my hands up his thighs, the denim rough against my skin.

"You don't have to ask twice." Dakota smiles, pulling his t-shirt over his head.

I need a second to let the sight of him naked sink in. His chest is broad and carved with precise perfection, each lean muscle defined like a work of art. I place my palm on the small hummingbird tattoo right under the left side of his ribcage and return his smile. "You really like hummingbirds, don't you?" My fingers stroke the inked skin.

"They're peace," he says. "In my next life, I want to be one." His eyes brighten.

"Do you believe you can choose what you can be after you die?"

"Right now, I want to be with you, Moonchild." He brushes his thumb over my bottom lip.

"Can I ask you a favor?"

"Anything."

"Will you turn on the hummingbirds?"

A smile tugs at the corner of his mouth. He slides from the bed and hurries to the switch panel. Seconds later, lights litter the ceiling above my head.

"Do you like it?" Dakota murmurs, returning to me.

I nod and rub my palms over his flat stomach. He reaches for my shirt to unbutton it and I let him. I let him undress me and I let him touch me where no one has ever touched me before. I let *him* carry me into the realm of sweet and sinful insanity.

We get rid of the rest of our clothes and explore each other unhurriedly.

His hand slips to my thighs and his fingers start rubbing circles around my clit, floating over me slickly and delicately, like water, as his mouth moves over every inch of me. Beginning at my neck, it slowly makes its way to my stomach, drawing out all my secrets.

When he kisses me between my legs, I'm uneasy at first, but the feel of his soft lips against my center makes me forget all about my nerves. Then his tongue flicks at my swollen spot and I can't contain a loud moan. His breath is hot and ticklish and his mouth is wicked, and I grab at the blankets, twisting the fabric, because the onslaught of new sensations is overwhelming.

"God, you sound perfect," Dakota whispers against my inner thigh, his lips lingering on my tender flesh, taunting me. His velvety voice vibrates against my skin. "I want to play you all night long."

"Please," I breathe out, tangling my hands in his hair. It's silky to the touch and I love the twinges it causes when the tips of it brush over my stomach

"Did that feel good?" Dakota rasps, moving up until his face hovers above mine as his fingertips trace the lines of my chin and neck.

"There are no words. It feels incredible to be with you," I tell him.

There's a pool of wetness between my legs and my heart's pounding like a drum. I'm nervous again, and I can't seem to catch my breath.

Dakota lowers himself onto me, our chests pressed together, our heartbeats shadowing each other's. He runs his palm over my hip and down my leg and hisses through his teeth. "God, I want to get lost in your body so badly."

"I'm not stopping you," I say, braving a small smile, but the truth is, I have no clue what to do to make him enjoy it. I almost asked Jess but ended up googling stuff, and now my brain has conveniently forgotten all the useful info.

"I'm so fucking gone for you." Dakota laughs against my cheek and reaches out for the bedside drawer to grab a condom.

I still under his gaze as he rips open the package and rolls it down his erection.

"I promise I'll be careful," he says, settling back between my legs. His body looks perfect on top of me. Stunning and tempting.

"Okay." A light tremor rushes through me, and I can feel a wave of panic brewing deep in my gut.

"Don't be scared," Dakota murmurs, palming my cheek. "Just relax." His voice caresses my face.

He enters me gently, the weight of him holding me in place, filling me slowly until he comes to my barrier.

"Are you okay?" he asks.

"Yes. I am. I really want this," I tell him.

He gives me a slight smile, and then he kisses me with everything he has as he pushes firmly yet carefully against my resistance until he's all the way in.

It's everything and nothing I thought it would be like. The pain is excruciating, more than I ever could have imagined. It's almost too much to take, and I can't make up my mind whether I hate becoming a woman or love it.

"Are you okay?" Dakota asks again, nuzzling the side of my face.

"Yes." I nod, sinking my teeth into my lower lip to subdue the sob clogging my throat. Every bit of me trembles with agony. My vision blurs and my heart leaps into my throat as I try to breathe through it.

His lashes sweep over my cheek as he closes his eyes and kisses the corner of my mouth. "You're so good."

I clutch his sweaty neck and pull him against me. Then he tenses as he draws back and slides in again, allowing me to adjust to his size. His breaths are heavy and loud, his pulse racing. He's so amazingly beautiful—I've never seen him this exposed before.

"God, you feel so fine." He groans, rocking into me with strokes that are measured and calculated. His hips roll against mine slowly, creating a perfect rhythm that continues until strange waves of desire begin to surge through me. It still hurts, but it's a hurt I can take.

"Here," Dakota utters, grasping my thighs and spreading them wider as our bodies start to move together. Our moans loud, our chests heave as he thrusts faster and faster. It's somewhat chaotic and I'm still nervous, but I like it. I like hearing him get to that point where he loses his breath for me. I like the feel of his every muscle growing tight when he shudders and stills. I like that I'm the one who makes him feel the way a man does when he comes. His release is sweet and wild. His body, slick with sweat, goes limp on top of mine, and we lie there for what seems like forever, panting and worn out.

"It gets better, beautiful," Dakota whispers in my ear, pulling out of me. "I promise."

I'm shaken up and my heart refuses to calm down. It feels like there's a bleeding wound between my legs, and I'm scared to move because it hurts.

He rolls onto his side and tosses the condom into the trash can by his bed. "Are you okay?" His fingers skim over the curve of my breast.

"Yes," I whimper, my eyes darting around to see if there's anything I can cover myself with.

There's a long pause where he just stares at me, his eyes shining with something new. Finally, he asks, "Do you want to take a shower?"

"Yes," I say. "I'd like that."

"Okay." He slides from the bed and goes to his closet to grab a towel.

My gaze follows his silhouette through the dark the room, studying his movements. His body is fit and elegant, as if it were made for sex, and I have no idea why he chose to have it with me.

The first thing I see when I step out into the hallway is a streak of light spilling from under the door of Mikah's room. A mixture of panic and shame rushes through me because we left the kitchen a mess, but what actually bothers me is the fact that he might have heard us.

Having another guy listen to me losing my virginity is not how I envisioned my first time with Dakota going. The idea of it makes me a little sick.

Clutching the edges of the towel that's wrapped around me, I tiptoe into the bathroom and nervously shut the door. My chest is heavy and I can't seem to catch my breath. My brain's still processing everything that just happen between Dakota and me. There's a twister of different emotions raging inside my head right now, and each one is fighting to be in the lead.

I turn on the faucet and splash cold water over my face, wondering if my parents will be able to tell a difference, but when I look in the mirror, my eyes look the same. They're big and brown with mascara smudged underneath. But that can be easily fixed. There's nothing in them hinting at my not being a virgin anymore. My mouth's still swollen from all the kissing, but that'll go away by the time I get home. There's a tiny red spot right above my collarbone from where Dakota's lip got carried away, but that won't be visible either.

My gaze darts from the mirror to the shower stall and back. I stand like that, motionless, soaking up all the new feelings possessing me, until a faint knock on the door drags me out of my daze.

"Alana?" Dakota's hushed voice calls from the hallway. "Is everything okay?"

"Yeah...yeah..." I clench at my towel harder.

"I brought you a t-shirt."

After a brief moment of hesitation, I go to the door and unlock it. He slips into the bathroom and hands me one of his oversized band t-shirts. "Are you okay?" There's concern in his gaze.

"Yes." I nod.

"Are you sure?" He shuts the door and reaches for my shoulders; his palms slide up to my neck and cradle my face. "Does it hurt that much?"

My heart drops to my stomach when I feel sticky wetness sliding down my inner thigh.

"No, no." I shake my head nervously, fisting the towel. "I'm fine. I'll be right out."

Maybe it's my eyes that give away my panic, or maybe Dakota's just that good at reading me. He scoops me into his arms and I rest my head on his chest. "What's wrong, Moonchild?"

I'm not sure if this is the reassurance I needed, but it feels nice—his warm body against mine, his gentle hands in my hair, and his soft lips on my forehead.

"It's just very overwhelming," I confess, wrapping my arms around his torso.

"My first time wasn't that great either. It's okay. It takes practice." He laughs a little, tightening his grip.

"I think I'm bleeding," I say quietly, feeling uneasy. "I need to take a shower."

"What a coincidence. I need a shower too."

"Are you going to get mad if I ask you to take me home after?" I ask tentatively.

"No, but I'll be sad."

"I don't want my parents questioning me about tonight."

"I barely got to have you and you're already running away from me, Moonchild." He sinks both hands into my hair.

"I'm not running."

"I know you're not." He gives me a dimpled smile.

After we take a shower and get dressed, we clean up the kitchen. Then I pack up some of the smaller things I brought with me, and Dakota drives me home.

My mind's still racing long after he's gone, and I decide to sort all the cupcake photos from today. The selfies he took of us in the kitchen go out to him at around five in the morning. Once the email is sent, I close my laptop and go to sleep.

***

Later that morning, I wake up to a throbbing pain between my legs and a bunch of Instagram notifications.

My phone's clutched in my hands and my heart's pounding, and I spend a good minute following a stray ray of light as it dances across my desk, because going downstairs terrifies me.

Parts of me still struggle with the fact I'm not a virgin anymore, and there's a dash of guilt lurking somewhere deep inside, but parts of me are happy we did it, because the wait was killing me.

I open my Instagram to see what's causing this sudden surge of likes and follows. Surely, people don't care about my photos of cupcakes.

My gaze scrolls down to the tag from six this morning that prompted the long string of notifications and I realize it came from Dakota's account. My heart jumps into my throat—the fact that he tagged me in his Instagram post hours after we had sex for the first time makes me feel a bit weird.

I click on the thumbnail and stare at the post. Dakota uploaded one of the selfies he took in the kitchen last night of our smiling faces next to each other, flour and all.

My insecurities come crashing in on me like a tidal wave. We've never posted any photos of us on social media and I'm not sure how to feel about it yet. My gaze drops to the bottom of the post to look at the caption. There's nothing there except for a bright red heart emoji. Emotions jam my chest.

Ignoring the comments, I close the app and dial Jess.

"Are you avoiding me?" Her tone is far from sweet. She's like my mother, my second mother who gets mad if I don't tell her all my dirty secrets.

I don't give her any sort of a warning. I just need to get this out. "We had sex."

"Oh...shit." Jess pauses. "Are you okay? You don't sound okay."

"I don't know," I confess. "It's odd. It was good until, you know... the important part."

"Did he go down on you before the important part?"

"Yes."

"Did you use a condom?"

"Yes."

"Okay, then you're fine, babe."

"I just feel so confused right now." I lower my voice. "Like there was something wrong with me because it didn't really happen at the end like it was supposed to."

"You didn't come. Is that what you mean?" I hear a sigh on the line.

"Girl, you can't expect your first time to be like in the books. It fucking hurts and it's not all that great until you try it a few more times. Practice makes perfect. I told you that."

"Yes."

"He's not some magician who knows what buttons to press right off the bat to make you orgasm every five seconds, but if he got you ready and didn't just stick it in, you're already ahead of the game. You'll get the hang of it."

I giggle at her choice of words.

"What are you laughing at?" she asks. "Always make sure he follows the checklist. First oral, then condom. If he's skipping at least one, he's a selfish prick in bed. Oh, and bonus points when he's not insisting on a blowjob if you're not offering."

"No, he didn't just stick it in and he didn't insist on a blowjob." I continue to laugh.

"I'm telling you. Some guys are like that. They don't care about your V-card. They just want to fuck you like you're a bag of potatoes. Austin was like that. Asshole never gave me oral. Not once."

My cheeks start to burn. Jess tends to get very explicit with her explanations at times, but she's never told me any of these details about her first boyfriend. Maybe because he was such a huge disappointment. She was fifteen when she lost her virginity and he was seventeen. They dated for about a month and then went their separate ways. I'm not even sure she's still friends with him on Facebook or has his number.

"He posted a photo of us on his Instagram at six this morning," I say.

"Really?" Jess cheers up.

"Yeah."

"I'm telling you he's in love up to his ears. You should call him."

"You think?"

"Yes. I think. And talk sexy."

"Okay."

"Okay, bye."

As soon as she ends the call, I dial Dakota's number.

His voice is sleepy and rough. "Hey, you."

"I'm sorry. I didn't mean to wake you up."

"No, it's fine." I hear him taking a long, deep breath and the sound of it stirs everything in me. "I need to get up anyway."

"I just wanted to hear your voice."

"Oh yeah?" He perks up.

"Yeah."

"How are you feeling?"

"I'm a little sore," I confess, thinking that a nice bath would probably help me feel better.

"I'm sorry, Moonchild."

"It's okay."

"Can I see you tonight?" There's longing in his voice.

"I still have to get the rest of my baking supplies from your place. Remember?"

"Yeah, I remember. Pick you up at six?"

"Six sounds good."

The moment I end the call, a new wave of emotions floods me. They're raw and confusing, and I believe I might be in love.

I have no idea what I'm doing anymore.

I must have still been high when I called C.J., because now, after mulling over Jess's words and everything that Mikah said to me the other night, I feel like I'm about to sell Dakota's memory, along with my soul, to the devil.

"Alana?" someone calls to me over the noise of the coffee shop patio.

I jerk at the sound and look away from my phone.

C.J.'s face comes into view. "May I?" He gestures at the chair across from me.

"Sure." I nod. My eyes slide to his hands first, then inspect his pockets. It doesn't look like he's carrying anything, at least nothing that might be a gun. Although I already determined he's harmless. I googled him last night after I got home. He's written a lot of articles. Why would he want to jeopardize his career now?

"Thank you for agreeing to meet me." C.J. sits down and his gaze lands on my face.

"Just so we're clear," I say quietly, picking at the corner of the napkin lying in front of me on the table. "I'm not here to talk about

Dakota just yet. I want to know more about what you're doing before I decide."

The truth is, there's this restless part of me that wants to spill everything, from Dakota's favorite band to the size of his underwear, because his own brother won't talk to me, but the rest of me understands it's not my place.

"Of course." C.J. puts on a small smile.

The second he begins to speak, my phone rattles against the table and I make the mistake of looking at it. Mikah's name on the screen sends my heart into a tailspin. I can tell from the preview that the message is long, and because Mikah's known for sending me nothing longer than two words at a time, it leads me to believe it's important.

"I'm sorry," I interrupt C.J.'s speech and tip my head toward my phone. "Do you mind?"

He gives me a voiceless nod.

My gaze flicks back to the screen and I open the text message. The letters in front of me begin to blur as I read. I feel the blood slowly draining from my face and my cheeks become numb.

"Would you like something to drink?" C.J. asks, the street noises muffling his words.

"I need to use the restroom," I mumble, grabbing my purse.

His eyes are wide with panic as he watches me getting to my feet.

I rush away from the patio like my feet are on fire and read the message from Mikah again once I'm in the parking lot.

I need you to know this. I miss my brother. He didn't deserve to die and if I could trade places with him, I would do it in a heartbeat. For him and for you.

I don't want you to be mad at me for leaving. But please understand that I had to. I needed to think about everything I said the other night away from you because looking at you makes me lose my mind. I stand by my words. I don't want you to seek me out if you can't fully commit to being with me...really with me. Only with me. I know this may be too much to ask, but I also know that if I can't have you the way he did—unconditionally—I don't want to struggle to live up to his legacy. So it's best we just say goodbye.

P.S. You can keep the hummingbirds. He would have wanted them with you.

The shock of the revelation makes all my emotions go haywire. I stand in the middle of the parking lot with my heart on the ground and my vision failing me until an obnoxious honking scatters the fuzziness in my head.

Hummingbirds? I don't have the hummingbirds.

Stepping out of the way, I look at my phone again, my heart beating harder and faster. Mikah has never said this much to me before. These words are miserable and disturbing and they stay with me like a mean shadow as I drive home, scrambling with my thoughts, which are a huge mess of Dakota's memories that range from insignificant to very important.

When I get to my house, I check our porch.

"Mom?" I rush inside, my eyes scanning the living room.

"What's wrong, sweetheart?" she calls out over the clanking of the dishes and the hum of the radio.

"Where's Dad?" I ask, walking into the kitchen, where there's a big box on the counter with a shipping label on it.

"He's in the back yard." My mother stops slicing turkey and motions at the window above the sink. "A package came for you." Her gaze follows me as I hurry to open the box.

My heart thunders like a caged animal as my hands rip at the top. Holding my breath, I begin to dig through the multiple layers of tissue paper. There, underneath all the packing material, are Dakota's hummingbirds.

"What is this?" my mother steps closer and asks over my shoulder.

Excitement swirls in my stomach. "Watch." I pull out one of the drawers to look for a small extension cord. "They're lights."

After we untangle all the hummingbirds, we lay the strand out on the counter, and I plug them into the outlet.

My mother's face takes on a strange expression. She seems surprised. "Well, this is pretty. Who sent you these?"

"Mikah." I brush my fingertips over the flickering birds.

"Did he now?" Concern hits her voice. "That was nice of him."

"Mom, I need to go somewhere for a couple of days."

"A couple of days?" She gasps, her eyes shifting to me. "Why so sudden? Who are you going with? Where to?" My mother throws a bunch of questions at me like a ball feeding machine as her mouth screws up in confusion.

"Seattle."

"What about work?"

"I'm not on the schedule until Sunday."

"What are you going to do in Seattle?"

"I need to see someone..." There's a rock in my throat. I don't know how to explain to her what I feel. I don't even know *what* exactly I feel toward Mikah. It's such a strong pull, a warped hold he has on me. What I do know is that I need to see him.

My mother takes a slow, measured breath. "This is probably best to discuss with your father around."

Anxiety begins to crush my spirits. I unplug the lights and hurry to put them into the box. "You don't get it, Mom. You never get it. You can't keep me here forever like I'm some pet."

"Honey. What are you talking about? You're not a pet." My mother's hand rests on my shoulder. "This is just so sudden. There's nothing wrong with taking a trip, but you haven't even packed. And you can't go without any planning."

I grab the box from the counter and rush to my room. To do both —the planning and the packing. My mind is spinning and my hands won't stop trembling as I stuff my clothes and an extra pair of shoes into one of my larger bags. I'm not sure why exactly I need nice shoes since this isn't prom we're talking about, but I suppose if a girl makes all this effort to chase down a guy in another state, showing up in front of him in a pair of worn-out sneakers may lose her some points.

After gathering all the trip essentials, I walk over to my nightstand and pull out the bedside drawer. Inside, there's a small velvet box with Dakota's hummingbird. I haven't worn the necklace since he died and part of me wonders if I should, but after staring at it for a good minute, I shut the drawer and move to my desk.

I open my laptop and type Mikah's name into the Google search bar. My palms begin to sweat when the results pop up on the screen, one by one. Stalking a guy I slept with feels weird, but what are the chances he'll actually want to speak to me after the screamfest we had in his apartment?

I click on the first link and stare at a dark flyer promoting Mikah's upcoming performances in Seattle. The image is moody, just like him. There's a tiny splash of light streaming across his face, and the only reason I can tell the photo is recent is from the faint line above the bridge of his nose that wasn't so pronounced before the attack.

Fifteen minutes later when I go back downstairs, my father and mother are in the living room waiting for me, their features pinched with distress.

"I'll be home in two days," I say, strolling to the front door as if I'm just going to another shift at the bakery, my heart hammering.

"You can't drive the Prius to Seattle." My father shakes his head.

I roll my eyes. "Watch me." My fist tightens around my car keys.

"Thomas." My mother rests her hand on his shoulder as if she's trying to hypnotize him. They rarely touch each other anymore, and it's bizarre to see this as their new method of communicating.

My father's gaze hardens. I can tell he's conflicted about the words that are going to come out of his mouth next.

"Why don't you trust me, Dad?" I ask, clutching at my bag and my laptop for dear life. "Why don't you want me to be happy? Why can't you let me do anything?"

"You're not well, Alana," he says, his voice quieter than usual.

"Maybe this is what I need to do to get well." My self-control begins to fail me. "Stop treating me like a child."

"Nobody's treating you like a child, sweetheart," my mother adds.

"Both of you do. Please let me figure out my life on my own. I'm trying to make sense of everything. I'm trying to understand where I fit in now and where to go from here, and all you do is keep putting a spoke in my wheel."

I don't bother to wait for their response, because emotions begin to clog my chest and I realize that if I don't leave now, it'll turn into another fight. I walk out the front door and my father catches up with me when I'm setting my laptop and my bag on the passenger seat. He grabs the door of the Prius and asks, "Do you have money?"

"What?" Puzzled, I blink at him rapidly.

"Do you have money for gas and a hotel?" he repeats the question. *Who is this man and what has he done with my father?*

"Yes," I squeak out. "I got paid last Friday."

"Okay." He lets out a heavy sigh. "I don't approve of this, but I don't want you to drive the Prius. You can take the Subaru under one condition."

My chest swells with clashing emotions—I never expected anything of this sort from my father.

"You need to text us at least every eight hours or before you go to sleep so that we know you're okay." He hands me his car keys. "That's non-negotiable."

I nod. "Sure."

My mother's silhouette lingers on the porch. Then she rushes over and shoves a few bills at me. "Just in case."

My gaze bounces between my parents and the Subaru keys and money in my hands. Tears begin to sting my eyes.

"Don't forget to fill up with gas before you get on the interstate." My father's gloomy voice hums in my head.

"Okay. I won't forget." I push the words out and throw my arms in the air searching for a hug and he reciprocates. I forgot how warm and safe my father's embrace was. I forgot how much I missed it.

28. AFTER

My heart begins to dance when I hit the Seattle city limits. The digital clock on the dashboard shows seven and the sun bleeding into the skyscraper-studded horizon is bright orange and furious.

I only stopped once near Chehalis to fill up the Subaru and use the restroom, and part of me regrets not planning this trip better. I want to at least take a shower before going to see Mikah, but deep down, I know a shower won't make a difference. The words will. That's why it's important I say the right ones. Luckily, three hours on an open road has given me some new perspective on things.

While I was at the gas station, I smoked a couple of cigarettes, sent my parents a mandatory check-in message, and googled a few hotels near the club where Mikah's scheduled to play his show tonight. Most places were charging an arm and a leg, and I almost changed my mind and decided to look for something outside downtown, but the idea of getting into a car again only fed my anxiety.

My parents once took me to Seattle to see the Space Needle, and although my childhood memories of that trip are vague, they're mostly bright and happy. The brooding city I'm driving through right now is nothing like the one I remember visiting. This city is dark and loud with sleek-looking buildings scraping the cloudy sky. The traffic is nerve-racking and the roads are insane. They're like rollercoasters, twisting and bending when you least expect it. Unlike Portland, people here seem to be in a hurry. The air is thick with urgency, and I wonder if it's because it's the weekend or if this is a typical Seattle night.

I can almost understand why Mikah would want to leave so badly. He'd fit in better here. He'd be a perfect addition to this mega puzzle.

At close to eight, I pull up to the hotel I randomly picked from my list. My panic is in full swing because, according to the venue's website, Mikah's set is scheduled to start at nine and he only plays for thirty minutes.

I rush to the check-in desk, fill out the paperwork, and get a room for two days, which pretty much eats my whole bakery paycheck.

At quarter to nine, I exit the hotel, showered and determined, in my light pink sundress and leather jacket. The air smells odd—exhaust fumes and summer rain. My eyes dart from the map on my phone to the long line of streetlights illuminating the busy sidewalk. Anxiety doesn't really begin to mess with my head until the marquee of the club across the street enters my line of vision as I reach the intersection that's humming with nightlife. Seeing Mikah's name flickering above the heads of people crowding the entrance sends cold shivers down my spine. I stiffen and stop for a second to regain my composure.

What if someone brings a gun?

Bang! Bang!

"You need a ticket?" A voice drags me out of my panic-infused daze, and I shift my gaze from the marquee to the person who's attempting to talk to me. He's older with a thin face and jumpy eyes, and his smile doesn't strike me as sincere.

"No, I'm fine." I draw a deep breath.

"Half-price." The guy tries again, motioning at the club.

"No, thank you."

"All right. Your loss, beautiful." He switches his attention to the couple standing to my left.

When the light changes, I cross the street and walk up to the line forming in front of the ticket window. My hands begin to shake and a surge of terror pings in my chest. The voices around me are distorted and unsettling, and the fear of going into a new place is bigger than ever.

After getting my wristband, I step aside to smoke a cigarette, but the high of the nicotine only lasts a few minutes. As soon as I get inside, panic ties my gut into a throbbing knot. The club is tiny and far from full. Small groups are scattered all over the main floor, and there's plenty of room near the stage, but I choose a spot in the middle. I don't want him to see me just yet.

The noise-filled darkness makes my heart go haywire. My gaze jumps from one person to another, scanning their jackets and hands, and then it flicks to the lonely guitar on stage. I fix my mind on the soft music playing in the background and try not to let panic ruin my evening.

A short time later, the lights in the club dim down and the whispers of anticipation disperse into the heavy air.

My anxiety has twisted up all my senses, and I'm not sure how to feel when Mikah's silhouette appears on stage. A few shy claps roll through the curious crowd as he walks over to the microphone and picks up his guitar. Under the spotlight, I can see that he's wearing a plain black t-shirt and a pair of faded jeans, and his hair falls loosely across his broad shoulders. The simplicity stirs me and my eyes devour every little detail, every move, every smirk, every blink. Every strum of the chord and every breath.

I'm in a daze as I watch him play and sing. His voice is a fine blend of tenor and baritone and is a perfect match to his acoustic guitar, the fusion of them bleeding across the room like oxygen. It's refreshing. It fills my cells with a strange buzz.

When the first song comes to an end, there's a wave of enthusiastic cheers, and a young man with a cell phone plunges to the front to record.

My chest swells with pride. I stand in my spot and listen to the music he's written until the very end of his set. I don't care that my legs are tired and my back hurts after the three-hour drive. He's devastating and stunning and I'm scared to move, because his songs have given me a moment of balance between all my worries and hurt, and I want to make this slice of peace in my heart last just a bit longer.

Mikah shifts on his stool and adjusts the microphone. "Thank you all." He slowly runs his palm across the scratched wood of the guitar body and clears his throat. "It means a lot to me that you came out to see me play. I have one more song left. I've never performed it live before, but I rehearsed the hell out of it yesterday." A faint smile tugs the corner of his mouth and laughter rumbles through the audience.

Mikah pauses, then his eyes slowly scan the crowd, and the lines in his forehead deepen. "A few months ago, I lost my brother." There's sadness in his tone. The whispers die and the silence is practically absolute. "We had a band and we made music together, and I didn't actually think I was going to do solo stuff at that time." Mikah's expression looks troubled. "My brother wrote amazing lyrics. I don't believe I'll ever be anywhere near his level so...this song I'm going to play isn't mine..." His voice trembles and I can see him losing himself in the speech. "I found these lyrics after he died and I wrote some chords. But it's really his song. It's called 'Moonchild.'"

I feel the blood draining from my face and a flash of panic burns my stomach. I'm not sure I'm ready to hear this, but I stand in my spot, motionless, waiting for the music to hit me, and when it finally does, my defenses crumble. The tears sliding down my cheeks are hot and unstoppable. My heart hammers so loudly that Mikah's words become muffled and I try to make out the lyrics, but the music cuts me raw, tearing my heart out. Every nerve ending in my body throbs with the torment of loss, and every inch of me burns with the need to hold Mikah close.

When the song ends and people begin to clap, he sets his guitar aside and shakes a few hands that are thrust at him from the front row. His expression is twisted with pain and there's a sheen of sweat covering his forehead. I've never seen him this nervous before.

I don't know if he realizes it's me when our gazes collide above the crowd, but my stupid heart jolts into a sprint and I bolt for the exit. The air outside is hot and misty, and a fine drizzle has already covered the asphalt. I have to stop in the middle of the buzzing sidewalk to calm my breathing. That's when Mikah's voice catches up with me.

"Alana?" he calls over the clamor of the city.

I turn around and see him hurrying in my direction, his gaze narrowing in on me as he pushes past a group of people near the club entrance.

"What are you doing here?" His face shows a mix of emotions, including shock, disbelief, and confusion.

A loud sigh rushes out of my mouth and the words bounce between us through the June mist. "I just wanted to see you."

Mikah slowly shakes his head, his eyes locking on mine. "You have this ridiculous habit of showing up without an invitation."

"I'm sorry." I smile meekly. The sound of my heartbeat booms in my ears. "I had to see you. I didn't like the way we parted. I was drunk and high... And we said a lot of really hurtful things to each other." I pause to get some more air in my lungs and realize people are looking at us. "I needed to see you."

"And you drove all the way here?" He stops right in front of me and raises an eyebrow in question.

"Yes." I nod staring up at him. The hazy glow of the streetlights dances across his stubbled cheeks. "I drove my dad's car." Although that detail probably isn't important.

"You drove your dad's car?" Mikah repeats after me, his Marlboro breath tickling my nostrils. His hand reaches for my cheek and the pads of his fingers brush across the wet trail.

"Uh huh." More tears fall from my eyes. Fear jams my throat, and I fling my arms around him, burying my face in the crook of his neck before people see me crying. "I'm sorry." My apology comes out in the form of a startled gasp. The taste of his skin on my lips and the thuds of his heartbeat against my chest make me feel as if I'm losing my mind. "I'm sorry." My fingers tangle in his satin hair.

"Why are you sorry, Alana?" Mikah rasps, his voice hoarse and shaky. His large palm slides to the back of my head to cup it.

"For slapping you."

"I deserved it," he says in my ear, pulling me closer.

We're a ball of emotions as we stop in the middle of the sidewalk, and I can hear whispering when people start swarming around us.

"Get a room, you two!" someone shouts, and a few scattered laughs come from out in the street, which brings Mikah and me back to our senses.

"I need to go inside to finish up a few things." Mikah's lips touch the tip of my ear and he pulls his hands away from me. "You want to wait backstage?"

"Yes," I tell him, pushing my hair away from my teary eyes.

I'll wait all night if I have to. I've done it before. Only, this time, you aren't standing me up.

As I sit in the corner of his small, stuffy dressing room, I watch Mikah being a rockstar. There's a cold can of Dr. Pepper in my hand and my pulse won't stop racing, but I force myself to stay collected. I don't want anyone to see me cry. People around me are dressed to impress in suits, jackets, ties, and dresses. Everyone's happy and colorful. It's nothing like the sea of leather and black found backstage at the Midnight Rust shows. I can't say who's here from the label and who's a fan, because Mikah takes the time to shake every single hand thrust at him and talk to every single person in the dressing room. It's exciting to witness.

One man in particular who I was briefly introduced to earlier is all over Mikah, and something tells me he's the one who calls the shots.

The band downstairs is rocking the house and the roar of the crowd makes Mikah's set look like it was just a soundcheck, but people seem to be interested in talking to him. I know why. He's got that mysterious vibe, dark and alluring, that pulls you right in.

We leave the club at around half past ten. By this time, the drizzle has stopped and the air is musty and thick with humidity. In the alley, Mikah hoists his guitar case over his shoulder and draws a pack of Marlboros from his pocket. He smokes with his eyes closed, his long dark lashes resting against his olive skin, and I watch him with fascination, wondering what he's thinking and relishing the precious high of my own cigarette.

"You were great," I say, masking my anxiety with a smile. I actually think he was phenomenal, but the words are stuck in my throat like a rock. I want to ask him things, but I don't know where to start. I wonder if he's aware Moonchild is what Dakota used to call me.

"Thanks." Mikah opens his eyes and looks at me. His penetrating gaze sends my heart into overdrive. "Where did you park?"

"I walked. I have a room at the hotel down the street."

"You really are nuts, Cupcake Queen." He sticks his cigarette between his lips and inhales sharply. "Hotels here are expensive as fuck."

I joke, "I wanted to get the full Seattle nightlife experience."

"You shouldn't walk alone at night." He blows the smoke out. "It's not safe. I'll take you back."

My stomach clenches with hope and worry. "I thought we could talk."

"We can." Mikah nods, staring at his cigarette. "We should. Just not here. And don't be a fucking weirdo anymore, okay?" His gaze flicks to me again.

"I'm not."

"You are." A slight smile tugs at the corner of his mouth and a flash of a dimple cuts through his cheek. "You have no fucking idea, Alana."

I'm not sure how we end up in my room. I suppose I asked Mikah to come up once he walked me back to my hotel, but I don't remember doing so. My brain has been on autopilot ever since the end of his set, and the anticipation of the talk we're about to have is turning me into a neurotic mess.

Mikah sets his guitar case on the desk and looks around. "You win the lottery or something?"

"No." I shake my head. I don't care about the money. It was worth spending this much and more just to see him perform. Even if he didn't want to talk to me, I wouldn't have regretted coming out here.

He turns around to face me.

"Are you hungry?" I motion at the menu sitting on the nightstand. "They have room service."

"I'm fine."

"Do you mind if I order? I haven't eaten anything." Truth is, I'm not even hungry. I'm just not sure what else is going to happen since we're in a hotel room.

"You don't have to starve yourself on my account." Mikah walks to the window and his gaze lingers on the flickering streetlights and neon signs.

The view of him against the backdrop of the Seattle nightlife ignites a flash of heat between my legs. The city suits him.

"Is this a smoking room?" he asks, fiddling with the latch on the handle lock.

"Yes."

Mikah pushes the sliding windowpane open and takes his cigarettes from his jacket pocket. The cool air streams inside.

I call room service and order some food while he smokes.

"Did he ever sing it to you?" Mikah asks when I hang up.

A spasm hits my chest. "No. I didn't know he wrote a song..."

"Did you like it?" Mikah looks at me over his shoulder, his arresting gaze scrutinizing my face.

I blink at him through the mist in my eyes. "Will you play it for me again?"

Mikah walks over to the desk and puts out his cigarette in the ashtray. After taking off his jacket, he opens his guitar case. With my heart in my throat, I watch him getting comfortable in a chair in the middle of the room. His fingers brush over the strings gently and he rips through a few chords.

I sit on the edge of the bed and let the music fill me with painful bliss. This time, I listen to the lyrics carefully, relishing every line and every note. It hurts hearing them, but at the same time, they pacify my anxiety like a warm balm, and the sound of Mikah's voice mixing with Dakota's words makes every part of me tingle with bittersweet delight. Knowing that he left us something so beautiful fills me with hope.

Pleasant heat hits my stomach and I have to grasp at the thick blanket because my hands begin to shake. I start crying and I hate myself a little for it, but I don't try to hide it.

Mikah's gaze settles on mine and he continues to run through the chords. His voice is low and deep and it cracks at times, but I like that he's making mistakes. Mistakes are human nature.

A strained breath rushes out of me when the music finally comes to an end.

"Why are you really here?" Mikah asks, not breaking eye contact. He sets his guitar aside and slides from the chair to move closer, and I wonder why he's still looking for reassurance that I've come to see *him*.

"Remember when you said that you felt like you didn't belong anywhere?"

Mikah nods, settling on his knees in front of me, his face level with mine.

"For a very long time, I felt like I didn't belong anywhere either. Even in my own house. It's like I was always misunderstood. With you, I don't feel that way."

Mikah draws a labored breath through his teeth and reaches for my hair. "I found a whole notebook of unused poems in his room." He carefully tucks a lose strand behind my ear, his gaze set to my lips. "I know 'Moonchild' is your song. And I know every time I sing it, you'll think of him instead of me. And that's okay. I want you to. But when you kiss me or hug me…you can't think of him. You need to think of me."

Serenity settles inside my chest. "You're all I've been thinking about lately," I confess. "I couldn't stop if I tried."

A smirk touches his lips. "You're so fucking weird, Cupcake Queen."

"Will you sing some more for me?" I ask, fisting the sleeves of his t-shirt.

Mikah grabs his guitar and plays song after song until a loud knock jolts us back to reality.

"Your dinner," he says. His hands freeze and the music stops.

Upset over a sudden intrusion, I hurry to the door and let room service in. I'm not even sure what I ordered. I just picked the first thing that stuck out on the menu without actually checking to see what it was.

Once we're alone, Mikah sets his guitar aside and walks over to the dinner cart. He peeks under the lid of one of the plates and shoots me a confused look.

"What is it?" I ask, horror filling my stomach.

"You really have to stop trying to impress me, weirdo."

"What do you mean?" I pull up the lid and glance at the food.

Mikah leans over and whispers in my ear, "Prime rib is expensive." His Marlboro breath skates across my cheek.

"I'm not trying to impress you." I cover the plate.

We stare at each other for a few awkward seconds, the air between us hot and tentative, until Mikah breaks the silence. "I thought you were hungry."

Panic coils my stomach. "Not anymore." My eyes never leave his.

"Why not?"

"I can't think straight when you're around and..." My words turn into shallow breaths. "Looking at you makes me lose my mind too."

"Is that why you came all the way here? To lose your mind with me?"

"Yes and no." I take a step back and move to the middle of the room. I need some distance between us so that I don't mess up everything I want and need to say. "I'm going to see the hummingbird tomorrow."

Mikah's quiet. He assesses me slowly and I can't tell whether this connection we managed to create today is falling apart or strong enough to withstand the storm.

"I need to see a place where he was happy," I explain. "I need to do this for me. Just like what you're doing right now is for you. I believe it's fair we do things for ourselves, because we don't know what's going to happen to us tomorrow. We might die."

"You know I'm not doing this for me." Mikah shakes his head. Do you think I enjoy being on stage after what happened? Do you have any idea what it's like to sit there surrounded by the dark and wonder if someone in the crowd has a gun?"

"I do," I say quietly, walking in his direction.

Mikah looks up at the ceiling. "I'm sorry. That's not what I meant." His voice breaks.

"It's okay." I reach up for his face and run my fingertips against his cheekbone. "I said some stuff I didn't mean either."

He doesn't move. His gaze, fiery and dark, returns to me and studies me for a few moments. "I still can't fucking believe you're here."

"I don't belong where you're not."

Mikah's hands rest on my hips to draw me closer, his warm mouth lingering on my cheek. "No, you don't. Because your weird only works really well with my weird."

Our lips brush and then our breaths collide. The kiss is uncompromising, full of hunger and pain, and I love it that we don't have to pretend.

Slick heat pools between my legs when his weight rests against me, pushing me gently across the room.

My ankles clash with the bedframe and we tumble onto the mattress, our mouths and tongues never breaking apart. Mikah settles between my legs and his calloused hands slip under the hem of my skirt. "You look beautiful in a dress, Cupcake Queen," he murmurs, his deep rasp vibrating against my cheek as his fingers crawl up my thighs, teasing me. "Very fuckable."

A nervous laugh leaves my mouth. Hearing him talk dirty does funny things to me. The warmth in my chest spreads below my stomach and I realize my panties are soaked.

"You love it, don't you?" Mikah asks, sliding his hands back to cup my ass. "When I talk to you like this?" He's grabby and a little rough, and his every touch is electrifying. "You're all light and proper on the outside, but you have a twisted mind...like me."

My head begins to spin. I nod, staring up at him.

He straightens up to get rid of his t-shirt. The artwork adorning his body is stunning, and now that I'm sober, I take my time to study all the designs scattered across his chest, stomach, and arms. My fingers tiptoe over the dreamcatcher tat covering his left side and slide down to an area of skin that feels different, tender. He must have gotten it recently. My gaze shifts to the design and I realize it's a small hummingbird, the same one Dakota had.

Mikah rasps in my ear, "You loved the way I wrecked you, baby?"

Heat pulses between my thighs. He's never called me *baby* before. It sounds almost too intimate. "I did," I confess, moving my hands through his hair.

"Do you want more?" He drags his mouth down to my neck, his teeth grating my skin.

"Yes."

"Say it, Alana."

The way he says my name sends a flash of fever into my chest and stomach.

"I want more," I whisper and palm his face to bring it to mine. "I want everything, whatever you have to offer."

He stares at me with wild eyes. His fingers fiddle with the drenched fabric of my panties and cup my sex. "The dress stays on." The corner of his mouth tilts up.

"Is this what *you've* been fantasizing about?" I bite back a timid smile. My core is throbbing against his palm.

"There's more." He brushes our lips together. "My imagination has no limits."

His body is molded to mine like a clay figure, filling in all my curves and shadowing all my movements. We kiss messily, our lips burning and tingling. Mikah slides to the side and peels off my panties, then gets rid of the rest of his clothes. I don't care that there's no foreplay or no items from Jess's imaginary sex list to check off. I want it dirty and fast because it fits us.

Reaching up, I grasp Mikah's shoulders and pull him down to me, needing to feel his warmth. Our bodies lined up and touching, his erection is pressed against my center as his hooded eyes rest on mine.

My hands slide to his ass to guide him, my heart tripping. Then he pushes in fast, hitting me deep, raw, and hard. His stubbled jaw brushes my cheek and his velvety moan fills the air.

I clench around his length and gasp for breath, letting a wave of need cascade through me. He pulls back and drives into me again, setting a frenzied pace as a low grunt rumbles inside his chest. My hips buck to meet his thrusts, looking to match his harsh rhythm. I tug on his hair, tangling it around my fingers and kiss him as our chests heave together.

I love the taste of his sweat on my lips, salty and sharp, and I love the feel of his skin on mine. He pounds into me like it's our last time. With everything he's got until the sheets are damp and there's not a single part of me that's left untouched. The sex is dirty and desperate, but it's honest and it's ours. It's a new messy memory for me to keep, and I like it. I like Mikah loud and powerful on top of me. I like him doing things to my body to make it sing. And I like him whispering my name in my ear when we come hours later.

His hands still in my hair, his legs twisted with mine, we lie there naked and breathless, panting to catch our breath, and it feels nice. It feels right and peaceful.

"I have to be up very early." I hear Mikah's rough voice. "I have a business meeting and a studio session." He rolls over to the side and runs his index finger over the contours of my face.

"Okay." I turn my head toward him and our eyes meet.

"Are you going to come to the show tomorrow?"

"Do you want me to?"

"Of course I want you to." He nuzzles my shoulder and kisses his way up to my mouth. "I just fucked you for two hours straight and you don't think I want to see you tomorrow?"

I swallow hard and bite down on my lip. My emotions are running rampant.

"I want you everywhere I go, Alana." His whisper simmers across my skin. His lips feather mine.

"Really?"

"Yes. Really." He pushes himself off the bed and walks across the room to grab his cigarettes and an ashtray. The food I ordered is sitting in the corner untouched and probably cold.

I feel a wave of heat pulsing through me as my eyes follow his movements. There's no doubt he's going to be a star—he sings heavenly and he's the devil on the guitar, and I don't want to miss anything, not a moment of this journey he's about to start.

Mikah sets the ashtray on the nightstand and lies down next to me. He lights up his cigarette with his usual finesse, his fingers elegant and his gaze concentrated.

"If they give you any shit about the smoke when you check out, let me know, okay?" he says, drawing the nicotine into his lungs.

"Okay." I nod. My sex is raw and swollen and my body is slick with the mix of our sweat.

Mikah pulls the cigarette from his mouth and hands it to me. "When are you going home?"

"The day after tomorrow." I close my eyes and take a long drag.

"You can't do this shit with your parents like you did to my brother," he says in an authoritative tone. "You're going to have to tell them we're together when you go back."

He's planting himself into my life deliberately and unconditionally. Marking his territory. And I love it.

"I will." I return the cigarette.

"If they don't like me, that's fine. They're not the ones seeing me, so they don't have a say in where, how, or what you do with me. You understand?" He stares at me, his gaze unwavering.

"I understand."

"It's like you said... We all may die tomorrow... I don't have time to persuade people to like me."

"I don't need persuasion." A smile stretches my lips.

"Good." He draws me closer, and I rest my head on his chest. "Because you get what you see."

I don't even know if he understands what I see is beautiful. I don't have any other words to describe him. He's everything I ever wanted in a man. I just didn't realize it until I got to *know* him.

Mikah continues to puff on his cigarette in silence, pushing the smoke out leisurely. His heart thump-thumps under my cheek, and it's peaceful. For the first time since the attack, it doesn't feel like the sky is falling or the earth beneath me is shuddering.

"Can I ask you something?" I whisper, my voice shaking.

"Yeah?"

"Why didn't you run like everyone else?"

I can feel Mikah's heart rate spike. "I don't know." He pulls the cigarette from between his lips and puts it out. "DK liked the lights dim. He wanted the shows to be intimate. Basically, when we're on stage, we don't really get to see the crowd. It's like playing to pitch black..." Mikah pauses. His hand slides to my head and he runs his warm palm over my damp hair. "I sensed the panic, so I turned my head to check on him and he looked like he'd been hit by something. I didn't know what it was at first. I glanced back at the crowd, and they were all screaming and there was so much noise...the floors fucking shook. I thought an earthquake had hit us. It reminded me of a scene from one of those horror movies DK loved, and then I noticed the gun. He...aimed at everyone who ran, so I didn't. I turned to DK, but he wasn't there anymore. That's when I saw you."

My throat catches and I'm scared to move or speak because the stillness between us is too fragile.

"You had this look on your face." Mikah has trouble getting the words out.

My spine stiffens. "What look?"

"Lost."

"I was scared."

"I was scared too, baby." He pulls me against him. "I was fucking terrified—I didn't know where my brother was or if we were going to make it out alive."

Mikah pauses. His hands move over my naked body, fingertips brushing my skin.

I shift in his arms and press my lips to his chest. He tastes of vulnerability and pain.

"What does your name mean?" I ask him, dragging my mouth across his inked skin.

"Nothing."

"How come?"

He chokes out an unhappy laugh. "I was an unsuccessful attempt to create a perfect child."

"No, you weren't."

"My mom wouldn't agree with you." A sad smile touches his lips, and his tone is sluggish. He's starting to fall asleep.

I swallow hard. "Why do you say you were unsuccessful?"

"I wasn't good enough, I guess. Or maybe she was pissed at my dad for ditching us and maybe she hated me for reminding her every day." His words hang in the air, bitter and depressing. "My brother...he was perfect."

I'm torn between asking him a question and letting it go. I know we have to talk about what happened the night I barged into his apartment drunk and screaming, but I'm not sure right now—when both of us are exhausted—is a good time to discuss our mutual feelings for Dakota. That seems like a conversation for another time.

Mikah's breath tickles the side of my face. He's quiet and the room is still, so we both begin to slip into the dark comfort of our dreams.

The next morning when I wake up, Mikah's already gone. The sheets on his side of the bed are cold and rumpled, the window's shut, and the curtains are drawn together. The room smells of Marlboros and dirty sex, and I lie there for several minutes breathing the scent of Mikah in like it's my oxygen, replaying every detail from last night and sifting through each word he said to me.

I know there's still a lot to talk about, but I'm not scared of my feelings. Not being confused about what he and I are anymore is liberating.

After texting my parents to let them know I'm okay, I take a shower and get dressed. Then I draw a backup map in my doodle-filled diary in case there's no reception at the park and set out for the drive up north to see Dakota's hummingbird. My body's sore and worn down from yesterday's drive and my wild night with Mikah, but my mind hasn't been this sharp in months—not since before the attack—and I love it.

The desperate need to hear Mikah's voice grips me when I'm near the creek exit, but I refrain from bombarding him with messages or calls while he's in the middle of a business meeting.

I arrive at the park at around eleven and hike up to the hummingbird using my handmade paper map. Just as I predicted, the reception is extremely spotty and the GPS doesn't cooperate, but the walk isn't what I thought it would be. The path snaking through the woods is easy and scenic, and I give in to my temptation and snap multiple photos with my phone. Oddly, using technology in the middle of the rainforest feels a little blasphemous. The lawn is small and sprinkled with streaks of sunlight that peek through the tall, thick trees surrounding the area.

I sit in the grass with my legs stretched in front of me and look up at the hummingbird. It's big, probably over fifteen feet high, and its wooden head is blocking the sun. Years of rain and snow have dulled the intricate carvings and have covered it with a layer of moss.

I lose track of how long I spend staring at it, but I'm determined to hear whatever it was Dakota heard. I keep my phone hidden away in my backpack, and my notebook is in my lap. I listen to the birds chirping and the subtle noise of the trees.

Dakota was right. This place is peaceful and a tiny part of me, the one that's still holding on to the memories tightly, would love to wish him near, but since I know he's not coming back, I use my wish that I never made at his funeral on other things.

I wish for Jess to be happy with what she's doing.

I wish for Luke to be able to play drums again.

I wish for Mom and Dad to stop worrying about me.

I wish for every person that was at The Crystal Room during the last Midnight Rust show to find the strength to walk through the dark.

I wish for Mikah...

29. BEFORE

"What do you think?" Jess squeals into the phone. "You like it?" Her voice pitches from excitement.

Is this real? Are we really going to live together?

"Hold on." I pull my phone away from my ear and glance down at the photo of the apartment she texted me a couple of minutes ago. My other hand grips the steering wheel of the Prius harder. The roads have been an icy mess since the middle of January when the temperature suddenly leapt up and all the snow melted, only to freeze a couple of days later.

"Tell me you love it, girl!" Jess presses.

"Yes. I love it!" I cry out, navigating my car through the gloomy gray mist. It's almost nightfall and it's strange to be driving home from college at this time. Last semester, all my classes were in the morning. This semester, they're all over the place.

"Remember, we're going to the mall on Saturday."

"Yes. I remember."

"You're buying that skirt I saw at Macy's."

"Yes ma'am." I don't argue with her, because it's usually useless.

Jess jumps back to discussing the apartment. "Did you see the kitchen? It's so fucking cute!"

"I know. I can't wait."

"I'm sure." She snorts out a laugh. "You can only use your blog as an excuse to come home late so many times a week, right?"

Pleasant shivers roll down my spine. Is it even normal to think about sex all the time? Being with Dakota has consumed me completely. He's like a drug.

"I'm pretty sure my mom is onto me," I say, straining my eyes on the road. The snow has been falling non-stop since last night.

"So what?"

"It's just weird. She's going to ask questions and then she'll tell my dad."

"You're eighteen. You're allowed to have sex." Jess groans. "He can sleep over every night for all I care. As long as he doesn't snore."

"He doesn't," I bite back, a smile breaking on my lips. Although we've never spent a night together, we fell asleep at his place once. It was amazing. I'd never slept in a man's arms before in my life.

"Good. Because Luke sometimes talks in his sleep. It's fucking creepy."

"No way." I giggle.

Jess laughs.

"What does he say—"

There's a loud pop and the car begins to skid across the road through a tunnel of swirling snow. I can hear the tires rebelling against the ice. My phone slips from my hand and drops on the floor along with my heart.

"Alana!" Jess screams from somewhere under my seat, but all my attention is on the road ahead of me. My fingers choke around the steering wheel as I fight for control of the jerking vehicle. The snowflakes blowing against the windshield blind me, and for a second, I feel like I'm floating through an abyss of time and space.

The Prius begins to limp and sputter and finally halts on the side of the road. My breath is stuck in my throat and my body's shaking. I sit with my hands locked on the wheel for a good minute until a noise coming from the vicinity of my feet snaps me out of my shock. I bend over and grab the phone, my blood roaring in my ears.

"Are you okay?!" Jess screams.

"I think I've got a flat tire. Let's talk later."

I step outside and round the Prius. The passenger side front tire is blown to pieces.

After a few unsuccessful attempts to get hold of my father, I call Dakota. I don't know why he's my next choice. Maybe because my mother knows just as much about cars as I do—how to drive them and how to fill up the gas.

"I have a flat," I say. "I can't get hold of my dad."

I don't really want to ask him to come and help me. Deep down, I know my father will probably see my missed calls as soon as he gets a free second at work. But this is something else. It's sharing a piece of information about what's happening in my life when Dakota's not around. Just like he shares things with me when he's playing a show somewhere I can't be. It's what "together" is like.

"Do you have a spare?" Dakota questions. The clanking of the silverware and a wall of voices I hear in the background tell me he's not home.

I tramp over the crunchy piles of dirty snow to get to the trunk and check inside. "Yes."

"All right. I'll be there in a second."

"It's okay. I'll try my dad again in a bit. He has a huge audit at his store today. He probably stepped away from the phone." The frost begins to bite at my face and skin.

"It's dark out and you're on the interstate," Dakota counters, his tone firm. "I'll be there in a second."

Obviously, it's going to be way longer than a second because I'm stranded in the wake of a snowstorm on the opposite side of town, but I do as he instructs—get back inside and lock the doors.

Twenty minutes later, a pair of high beams crawl past me and a truck pulls over a few feet in front of me. The doors swing open and Dakota steps out of the passenger side. Then my eyes move to the driver's side and I recognize Mikah's broad frame trudging through the snow. His hands are thrust in his pockets, his coat undone.

Strange delight settles deep in my stomach. I don't understand the reasoning behind this reaction, but I revel in it, nonetheless. I've never been rescued in such a collective chivalrous manner before.

"Someone call for roadside assistance?" Dakota yells, approaching me.

I get out of the Prius and fall into his arms for a brief moment, my peripheral vision catching a glimpse of his brother behind a cluster of snowflakes. Dakota's disgustingly affectionate in public. He likes to hold my hand, touch my face, and play with my hair, and I love every second of it, especially when we're out. I love that everyone knows I'm his girl. We might be one of those overly cheesy and a bit mismatched couples you'd find on Pinterest when you type *cute stuff* in the search bar.

"What happened to your car?" I motion at the truck as we break our hug.

"It's in the shop until tomorrow," he explains. "Will you pop your trunk?" He heads behind my car and I push the button on my key fob so that he can get my spare.

"Just say it, DK." Mikah shakes his head and moves closer. He gives me a nod in place of hello.

"What?" My gaze ping-pongs between the two.

"He doesn't know how to change a tire. That's why he brought me," Mikah says with a solemn face, his hands never leaving his pockets. He's not wearing a sweater underneath his jacket, just a t-shirt. Narrowing my eyes, I scan part of the design that's spread across his chest.

The spare falls onto the snow with a low thud and Dakota's voice drifts at us from behind the car. "Hey, man. It's all yours." His head pops above the lid of the trunk and he flashes us a sly grin.

Mikah rounds the Prius and stands next to his brother, looking at the contents of my trunk and then at Dakota. They glance at each other but say nothing.

"You don't have a jack?" Mikah inquires, rubbing the back of his neck.

"I don't?" I'm struck by this revelation myself.

"Nope." His lips twist. "Good thing I have one."

He walks over to his truck to get the jack while Dakota grabs the lug wrench.

I hold up my phone and point the flashlight at the front tire. The snow twirls and spins above their heads like crazy as they jack up the car.

"Just so you know, this asshole lied." Dakota motions at Mikah, wrench in his hand. "I know how to change a tire." He pushes his hair aside and returns to removing the flat.

"I can see that." My eyes dart to Mikah. The thin line above the bridge of his nose twists in concentration. My fingers are frozen solid around my phone. My cheeks tingle and my lungs sting from the cold air.

"I just like to fuck with him." Mikah punches his brother's shoulder.

A smile stretches my lips. I like watching them together. There's something immaculate about the connection they share. Honest and real. In a way, it saddens me that I have no idea how it feels to have a sibling, to have someone else who's a part of your mother and father. It must be magical.

When they're done with the tire, Dakota takes the wrench back to my trunk.

Mikah grabs a handful of fresh snow and slowly rises to his feet. My flashlight lingers on the design on his t-shirt as he crushes the snowflakes between his fingers and they fall slowly onto his boots.

Dakota pats his pockets, his gaze flicking to me. "If you have an emergency and your dad or I don't pick up, call my brother, okay?" He reaches to grab my phone and quickly punches something in. The next thing I hear is muffled buzzing coming from Mikah's pocket.

He pulls out his phone and looks at it with his face screwed in confusion.

"DK's girl. Emergency." Dakota slaps his back energetically and bends over to grab the jack. "Hold on a second. I believe my phone's in the truck." He returns mine to me and walks off, leaving me with his brother.

"Is that Gary Oldman?" I ask, motioning at Mikah's t-shirt.

"Yeah. *Bram Stoker's Dracula*. Classic from 1992." He draws a pack of Marlboros from his other pocket and lights up a cigarette.

"Is that the one with Annie Lennox's soundtrack?"

"Yeah." His eyes land on my face. "The nineties were great. That was what? Eight years before you were born? You missed all the fun."

This is the most he's said to me since we met, and I wonder if I've hit the jackpot. He likes the nineties. "'Love Song for a Vampire,' right?" I say, watching him blow a cloud of smoke into the snowy air. I can feel his gaze on me through the hazy veil that hangs between us.

"Yeah." He nods. "You read the book?"

"No."

"Read the book. It's better than the movie."

"The book is always better," I mumble under my breath.

"Movies are tailored to the audience. A bunch of dudes with money who call themselves producers take the source material and chop it to their liking and do what the industry demands. But a book is a time capsule. You can't change it to match the present era or the expectations of consumers." Mikah takes the cigarette from his mouth and taps it gently. Tiny flecks of ash fall to the white snow next to his boots.

"You're still wearing a t-shirt with the movie character." I grin at him.

"Yeah. I like movies too when they're done right, but some of those classics are too immersive to be put on screen. This one was decent. It retains the dark, creepy feel of the novel."

"I believe you."

"It's the best horror novel you'll ever read," he says, sticking the cigarette back between his lips. His gaze darts to Dakota heading toward us through the snow. It's coming down hard and fast and I realize that if we don't leave now, we're risking being stuck here all night.

"I'm gonna drive her home," Dakota tells Mikah, ushering me to the passenger side of my Prius. "See you later."

"Yeah, later," Mikah mutters, waving at us. A trail of smoke shadows him as he starts walking toward the truck.

We hurry inside and turn on the heater. I'm trembling and wheezing and my lungs feel like they've been stuffed with chunks of ice. My phone rattles in my pocket when Dakota's blowing hot air into my fists that are cramped up from the cold.

I withdraw my hands from his grasp to check who's calling. "Sorry, it's my dad. Let me take it."

"Where are you?" my father yelps, his voice full of panic.

"It's okay, Dad. Dakota's already here. It's just a flat. I'll see you at home in a bit," I explain.

"Okay." There's a pause and I wait for a snarky comment to drop at any second, but surprisingly, he follows with, "Drive carefully."

"We will. See you soon. Bye," I say and end the call.

Dakota looks at me, and his eyes study my face carefully.

"Hey." He reaches for my hair and pushes a loose strand back. "If something ever happens and neither your dad or I answer, call my brother. Flat tire, dead battery. Whatever."

"It's fine," I counter.

"I'm just saying," Dakota insists, palming my cheek. "If I'm not around to help, you can call him. He's not that scary." The corner of his mouth curls up.

"What do you mean if you're not around?" Panic crawls over my skin. "Where are you going?"

"Nowhere." He shakes his head, smiling. His dimples are driving me mad. "I'm not going anywhere except for playing shows around the world... This is just in case. If something happens. In case of emergency. You can call Mikah. Okay?"

"Okay." I throw my hands around his neck. "But don't leave me." It's childish to say these things to him, because we both know he's not leaving me, but the fact that he thinks ahead and plans for the worst gnaws at my gut. It's frightening. One minute you're living in the moment and the next, you realize everything ends at some point.

"I'm not going anywhere." Dakota laughs, wrapping his arms around me. His cheek brushes mine. "You couldn't get rid of me if you tried."

"Why would I?" I whisper into his hair. "I love you."

"I love you too." He presses his lips to my temple and we sit like that for a while, relishing each other's warmth as the snow outside works hard on hiding my car. "You want to come see us rehearse next week? Mikah and I wrote a new song."

"Of course!" I pull back and look into his eyes. "You don't even need to ask. I'd watch you rehearse my mom's grocery list."

Dakota cocks a brow. "Can that be arranged?"

"Yes, it can." I giggle, touching his face.

He makes me so happy that I'm scared it's going to hurt too much if we fall apart.

30. AFTER

I get a strange inkling something's off when I get back to the city limits and all three text messages I sent to Mikah are still unread. The lack of response does fit his typical behavior, but it seems like after last night, things should be different, shouldn't they?

I hit a lot of traffic and spend a good hour struggling to get out of an industrial area that the GPS chooses to send me to, thinking it's a great detour. After circling around the neighborhood of warehouses for what seems like hours, my mind isn't in a good place. I arrive at the hotel at around six and rush to my room to clean up and change.

Once I get to the club, there's no pass left for me at the Will Call window, and I have to pay for the ticket to get in, which only feeds my anxiety. I was under the impression Mikah would put my name on the list. My stupid heart that's head over heels for him blames his busy schedule, but my gut tells me I might be giving him too much credit.

Inside, the floor is buzzing. There are way more people here tonight than yesterday. I recognize some faces from last night, but they're mostly all new.

The band on stage is playing something very jazzy and people don't seem too enthusiastic about the set. Forcing my panic down, I push to the opposite side of the club and approach the security guard.

"My friend is performing later on tonight and I can't seem to get a hold of him!" I scream over the racket of the music and motion to the backstage area.

"Sorry, ma'am. Only if you have a pass."

"Can you at least get him for me?"

"Sorry, ma'am." The security guard shakes his head, his face expressionless.

Swallowing down my defeat, I step aside and dial Mikah's number again. The line rings and goes to voicemail.

My anxiety levels are sky high and my mind's racing. Part of me hates him, but part of me is just pissed at myself for being so stupid to believe that after last night, something would change.

Mikah Bennett is a jerk and always will be.

I stand against the wall and watch through my tears. My hands are trembling and my phone is charcoal hot in my palm, burning through my bumpy scars. When the band finishes their set, the crowd begins to thin out. People trickle outside one by one to take a quick break while the crew is resetting the stage. My nicotine craving is battling my Mikah craving, and I decide to give it one last shot. Drawing a deep breath to push back the tears, I return to the backstage entrance and ask security to get Mikah again.

If he chooses to continue his ignore game after this, I'm driving home.

"Ma'am, I really can't," the guard says, giving me a lazy headshake.

"I'm sure you get a lot of girls like me, but this *is* actually important." I try to keep my voice steady, but something tells me I sound just like any other groupie who wants to sneak in backstage, because right now, I *am* a groupie.

The door swings open and a cluster of people pour out onto the main floor, their chatter mixing with the clamor of everyone in the bar and the stage crew. My gaze catches only a glimpse of the back hallway, and it's packed with some suits from last night but no Mikah.

"Could you please step aside, ma'am." The security guard flashes his light at me. I do as he says to let another group out. They're arguing, their voices pitching and jumping over all the noise.

"Hey!" Someone's hand grabs at the sleeve of my jacket. "I'm Al. You're Bennett's friend, right? You came yesterday?" The man's face swims into view and his eyes seek mine. They're small and squinty and barely show from behind his plum cheeks. He's not the kind of person you'd easily forget. I remember him fawning over Mikah last night. He's the man in charge.

I nod, my heart jolting into doing insane acrobatics. "Yes."

"Okay. Come on." Al hooks his arm through mine and flashes his all-access pass at the guard.

Backstage is humming. I can feel the tension rising as we walk through the hallway in the direction of a door with an exit sign.

"What's your name, babe?" Al asks, ushering me to a staircase.

My knees weaken at the sight of numerous security guards and the rest of the backstage crew and guests gathered at the bottom of the stairs.

"Alana," I say, swallowing past the tightness in my throat.

"Okay, Alana." Al stops and rubs the back of his neck. "Maybe you can talk to your friend. He has a show in forty minutes."

"What do you mean?" My gaze darts around the crowd. Their faces, twisted with concern, send shivers down my spine.

"I think you should call the police," someone barks from the back.

"I'm not calling the police." Al lifts his hand in the air and shakes his head just like my father would. He even sounds like my father— condescending. "I've dumped a lot of money into this guy. He needs to stop this nonsense."

"He's not stable," a woman in solid black puts in. "Better let the professionals handle it."

Al starts up the stairs and motions for me to follow him. "Just see if you can talk to him." He draws a tissue from his pocket to wipe off the line of sweat coating his forehead. "Alana, right?"

I nod.

"That's a great name. You folks from Portland have really great names. Very poetic."

We climb up what seems like at least ten flights of stairs. Maybe fourteen. My fuzzy brain can't keep up with the count. My legs begin cramping somewhere around flight three. I'm sweating buckets when we finally approach another group of people. They're gathered near a massive metal door that opens to the roof. They give us worried glances.

Giving me a tight smile, Al points at the exit. "He needs to come down, dear. It's important we don't involve the police, because this is going to ruin his career." He sounds like Professor Pollock giving me a lecture on how bad my grades are. "I've risked a lot of money on your friend. He's the next James Bay. He better stop with the theatrics right now."

A spasm of panic rolls through me. "Come down from where?" I ignore the James Bay comment, my gaze darting from Al to the rest of the waiting crowd. My heart pounds so hard that my ribs are about to crack open. Pushing the heavy door open, I step over the metal threshold.

Al stays inside but a few nervous whispers follow me as I silently walk to the middle of the roof and let the disturbing view set in. The dark of the night has consumed most of the sky. There's just a thin blue line remaining right above the ragged flickering horizon, and that's where I see Mikah's silhouette—drawn against the last of the light. He's sitting on the ledge, facing away from me, his legs dangling over the city. There's a pack of Marlboros and a bottle of beer next to him, and clouds of smoke are floating above his head.

My heart stops beating. I wait a few seconds, then push his name out. "Mikah?"

He doesn't react.

"Mikah?" I call again, this time forcing myself to speak louder. "What are you doing?"

"What does it look like I'm doing?!" he barks, drawing his cigarette from his mouth and lifting it up in the air.

"It looks like you're being stupid." I thrust my hands in the pockets of my jacket and make them into fists.

"Well, sorry to disappoint, Cupcake Queen."

"Why weren't you answering my calls?"

Mikah gives me a one-shoulder shrug. "Did you hear what the trees said?"

"Maybe."

A sour chuckle. "I never heard them. I always thought DK was an idiot."

"Can you come down please?"

"Why?"

"Because I can't talk to your back, jerk." I try to sound unfazed to match his mood, but the truth is, I'm nowhere near unfazed. I've only been this scared once in my life—the night Dakota was killed. And now I'm standing on the roof of a seven-story building watching his brother being completely stupid. And the fact that I have no idea what's going on in Mikah's mind terrifies me.

"Sorry. You get what you pay for." He shrugs, returning the cigarette to his mouth. The soft evening wind ruffles his hair.

"I'm serious, Mikah. Can you come down please?" I go toward the ledge and stop a few feet away from him, right before my sanity's point of no return. My head begins to spin.

He smokes slowly, extending his love affair with nicotine for as long as the cigarette lets him. My eyes are trained on his head because I'm afraid to look past his shoulders. I have no idea why he's not scared and how this ridiculous idea even infiltrated his mind.

The silence between us drags on and on.

"Can you please come down?" I ask again after a while. "There are a lot of people downstairs waiting for you." My desperation begins to get the best of me, and the things that come out of my mouth stop making much sense.

"No, they're not." Mikah puts out his cigarette, pats the front pocket of his jacket, and holds up a small piece of paper. "I found it in the bathroom when I was getting ready to leave this morning." He pauses, and then he sounds bitter and broken. "It was just sitting there next to your toothbrush."

I move closer and realize it's the business card C.J. Barnes gave me. Horror and panic grip at my gut. I must have slipped it into my makeup kit by accident while packing.

"Do you feel better now?" Mikah asks, his harsh tone sifting through me like a river of acid. "What newspaper am I going to read about my brother's dick size in, huh?"

The accusation cuts me open. "I-I...didn't talk to him." I trip over my words; my tongue feels thick and heavy in my mouth and doesn't want to collaborate with my brain. "I only met him once, and I didn't say anything. I changed my mind." Heat hits my face and angry tears begin to pool in my eyes.

"Why did you keep it then?" He tosses the card in the air and watches it spiral down along the breeze.

"I don't know." My breath comes out in fast, shallow bursts.

"Why?" Mikah's voice grows louder. He shifts on the ledge and looks at me over his shoulder, and I can't tell whether he's going to come down or jump. His face is blank and his eyes are void of emotion. "Why did you keep it, Alana?"

My heart almost flips out of my chest. "I don't know...because you didn't want to talk about him."

"So you decided to go talk to some fucking reporter instead? There are support groups, you know. To talk to about this shit. Jess runs one, for starters. You don't have to go tell the whole fucking world how good of a person my brother was and what cupcakes were his favorite."

"That was before." I shake my head.

"Before what?" Mikah resumes staring at the sidewalk beneath him.

"Before last night! You never wanted to talk before last night!" I'm screaming in hopes that it'll make him believe me.

"So you just expected me to fuck you and then discuss my brother afterward?"

"No, for God's sake!"

Mikah's body begins to shudder and I realize he's crying. "Yesterday, I sat on that stage and I looked at all those people and I was fucking terrified someone would start shooting. I don't remember a single song I played. It was just darkness. Miles and miles of it. I just wanted to get out of there. And now I'm not sure if I can do it without him. Not after the way he died."

There's a long pause and I watch the wind blowing through Mikah's hair as he tosses his head back and covers his face with his palms.

"My dad got me a guitar when I was eight," he says quietly, but I can hear his sobs. "I sucked, but I wanted to learn so badly. One time, I came home from school and found DK playing with my guitar, and the next day, our mom took him to the shop and bought him his own."

I don't dare move. I just listen.

"It's funny"—Mikah reaches for another cigarette and flicks his lighter—"we both played. She never took me anywhere, but she signed him up for every single talent show within a hundred-mile radius, and I hated him for taking all the attention. I hated him so much it hurt." The smoke dances in the air around him like a tease. "And then when he was fourteen, he won this big ass state competition and they gave him an award, and he came up to me and asked if I wanted to be in a band with him. He was better and he was going to be a fucking super-star, but he wanted to play his weird music with me. His loser brother."

"You're not a loser," I choke out. "People loved your show last night. I loved it too. You're really talented."

"Do you think this is a coincidence the label got in touch with me after The Crystal Room?"

Moisture hits my eyes.

"You know when I saw you that night in the dressing room, I wanted you for myself, but he was first. He was always first."

Tears begin to fall down my cheeks.

"I told him if he was going to fuck it up, I was going to beat the shit out of him, but he didn't. He was like a puppy and I hated him for not failing at being so fucking good for you."

A sick flash of relief bursts through my horror.

"He had to fucking die so that I could get a record deal and you. And it feels like shit that I ever wished he didn't exist. It feels like shit to be alive, because I don't fucking deserve it."

Mikah's words hit me hard, like a punch in the gut. "Can you please come down?" I say breathlessly, my body shaking.

Mikah shifts in his spot and swings one leg over to the inside of the ledge. The sight of his tearstained face breaks me a little more. I've only seen him cry this much once. At Dakota's funeral. But they were shy, skimpy tears, and they made me believe he wasn't the type to get overly sentimental.

Mikah puts out his cigarette and takes a swallow of his beer.

"Can you please come down now?" I step closer.

"Why?" He turns to look at me, his eyes bloodshot.

"Because I don't want you to jump."

"Why?"

"Because I love you."

His gaze roams around my face as he sits there, still as a statue.

"Please come down." I draw my hands from my pockets and wipe my wet cheeks.

Mikah swings the other leg over the ledge to face me and rests his elbows on both knees. "Why are you telling me this now? Why didn't you tell me this yesterday?"

My emotions clog my throat and all I can manage is a pathetic headshake.

"I can't compete with him, especially now that he's dead. And I can't read your fucking mind. If you can't explain why you said what you said, how do you expect us to work?"

I gulp past the knot in my throat and rub at my watery eyes. "I don't want you to compete with him. You're a different person. What we have is different. And I love you differently. I want to be there for you and with you."

I have no clue what I'm thinking when I jump at him. All he has to do to end this is lean backward and let go. And I think part of me wouldn't be too upset if we both fell, but I still throw my arms around his neck and pull him to me. "Please, don't jump." My whisper muffles against his hair. "Please don't."

We tumble over, away from the ledge. He eases into me and snakes his arms around my frame, his face buried into the crook of my neck. His body is rigid and warm against mine, his heartbeat strong.

"I love you." My sobs are loud and endless and I don't remember the last time I bawled like a baby. Not after the night at The Crystal Room. What I do remember is how it feels when I'm on the floor with shards of glass in my face and palms, with my cheeks and hands bleeding. "Please don't scare me like this again." I cry ugly. I cry for Dakota and for the other twenty-three people and for their families and for all the candles my father lit at church every single Sunday after the attack. I don't know if Mikah's broken like me or in a different way, but I can feel his sadness and I know he understands mine, and I want to do whatever is in my power to help him get better. "Please don't scare me like this..." My words are mixed with my sobs and sound like drunken slurs...and it fits us. We're blissfully miserable in our pain.

"You started it." Mikah cradles my head. "You jumped out of a moving car, weirdo." His voice is a hot rasp near my ear and he's trembling, but his embrace is comforting. It's not the embrace of a person who's going to jump off a seven-story building. It's the embrace of a person who's *scared* to jump off a seven-story building.

"I won't do it again if you promise me you won't get on any ledges."

"I won't," he agrees.

"Okay." I pull back and touch his wet face with my fingers, and then I kiss him everywhere—his mouth, his cheeks, his chin, his dimple. I don't care if his hair's on my tongue. "I love you. I'm sorry I'm so weird. I'm sorry..."

"You're my weird, Cupcake Queen," he mumbles against my lips. "You're my weird and I don't deserve you."

"Don't say that...don't say that." I shake my head. "You belong with me. You're not going anywhere."

"Hey, rockstar!" Al's chalky voice penetrates the misty Seattle air. "Are you all right? You want anything?" He steps out onto the roof and marches toward us. The expression on his face is a strange blend of relief and agony. I suspect he's happy his shiny new toy didn't jump, taking the money his label's planning on making along with him, and perhaps he's a little upset over the excessive exercise.

I watch him from the corner of my eye with my arms wrapped tightly around Mikah's body. My cheek is resting on his broad chest, and I'm terrified to let go. Everything between us changed in a matter of seconds, and it feels different to hold him now. Desperately exhilarating and painfully beautiful. Knowing he's not what he led me to believe is a relief. He's not made of stone and paper. He's flesh and blood like me and he feels everything, every second of every day. He's reliving it all the same way I do, and in a sick way, it seems as if we're made for each other. To fill each other's gaps that exist where we're broken and where our hearts shattered.

"You scared everyone, big guy." Al wipes the beads of sweat rolling down his forehead and moves closer. "It's a full house tonight, buddy. I hear Ned Morton's here."

Mikah draws back a bit and runs his palms over his cheeks. His eyes are bloodshot but curious, and I have a feeling Ned Morton is an important man.

"I'll make you a star, boy," Al says proudly, his gaze sweeping over to me for a second and then to Mikah. "Just don't do this to me again. Deal?"

Mikah gives him a curt nod. "Yeah, sure." His voice is weak. He seems withdrawn and somewhat lost, but I know it's his protective mechanism. He likes to build walls around himself.

"You take your medication? You need anything?" Al throws his hand over Mikah's shoulder and nudges him toward the staircase exit.

Grabbing Mikah's hand, I glance at the glimmer of the fading horizon. The night sky has blanketed the city for as far as the eye can see. As we follow Al silently, my heart's still out of control, restlessly hammering in my aching chest.

The people hanging out in the staircase watch us with judgment, shock, and curiosity. Al's footsteps thump down heavily as he continues his pep talk on our way downstairs, where Mikah locks himself in the restroom to clean up.

I patiently wait for him in the hallway, ignoring the buzz of the crew and stares of the performing bands' guests. My phone is hot in my hand and my dress feels thick and scratchy against my skin. I picked it because I wanted to wear something nice for Mikah tonight and because the dirty parts of my mind probably hoped for him to get creative with it again after the show. These things seem a little trivial right now.

"Is he out yet?" Al shouts from afar. His round silhouette lingers among the crowd as he makes his way back to me.

I shake my head and check the time. The set's about to start.

"Here, babe." Al hands me a laminate with a strained smile on his lips.

"Who's Ned Morton?" I ask. My phone pings a couple of times as I put the lanyard around my neck. The texts are from Jess.

The shocked expression on Al's face tells me I'd be better off asking Google.

"Honey." He squeezes my shoulder. "If you're going to date a rockstar, you need to know these things."

I respond with a meek smile. My stomach squeezes from the mere idea of being on a date with Mikah. We've never had one and I wonder what it would feel like to be out with him, to hold his hand in public and to kiss him on the lips in the middle of the street in the pouring rain.

Al presses his ear to the restroom door and knocks. "Everything all right, big guy? You're on in ten."

Mikah steps out into the hallway a few moments later. His five o'clock shadow and the glint in his bloodshot eyes make him look tired, but probably not many will notice.

Al leads us through the backstage maze toward the stage area. The curtains are up and the lights are dimmed down just like during the Midnight Rust shows, but I can still see the heads of the audience through a small opening on the side. Panic is slowly rolling through me, wave after wave. I can't tell if anyone appears sick enough to have brought a gun and it terrifies me.

One of the girls who works for Al hands Mikah a bottle of water. He drinks half of it, his face tense and serious.

Swallowing my anxiety, I reach up for his cheek to palm it. "It's going to be okay." There's a tremble in my voice and my stomach is all knotted up. "You'll do great."

"I'm fucking nervous," he mouths at me.

"Don't be. You're amazing." I grab his hands and squeeze them in encouragement.

The hum of the backstage area muffles our whispers.

He leans in and presses his lips to mine. The kiss is innocent. It's sweet and a little tingly with a pinch of cigarette smoke, and I relish the feel of it until the end of Mikah's set. Until he's back with me. Until we walk out into the busy street hours later, until his mouth finds mine again and we kiss for a long time on the crowded sidewalk. We kiss in front of everyone, we kiss slowly, like in the movies. With our lips barely touching, with our hands on each other, with our hearts tethered.

EPILOGUE

Three Months Later

I slide my notebook in my bag and turn to Jess. Her face is the definition of bored.

"I don't understand why we need to take economics again if we took it in high school," she whispers, rolling her eyes. Although I don't believe the professor can hear her complaints or even cares, because ninety percent of the sophomores are of the same opinion.

Besides, we're at the very back of the noisy classroom and whatever happens in the back usually stays there.

"Hey, birthday girl," someone calls from behind me. "Invitation for tonight still open?"

I glance over my shoulder and see Mallory. Somehow, we ended up taking a bunch of the same classes this semester again.

She flashes me a big smile, and I return the gesture. Mine may not match hers, but I try. It's something I promised myself I would do more often. I promised I would smile and be nice to people because there's enough rudeness and ignorance in the world already.

Jess perks up. "Totally. Bring your boyfriend."

I'm not entirely sure how the two became friends.

Mallory motions at Jess's hair that's now the color of blue orchids. "I love the new shade."

"Thanks. I think I'm keeping this one for a while."

During the summer, Jess attempted three different looks. I was shocked when she showed up for one of the meet-ups and it was bright green. It took some getting used to, but as soon as I started to feel adjusted to it, she changed the color to yellow. I don't know if this is her idea of trying new things or just trying to find herself in the midst of all the chaos with the Joseph Miller case, but I do know I've gotten to love this version of Jess Tiller. I've gotten to love her drive and determination just as much as I used to love her obsession with finding me a suitable boyfriend.

Now we have a different kind of friendship. Less co-dependent and more genuine.

After saying our goodbyes to Mallory, we pack the rest of our things and walk out into the busy hallway.

"Am I driving you home?" I ask, hoisting my bag over my shoulder.

Today, I took Jess out for breakfast as part of my birthday present to her. The second half of that present is in my bedside drawer back home, and I'm beyond nervous because I'm not sure if she still feels the same as she did about Black Rose. Her music tastes changed a lot over the course of last year. But I acted on a whim and asked Mikah to get the tickets anyway, even if she and Luke can't find the time to drive to Seattle to see the show.

Jess tears her gaze from her phone and scrunches up her nose. "Luke's here." There's a mischievous spark in her eyes.

My heart flips. "What?" I gasp for air. "Is he driving?" It's hard for me to believe this is possible. He's been in intensive physical therapy all summer and finally began walking in August.

"Don't forget"—Jess dodges my question—"you're wearing the blue dress to match my hair tonight." She hooks her arm through mine and pulls me in the direction of the lobby.

"Yes ma'am."

"Silver sandals," she continues with her instructions as we make our way to the exit.

"You know they're the most uncomfortable pair of sandals I've ever owned." My shoulders slump from the mere idea of wearing them. They were Mom's present for my high school graduation and cost a fortune, but I've only been able to bring myself to put them on once.

"Beauty requires sacrifice."

"But it doesn't require torture," I counter. "I feel like my little toes fall off when I wear those sandals." I pout.

"It's okay. You have eight more toes." Jess giggles.

I giggle back.

We walk out of the building and rush down past the clusters of other students nesting on the steps. Crowded hallways and spaces with not enough doors and too many people still make me nervous, and this moment—the moment of leaving the confines of a campus building— always causes something inside me to snap. I don't like it. I don't like that there's a switch that I can't quite control, but I'm used to it and I don't allow it to define me. I don't allow my fear to rule my life. I can't. Because it's just like Mikah said. We don't know how much life we have left.

The air outside is warm and the sun is gentle, and I breathe in deep and hard, feeding my lungs with September oxygen.

"Did I tell you my dad is buying me a Mercedes?" Jess says.

"What? No!" Although I'm not surprised. The Tillers can afford to get their daughter a fancy car for her nineteenth birthday. I don't expect anything like that for my birthday next month; I'm fine with my Prius—it runs great. Dad doesn't let me drive it to Seattle, but for that, we have the Subaru.

"Yes. We're going this weekend." Jess turns to face me. There's a huge grin on her lips and her gaze darts over my shoulder.

"What?" I spin on my heels to see what she's staring at.

Luke's blond hair lingers above the heads of the other students roaming around the courtyard. Not bothering with the passersby, he thrusts his cane in the air and waves at us. "Yo! Over here, birthday girl!"

My heart begins to gallop and my knees weaken because Mikah's standing next to him. Not able to contain my excitement, I barrel through the crowd and fling my arms around his neck. He picks me up to spin me and I respond with an enthusiastic squeal. Our bodies clash hard against one another and our lips collide in a mad kiss. It feels incredible to be able to hug him after a three-week break. A small fraction of me hates the separation and the fact that he's a hundred and eighty miles away, constantly surrounded by tons of people, and always busy. But for the most part, I'm happy. I'm happy he's doing something he's passionate about.

We kiss like high school kids, until our lungs are out of air and the whistles of other students in the courtyard grow louder.

"I was under the impression it was *my* birthday!" I hear Jess laughing as Mikah puts me down.

"You two are disgusting." Luke snickers, winking at us.

"What are you doing here?" I ask, staring up at Mikah. My hands slide across his chest and I straighten his t-shirt that reads *Bite Me*. "I thought you said you'd be home next week?"

"Are you not happy to see me, Cupcake Queen?" He chuckles, moving his fingers into my hair. "I can go back to Seattle."

"No!" I wrap my arms around his body, press my cheek to his chest, and squeeze. "I'm just surprised is all."

I stand like this for a few seconds, hugging him as he's drawn tight in my embrace.

"Don't forget, man." Twirling his cane, Luke glances at Mikah. "You're famous now. Don't let her seduce you into making a sex tape in the middle of the day."

"She can do whatever she wants." Mikah scowls, his gaze returning to me. "Right, baby?" He brushes my hair.

"Okay, you can make out later," Jess says, "but I need to get home and get ready for my party. Who's driving?"

"I thought your boyfriend was." I motion at Luke.

"We Ubered," Mikah explains. "There's no way I'm letting this fool get behind the wheel."

"You'd be surprised what I can do with one good leg." He bats his eyes at us and throws his arm over Jess's shoulder.

Seeing him smile and joke makes me feel light and happy. He used to refuse to leave his wheelchair. At some point, all of us refused to move on.

"Okay." Jess slaps Luke's chest playfully. "We better get going." Her gaze shifts to me. "I'll see you two later."

"Don't let him drive," Mikah growls out, drawing his cigarettes from the back pocket of his jeans.

"Thank God for Uber," she agrees.

After we say our goodbyes, Mikah lights up his cigarette and we head to the parking lot. The scent of his aftershave and Marlboros makes my head spin. It's a fine blend of humble and taunting, and it reminds me of all the times we've shared.

"I thought Al told you to quit," I say, wrapping my fingers tighter around Mikah's hand.

"Al can go fuck himself."

I don't argue, because I know Mikah will bend for the label only so much. He's already given up all his time.

"Oh, did I tell you Anna's Pastry is going to be on Food Network?" I jerk his arm as excitement rolls through me. Someone contacted Mrs. Kaminski last week. One of the producers came across an Instagram photo of a wedding cake I took a couple of months ago.

"For real?" Mikah exhales the smoke into the warm air.

"Yes. I might end up being on TV before you." I tease him.

"Nice. That's my girl."

A pleasant shiver races up my spine. I like hearing him say that I'm his.

"You're sure you want your dad wasting money on your college tuition?" he jokes.

"I want to finish it. I don't know if I'm ever going to need the diploma, but I want to finish it."

Mikah pulls me toward the trash can and puts out his cigarette before we get into my car.

We sit in silence for a few moments, staring at each other, studying each other's faces. Watching him is like waiting for sunrise. Excruciatingly breathtaking.

"I missed you." My voice is small and shaky and all my fears are exposed.

"Of course you did." Mikah reaches for my hair and tucks a loose strand behind my ear. "Otherwise, you wouldn't be texting me every five minutes."

"Is it too much?"

"Nah." His eyes align with mine. "It's perfect." There's a pause. "My mom's coming to my show next month."

"Oh." I gasp softly, anxiety tampering with my calm. Mikah and his mother became distant after Dakota's death. I didn't know any of this until after he moved to Seattle permanently. It took him a little while to open up.

"Yeah." Mikah relaxes in his seat and runs his palm over his face.

"She'll love it."

"I hope she does."

The static on the radio crackles as I start the engine. Mikah's fiddling with his seatbelt when the host's voice fills the car.

"...it's clear the defense will keep insisting the evidence is inadmissible. It'll be interesting to see how the prosecution responds. This is a really sticky situation, and the community believes families of the victims deserve justice. There's a lot of heat online in regards to why the death penalty is dismissed in cases like these. The students are..."

Mikah reaches for the volume control to turn down the news.

My chest stiffens and lean over and I rest my head on his shoulder.

"It's fucked up, isn't it?" He looks at me, the blood draining from his face. The corners of his lips curl into a sad smile.

"I know. I'm sorry."

We rarely talk about the case. I follow the news and I read the updates online, but I don't want it to consume me like it consumed Jess. I don't want it to dictate my life.

"What are you sorry about?" Mikah kisses me on the cheek. "Let's go before your dad thinks I kidnapped you and calls the cops on me."

"He would never do that."

"Come on. You know he hates my guts."

"No, he doesn't. He's just getting used to the idea of me dating the next...umm...what did Al call you? James Bay?"

Mikah tosses his head back and laughs. "Let's go, weirdo."

We leave the campus and jump on the interstate with our windows rolled down and music blaring from the speakers. Mikah's hand is resting on my thigh. It's a nice drive. Warm, windy, and scenic.

"Pull over! Pull over!" He sticks his other hand out the window and spreads his fingers to let the air breeze by.

"What, here?" I huff, stiffening in my seat.

"Yes. Here."

I do as he says. I change lanes and we veer to the side of the road. Mikah gets rid of his seatbelt and steps out of the car. He moves through the tall grass slowly, his gaze darting around the trees edging the highway.

I put the Prius in park and round it. "What are you doing?"

Mikah swivels to face me, his eyes seeking mine. "You remember this is where you had a flat tire?" He gestures at the stretch of grass.

"Yes." How could I forget?

"You remember you asked me about my t-shirt?"

"The Gary Oldman one? Yeah, I remember."

The loud traffic drowns out our voices.

"You remember DK punched my number into your phone?"

My heart begins to sprint. "Yes."

"And then he died two weeks later." Mikah moves closer, his words lingering between us like the broken pieces of our lives.

Unable to speak, I nod in response.

"I keep thinking about it, you know." He grasps a handful of grass and plucks it out of the ground. "About why he did it... Like he felt he was leaving and he didn't want you to be alone."

Emotions begin to clog my chest and I feel tears welling up in my eyes.

"That's why he did it." Mikah flashes his dimple at me. "That's why he was better. Because he was going to burn too bright and too fast."

I draw a deep breath through my teeth and cover my face with my palms.

"Don't fucking cry now." Mikah walks over to me and tickles the side of my cheek with the grass. "I love you."

"I can if I want to," I mumble, looking at him through the openings between my fingers.

"It's not your party. It's Jess's," he counters. "So you can't."

"You aren't supposed to talk to me using song lyrics. We had a deal." I move my hands away from my face and blow at the grass.

"You started it." Mikah smirks, and his hands slip to my sides and he pulls me closer.

Our bodies press against each other hard. I love the feel of us together surrounded by the roaring of the cars and the noises of the wind in the trees. I love the feel of the grass prickling my ankles and the smell of mint or cigarettes when Mikah breathes on my cheek. I love that he's mine and I love that he doesn't mind my weirdness.

I love that we're alive.

THE END

Thank you so much for reading Alana's story. If you'd like to get a peek into Mikah's future and get your hands on the lyrics of *Moonchild*, use this link to download your gift: BookHip.com/PTLDXT

If you enjoyed the book and have a minute to spare, please consider leaving an honest review.

ACKNOWLEDGMENTS

I would like to thank my family for their continued support.

I would like to thank my editors – Loredana Elsberry Schwartz and R.C. Craig. These ladies are true magicians.

I would like to thank my beta readers – Sue, Shannan, Karen, Naadira, and Jason.

I would like to thank my street team and my book besties – Shauna, Krysta, Shannan, Denise, and the amazing Robin Hill. I highly recommend you read her Waiting for the Sun duet.

I would like to thank my assistant, Tiffany, for everything she'd done to help me with this release.

I would like to thank all the bloggers and readers who are taking a chance on this book. It really means the world to me. You are the true rockstars!

Lastly, I would like to thank all the artists for creating the music that inspired me to write *Severance*. Thank you so much for everything you do.